DEATH PLUS
TEN YEARS

DEATH PLUS TEN YEARS

Roger Cooper

HarperCollins*Publishers*

HarperCollins*Publishers*
77–85 Fulham Palace Road,
Hammersmith, London W6 8JB

Published by HarperCollins*Publishers* 1993

9 8 7 6 5 4 3 2 1

A catalogue record for this book
is available from the British Library

ISBN 0 00 255045 8

Set in Linotron Perpetua by
Rowland Phototypesetting Ltd
Bury St Edmunds, Suffolk

Printed in Great Britain by
HarperCollinsManufacturing Glasgow

*To the land and
people of Iran*

LIST OF ILLUSTRATIONS

Note on names

SCHOLARLY SYSTEMS OF transliterating Arabic and Persian are not well suited to a book like this. My general policy is to spell words so as to reflect their actual pronunciation, and this convention is useful in differentiating between the Hizbullah of Lebanon and the Hezbollah of Iran, the Azaris of Iran and the Azeris of the former Soviet Union. Where there is a familiar English version, however, such as Isfahan or Ahwaz, I prefer that to the more 'correct' transliterations Esfahan and Ahvaz.

Similarly, the Imams of Shia Islam are traditionally written with an 'I', and this word should not be confused with Ayatollah Khomeini's courtesy title of 'Emam' (meaning, roughly, 'leader') as he is usually styled in Iran.

Before the Revolution, the Shah's main non-military security apparatus was known as Savak, an acronym standing for National Organization for Intelligence and Security, and reported nominally to the Prime Minister. Renamed Savama, it was merged into the Ministry of Intelligence when this was set up in the mid-1980s, headed by a cabinet minister. The new regime's security personnel included large numbers of former Savak agents, who referred to themselves as being from 'the Prime Minister's Office', possibly even after the post of Prime Minister was abolished in 1989, although in Evin the interrogation staff were referred to collectively as simply 'the Ministry'.

In the Shah's day, the body responsible for controlling the domestic and, as far as possible, the foreign media was known as the Ministry of Information. After the Revolution this was misleadingly renamed the Ministry of Islamic Guidance, while the Ministry of Intelligence took advantage of the ambiguity of its Persian name (*ettela'at* means both 'information' and 'intelligence')

9

to call itself in English the Ministry of Information, which it obviously considers less intimidating.

I have opted for 'Persian' rather than 'Farsi' on the basis of common sense and consistency; English-speakers, after all, conventionally use 'German', not 'deutsch', and 'French', not 'français'.

Finally, I have not always used people's real names for reasons which must be obvious.

DEATH PLUS
TEN YEARS

IRAN AND NEIGHBOURING STATES
(LATE 1980s)

Tehran, 7 December 1985

THE DAY BEGAN like most of its predecessors. I was on a business trip to Tehran, the Iranian capital, and that morning I took a hotel taxi soon after breakfast and set off for an appointment.

The traffic seemed particularly bad that Saturday, the first day of another Iranian week, and as the car moved sluggishly along Avenue Motaheri, one of Tehran's main streets, I realized I was going to be slightly late. Not that it really mattered: I was ninety per cent sure that nothing useful would come of the meeting. These mysterious phone calls from Iranian businessmen, anxious to discuss projects with me, were becoming monotonous. Tehran in those days, and I am sure things are much the same today, was full of wheeler-dealing commission agents.

I noticed a car trying to cut in on us. It was a smart blue BMW coupé, a rare sight in Tehran since the Revolution, and it came boring in from our right. This is not an unusual experience in Tehran, and at first I assumed the BMW was paying us back for some perceived driving insult on our part. My driver began to speed up and take evasive action, but I told him to ignore the BMW and let it go by – I even turned to the young driver and his companion and signalled them to go past. Life's too short to get into fights with crazy drivers, I thought.

The BMW continued to nudge us over to the left of this one-way street until our wheels were practically on the kerb of what passes for a pavement in Iran. With a final burst of speed the coupé got its nose in front of us and forced us to stop. The two young men leapt out, came up to my window and told me I was under arrest. One of them got into the back seat with me, the other into the front passenger seat. I was still thinking in terms of some alleged driving offence and could not understand why they were arresting me and not the driver.

The man in front produced a typed sheet of paper, headed with the emblem of the Islamic Republic of Iran, and said it was my arrest warrant. When I leaned forward to read it he snatched it away and pocketed it. He then told me to get out of my car and into theirs, bringing my briefcase.

By now I had guessed they were security police of some sort, and I could see the bulge of a pistol under the jacket of one of them, so I decided it was wise to obey. For some reason, though, I became quite obsessive about my meeting. I began giving the driver the exact address, asking him to go there and explain that something urgent had cropped up, and that I would be in touch shortly. But this was immediately countermanded by one of the plain-clothes police, who told him to go back to the hotel and tell the taxi desk that he had dropped me off at my meeting. On no account must he tell anyone what had happened or it would lead to big trouble for him. They would find out if he ever spoke about it, even to his own family.

So I got into the BMW and reviewed the situation. By now I thought I knew roughly what was going on. I had arrived in Tehran some four months earlier on a two-week visa, but when I applied for a routine renewal, supported by a letter from the Oil Ministry, it was refused. Nor was I allowed to leave the country. My friend at the Foreign Residents' Bureau, a police colonel I had known since he was a lieutenant, told me the problems came from 'the Prime Minister's Office', a euphemism for the secret police. In due course I was summoned to the Foreign Residents' Bureau for an interview with a security official, who asked a lot of questions about my life in Iran before the Revolution and my visits since then, including names of all my contacts. He seemed reasonably satisfied with my answers, but asked me to prepare a statement on what we had discussed.

I had not written Persian for many years and quite enjoyed the task. Having got an Iranian friend to check what I had written, and had it typed at an agency, I submitted the statement to the Foreign Residents' Bureau. Then I simply waited. Nobody would tell me what, if anything, was happening, but I did understand that there would be a further meeting with the security service; after that, '*Inshallah*, your case will be resolved.' So this, I thought, was it. Rather a rude way of getting me to an interview, but at least the problem would soon be over, whatever it was, and I could get back to Dubai. In fact, one of the secret policemen, a fat young man oozing with self-confidence, had become a little more friendly. 'This will only take one or two hours,' he said, 'then you will be free to return to your hotel.'

What happened next seemed a blend of the Keystone Cops and the Theatre of the Absurd. An argument had developed between the two secret policemen as to who had the *cheshmband*. Although this article would play a vital part in my life over the next five years, three months and twenty-five days, I could not at first think what they were talking about, or that it had anything to do with me. Literally, *cheshmband* means 'eye-closer', and for a moment I wondered if it was a new Persian term for sun-glasses or a sun visor. It was a bright morning and we were driving east. Then it dawned on me that a *cheshmband* must be a blindfold, something I had not seen, read or heard about in all my years in Iran. Could they possibly be proposing to blindfold me on the way to wherever they were taking me? Whatever would other drivers and pedestrians think?

On the various occasions when I had been summoned by Savak, the Shah's secret police, for an interview, they would send a uniformed policeman from the local station to my house, with orders to present myself at such-and-such an address and precise instructions as to how to get there. The surest way to upset the policeman, a fatherly figure I came to know quite well, was to write it all down carefully, repeat his instructions, and, at the end, ask him innocently, 'And who is it who wants to see me there?' There would be squirming noises and a shuffling of the feet, but no real answer. That was the time to say, 'Is it Savak?', a word no Iranian liked to hear, even a policeman. The first time I tried this the pot-bellied cop sighed with relief when I uttered the dreaded word. 'You said it, Agha, not me!'

This time it was different, however. There was no real embarrassment, just bickering about whose fault it was that the *cheshmband* had been forgotten. Eventually the younger, fat-faced

17

man suggested they go to a chemist's shop and buy a bandage, but as we drove along it became clear that they did not know where to find one. I had lived in Tehran, off and on, longer than they had, judging from their apparent ages, and they probably came from far south of the rather wealthy district we were in, so I was immediately able to direct them to the nearest pharmacy. The fat boy went in, emerging ten minutes later with a piece of dark cloth, more like a large bandanna handkerchief than a bandage, perhaps an arm-sling.

Up to now I was, in a strange way, pleased at what had happened: I had been in Iran for months, my passport stamped *Mamnu' al-Khoruj* – 'forbidden to leave'. Now, whatever the fuss was all about, I could get it resolved, just as in the old days my clashes with Savak had resolved themselves into an annual battle of wits with Mr Hoseini, as he termed himself, an insecure young man who had handled my file for the last five years of the Shah's reign. He always gave me a hard time, blustering and threatening, but I knew, and he knew, that he lacked the authority to expel me from Iran, even if he did think I was an 'illegal', a British spy refusing to co-operate with Savak. As in other countries such as Russia and East Germany, when the regime changed the security police had simply switched allegiance, and Savak had been renamed Savama. I might even find myself facing Mr Hoseini again. Although relations between Britain and Iran were at their lowest point in thirty years, I could not foresee any serious problems arising. At the worst I might waste a day with more questioning, but by tomorrow I would be free to leave the country. I might even get back to England in time for Christmas with my family.

Having blindfolded me, the fat boy told me to lie down on the floor behind the front seats, which, with difficulty, I managed to do. The BMW sped off, to my surprise southwards, as I had always associated Savak with north and central Tehran. The driver spent some time driving aimlessly around, presumably to ensure that I would not know our destination, but I had a fairly clear idea of where we were going. I know Tehran rather better than the back of my hand, so I could easily guess our route until the very end. The fat boy had not tied the *cheshmband* very securely, and by raising my eyebrows a few times (a technique I was to perfect in

18

the coming months) I could soon see daylight, which helped me to confirm our direction and the route itself. About an hour later I knew we had completed a large quadrilateral, with a few minor diversions, and we were now approaching my hotel from the south.

I expected the driver to continue northwards, as Savak used to have a place at the top of this road, a small, isolated building near where a foreign correspondent friend of mine lived. He told me he could sometimes hear screams late at night and see unmarked Black Marias arriving or leaving. It seemed likely that Savama was still using this building for interrogations. Instead we turned left along a street I was less familiar with, although I knew that Tehran University's hospital was on it. Once, when I was studying Persian literature at the university in the late 1960s, I had gone to see a Danish fellow-student who had contracted hepatitis. I remembered there being a small army barracks nearby, one of dozens scattered around Tehran by the paranoid Shah and his father.

We seemed to stop at a gate or checkpoint and shortly afterwards the engine was switched off and I was told to get out. The fat boy tightened the *cheshmband* and led me by the arm up some steps and into a building, then ordered me to stand facing a wall with my palms touching it.

He went off, and I never heard his voice or saw his face again. A new, harsher voice told me to follow its owner by placing my hand on his shoulder. We moved off, through a series of locked doors which either he or someone else unlocked. When the last one opened a wave of cold, damp air hit me and I knew I was in a cellar. Down the steps we went and along a corridor, with a different person leading me now. One final door was unlocked and I was pushed inside and told to take off my *cheshmband*. I did so, the door clanged to and I found myself in a small, dirty cell, roughly carpeted, with a thin piece of foam mattress on the floor: nothing else. The guard was now looking at me through a small eye-level metal window in the door and telling me to take my clothes off.

I did not like the sound of that at all. If they merely wanted to interview me for an hour or two, why should I take my clothes off? Besides, the place did not seem like a regular prison, so why should I put on a uniform, if indeed that was the idea? Perhaps

19

the object was a body search. I therefore did nothing, which earned me a sharp rebuke from the guard when he returned ten minutes later with two blankets and some strange-looking clothes.

I stripped to my socks and underwear, which after a perfunctory body search I was allowed to keep, then put on a jacket with grey and blue vertical stripes and shiny metal buttons. The jacket was far too small for me, while the khaki trousers must once have fitted a man with a huge paunch and bandy legs. The guard also stuck a small piece of adhesive tape on the breast pocket of the jacket, with the number 369 on it, telling me to learn it by heart and never take it off. It seemed a friendly number and I took this as a good omen.

My briefcase had already been taken. Now the guard went through my pockets and carefully wrote down the contents, counting out the large amount of cash I was carrying and asking me what make my watch was. He then took all my belongings away. I tried on the pair of old plastic flip-flops he had left me, both too small for my size 12 feet, though one was rather more so than the other. None of these items were really dirty, but nor were they exactly clean. What worried me more was that the cell was unheated, with a large barred space above the door for ventilation, and the clothes were inadequate for the cold Tehran winter.

I was examining the graffiti and other marks on the wall when I heard the clanking of a trolley and lunch was served. I was given a plastic bowl, a mug, a water jug and an aluminium spoon, but the food itself looked surprisingly good: it was *pollow khoresh* of some kind, the standard combination of fluffy long-grain rice and a ladle of sauce containing herbs, vegetables and two large lumps of meat. There is not much variety in Persian food, but it is usually tasty and the rice is always good. It is only when attempts are made to copy Western dishes that things go wrong.

The guard serving the food was friendlier than the first one, but knew nothing about why I had been brought here and what was going to happen to me later, or if he did he was not going to tell me. I did not have much appetite, but decided to eat anyway. The food would not be good cold and I might not see any more for some time. The friendly guard then came back with a large piece of *barbari,* my favourite of the four or five different kinds of flat Persian bread, explaining that I had missed the bread issue earlier in the day. By the number of times the apertures in the cell doors were opened to hand in the food I knew there were eight cells in the corridor, and when all these had been served the trolley was taken to another corridor, longer than mine to judge by the time it took. I was in the third cell from the foot of the steps. There could not have been more than twenty cells in all, while upstairs had seemed to be more of a staff or administrative area. Not much of a prison, really.

After lunch I was taken to the ablutions area, three sinks for washing oneself and one's dishes, and two WCs (the oriental kind, with a hole in the floor over which you squat), not as dirty as I would have expected. In the back there were apparently some showers, one of them constantly running, which must have contributed to the dank atmosphere in the cells. Another guard told me I could only go there three times a day, after meals, 'unless it's an emergency, and we don't like emergencies'. A sign said the maximum permitted time was seven minutes, but when I got my watch back later I found the guards routinely told prisoners that time was up after only three minutes, so there was no time to lose. The guards even blindfolded me for these ten-yard trips from my cell, using a towel kept on a nail outside the cell door, and they were much more thorough than the fat boy had been. Some of them made me tie it myself and then inspected it for tightness, the nastier ones making sure I could not see a thing, the nicer ones allowing me at least to see my own feet.

About three in the afternoon, although it was not easy to judge the time, I was taken upstairs and led through a series of rooms into one that had double doors. I discovered later that most interrogation rooms in Iran have double doors, presumably to prevent people outside from eavesdropping or hearing cries. A little while later a man came in and told me to remove my *cheshmband.* He was quite short, perhaps five foot two or three, and he wore a close-fitting white mask over his face with slits for the eyes. It was a frightening sight, reminding me of the famous photograph of the armed Arab terrorist taken at the Munich Olympics in 1972, and it is an image that has stayed with me ever since,

21

regularly haunting my dreams and occurring in flashbacks during waking hours.

This man turned out to be my interrogator, the person who was to have almost total control over me for the next three years. He could and did beat me whenever he felt like it, and I could do nothing to stop him. He could order my scanty possessions to be taken away, as he had already done, and he could restore them to me. He could let me receive letters and parcels, write to my family, and have a short daily exercise period. For almost three years he denied me these basic privileges.

At this first meeting I was not beaten. He told me to sit in a wooden chair with a broad armrest, of the type used in Iran for school examinations. After studying my face at some length, he began to ask me questions such as 'Why have you come to Iran?' and 'What instructions did you receive before coming?' in an extremely hostile tone. He took no notes of what I said, in fact considered my replies irrelevant, raising his voice and calling me a liar whatever I said. Then suddenly he told me to move my chair into a corner of the room and face the wall, like a naughty schoolboy.

'Listen, Cooper, listen very carefully to what I am going to tell you. We know all about your espionage career in Iran, both before and after the Revolution. We know the outline, but there are some details which are very important to us. This is the end of the line for you as a British spy, but if you co-operate with us, we won't punish you, we'll let you go, and the British authorities won't even know you have spoken to us. But if you do not co-operate you will stay here until you do, or until you die. I will give you tonight to think about this and will see you again tomorrow. Now go back to your cell.'

1

I FIRST ARRIVED in Iran in 1958, at the age of twenty-three, intending to work as a journalist – I had trained in the Toronto bureau of United Press – while studying for a degree in Persian literature. I had always enjoyed learning languages: as a schoolboy at Clifton College in Bristol I studied French, German and Spanish, as well as Latin and Greek, which led to my being assigned to a Russian interpreter's course during National Service. I had picked up fluent Serbo-Croat working as a travel guide in Yugoslavia during university vacations and that, with Russian, made it easy to read and communicate in other Slavonic languages such as Bulgarian, Slovene, Polish and Czech. On my overland trips to and from Iran I learned to get along in Turkish.

For many years the West had shown little interest in Iran as a news story, although in the early 1950s under Dr Mossadeq, the improbably charismatic prime minister who had nationalized British oil interests in Iran, the country had become better known to newspaper readers. In 1953 a CIA coup toppled him from power and restored the Shah, who had lost his nerve as the coup got under way and fled the country a few days before it succeeded. Iran then entered a 25-year period of growing prosperity – sadly combined with growing authoritarianism and disparity in the distribution of wealth.

I soon discovered that life was not easy for a foreign correspondent in Iran. There was trouble with Savak, the Shah's secret police, over an article I wrote for the *New Statesman* on opposition politics and human rights abuses. Over the years a number of colleagues were expelled for writing articles critical of the regime – even for referring to the Arabian Gulf, or simply the Gulf, instead of the Persian Gulf – so any journalist wanting to stay in Iran had to give up the idea of reporting the political scene, unless he was prepared to turn a blind eye to the regime's excesses and the undercurrents of opposition. I concentrated on writing about economic and cultural affairs, and turned to other activities altogether, such as teaching, translating and later, briefly, business.

In 1960 I married Guity, whose prosperous upper-class family welcomed me warmly into their ranks, and our daughter Gisu was born in 1962. Even though Guity and I were divorced three years later, we all remained on friendly terms. I stayed on in Iran, writing and teaching, until the last year of the Shah's reign, when I returned reluctantly to England, guessing that the country I loved so dearly would soon lose the ambience I had enjoyed for nearly twenty years.

As interest in the area began to pick up I gained something of a reputation as a specialist in Iranian politics and, increasingly, Islam. Journalists I had befriended on their visits to the Middle East started to mention my name to their editors as someone who understood what was going on in Iran. I was asked to do a few broadcast interviews and commentaries for the BBC World Service, the start of a romance with radio that continues to this day.

Late in the summer of 1978 the *Sunday Times* commissioned me to go to Iran for its colour magazine, together with Britain's best war photographer, the legendary Don McCullin. Don is famous for being in the right place at the right time, and he certainly was then. We met some of the leading opponents of the Shah's regime, including senior ayatollahs, and we were at Jaleh Square soon after the Bloody Friday massacre there, when on the first day of martial law soldiers shot dead hundreds, perhaps even thousands, of peaceful demonstrators at a political rally, thus pushing the country irrevocably along the path to revolution. We were visiting Kurdistan when we heard news of the Tabas earthquake and drove across Iran through the night, reaching the devastated desert city with the first group of journalists a full day before the Shah got there. Finally, after Don had left, my patience was rewarded with an exclusive interview with the Shah, the last one he gave before fleeing the country a few weeks later. I also secured an interview with Ayatollah Khomeini during his brief stay in France after Iraq had obliged the Shah by expelling him.

Wrongly as it happened, I guessed that as a news story Iran might play itself out, and I had no wish to leave myself stranded journalistically as an Iran-only expert. During my years there I had travelled widely elsewhere in the Middle East and could read and speak a little Arabic, so I thought it was time to study it properly. Although I had always been somewhat daunted by this beautiful but difficult language, I knew it to be essential to a proper understanding of Islam and the Arab world. So when I returned to London I enrolled at the Polyglot School in Kensington, along with two Japanese bankers and an Australian diplomat. Studying under two brilliant teachers for six hours a day, with lots of homework on top, I could soon speak and read reasonably fluently.

It must be remembered, however, that spoken Arabic varies greatly from country to country, although the written language is virtually the same everywhere. For example, in the mid-1960s I was in Rabat, interviewing Morocco's minister of information for the *Financial Times,* when a Kuwaiti journalist arrived early for his appointment. The minister suggested he should join us, and I agreed. After a few conventional greetings the Kuwaiti began to ask questions in Arabic, but the minister could not follow him. The Kuwaiti tried English, and the minister replied in French that he did not understand. So I found myself interpreting for two Arabs. Ever since then I have been suspicious of the concept of 'the Arab world' or Arab unity. Nationalism is, I believe, more important in trying to understand the Arabs, and within most Arab countries there are further vital differences of a tribal, religious or social nature.

My knowledge of Arabic led in 1982 to a commission for an article on Islamic banking and economics for *Euromoney,* the British financial journal. I travelled to half a dozen Arab countries researching it, and turned in a 4000-word article. Padraic Fallon, the editor, read it carefully and told me it had good material, but he wanted something heavier. 'Include more of the theoretical base,' he said. 'Go back to the Quran.' To sugar the pill, because no journalist likes to have an article rejected, he told me I could go to 7000 words if necessary, a huge length for a freelance writer. So off I went to London University's School of Oriental and African

Studies and immersed myself in Islamic texts. The resulting article was well received, and I was soon being contacted by international banks that were looking for ways of getting into the lucrative business of Middle Eastern finance. But for every financial agency prepared to pay me a consultancy fee, there were three or four that thought they could find out all they wanted to know free of charge over a City lunch. I used to wonder what a QC would say if you tried to get counsel's opinion on the cheap in this way. Journalists are considered fair game, however, and being on the whole amiable and sociable creatures, they are usually willing to have their brains picked.

I was also asked to address an international banking conference in London and was puzzled when the organizers asked if I wanted to be paid in cash or wine. The explanation was that many bankers preferred 'a case or two of chateau-bottled claret' to a speaker's fee, because it was 'more tax-efficient'. I replied that my efficiency was not so great and a cheque would do fine. The sad truth was that although I was beginning to make a name for myself as a journalist – not only on Middle East affairs, but using my knowledge of Russian to get interesting assignments in the Soviet Union, and persuading *Euromoney* to send me to francophone Africa – I was not earning enough money, especially with my new obligations to my daughter.

The British authorities had refused to recognize my marriage to Guity, claiming it was 'potentially polygamous': ironically, in Muslim Iran we had not been allowed to marry until I produced a certificate from the British embassy stating that I was not already married. Gisu was born in London, however, which automatically entitled her to British citizenship. She grew up in Tehran in her mother's care, as a Muslim, amid a typically vast Iranian clan of uncles and aunts and cousins. There is no single word for 'cousin' in Persian, which instead spells out precisely the eight kinds of first cousin — son or daughter of maternal or paternal uncle or aunt — and there were plenty of each kind. Her second cousins and collateral relations were also numerous, and there was constant to-ing and fro-ing between the various relations, who always looked on Gisu as something special, the only member of the family with non-Iranian blood. She was expected to do well in life and was under considerable pressure to live up to these expectations.

In Tehran, Gisu went to the Jeanne d'Arc girls' school, where Farah Diba, who later became Empress of Iran, had once been a pupil. It was run by French nuns, and the pupils followed both the Iranian state education curriculum and its French equivalent, or much of it. She always did well at her lessons, and was usually class prefect as well. If she slipped below top of her class both her mother and grandmother would scold her. I used to think they made her work too hard, but had to recognize that she had a much more stable family environment than I could have given her, even though Cherlee, my second American wife, and I, with no children of our own, would have modified our rather bohemian lifestyle if she had lived with us.

At the time of the Islamic Revolution in 1979, Gisu was sixteen and by now in the Lycée Razi, Tehran's French high school. Foreseeing the fanaticism that was about to be unleashed on the westernized middle classes, we both decided that she should come to London to continue her education in my custody. I was delighted, while realizing that there would be problems. Cherlee and I had separated, and I was sharing my flat in Kensington with an English girlfriend. It was within walking distance of the Lycée Français, London's top French school, where I had reserved a place for Gisu the previous autumn, but there was not enough room in the flat to accommodate her properly.

The problem was partly solved when the Lycée at the last minute declined to enrol her. There were so many Iranians flooding in because of the Revolution that the school decided not to accept any more, and by the time Gisu and her mother arrived the quota was full. I am a great believer in the French baccalauréat system, which gives high-school students a much wider education than the British A-level, so we looked for a school offering the international equivalent, in English since French was now not possible. She was lucky to find a place at a teacher training college in south London that was experimentally offering a sixth-form residential course based on the international bac.

Gisu arrived at the college with hardly any English, hoping to get into medical school two years later. She did extremely well and I think I was proudest of all that she finished second in English literature. Unfortunately, British medical schools are not familiar with the baccalauréat system, and with intense competition for places they look for high A-level grades above all else. So reluctantly Gisu had to go next to a tutorial college at Oxford, where she spent a happy time getting good A-levels and enjoying a lively social life.

I had gone to St John's College, Oxford, on a State Scholarship, but was sent down for going to Hungary during the 1956 uprising. Many people at the time thought it was unfair, but there was no appeal and I had had to enrol as an external student of London University, taking English, French and classical Persian literature for my BA degree. Years later, thanks to the intervention of the Bishop of Oxford, who had been the college chaplain in my day, the new president of St John's investigated my case and decided I had been wrongfully sent down. After some negotiations over the port I agreed to have my name restored to the college rolls on two conditions. One was that I could return one day to take up any course of study I chose, the other was that my daughter would receive favourable consideration if she wanted to apply for a place. The college kept the bargain, but they only had two places for medicine in 1983, and both were already promised to outstanding applicants. St John's did offer Gisu a place to read Persian or even English literature, but her heart was set on becoming a doctor, so in the end she went to the Royal Free Hospital, one of the teaching hospitals attached to London University.

Because she had lived for so much of her life in Iran it did not seem likely that she would get a government student grant, so I had to think how I could pay her tuition and living costs myself. Early in 1983 I was offered a job in Dubai with McDermott International Inc., reporting to an Iranian vice-president, Homayoun Beklik, an old friend for whom I had worked in Tehran some twenty years earlier. As his assistant I would be able to save most of my salary since almost all my expenses would be paid for by the company. Soon after I joined McDermott, Beklik resigned and, against some competition from existing staff, I succeeded in taking over his job, though with the more humble designation of Sales and Marketing Manager. This was what I was doing when I was arrested, and why I was always described in press reports during my captivity as a businessman, not a journalist.

McDermott was the world's leading marine construction company, its chief market being offshore installations for the oil industry. Before the Revolution the company had completed a number of contracts in Iran, but by 1985 we were facing several serious problems in doing business there.

First, it was a major disadvantage being an American firm, even though we were registered in Panama to avoid double taxation in the United States and the countries we operated in overseas. Secondly, our hands were tied in the matter of agency commissions: after some financial scandals in the 1970s McDermott had been rapped over the knuckles by the US Department of Justice and now had to follow Washington's guidelines to the letter, particularly the Foreign Corrupt Practices Act. As Middle East sales manager I was obliged to sign a formal declaration every year that I knew of no illicit payments or secret agreements with competitors, so the idea of paying a bribe, even if superficially designated as commission, was out of the question. We had an agent in Iran, whom I kept on a very tight lead until he had proved his ability, but his contract gave him a mere 5% commission on small contracts, and as little as 1% on the very large contracts I was after. So when a would-be middleman told me: 'If you agree to 20% you will win the contract', I smiled sweetly and referred him to our agent, while trying to find out what he knew about a particular project, or the internal politics of the Ministry of Oil, or indeed the internal politics of Iran. If pressed on the commission question I would say, 'But who would we pay the five million dollars *to*?' One of these middlemen replied, 'The Qom football team', Qom being the Shi'a holy city where all the top clergy, including Ayatollah Khomeini, were trained or had taught.

There was also the question of our quite substantial claim against Iran for unpaid pre-Revolution bills. This was limping along before a tribunal at The Hague, set up in the wake of the US embassy hostage crisis of 1979–80 to resolve Irano-American financial disputes. The Iranians had predictably counterclaimed with some rather spurious demands for social security payments going back

29

a dozen years or more, which they had boosted with punitive fines and interest charges, although even then they could get nowhere near the $10 million or so which we were claiming for work done and approved during the last year of the Shah's reign. Then there was the slump in the offshore oil industry, resulting from stagnant oil prices. In times like these, countries such as Saudi Arabia and Abu Dhabi which had both onshore and offshore oilfields were naturally reluctant to start more expensive offshore operations and generally restricted themselves to essential maintenance work. Our only reasonably healthy Middle East markets were India and Egypt, because their onshore fields were negligible. Several of our competitors had already cut back their workforces drastically and mothballed equipment.

During the first half of 1985 my number one sales priority was a pipeline project vital to Iran's economic survival. Oil exports were the only way it could pay for food, industrial goods and, above all, the arms it needed in the war against Iraq, which had dragged on since September 1985. Almost all Iran's crude oil exports pass through Kharg Island, flowing by gravity from wells high in the Zagros mountains of south-west Iran. Kharg is a large coral reef in relatively deep water off the Iranian coast. Oil is stored in a vast 'tank farm' built on the high ground, each of the score of tanks larger than a football ground. When a supertanker arrives at the berths of the man-made island, a terminal in even deeper water where the largest crude oil carriers can moor, the valves open on the 56-inch lines and oil gushes down into the holds, but even then it can take twenty hours to fill them.

By 1985 Iraqi air supremacy meant that these vital facilities could be attacked whenever Saddam Hussein gave the word. True, it was quite easy to patch up the storage tanks and start the flow again, but one by one the Iraqi air force was knocking out the mooring berths, and Iranian strategists were belatedly making provision against further destruction. The long-term plan was to lay a new pipeline along the coast down to a proposed new terminal on the Strait of Hormuz, the narrow entrance to the Persian Gulf, or even further east in Baluchistan. This would give the Iranians direct access to the Indian Ocean and be well out of range of Iraqi fighter bombers.

Such a project would take years to complete, and meanwhile a quick fix was required. One solution was to lay a new submarine pipeline from the coast halfway across to Kharg Island, parallel to the existing lines and ending at an SPM (single-point mooring) system some twenty miles offshore. Tankers would tie up to special buoys, connect the flexible end of the pipeline to their holds and start loading at once. The process is slightly slower, but the SPM presents a far smaller target than a jetty or terminal berth and even if damaged can easily be replaced.

McDermott was one of the few established international contractors prepared to bid for this dangerous job. It would mean towing one of our barges into the war zone and laying the pipeline as quickly as possible. This is done by welding forty-foot lengths of steel pipe into a long string, and gently lowering the string to the seabed in a continuous process. No other firm had the equipment, the expert personnel and, above all, the willingness to do this hazardous work. The only reason we were prepared to bid for it was the desperate state of our Middle East order book.

Even making the bid was bedevilled with problems. McDermott was understandably considered an American company, and there was legislation prohibiting the award of contracts to the Great Satan. In a small way, working ostensibly as subcontractor to firms registered in Dubai or Singapore, we had already done some jobs for the National Iranian Oil Company. These were in the border waters between the United Arab Emirates and Iran, however, and escaped the notice of the fanatics in Tehran. Working in the war zone, with a contractual obligation to lay several miles of pipe on Iranian soil, would be something quite different, and the pragmatic NIOC engineers needed all the help they could get to protect themselves from political repercussions. My in-house research told me that, while we were confident of winning at The Hague, the suit was not likely to be settled for several years, and the lion's share of any award would probably be absorbed by legal fees. From the accounting point of view, the sum we were claiming had already been written off, so it was not difficult to persuade top management in New Orleans to drop the case, provided our name was removed from the blacklist and we were genuinely allowed to bid for new work in Iran.

After months of delicate negotiations I got head office approval for an 'equal offset' along these lines, with both sides dropping their claims and McDermott's name formally being added to NIOC's list of approved contractors. The claims were withdrawn from the Hague tribunal and I succeeded in producing a document acceptable to the Iranian lawyers that confirmed the fiction that we were a fully-fledged Panamanian company, not a US one. Even this had not been easy: all our normal registration documentation was in English, spattered with State Department seals and the validatory signatures of persons like Secretary of State Al Haig, scarcely likely to impress the hardliners in Tehran, so I had to obtain new papers in Spanish for official translation into Persian.

Late in 1984 I travelled to Ahwaz, the centre of Iran's oilfields operations, made our submission, and next day attended the opening and reading of the bids, ours and those of two competitors from Italy and Singapore. It was an exciting moment, for we were not only the lowest bidder, but the only one to have submitted a bid bond, a bank guarantee for 5% of the price. Since this had been a condition of the invitation to tender I argued that we should at once be awarded the contract, but things were not so simple. For months the bids were evaluated, until the Italian firm effectively dropped out and it was between us and a small Singaporean firm with no track record for a project of this size. We had in fact fabricated and installed a production platform in their name in Iranian waters, and I remember laughing when I heard that their managing director had insisted on our workers posing for photographs wearing their uniforms. Now, it seemed, they were using these photographs as evidence of their capability. That particular job had gone sour, as it happened. We were not responsible for the design or engineering of the platform, although our own engineers had queried some of the specifications and considered them inadequate. Sure enough, the project had gone wrong and the entire platform was going to be written off or expensively refurbished.

This firm was now proposing a novel approach to the vital new pipeline project. Instead of laying it with a conventional lay-barge, they wanted to fabricate the whole line onshore and pull it out bit by bit. The advantages were obvious: lower costs and greater security. One snag was that the pipeline route was a dog-leg (to avoid some fishing grounds), and you can only pull in a straight line, whereas a lay-barge can lay pipe in an arc if need be. Even more serious, however, was that nobody had ever pulled such a long and large (26-inch diameter) pipeline before. From our old pre-Revolutionary work in Iran we had access to soil studies in the area and knew how fine the seabed sand was. The trench which would have to be gouged out ahead of the pull would silt up before pipe-pulling was completed. This would not happen if a lay-barge were used because the trench cutting would be just ahead of the pipe-laying.

Against us, on the other hand, was the question of insurance. It was prohibitively expensive to obtain Lloyd's cover for the three months or so we would have to operate in the war zone, so we suggested that the client, NIOC, should make its own arrangements, either through an Iranian government insurer or on a self-insured basis, giving us an indemnity to cover the risk to our personnel and equipment.

I was back in Dubai when the news reached us – more on the grapevine than as an official communication – that our rival was to be awarded the contract. It was a nasty shock for me personally: I had been expecting us to win and was looking forward to playing an important role in the project. We already employed a score or so of Iranians in Dubai, all good workers, mainly at foreman level, and although all personnel were going to be chosen on a volunteer basis we expected that at least some of these men would have been on the barge, which would have been good PR and useful for dealing with day-to-day problems involving NIOC or government personnel. But I would have been the main link between client and contractor, with an office in Ahwaz already being planned for me by our agent, while also making frequent trips to Tehran, where major decisions were taken. Everybody working on the project would have got double pay, which was an attractive bonus to the pleasure I anyway derived from working in Iran.

It seemed a good idea for me to go to Tehran to see if there was anything to be done to retrieve the situation, at least to find out officially why we had not won, and perhaps to make a formal complaint through political channels if I smelt a rat. Wrong as it

33

would be to make accusations without clear proof, there is no doubt that if a Singaporean firm wants to give a donation to the Qom football team there is nothing to prevent it, whereas a US firm, at least a major listed corporation, has had to be squeaky clean ever since Jimmy Carter pushed the Foreign Corrupt Practices Bill through the US Congress.

All this was known to people within NIOC and, of course, to our rival's agent. The last thing he, and possibly they, wanted was for Roger Cooper to go the rounds of his contacts in the Ministry of Oil and perhaps other government agencies casting a shadow of suspicion over this highly lucrative contract. If our rival had won fairly and squarely then that would have been the end of it from our point of view – 'You win some, you lose some' is a cliché of the construction business – but nobody likes to lose unfairly, especially after hundreds of thousands of dollars have been spent on bid preparation and a bid bond, and with hundreds of jobs at stake. So McDermott were as keen as I was myself to find out what was going on in Tehran.

In Iran's Dubai consulate I was politely refused a visa, for no very clear reason. Our agent in Tehran could not help, so I went to London to try my luck at the Iranian consulate there. I re-established some contacts from my days as a journalist, and was even invited to dinner at the embassy. The chargé d'affaires turned out to be charming, and it was encouraging to see that intelligent, pragmatic men were rising to positions of importance under the new regime.

Dinner was a curious occasion. We sat surrounded by gilt mirrors in the plush Iranian residence overlooking Hyde Park, with fine carpets under our feet. But the meal itself was somewhat rough and ready, the kind of food you might find at a truckers' pull-up on the Tehran to Isfahan road, and the host was tieless, with a few days' growth of beard. The cook, having served the meal, sat down and ate with us.

I was mildly shocked to find that the embassy had almost no contacts in British political or social circles. Admittedly, relations between Britain and Iran were poor, but embassy staff had developed a ghetto mentality, unnecessarily in my opinion. None of them ever seemed to meet MPs, trade union officials, students

34

(other than officially sponsored Iranian students) or church leaders.

'How could I meet an MP?' asked the chargé.

'Easy,' I replied, 'invite him to tea.'

'But he wouldn't come. They all hate us,' he objected.

'I don't think that's true,' I said. 'Our politicians are pragmatic rather than ideological, and if you invite five of them for tea I'll bet – sorry, that's not allowed in Islam, is it? – I'm sure at least one of them will come, if only out of curiosity. Work your way through the whole House of Commons.'

The chargé was intrigued by these and other ideas and asked me to come to the embassy the next day to discuss them with his political first secretary. At this meeting I introduced a detailed list of ways to widen the Iranians' network of contacts. The first secretary was a pleasant young man who spoke reasonable English, having studied agriculture at a British university, and when I told him how much I liked Damavand, his small home town, the atmosphere quickly became cordial. In the course of an hour I made various suggestions for improving Irano-British relations, and when I left he told me I could collect my visa that afternoon. It would be signed personally by the chargé, a rare honour, without reference to Tehran.

Next day I flew back to Dubai, well pleased with the way things were going, especially since my boss had recently indicated that Iran was our most important target area. If I had not even been able to get a visa for Iran, my usefulness to the company would have diminished substantially. Heads were rolling all around me, and although I did not want to make a permanent career in the oil industry I did enjoy the challenge, while the $4000 or so I earned each month, tax-free and with almost all my expenses paid, had already revolutionized my finances. I now had some cash savings for the first time in my life, and was looking forward to at least another year in Dubai, unless, like so many of my colleagues, I was made redundant.

Travelling on the two-week visa I had obtained in London, I arrived in Tehran in August: four months later I was in gaol.

2

IN MY CELL, which was colder now that the wintry sun had set, I sat down on the foam mattress with a blanket over my legs and reviewed the situation.

At first sight the outlook was bleak. Here was this crazy man, convinced I was a British spy, threatening to keep me in gaol indefinitely unless I 'confessed'. It was not the first time I had been accused of being a spy. The Shah's secret police had often made this charge and, more seriously, it had happened when, still at Oxford, I had ferried a large supply of antibiotics to Budapest hospitals. Just after the Hungarian uprising in 1956, the new government installed by Soviet tanks and bayonets was extremely jittery. They wanted to find foreign scapegoats to cover up the fact that their own people had risen against Communism and the Soviet occupation.

But even in No. 1 Fö Utca, the notorious state security prison in Budapest, there were vestiges of legality and human rights. The interrogation I underwent was always courteous: both the nameless interrogator and Ilonka, the young interpreter, treated me with respect, never beating me or raising their voices. Although conditions in Hungary were understandably uncomfortable in midwinter, so soon after the Soviet coup and with the economy crippled, I always felt the comfort of being in European hands, even if Communist ones. My interrogation, which lasted seventeen days, was a true battle of wits, one that I nearly lost when I was caught hiding the fact that I had been a Russian interpreter – information they discovered from a news item in the *Daily Express*. In Tehran, however, I found myself up against a much more dangerous adversary, a man who would not listen to what I said but simply ranted and accused me of lying.

Then a ray of hope struck me. How silly not to have thought of it before! This had to be bluff, crude bluff at that, the sort of tactic Savak might have tried had they not been afraid of it back-firing, for in the Shah's days you could not ill-treat a European with impunity. The masked man, whoever he was, was simply trying to frighten me into a confession. Given the various factions within the Iranian government – God knows how many rival quasi-police forces there were in Iran then, each with its own uniform and command structure – it was quite likely that this man did not even have jurisdiction over my file. He had simply heard about it, pulled me off the streets without a valid authoriz-ation – why else had they not let me study what they said was an arrest warrant? – and was hoping to scare me into some juicy intelligence gossip that his particular group could turn to their advantage. If I toughed it out for a day or two – surely that would be the longest they could keep me in this tinpot gaol – I would be released only slightly the worse for wear. Once the psychological shock had worn off it would make an amusing story to dine out on. I would enjoy telling it to my new friend the Iranian chargé, when I next passed through London.

With my spirits thus raised I ate my supper with something close to enjoyment and resumed my examination of the cell. The walls were of mud, with a thin coat of limewash applied a long time ago. Earlier occupants had left their marks, some by tallying in vertical lines the days they had been here, the longest time being about six weeks. There were passionate pleas to God, to the authorities, to the family, proclaiming the writers' innocence. There were defiant emblems of the National Communist Party and other banned organizations. There were dozens of red smears where mosquitoes engorged with blood had been squashed with the palm of a hand. There were some aimless holes, apparently gouged out by finger-nails.

Most prisoners had used pencils or ballpoints, but those like me who had neither were still able to write, using a *mohreh*. This is a small compressed clay tablet supposedly made from the soil of the holy cities of Najaf or Karbala in Iraq, where Imam Ali and Imam Husain, son-in-law and grandson of the Prophet himself, are buried. You will find a *mohreh* in every Iranian hotel, rather like a Gideon Bible. It is used by the Shi'as when they prostrate themselves in prayer, the tablet being placed on the ground and the forehead touching it in each prostration. It symbolizes the soil itself, to which we must all return, and what purer soil than that where Ali or Husain lies? Apart from this religious use, a *mohreh* makes a handy crayon, somewhat crude when worn down, but with careful moistening and honing you can get a decent point on it. This may seem sacrilegious to the orthodox, but I never saw a *mohreh* in an Iranian prison cell that had not been used in this way.

I was still trying to decipher some of the more faded messages when the cell was plunged into darkness. Lights out had come without warning, not long after the last toilet call. A dim light in the corridor threw a distorted shadow of the nine bars of my cell on to the wall above my head, and I dozed off, still wearing my uniform against the cold, with this hostile image imprinted on my mind. If I close my eyes I can still see those nine bars above me today.

Next day I woke with a start before dawn when a guard clattered into my cell, telling me to get up for *vozu*, the ritual ablutions a Muslim must perform before praying. I thanked him and said I was not a Muslim and did not pray like that.

This was a decision I had no time to consider properly. Technically, I might be considered a Muslim, because when I married Guity a quarter of a century earlier I had been obliged to become one: there is no civil marriage in Iran and even in the Shah's day all marriages had to be between co-religionists. It was unthinkable for her to become a Christian: the penalty for apostasy is death, and since I myself no longer believed formally in Christianity it would have been hypocritical as well. Besides, as a student of Persian literature and philosophy I was already strongly attracted to Islam, especially Sufism, the mystic element of the religion that pervades most of Iran's poetry, so it was easy for me to take the plunge.

The most difficult condition, in fact, had been the obligatory circumcision. Among non-Jews and non-Muslims this minor surgical operation has had its fashionable ups and downs. In England when I was a baby it was not normally performed, although one of my brothers had it done when very young on medical grounds. I understand that in infancy, when Jews and most Muslims are circumcised, it is relatively painless and problem-free, less so at ten or eleven, which is when young Turks have it done. In Turkey it is a major rite of passage, and boys are given impressive military or police uniforms to help them overcome the undoubted trauma they suffer.

I was 25, not at all the normal age to be circumcised, so I tried to obtain sound medical advice beforehand. Because it is so unusual an operation in adults in Iran, occurring perhaps only when a rare Armenian Christian converts to Islam, I could not find a surgeon who had actually done the deed. The best advice seemed to be to find a good gynaecological surgeon. This led me to Dr Mossadegh, not the famous politician who nationalized Iran's oil industry in the 1950s, but his son, a much respected gynaecologist with his own hospital.

I had always admired Mossadegh *père*, loathed though he was by politicians like Churchill and Eden and portrayed by the British press as a pyjama-clad hypochondriac. He was still alive in those days, living in house-arrest outside Tehran. Although in practical terms his policies had failed, he was a great statesman. Without him the colonial age in the Middle East would have lingered much longer, and Arab nationalism, as developed by Nasser, with the nationalization of the Suez Canal its greatest initial achievement, might never have blossomed.

On the day in question I presented myself at the hospital and was given an anaesthetic by injection. The anaesthetist told me to count to ten, which I did without difficulty. He looked surprised, and told me to count to twenty. I think I got to nineteen before dozing off, but once the operation began I returned to at least partial consciousness. I could see and feel everything, and it was the most excruciating pain I have ever experienced, before or since. I entered Islam the hard way.

Guity's mother was, in fact still is, devout. True, she did go through a stage early in the Revolution when she stopped praying, but that was when her eldest son Mohsen, a major in the Special Forces, was convicted of complicity in a coup attempt and sentenced to life imprisonment. Touran concluded from this that Islam itself must be wrong, though later she changed her views again. When Guity and I were living in England, and she came over to help with the birth of our daughter Gisu, she made me carry out the regular prayers, at least for the first few days of Ramadan, but apart from that I have never practised Muslim rituals, although I have studied Islam extensively and respect it greatly. But, not knowing how long I might remain in gaol, I did not want to become involved in its day-to-day practices – forced to pray morning, noon and night and fast in Ramadan.

Meanwhile there was noise and clatter as one by one the other prisoners were taken out, for an even shorter time than usual. *Vozu*, at least as it is practised by most Iranians today, is at best perfunctory. The Prophet Muhammad is said to have been unusually particular in matters of hygiene, and originally the compulsory washing of hands, feet and face five times a day (the Shi'a have condensed this to three times), using sand if no water could be spared, must have done wonders to improve personal cleanliness among converts to Islam, and doubtless health standards too. But today it is the form, not the content, that matters. If you have just had a shower you still have to perform *vozu*, even if the water you use is contaminated, as is often the case in the pools in mosque forecourts used for this purpose.

It was impossible to go back to sleep, and after tea had been brought round I began to regret having missed this early opportunity of going to the lavatory. By the time my turn came my bladder was bursting, but I was determined not to ask for emergency relief.

My interrogator did not arrive until about 11.30 that morning, and seemed in a much better mood than the day before. He asked me questions in a methodical way, took some notes and generally seemed pleased with himself. I began to think my theory must be correct, and that if this continued for a few more sessions everything would sort itself out. For some reason he could not stay long. As soon as the noon call to prayer came over the Tannoy system he sent me back to my cell, saying he might come back in the afternoon. This pleased me: the sooner I got the whole thing over the better.

He was back almost as soon as I had finished lunch, but his mood had changed again. He asked me questions about Pauline Jackson, a journalist friend of long standing, asserting that she too was a British spy. This annoyed me, and I began to tell him why he was wrong. One of my main points was that Pauline, like many freelance journalists, was often in financial difficulties. She now lived in rented accommodation in south London, a nice old house but needing major renovation, which the landlords were unwilling to carry out. She had taken her two children out of public school because she could not afford the fees. It was hardly likely, therefore, that she was working for British Intelligence as an expert on Iran, as he claimed. Surely, I argued, an MI6 salary would cover school fees. I added that Pauline loved Iran as much as I did and would never do anything against the country's interests.

I was once again sitting in the corner of the room, like a dunce, and talking about Pauline, when suddenly the interrogator struck me hard across the side of the head. The surprise and shock were as strong as the actual pain, and I felt a powerful instinct to turn round and hit him back. In a fair fight, unless he was trained in judo, I think I could have won, since my extra height and weight would have overcome his fifteen or twenty years' age advantage, but I knew at once this would not be wise. There were colleagues of his outside, and after they had beaten me into a pulp he would claim I had hit him first. Over the years, though I am glad to say less and less often, I have got into occasional punch-ups either with drunks or when drunk myself, but on such occasions the adrenalin or the alcohol, or simply the human instinct for self-protection, has prevented me from feeling pain or anger until later. To be hit, and unable to hit back, was a totally new experience.

The interrogator carried on with his questioning for another half-hour, but he could see I was no longer in the right frame of mind and sent me back to my quarters. While I was away someone had left a Quran and Ayatollah Khomeini's treatise on Islam in my cell. Whether this was standard equipment, or whether my refusal to perform *vozu* had sparked it off, I did not know, but I was grateful anyway. At least I had something to read now. I do not often watch television, and have only seen one or two videos in my life, but I am a compulsive reader, especially of newspapers, and a regular listener to the BBC World Service. Like most visiting journalists and businessmen in the Middle East, I always travel with my short-wave Sony to keep me in touch with the news, and I was already beginning to feel withdrawal symptoms.

In fact, there was radio of a sort. Just outside my cell, unfortunately, was a loudspeaker, and after breakfast and lunch, as well as at prayer times, it would leap into life. The sound quality was so bad that it was difficult to follow, and the quality of the news itself was little better. I had never listened to the Voice of Islamic Iran much, except when I came across a broadcast by chance while driving to or from work in Dubai. Now I was obliged to listen to it for half an hour twice a day. I was shocked at how biased it had become since the time when I was working as a correspondent in Iran soon after the Revolution. In terms of news selection and emphasis, and in the merging of fact with commentary, it was reminiscent of Eastern bloc propaganda at the height of the Cold War. I remember one item in particular. A plane carrying US troops on a training mission had crashed in Canada with heavy loss of life. The newsreaders could hardly disguise the pleasure this news gave them, and two or three days later they were still dredging up the story and giving it prominence. Much later, when I was allowed local newspapers, I noticed this bias again. Any accident or disaster in the United States or Britain was front-page news, even if casualties were minimal. But if a truck crashed into a bus in Iran – a not infrequent event – and scores of people were killed or injured, this would be relegated to a brief mention on an inside page.

Now, with no reading material of my own, I was grateful to have the Quran, a book I had browsed in rather desultorily but never read properly, and I also welcomed the chance to read Ayatollah Khomeini's treatise on *fiqh*, the legal and social code of Islam.

Every ambitious ayatollah is supposed to write such a work, setting out for his followers what to do in a bewildering set of circumstances. It is easy for Westerners to laugh at the idea of a modern nation looking to religious leaders for guidance in everyday life, but before the Revolution there were clear discrepancies between the civil law enacted under the Pahlavi dynasty between

42

1921 and 1979 and Islamic *fiqh*. Ayatollah Khomeini and other fundamentalists were trying to re-establish the proper Islamic position, which was gradually being forgotten or ignored as Iran westernized, and the publication of their interpretations of the law was part of this process. At the time of Khomeini's short exile in France in 1978, some journalists obtained translations of his treatise and held it up to ridicule. It was alleged to include the advice that one should not have sex with a camel, while specifying what steps should be taken to purify oneself ritually if this eventuality occurred, although I found no such references during the short time I had the book in my possession.

I had read an English translation of the treatise of Grand Ayatollah Shariatmadari, who was senior even to Khomeini, and it certainly contained nothing on that score, although it did have quite a lot of down-to-earth advice on sexual matters. In any case, although neither the Quran in Arabic with Persian subtitles (the term translation is never used since it is deemed impossible to 'translate' the word of God) nor Khomeini's advice on matters of Islamic practice would be on my list of books to take to a desert island, I was nevertheless glad to have them. Any port in a storm.

Later that day another thought occurred to me. There was something fishy about this gaol, and the more I looked at the evidence, the fishier it became. For a start, there was a total ban on sound, except for loud radio at limited times. If any prisoner began to talk to himself, or pray aloud, or cry, as did sometimes happen, a guard would immediately hurry to his door and order him to be quiet, but without raising his voice – in fact in little more than a whisper. Then there was the constantly running shower. In a country desperately short of water, where even in winter appeals were made to economize on domestic usage, why would this tap not be mended? Perhaps it was left on deliberately to muffle other sounds, as happened in the Soviet Union when people wanted to have a discreet conversation in a hotel room.

From a corner of my cell I could see the tops of some buildings that looked like the back of a row of suburban houses. I could not see any people or movement, but that might be because it was winter. Also there was something strange about the guards. There seemed to be a lot of them, but they did not have a standard uniform. They wore mainly khaki, but in all sorts of variations. Since the Revolution, and especially since the war with Iraq, many young Iranian men wore military-type clothing, but if this was a prison surely there would be some sort of guards' uniform? My own clothes could hardly be considered a prisoner's uniform either.

Another mystery was that from time to time I could hear what sounded like soldiers being drilled. But if this was an army barracks, why did I also hear the voices of women and children? One possible explanation was that it was a camp or safe house of a fundamentalist group, less formal than the Revolutionary Guards, who now came under their own ministry. I was familiar with the Revolutionary Guards, and felt fairly sure that the prison warders were not part of that organization or any other group I had heard of.

Then it struck me. They must be MKO, the Mojahedin Khalq Organization, the main urban terrorist group opposed to the regime. They had kidnapped me, both to obtain information, as they hoped, about British involvement in Iran, and perhaps also to gain some leverage with the British government. This would explain the BMW, hardly likely to be an official car, the absence of uniforms, the insistence on silence in case neighbours reported them, the running shower. The only fly in the ointment of this argument was Khomeini's treatise, since they had become his mortal enemies after he refused to share power with them.

Next day, 9 December, I was interrogated again, and I decided to test my new theory. Almost as soon as my interrogator came in I said, 'I know you are a member of the MKO and I must tell you that when it gets out, as it will sooner or later, that you are holding me, the British government is going to get very tough with your people in London. They know them, and you can be sure that at least your leaders there will be deported, perhaps back to Iran.'

Instead of showing panic and dismay at my words, as I had hoped, he burst out laughing, not something I had seen him do before or was to see often again. He seemed to think this was the funniest thing he had ever heard. Much later I deduced (I still believe correctly) that a close friend and colleague of his was in a British gaol for involvement in a bomb attack on MKO headquarters in London; I realized then how my theory must have amused him, although he did see the force of my logic when I explained my reasons.

Strangely enough, my remark seemed to put him in a good humour, although he could not help saying that it provided further proof that I was a spy. 'Only an Intelligent agent would think like that,' he said. The Iranians, by the way, always get the name by which the British secret service is best known slightly wrong, calling it with unconscious flattery the 'Intelligent Service'. I never corrected my interrogator on this as it was a secret source of amusement.

3

THE PACE OF the interrogation now began to increase. Apart from the daily summons to the interrogation cell upstairs, I was given a sheaf of questions to reply to in writing every day. The beatings and the shouting continued, but were interspersed with occasional episodes of normal Persian civility, making me think my interrogator must have some unresolved psychiatric problems. In layman's terms he seemed to have a split personality. Once he even apologized for knocking me off my chair.

Quite early on in the interrogation, perhaps after only a week, he decided he no longer wished to wear his white mask, but was determined that I should never see his face. As I sat in my regular dunce's corner he put his hand in front of my face from behind, holding a ballpoint pen.

'What is this?' he asked.

'It's a pen,' I replied.

'Good,' he said. 'If you ever see my face, even by accident, or even try to see it, I will push this pen in one of your ears and out of the other.' As he said this, he inserted the point of the pen in my right ear so that I could just feel it.

It was the most effective way he could have chosen to convey his meaning. From that moment on I went out of my way to avoid any chance of ever seeing him. If he knocked me over I got up, dizzy perhaps, but always remembering to cover my eyes until I was back in my chair facing the wall. If I was alone in a room and someone came in, I turned away or covered my eyes, often to the amusement of other interrogators, since he was the only one who ever insisted I should do so.

In the end I did glimpse his face for a split second, but luckily he was in a good mood and I somehow persuaded him I had not really seen him. I had a good idea of his features from when he wore the mask, and hearing his voice for over three years enabled me to assign him a face in my imagination, which turned out to be surprisingly like the real thing. From the colour of his hair, which I sometimes saw surreptitiously from under my blindfold when he led me back to my cell block, I had not, however, expected that his beard would be quite so gingery as it was.

I was also naturally keen to discover his name. At first he refused even to give me a false name, as many interrogators and guards do. 'There's no need for you to call me anything,' he said brusquely. 'I'm your interrogator, and that's all you need to know.'

I argued with him on this point and said, 'In that case I shall give you a name myself. I have to think of you as having a name.' He became curious and asked what name I had chosen. I replied, 'Ali. You sound like an Ali to me.' He flew into a temper at this and said foreigners always assumed every Iranian was called Ali. I said to myself, 'Now, my friend, I'm sure your name is Ali.' After a few moments of silence he said, 'My name is Hosein.' I felt some pleasure at this small, perhaps insignificant victory, especially when, some months later I did discover his real name, and it was Ali.

Many of his questions were similar to those I had been asked by the security official at the Foreign Residents' Bureau, and I told him so. He claimed not to know what I was talking about, and I could not immediately make up my mind whether he was lying. He might well think it worth while to ask me the same questions a month or two later and compare my answers, looking for discrepancies. On the other hand, he might just as easily belong to a different branch of the Islamic Republic's security apparatus and not have access to the dossier on my earlier interrogation.

I quickly came to the conclusion that he was neither an experienced interrogator nor a naturally gifted one. He did not follow any particular course of enquiry but jumped backwards and forwards in an often haphazard way. There may well be cases where this method is effective, say if the interrogator is trying to catch the prisoner off guard with an unexpected question, but he never did this, and his line of questioning would simply fizzle out.

Hosein (to give him the name that I had to use the whole time I was in prison) proved extremely anti-Western, with a particular

47

dislike, amounting to hatred, for the British.

'If I received an order to take a hundred British spies out into the courtyard one by one and shoot them, it would be the happiest day of my life,' he told me early on, and sounded as if he meant it. On another occasion, talking about the British, he said, 'You're all spies.' That remark gave me a certain amount of encouragement, contrary to his presumed intention. For if we are all spies, then there might be nothing especially spy-like about me. It would be enough for me to be British to be a spy, and even in Islamic Iran being British cannot in itself be a crime.

Another characteristic of Hosein was his self-importance. He boasted once that he had single-handedly made the decision to arrest me, and had gone through my file for weeks getting to know me. If that was true he had not done a particularly good job, and as the weeks and months passed I was always having to correct him on matters of detail that arose during the interrogation or to remind him of a name or a place. I think it was on that occasion that he told me about my Savak file, now in the hands of the successor organization Savama. I said that I had once seen my file when summoned to Savak in the 1960s, and it was rather large. 'Large?' he said. 'You should see it now. Two men cannot lift it.'

The beatings were unpleasant enough, of course, but not seriously damaging. Occasionally Hosein would draw blood from my nose or lip, and twice he punched my ear so hard that it was painful to sleep on that side for a few days. Despite this, I suffered no permanent physical injury, as far as I know. Worse than the blows themselves was the anticipation, waking up in the fair certainty that before the day was out I would be hit or punched and unable to defend myself or fight back. Then there was the relief of being taken back to the cell and flopping down on my mattress and trying to shut my mind off from it all, at least for an hour or two, before having to start answering the written questions I had been given. Friday, when he never came, was pure bliss.

The written questions had the advantage of allowing me pen and paper, but the sheets were numbered and I could not at first get hold of any for my personal use. One day, however, Hosein must have numbered the pages in a hurry and I found an unnumbered one in the pad, which I was able to extract and keep. This was such a treasure that at first I did not know what to do with it. The pads he gave me usually had only a dozen sheets, without any cardboard backing, and I had difficulty writing on my knees in my cell. Khomeini's treatise was too small a format to rest on; the Quran served perfectly until a guard caught me and took it away from my profane hands. I got it back from a different guard the next day.

My written Persian was poor at first. I had not written more than the odd note or memo for years, although I could still read and speak fluently enough. But reading and writing are quite different, and sometimes I would rack my brains searching for a word or how to spell one. One of the problems of Persian is that there is a wider gulf between the written and spoken forms than in most European languages. If you write as you speak it is considered quite barbaric. Instead, you have to use a more formal, stilted mode, which in turn would sound ridiculous in everyday speech. During the three years I studied Persian literature and philosophy at Tehran University, the professors would hardly ever set the foreign students written work, presumably because it would mean they would have to mark or correct it, and most of them were too lazy or too grand for that. It was only at the end-of-term examinations that we wrote much, and even those were predominantly oral.

In a curious way, therefore, I quite enjoyed this exercise. At least I was keeping my mind active, and although Hosein never corrected my answers because he said they were fine for his purpose, I could feel I was making some progress, above all improving my writing speed and gradually my handwriting, too. In the early stages of my interrogation it would take me an hour to write a page, and perhaps half an hour to check it over. Later I got the whole thing down to 15 or 20 minutes, and with fewer mistakes.

After a few days, and as the first shock of being thrown into gaol wore off, I began trying to establish some rapport with my guards. The first thing was to learn to differentiate between them, and then to give them names or nicknames. They were an extremely taciturn bunch, and with most of them it was impossible to have any conversation. One or two were downright sadistic, clearly taking pleasure in putting on my blindfold and shouting at me to hurry up when I was washing. Whenever Hosein drew blood I used to ask the guard on duty to let me wash my face before going back to the cell. They usually agreed to this, since blood is *najes*, a pollutant, in Islam, but there was never any sign of sympathy: clearly beating was considered a normal part of the interrogation process.

Nobody told me about the shower rules. Apparently my cell's turn was on Saturday, but I had arrived too late on my first day. A few days later I decided to investigate that running shower tap, and found to my surprise that the water was warm. Knowing I was taking a risk, I slipped off my clothes and got under the shower. I had no soap, but the 'feel-good' factor was certainly present, until the guard came in and caught me. I deadpanned that nobody had told me this was illegal, that cleanliness was next to godliness in Islam, and that the Emam himself (as Khomeini is normally termed in Iran) had told us not to waste water. My act was therefore triply Islamic. The guard did not admire my theology, however, and I was punished by not being allowed a shower when my official day next came round. (A couple of weeks later a plumber finally arrived to replace the washer of the trickling shower.)

Early next morning, perhaps about 5 AM, I was woken by a guard, ordered to the ablutions area and told to start cleaning it. Still half asleep, I had the presence of mind to say, 'What with?' He showed me where the mops and brushes were kept and left me to it. At first I thought this was a punishment for my illegal shower, but then I remembered waking up the day before when my neighbour was hauled out of his cell at about the same un-godly hour, so I guessed there was a cleaning rota based on cell numbers.

To my surprise, I found myself quite enjoying the job. It was a pleasure simply to be out of the cell, without a blindfold, doing some physical exercise that was also useful, for, truth to tell, the whole area needed a thorough spring-cleaning, especially the lavatories. This guard was one of the friendlier ones, and when he came round to collect me half an hour later he was pleasantly surprised at my zeal. I asked for a further ten minutes to finish what

50

I was doing, and he even let me have a quick shower afterwards, so I was well rewarded.

As he hurried me back, with the muezzin about to call the dawn prayer, he told me that this day was my cell's turn, so I would not be detailed for duty till the same day next month. This indicated that there were about 30 cells in the whole prison. To his surprise, I said that if anyone was sick or did not want to do the job, or if a cell was empty, I would gladly volunteer. He said that cells were rarely empty, but thanked me for the offer and said he would tell the other guards. From then on, I was called about once a week, and by the time I left that gaol the ablutions area was spick and span.

Apart from the bonus shower and physical exercise I must have earned some brownie points from the guards. I used to tell them earnestly, 'You see, in our religion cleanliness and hygiene are very important,' to which they would reply, 'In ours too', at which I would look surprised or sigh enigmatically.

As I learned to differentiate between the guards and give them nicknames (occasionally a real name, if I could be sure who was being addressed as 'Hasan' or 'Asghar' by another guard), I decided that my theory about this being a secret opposition group was unlikely to be correct. Members of such a group would be more intelligent, or at least ideologically more aware. They would also switch the radio off when Khomeini's voice came on, and would not let us hear Friday prayers, at which one of the top religio-political leaders, such as Ali Akbar Rafsanjani, Speaker of the Majlis (the Iranian parliament), or President Khamene'i, would preach to the nation.

These guards were true lumpenproletariat, many of them villagers to judge by their accents, and almost certainly doing their two years' military service, to judge by their ages. Most of them sprouted adolescent beards that scarcely needed the three-day blunt scissors job that gives the true designer-stubble look. I was not surprised to find out much later that they were trainee military police, so doing shift-work in this makeshift prison was good practice for them. If I had thought harder I might have guessed this. They had orders not to talk to the prisoners, but one could sometimes gather scraps of information from them. Gradually I worked out their duty roster, and it gave me great pleasure when I guessed correctly, for example, who would be serving lunch or who would be on the first shift of the day.

On the interrogation front, Hosein was now increasingly offering the carrot as well as the stick. He told me that if I 'co-operated' with him I was in no danger, and could even expect to be freed shortly. If not, well, it was up to me, but I would simply linger on indefinitely. On one such occasion I decided to be rather more forceful. I said, 'By now my company will be wondering where I am. When they find I'm not in the hotel they'll get on to the British embassy, who'll take it up with the Foreign Ministry. Dr Velayati will start an investigation and you will have to let me go or bring me to trial without any evidence.' (Ali Akbar Velayati was, and at the time of writing still is, Iran's Foreign Minister. He is a paediatrician, and is generally considered a moderate.)

Hosein snorted at the name. 'Velayati? He's nothing. I could bring him in here tomorrow if I wanted.'

I did not, of course, believe this piece of Hoseinly bravado, but the truth was that by bad luck on the day of my arrest I had just had long conversations with my staff in Dubai, with our agent, and with our prospective partner for a reconstruction project on Kharg Island itself that I was interested in. With nothing much happening it might well have been a week or more before anyone began to wonder where I was.

I asked Hosein what the hotel would say if somebody called me. He said they had already been told to reply that I had checked out and had not said where I was going. Although this would have been contrary to company policy, Dubai might just think I was following up some unexpected piece of business, and therefore not worry about me for a while. My daughter and mother would not start worrying until a few days before Christmas. I had promised to try to get to England for a brief stay over the holidays, but they knew how hectic my schedule was and would not expect news until the last minute.

I had already managed to get a confidential message back to Dubai through a visitor from a company we did business with, so McDermott knew the difficulty I was in over my visa even before my arrest, although no one could have foreseen what actually happened. In point of fact there is some evidence that they were aware of the risk I was running, but this did not emerge until I was already in Iran and unable to leave. I could not be sure whether the Iranian government would be prepared to deny any knowledge of my whereabouts when I was presumably being held by one of its executive agencies.

In December 1979 the referendum on the Constitution of the Islamic Republic upheld the principle of habeas corpus. But I knew that the Shah and his father had consistently ignored the democratic elements of their constitution, so I could not feel confident that my rights would be respected under the new regime. It was all too likely that Hosein could get away with keeping me for months, until I 'co-operated' with him or he received orders to let me go. It might even be less embarrassing to kill me and hide the evidence. At best, my illegal detention would be brushed aside as an 'administrative error', or 'in the higher interests of the state', and all concerned, including me, would be too pleased with the outcome to make much of a fuss.

Some months later, Hosein did admit that the British embassy had been asking for information about me, as I knew must be the case. Hosein laughed as he told me the government had denied all knowledge of me. 'Nobody knows you're here, and they probably think you've been murdered by Forghan,' he said, a reference to an extreme religious group that had already kidnapped and murdered the son of the Anglican bishop of Isfahan, whom I had met shortly before his abduction.

On Friday 20 December 1985, at the end of my second week in gaol, I was told to come out for exercise. I was led to a small yard, where I was allowed to take off my blindfold and walk around a circular track for a quarter of an hour, under the watchful eye of a guard. This gave me enormous pleasure, as my cell was only about nine feet by five, too small to take more than three or four short steps. I love walking, in the mountains or woods or in an unfamiliar town, but this was positively therapeutic. In less than two weeks my leg muscles had already begun to stiffen, and I determined to start a proper exercise programme and keep it up until I was free. That, together with a brisk walk, even a brief one once a week, would keep me in shape.

Another great joy was that I could now see where I was, and felt pleased at having worked out the location so accurately. Above me like a great wall stood the Alborz mountains, already thickly blanketed with fresh snow above the 8000-feet line, and from a few buildings and open spaces, and the sound of traffic, I knew exactly which street I was on. There was no doubt that I was in an army barracks. Being Friday there was little activity, and my view was restricted, but the architecture was pure Pahlavi military. The buildings I had thought might be suburban houses could now be seen as part of the barracks, perhaps married quarters, and on reflection I realized it would be impossible for an opposition group to run such an operation in the centre of Tehran without being detected. This still left unsolved the mystery of why I had been taken to a military camp instead of one of Savama's own detention centres, taken over from Savak, where my friends Narsi and Louise Firouz had been questioned for a week, or to Evin, the maximum-security prison in the foothills of the Alborz mountains north of Tehran where most detainees on spying or anti-state charges are held. Something was wrong.

It was a beautiful early winter's day, in fact just two days before the official start of winter, with autumn lingering in the air. Some of the poplars still had their leaves. Although it was almost noon, the sun was low. Tomorrow night would be Shab-e Yalda, the celebration of the winter solstice that goes back to pre-Islamic times, an evening when families traditionally sit around eating water melons, carefully kept since late summer, and dried fruit and nuts, telling jokes and stories to while away the longest night.

The Emam (as I was always careful to say when referring in Persian to Khomeini) disliked these old traditions, which he considered un-Islamic, and was doing his best to discourage them, even Now Ruz, the spring festival and Persian New Year. The official excuse was that celebrations should not take place until after the war with Iraq was won, but when the war did end in 1988 the religious establishment found other excuses to play down the festivals, so that a whole generation was growing up with little knowledge of this traditional part of Iranian culture.

I love the Persian calendar, and would like to see it replace the

West's ridiculous hotchpotch in which the year begins on a nothing day that comes only a week after Christmas. The twelve Persian months match the seasons and the signs of the Zodiac, and are named after Zoroastrian angels (angels, incidentally, are also an Iranian invention). The first six months all have 31 days, the next five have 30, and the last one has 29 days plus an extra one in leap years. These lengths actually correspond to the seasons, as spring and summer are about a week longer than autumn and winter, and so the equinoxes and the solstices are accurately reflected in the Persian calendar. Omar Khayyam is said to have been one of the scholars who worked on perfecting this system in the eleventh century, at a time when the Julian calendar which we inherited from the Romans was beginning to get seriously out of synch with the seasons, and some 500 years before Pope Gregory XIII introduced his half-hearted reformation, which we still use in the West. What a pity he failed to look East!

I was still musing about dates and calendars when the guard called for me to come in, and I took one last look at Towchal, the highest peak, at about 13,000 feet, in the range overlooking Tehran. The perpetual Tehran smog, at its worst in winter when millions of kerosene stoves add to the exhaust fumes to create a huge black cloud that is visible as one approaches the city, prevented me from seeing Mount Damavand, the 19,000-foot dormant volcano to the east. I had climbed Damavand some twenty years earlier and would like to have tried it again, but this time without the village guide, whose advice made the climb more difficult than need be, even allowing for the shortage of oxygen and the sulphur fumes as one nears the summit.

In a high valley quite close to Tehran, I had helped in 1966 to build a small stone shelter beside a rushing stream, and until the early 1970s had used it as a year-round base to climb from. Arthur, my climbing partner, and I brought the stones to the site, mainly by rolling them down from above, and we found a dry-stone mason who magically created walls from them. Then came wooden beams, some straw matting and a thick coat of mud for the roof. A crude window, usually blocked up against the cold, and a stout lockable door completed our little hut, which we could reach in an hour from where we parked in north Tehran, even in fresh snow. In autumn we took fuel, potatoes and onions up by mule, and the hut was equipped with cooking and eating utensils, bedding, a lamp and a chess-set, so that we could travel light when we finished work on Thursday afternoons. I would get a simple stew going while Arthur lit his pipe and set up the chessboard and a quarter bottle of vodka. The next morning we would wake up early, often to fresh snow crisscrossed with the tracks of animals we never saw, consume vast quantities of tea and porridge, then set off up to the ridges, with Tehran behind us and the Caspian Sea far away to the north, usually hidden by cloud or other mountain ranges. A whole day in the mountains set us up for the six days that lay ahead.

Sadly for us, the Shah decided to change palaces, and the one he (or more probably the Empress Farah) picked for the main imperial residence was close to the mouth of our valley. Security considerations soon put the whole area out of bounds except to a few known shepherds. We did manage to get to our Shangri-La a few times after that but were usually spotted by the guards on the watch-towers, and the trip was simply not worth the hassle. On my visits to Tehran after the Revolution I was free to go there again, and although the valley was just as beautiful I was distressed to find our hut vandalized, the roof now missing and open to the elements. I could have rebuilt it, but I was not now likely to be in Iran long enough to make it worth while, although I did leave a pair of boots with friends and always tried to fit in a short climb on my business trips.

I went back to my cell, refreshed in body and spirit, quite unaware that my short spell in the open air had been without Hosein's knowledge and consent. He soon found out, and that was my first and only outing. It was to be more than two years before I saw the mountains again, or even walked in the open air without a blindfold. Outside my cell I could only take the thing off during interrogation when I faced the wall, or when I got to see a medic, or was actually inside a shower cubicle. The two cells I lived in for the first three years of my captivity received little daylight, and almost no sunshine at all.

The weather turned cold bang on time, as it usually does in Iran, and I was soon feeling the blasts of winter in my cell. The

56

guards had orders to open the corridor window into the courtyard for a few hours every day, and while I approved of this change of air, it did make my cell particularly cold since it was right opposite the window. My prison clothes were inadequate, so I asked Hosein if he would give me the black cashmere pullover I had put inside my briefcase on the day of my arrest. To my surprise he agreed, though adding that it would depend on the quality of my written answers next day, so I took extra care with them. He even agreed to my watch being returned, when I told him it would help me to plan my writing every evening and not be plunged into darkness with papers scattered about the cell when 'lights out' suddenly came.

That pullover was a life-saver. I wore it night and day, and slept better without the metal buttons of the jacket cutting into me. It was the most wonderful garment I have ever owned, even though it was bought in a sale and was not quite my size. It was made in Scotland by Pringle, who, as manufacturers of knitwear to the Queen, had put the royal coat of arms on the label. Despite my republican leanings, that gave me a warm, patriotic feeling, and somehow renewed my dwindling hopes that Her Majesty's Government were trying to trace me. I liked my pullover so much, in fact, that when the fruit trolley next came round and I got my 125-gram ration of apples and oranges (usually one of each, but the guards were meticulous about weighing out the fruit), I asked the astonished guard to weigh it. I then calculated the value of an equivalent weight of gold and found that if I stayed in gaol much longer the pullover would literally be worth its weight in gold, or even platinum, since I would gladly have paid ten dollars a day for its comforting warmth. The only trouble was that cashmere pullovers are not designed for hard gaol use, and within a few months the right elbow began to wear thin. I patched it with some coarse blue cloth, all I could get, but thereafter it was not quite so House of Windsor as it had been.

I was more than usually conscious of the approach of Christmas, which is always a last-minute operation as I rush out to do my shopping on the last day possible. Somehow I felt sure that if I was going to be freed it would be before or at Christmas, or at worst by New Year's Day, since Iranians always get confused about which is which. Whether this happened or not, I decided to practise a few carols so that I could have a carol service on Christmas Eve. I must have had this idea on 12 December because I remember noticing when I began trying to remember 'The Twelve Days of Christmas' that there were exactly twelve days to go. At first I could not remember all the verses or their order, so I decided to sing one verse a day while I worked out the next one, finishing up with the full last verse on Christmas Day.

This was one of those superstitious habits which I found most prisoners succumb to, saying things like 'If X happens, then I'll be released by such and such a date' or 'If Y is on duty in the morning I won't be taken to interrogation.' These superstitions rarely work, but prisoners go on making them up and believing in them.

I was already preparing myself for being in my cell for Christmas, and as it approached I began saving titbits of food for my Christmas dinner. We were lucky to have chicken stew a day or two before, so I kept the best piece for a symbolic 'roast', and decided to put some hoarded fruit into a sock to make a Christmas stocking the night before. By then the prison shop, in the form of a trolley, had come round, enabling me to buy spare socks and underwear and a second towel. I also acquired a toothbrush, toothpaste and a peculiarly Iranian implement, something between a brush and a comb, which I am sure would catch on if marketed in the West. The Christmas tree and decorations were my main problem.

My voluntary work in the ablutions had the advantage that I could pick over the trash-can at my leisure. The guards often threw away quite useful things, which I could then smuggle back into my cell. On one of these siftings I came across a large piece of cardboard, and even some green paper and other coloured items. With these, on Christmas Eve I erected a tree of sorts, propped up in my trash bucket. The guards were suspicious at first, but I explained it was a religious ceremony and they became both respectful and curious about such a strange custom. I told them that many of our religious ceremonies went back to the pre-Christian era, and that they often echoed old Persian traditions like Now Ruz. Iranians, for example, bring green plants into the house before New Year, such as sprouting wheat and hyacinths, but to avoid bad luck must throw them out on the thirteenth day, just as Westerners take down their Christmas trees on Twelfth Night.

I discovered from the blank stares I received from the guards that they knew nothing about their own traditions, but were nevertheless interested in mine. As I began to have conversations with some of them I heard extraordinary stories about England, clearly black propaganda spread by fanatics. Apart from AIDS being endemic, our drinking water was recycled sewage, and homosexual marriages were commonplace. The Queen, or possibly Mrs Thatcher (the two were sometimes confused), decided who the next President of the United States would be, because Americans were very weak in politics and the British were extremely clever. This made Britain a more dangerous enemy than America. They even misquoted a famous saying of the Emam, which actually goes 'America is worse than Britain, Britain is worse than America, but the Soviet Union is worse than both,' making Britain the arch-villain.

One day a medic came round to vaccinate us against tuberculosis. I was willing to have this done – in fact it seemed a sensible precaution if I was to stay for any length of time in this damp and insalubrious environment – but there were strong objections from several of the prisoners in nearby cells. The guards had to hold one man down, and the others only acquiesced when they saw that resistance was useless. I could hear the man after me grumbling that he did not believe it was really a TB shot, it had to be for something else. In any case, he was not going to be here long enough to get TB. He was innocent, and in the Islamic Republic an innocent man could not be kept in prison, as used to happen in the time of the Shah. (In fact he did not refer to the Shah by his title, which is rarely heard in fundamentalist circles. Instead he said 'taghut', a Quranic word used to describe a particularly nasty devil.) The guard's reply – one I was to hear again and again in the course of the next five years – sent a shiver down my spine: 'You wouldn't have been brought here if you were innocent.'

A few days later the prisoner in a cell two doors down from mine went berserk. He began shouting and screaming, and the duty guard could not get him to stop. He threw his few possessions at the walls and ceiling, breaking the light; some of them sailed through the bars and clattered down the corridor in front of my cell. The guard went for help, but two men could not subdue him. The medic was called to give him a shot of something, and soon the prisoner was lying down, quietly sobbing. The drama was over. I was impressed that the guards had not solved the problem by beating him into a pulp, as happened once or twice later in my block in Evin when prisoners went out of control.

I had acquired another book, a work on Islamic economics which had been brought to me by a guard, in addition to the Quran and Khomeini's treatise, but one day I was told to come to the library. The guard who took me was particularly strict with my blindfold, so I saw nothing en route, but noticed that we went upstairs by a spiral staircase, not by the usual steps. When I got there the library clerk asked my prison number and was obviously looking me up in a register. Suddenly his tone changed and he said to the guard, 'This prisoner has been denied library privileges. Take him back to his cell.'

That little outing made me appreciate the economics book all the more. The guard failed to notice I had it, and I guessed the two religious books would not be taken away.

One problem with reading was that Hosein would not return my glasses. Perhaps he was afraid that I would break a lens and slash my wrists, because it was clearly in his interests for me to see properly to answer his endless questions. He said, 'You've only recently bought your glasses. I'm sure you can see well enough without them.'

This was true, and confirmed that I must have been under constant surveillance in the weeks before my arrest. I had in fact bought my first pair of glasses only a month or so earlier from a local optician who tested my eyes and gave me the minimum strength of lens to help me read fine print, which had begun to be difficult. In the cell, with only one low-powered bulb, I could not easily read the small type that Khomeini's words of wisdom were set in, nor the Persian version of the Quran, printed in beautiful calligraphy beneath the more legible Arabic. I could read the economics book quite well, however, and after the library incident I got on more quickly with it, afraid that the guard would come to confiscate it.

Already I was beginning to wonder whether a false confession might not be the best way of gaining my freedom. It was a dangerous idea, and if I got it wrong I would be in a worse position than I already was, but if nothing happened soon I might very well be in for a long haul. Although I had by no means decided to make a confession I thought it might be best to start thinking about this as an option, and to use my precious sheet of paper to make notes on, which I could then commit to memory. The only way would be to confess to something extremely minimal, not in fact to espionage at all, for example to having some tenuous links with people who might, without my fully realizing it, be part of British Intelligence. It would not be easy, but with luck I might be able to strike a safe balance between giving Hosein enough material to save face and actually incriminating myself. At least, I thought, I could begin working out the bare bones of such a story for possible use if the going got really rough. The worst situation to be in would be to undergo torture without a convincing story that might induce my persecutors to stop.

So I began making notes, trying out various possible lines, crossing some of them out, changing them, always trying to think of things that looked right for this purpose but in fact were never against Iran's interests. For several nights I sat up working on this after I had done my 'homework' of questions and read my daily chapter of Bagher Sadr's *Our Economy*, an interesting work by a relative of the Lebanese Shi'a leader Imam Musa Sadr, who disappeared while on a visit to Libya and is now assumed to have been killed on Qadafi's orders, because while taking Libyan money he was not following the Libyan leader's line closely enough.

One evening just before Christmas a guard suddenly opened the door and told me to pack up all my things. 'Hurrah,' I thought at once, 'I'm going to be released. The British chargé d'affaires is probably outside the prison gates in the embassy Jaguar, and this nightmare will soon be over.'

I told the guard that there was nothing in the cell I wanted, and I was ready to come as I was, though preferably in my own clothes, please. He insisted on my taking the plastic bowl and water jug and my other possessions. This perturbed me, but perhaps there was a bureaucratic check and I would formally have to return all my prison items. He led me blindfolded down the corridor, worryingly not up the usual steps or even the spiral staircase, but into the second corridor behind mine where he opened a door and pushed me into a cell.

When I took off my blindfold I found myself in a cell about the same size as the one I had just left with two Iranian prisoners already in it. They had intelligent and friendly faces, but were obviously as surprised to see me as I was to see them. I told them my story briefly, and asked them theirs. One had been there a little longer than me, the other only about a week. One said he had heard nobody stayed more than a month in this gaol, but I said a previous occupant of my cell had been there at least 58 days, judging from the graffiti.

As I asked them more questions I noticed a slight reticence developing, and I sensed that, understandably enough, they did not fully trust me. There would be time for us to get to know each other, so it would be silly to ask them about their personal cases until they were ready to talk. What worried me most was the lack of space. Sitting cross-legged on the floor – something I am not very good at – we had room enough. But at night, although both men were quite small, we would only just about be able to stretch out on the floor. I had not brought my bedding, but presumably the guards would let me fetch it or bring it themselves.

One thing I liked about the cell was that it was spotlessly clean, certainly cleaner than mine. I asked them how they kept it like this, as I had tried unsuccessfully to borrow a dustpan and brush. They showed me how they had broken off a piece of foam mattress and used it laboriously to clean the thin Chinese carpeting on the floor. This explained why my mattress had a chewed look at both ends and was a good eighteen inches shorter than my height.

We were chatting away about neutral subjects when the guard reappeared. 'A mistake,' he said, looking slightly worried and clearly thinking he might get into trouble. The two men stood up politely and shook hands with me, and less than half an hour after I had left it I was home again, sorry to have lost an opportunity of finding out more about the prison, but at the same time glad to be back in my own cell, which suddenly seemed luxuriously spacious.

Christmas Day fell on a Wednesday that year, and I hoped against hope that Hosein would not send for me. Surely he must know it was a special day and would leave me alone?

I was up early, as usual, thinking of the carol service that I had sung sotto voce the night before. I had left two carols for the day itself, 'I Saw Three Ships Come Sailing In' and, of course, the last verse of 'The Twelve Days of Christmas', with the lords a-leaping and the maids a-milking all in their proper place. I admired my Christmas tree and opened my stocking. My special Christmas dinner was a treat in store.

And then Hosein did send for me. I decided to put on a jaunty air, and wished him a happy Christmas. In case he did not know of Christmas, I explained the significance, suggesting that he should postpone the interrogation for a day. It was not to be. In his coldest voice he replied that Muslims did indeed revere Saint Jesus, who was one of the greatest prophets before Muhammad, but whose message had been distorted by the Europeans. It was blasphemy to call him the Son of God.

This led us into theological disputation, and I noticed that Hosein was beginning to speak more rapidly and the tone of his voice was becoming shriller, sure signs that he was losing his temper. Suddenly he clouted me on the side of the head and told me to shut up and answer his questions. It was a particularly unpleasant session, and I came back to the cell shortly before lunch, psychologically drained and with my head still ringing from his slaps and punches. I flopped down on to the mattress, crushing a tangerine that was still in the sock. I took my lunch, but could not eat it. When I recovered an hour later, there was a thick coat of congealed grease on top, which I could not face. Instead, I ate my little morsel of chicken, with some bread, and felt very sorry for myself.

4

HOSEIN HAD KNOCKED the Christmas spirit out of me. By Boxing Day my 'tree' had begun to look ridiculous, so I dismantled it. It was Thursday, the Muslim equivalent of Saturday, a day when Hosein might or might not come: I was glad when he did not. On Friday, my third Friday in gaol, I knew he would not come, but neither did I get the walk in the yard I was expecting. Instead, I got Friday prayers played full blast over the speaker outside my cell. Saturday was not a day to look forward to, the start of my fourth week of interrogation, but miraculously Hosein did not come.

On Sunday morning two guards appeared in my cell and demanded all my writing materials: writing pad with half-hearted answers to my Christmas Day questions, my own ballpoint pen, even more worryingly the Quran, the Khomeini treatise and the economics book. The ultimate humiliation was when they demanded my watch. I dreaded that my pullover would also be taken back, but it was not.

How clever of me, I thought, or how lucky, that I had put my 'confession' notes under my mattress. They might take everything away, but this they would not find. After lunch, or perhaps in two or three batches, since I could not rely on the absorbtive capacity of the WCs, I would shred and dispose of this potentially incriminating document. But my luck was out. After taking the obvious items they then searched the cell thoroughly and, of course, found my hidden sheet of paper, full of half-baked ideas. The most ridiculous of all, it now seemed to me, was an imaginary trip to Johannesburg at the invitation of BOSS, the South African security service, who had consulted me on ways of buying Iranian crude oil. I had said that Iran would never sell oil to South Africa while apartheid was in place, but I might be able to arrange some one-off tanker-loads from smaller Persian Gulf producers, at a price of course. This was the kind of spy-image I wanted to promote for myself, rather harmless and always pro-Iranian. Originally I quite liked this story because Hosein would not be able to disprove it, since no Iranian could have visited South Africa, at least officially, since the Revolution, when diplomatic links were cut. I could therefore probably describe my brief stay as the guest of BOSS – night arrival, night departure, car to a private villa – convincingly enough, and I knew enough about the marketing of Persian Gulf crude oil to make my thirty krugerrand fee sound plausible. I remember I toyed with various amounts and methods of payment before hitting on the Judas number. Now Hosein would have all these draft versions, and plenty to grill me about later that day or the next.

Monday came, and Tuesday, and still no summons from Hosein. What did this mean? Tuesday night was New Year's Eve, and one or two of the guards, having heard on the radio that for me this was the last day of the year 1985, dropped in to see what pagan ceremonies I would be performing. To their surprise, I said 'None'. The 'Eskotlandis', I told them, performed special rites on this night, which they called 'Hogmanay', perhaps because on that night they killed and ate a pig – shock and horror from the guards – but the 'Englisis' hardly recognized it, my family certainly did not, and in any case it was not part of our religion.

Perhaps, I thought, Hosein has checked his diary and thinks, like the guards, that 1 January is a day when I would feel particularly vulnerable, and hence ideal for interrogation. But New Year's Day came and went, and the next day, then it was Friday again. Surely on Saturday; but no. Nothing from either Hosein or the guards. Time simply passed.

I was not idle during this period. Some time during that week I was allotted a new prison number. It was an unfriendly number, 381 I think, divisible by 3 and nothing else, and with time suddenly on my hands, and nothing to read, I began to consider the question of prime numbers, the very concept of which I had not thought about for almost forty years. How exactly did they occur, was there a pattern, could one predict their occurrence or frequency?

I decided to investigate these questions.

Without pen, paper or a calculator it is not easy to do even simple maths, and the first problem was to find substitutes. My initial idea was a crude quantitative system of numbers using orange pips. A Persian orange can easily provide two dozen pips, but on a one-to-one basis this soon became a cumbersome way of deciding whether a number was divisible by 17 or 23. Instead, I began to collect prune-stones from the stews, using them as fives, like the roman numeral V. My next breakthrough came when I decided to give my numbers a positional value as well as a quantitative one, just like our decimal system. Finally, I hit on the idea of using an apple pip as a zero. The Romans, to their eternal shame, failed to invent the zero, a concept coming much later from the East, probably from India to the Arab-Persian scholars of central Asia, who called it *sifr*, 'yellow' because more parchment could be seen in the blank space. If the Romans had developed a zero and built upon the Greek and Babylonian traditions of geometry and astronomy, who knows what technological breakthroughs they might not have achieved?

With my *mohreh* for a crayon I was soon able to record, on the wall behind the door – guessing that if a guard entered my cell he would never close the door – all the prime numbers up to about 2000. I then tried to find a theory that explained their occurrence. Since then I have not had the time or the inclination to repeat the exercise, but I remember being surprised that their frequency does not diminish on a straight-line statistical basis, as I had expected. Instead they occur in apparently random bursts, such as 461, 463 and 469, which are all primes. I failed to find a satisfactory explanation for this, but as a working analogy I compared it with the electronic game of 'Space Invaders'. As each new number is thrown up by our decimal system (say, 272, 273, 274, 275, 276) most of them will be 'shot down' by earlier primes, in this case to take the lowest prime only, by 2, 3, 2, 5, 2 respectively. The next one in this little series, 277, however, will 'slip through the barrage', as a prime, to join the surface-to-air defenders itself in due course, although it will have to wait until 77,837 for its first direct hit. These mathematical musings are of little or no scientific interest in themselves, although they did pave the way for some more exciting experiments and discoveries later, once I had proper writing materials.

At about the same time I began to feel the need to play some kind of game. When Hosein brought my sweater he also gave me the airline eyeshade that I always carry in my briefcase. I use it whenever I am on a long car or train trip and want to take a cat-nap, and I think Hosein originally brought it to ask me what it was, since Iran Air, probably the only airline he had ever flown with, did not provide its passengers with these useful giveaways. For some reason, perhaps because it was foreign and therefore gave him status, he preferred it as a blindfold to a towel, and let me use it when he summoned me, although the guards banned it for the ablutions run: they knew that it was easier to cheat with than a towel.

One afternoon I was sitting with my back against the wall and my calculating prune-stones and orange pips in my hand, when I idly flicked a stone at the eyeshade with my thumb. I missed, but at that instant the game of flicket was born, just as rugby football came into existence at the precise moment in the year 1823 when William Webb Ellis picked up a football and ran with it. Flicket is not, as yet, widely known, but one day I am sure it will sweep the world, as football has done, since it requires little in the way of equipment or space, yet is competitive, demanding and fun. I am proud to say that since no one has so far challenged me, my claim to have been the sport's world champion for the past seven years must be valid.

Over the next few weeks I evolved a complete set of rules for flicket, together with the special vocabulary that all proper games have. To be honest, I cannot now remember them all. Flicket is played between two walls about five feet apart, and once I left solitary confinement for a larger communal cell I had to stop playing it. This disadvantage might have been overcome by the use of portable boards, but in gaol this was not easy to arrange, and, frankly, my cell-mates did not seem as enthusiastic about flicket as I was.

Briefly, the game is played between two players, or any combination of teams or individuals, each of whom is armed with 17 prune-stones, two of which are coloured red with pomegranate

67

juice. These are known as 'pommies', and score double or triple, depending on when they are used. The object is to flick your stones on to the eyeshade either directly (a 'straight'), or off the wall (an 'offer') and different scores apply. There are bonuses for hat-tricks ('hatters') and ones that strike other stones first ('strikers'). As can be seen, the game is not very sophisticated (it has some affinity to tiddlywinks), so the scoring brings variety. I never achieved a perfect run of flicking all my stones into the eyeshade, but I did once get 13 of them in, including both my pommies, and on another occasion got a ten-hatter early on, then blew the rest of the round. Once I am dethroned as champion I expect to settle down as a good average club player.

Backgammon has been a passion of mine ever since I learnt the game at the age of eleven. My then housemaster, Major Read, had served in the Indian Army, where it was a popular, low-stakes gambling game, and with none of his old cronies around to play he decided to teach me. I doubt if I gave him much of a game, but years later I found another instructor in Guity's stepfather, 'Shazdeh' Jalali Qajar, one of the best players in Tehran. If he had stuck to backgammon he might have preserved, or even increased, the family wealth, but sadly he lost more than his backgammon winnings at chemin de fer. He played this card-equivalent of roulette several times a week at the illegal gambling clubs that were a feature of pre-Revolutionary Iran, and resembled the floating crap-games described by Damon Runyon.

'Shazdeh' means 'prince' or 'princeling' in Persian, and my father-in-law was a grandson of the Qajar monarch Nasser-ad-Din Shah, whose reign roughly coincided with Queen Victoria's. His father had been for many years Minister of War, but the advent to power in 1921 of Reza Khan, later Reza Shah, greatly diminished the Qajar family's influence, although 'Shazdeh' was given a sinecure job as inspector of railways, which he still held when I married Guity. He had such a reputation for gambling and enjoying the good life that even his brothers called him by this slightly disparaging nickname.

At my request he took me along to a few all-night sessions of the 'Gazelle' chemin de fer club, and I discovered that the owner of the house got a fat fee from the organizers for permitting sessions to be held once or twice a month. I suggested to Shazdeh that instead of losing his money at the tables he should offer to host the club occasionally. At the time my in-laws' family house had just been sold and they were staying with Guity and me while house-hunting. Guity and her mother Touran both objected, but Shazdeh and I pressed the point and a few sessions were held in our house. I was glad that this never came out in my interrogation as I could have been sentenced retroactively to 72 lashes for incitement to gambling, which Islam rightly abhors.

It did not take me long to set up a backgammon system in my cell. A pair of dice was soon moulded from bread dough, with apple-pips for spots, and a complete flat loaf of *barbari* bread cried out to be used as a backgammon board. The men were prune-stones and orange-pips, and they proved evenly matched, from the first rubber to the final rubber of rubbers of rubbers, which the prunes narrowly won. Later on, in Evin, when I got a packet of dates, a third side could enter the fray. To my surprise, they carried all before them, proving perhaps the oriental origins of the game. Legend has it that a sixth-century Indian monarch sent a chess set to Khosrow Parviz, the Persian King of Kings, but without explaining the rules of the game. Bozorgmehr, the clever vizier at the Persian court, worked out the rules himself and sent an ambassador with backgammon as a return gift, together with the first-ever chess problem. This amazed the Indians, according to the story.

I was playing backgammon in the corner of my cell least visible through the spy-hole when the door suddenly opened and a guard demanded to know what I was doing. There was no time to get rid of the dice, which he took from my hands to examine in the corridor. Knowing that since the Revolution backgammon was banned in Iran I was quaking at what the penalty would be. Luckily, he was either a friendly or a stupid guard. He dropped one of the dice, which shattered on the floor, and then handed the other one back with an apology. I immediately crushed it in my hand and said it was quite unimportant; I was just fiddling about with a piece of old bread. I stopped playing for a few days and thereafter took greater precautions when rolling the dice. Usually I could hear the guards clumping up and down the corridor

69

or sitting down by the radiator, but there was no defence against a guard who tiptoed up to the spy-hole.

As the days of January slowly passed, my optimism faded, but one of the strange aspects of this dark period of my imprisonment, in fact perhaps of the entire period, was that my dreams were always cheerful and optimistic. They were full of parties and gatherings of friends, there were flashbacks to playing tip-and-run cricket on a corner of the famous Close at Clifton College, when I was fifteen or so, the weather was always warm and sunny, the music, food and drink were first class. Before my arrest I had been working in any free time I had on a guide to the seafood of the Persian Gulf, cooking my way through the 243 edible marine species found there, or at least representatives of each genus. I used to eat fish or shellfish at least once a day. In prison, except for the odd can of mackerel or Caspian sprats which came my way in the last two years, I did not eat any fish, but in my dreams there were often bowls of mussels or prawns, and plates of silver pomfret on the bone, or a nice fillet of *hamur*, two of the best fish to be found in the Dubai market.

These dreams were a great comfort, getting me off to a good start on otherwise boring or unpleasant days. Later, when I had writing materials again, I began to record them, and these notes were like a library of home videos that I could play again and again and ponder their significance. One schoolmate of mine, for example, whom I had not been particularly close to, kept recurring in my dreams, even though I had not seen or heard of him for almost forty years. A few weeks after my release I was walking down a street in a small Surrey town and practically bumped into him. He was now a successful painter and looked exactly as he had done in my dreams. A true test of a prophetic dream is, I suppose, if you write it down or tell somebody before the event happens. Of the hundreds, perhaps thousands of dreams I was to record only two fell into that category, both of them previews of rather insignificant but unusual events that actually happened later that day.

The other side of the dream coin came after my release. For the first few months, and indeed even two years later, I regularly had nightmares or at least dreams full of angst and unpleasantness.

My own theory about this is a financial analogy: in gaol I was drawing heavily on the bank of my subconscious; later, like all loans and overdrafts, this credit had to be repaid.

At a more mundane level I still suffered for a time from limited access to the toilets. After the TB drama I got on friendly terms with the medic and explained to him that because of a chronic digestive problem I needed more than one cup of tea per day. My doctor, I told him, recommended at least a litre of tea or other warm drink to irrigate my digestive tract. He nodded sympathetically and wrote a note on the card outside my cell authorizing me to have extra tea when available. Not all the guards honoured the request, but I often got more tea than my bladder could comfortably hold until the next toilet call. The solution came when I found a small bucket in the washroom, obviously left behind by a prisoner. There was one of these in every cell, and the strictly honourable thing to do, perhaps the wisest one too, would have been to have handed it over to the duty guard. I pondered the problem for a while and decided the guards would anyway have to replace the missing one, whereas if it was traced to me I could simply say I thought it had been discarded. So I left it conspicuously in my cell for a day or two, and when I was sure no search party was looking for it I hid it. From then on I had a chamber pot, which I could cover with a dish and empty surreptitiously, while taking my actual trash to the bin on other occasions. It seems almost unbelievable now that such subterfuges were necessary or important, but at the time they certainly were, and they also proved to be good training for the more rewarding ways I found of bucking the prison system later on.

It would be misleading to give the impression, in describing my activities and feelings in these first few weeks of captivity, that my morale was consistently high. True, I always tried to put a brave face on events, and my public-school education, followed by two years in the British army, had instilled the stiff-upper-lip convention into me in my formative years. But deep down inside me I felt surges of panic and desperation. Later on, and even to some extent at that time, I guessed that Hosein was staying away deliberately, hoping to make me nervous and so more amenable

71

to his offers. I was determined not to let this happen, yet could not help it, and by 29 January 1986, my fifty-first birthday, I was seriously depressed.

I do not normally make much of my birthdays and have not held a party for one in years, except occasionally to join forces with Chris Powell, a New Zealand journalist friend almost exactly my age, to give a joint one. My fiftieth birthday, supposedly a major milestone in life, had been spent in our agent's guest-house in Ahwaz. I had managed to get a quart of 'rocket-fuel', as we called the fierce moonshine liquor made illicitly since the Revolution by Armenian Christians, plus a bottle of Scotch bearing the label of the Iraqi state liquor and tobacco monopoly. It amused me that even though Iran and Iraq were locked in the bloodiest war since Vietnam the black market – or free market as I prefer to call it – was somehow able to deliver this product across the front lines, presumably by pack animals through Kurdistan. So I treated the other expats in the guest-house to a celebratory supper of Persian Gulf shrimps and fruit salad, and they drank to the success of my second half-century. The way things were going, their wishes now looked wildly unrealistic, I thought. I also missed the letters or cards that my mother and daughter always sent, which suddenly seemed terribly important.

By now, as the end of my second month in gaol approached, I had begun to think of basic religious matters, asking myself what I really believed in. Is there a divine purpose to life or are we just a freakish blip in the vastness of a lifeless universe? By defining life in purely physical and chemical terms, are the scientists really getting any closer to the mystery of creation? Are we something special or just the most successful species to have emerged from the evolutionary process? And does bringing God into it really make things any different? Calling God 'uncreated', as all religions are bound to, hardly alters the underlying question: how did the whole programme start in the first place? I found myself baffled by these fundamental questions, and in my agnostic, if not quite atheistic, way asked the most pressing question of all: 'O God, if there is a God, why are you doing this to me?' The silence was deafening, even when I politely rephrased it as: 'Why art Thou doing this to me?' These questions continued to haunt me for the next five years, but by the end of that time I had found some partially satisfactory answers.

The other and more practical question was: 'Why am I not a paid-up member of the Intelligence Service?' If I had been, I would have been briefed, presumably, on how to behave in my present predicament. I would have been told what to say, how to say it, which 'secrets' to reveal, which to guard at any price. I might even have been issued with a cyanide pill, as I recalled James Bond had been on the eve of one of his assignments. It was not enough to think that I would probably have done what the intrepid commander did and flushed it down the nearest lavatory. Wallowing in self-pity, I came to the conclusion that my position was much worse than any he had found himself in.

I did, in fact, consider the question of suicide then, and once or twice later. Not that I believe I would ever have done it, but I did consider it in philosophical and practical terms. I remembered arriving in Spain once at the urgent request of my uncle Christopher, a doctor who had qualified while in an iron lung suffering from tuberculosis, from which he only partly recovered. Later, having moved to Spain for the climate, he contracted severe arthritis, and by the time I arrived at his villa he was depending on aspirin and alcohol for pain-killers, one knee now held together by a metal pin and the other about to require the same treatment. This would mean the end of his driving, and the destruction of his already threatened life-style.

Almost the first thing he asked was 'Have you read Montaigne on suicide?' I racked my brains, but had to admit that this particular essay had not been on my A-level or Oxford French literature syllabus. He handed me a copy, and next day I told him that while I found the eighteenth-century philosopher's arguments powerful, there were important counter-arguments he had not touched upon. By now, my uncle had hinted that the reason for his summons was that he was contemplating putting an end to a life he considered unproductive and self-indulgent. In the war he had cleared a record six feet to win the RAF high jump; now he could hardly walk. Far better to die now and pass on his patrimony to his nephews – he had never married – before it was all dissipated. I told him he was one of the best-loved members of the family, a source of intellectual and practical inspiration to his wide circle of friends, and that his death would be widely mourned and even considered selfish. He perked up at this, and when I left him three months later he seemed to have acquired a new lease of life, not the least reason being the question of whether I would ever repay the £2000 or so I had borrowed from him. I did so, and regret it to this day, because within a month he took an overdose of sleeping pills while staying with my father, ironically himself a psychiatrist.

I felt, and still feel, that suicide is often the coward's way out. My life would have to be extremely bleak, on a different scale of bleakness even than the black moods I was now sinking into, for me to take my own life. Yet I had to consider the very real possibility that things might reach that stage. Under serious torture, as opposed to Hosein's spiteful punches, what would I be able to do? I had nothing to confess, to buy time with, so it could go on indefinitely and I might find myself in those Stygian depths of depression that make people give up. The answer, it seemed to me, was twofold: first, to prepare a confession, work it out as thoroughly as possible and learn it so that to me it actually became the truth, without which it would never be plausible; and second, to think about how to end it all if life became intolerable. The second option was easily thought out. I was tall enough at six foot two just to reach the bars above the cell door, and it would be quite easy to fashion a rope with a slip-knot from my clothes or strips of blanket. I knew the habits of the guards, which almost always involved their going off duty ten minutes before the end of a shift, with the next one arriving ten minutes after it had begun. That would give me plenty of time to get my head into the noose and throttle myself, not the most pleasant of ways to die, but one with a long history of success.

The more important question took a little longer, but once I had made up my mind it became an interesting intellectual challenge to make a history for myself, complete with names and dates, facts and figures, as a British spy.

Early in February I was abruptly summoned to Hosein. He seemed in a good mood, but gave no reason for the six weeks or so that had passed since our last meeting. I felt he wanted me to ask him,

74

so deliberately did not do so. Later he was to tell me that he had been to the front, something Iranian officials liked to do from time to time, although whether they saw any action and how effective in military terms such short visits by older, often unfit and untrained personnel actually were I could never establish. It obviously added to their personal kudos, however. Throughout the time I knew him Hosein never admitted to taking even a week's leave. Any long absence was explained as being a 'visit to the front', yet when I asked another interrogator whether he ever went to the front, like Hosein, he gave me a surprised look that implied Hosein was no soldier. He himself had volunteered some years earlier, he said, and showed me his battle scars to prove it, but his family had suffered so many dead ('martyrs in the struggle of good against evil', in the terminology commonly used to describe battle casualties) and wounded ('living martyrs') that he was not now allowed to go. Or so he said.

After some small talk Hosein got down to business. 'I hope you have been thinking carefully about what I said to you. If you co-operate all will be well, and you could be free by Now Ruz. If not . . .' and I sensed he was shrugging his shoulders behind me.

I made some noncommittal reply which seemed to satisfy him and he added: 'Good. I shall make arrangements to move you soon to another prison, perhaps even tomorrow, where conditions can be either better than here or worse. It will be up to you.'

'Evin?' I asked, but he sent me back to my cell without replying.

Early the next day, 3 February I think, I was told to get ready, the work of a moment. My clothes and watch were returned, and my cash carefully counted out with deductions for my few purchases. Then I was taken into a small courtyard, without a blindfold. It felt good to be out in the open again and to see the world around me. After a long wait a Nissan Patrol, the standard vehicle of the more important government agencies, arrived to collect me. We set off north, towards the mountains, as I had expected. There were two guards, both in khaki fatigues, one driving, the other in the front passenger seat, with me behind. When we reached the freeway they confirmed that our destination was indeed Evin.

As we drove up the hill, going far too fast for my liking, we approached an unusual convoy. The rear car had diplomatic plates, but because of security considerations these no longer identified the embassy concerned. Up in front I could see what looked like the West German flag fluttering on the front of a big Mercedes Benz. The two guards discussed this, then asked me if I knew which country the convoy represented. I replied 'Germany', and when they said 'East or West?' I stupidly replied 'West'. Immediately the senior guard told the driver to slow down, just as he was about to overtake. He had obviously foreseen that I might somehow communicate with these Westerners.

The idea had in fact just occurred to me. A short time before my arrest I had been invited to lunch by the West German cultural attaché to meet Franke Heard-Bey, a German who lived in Abu Dhabi and had written an academic history of the emirate, using Sheikh Zayed's own documents and resources. I had read the book quite recently and enjoyed discussing it with her, and Persian Gulf politics generally. It seemed probable to me that if this convoy was an official visit by a high West German official my host at that lunch, who also acted as press attaché, would be in one of the cars. I even thought I could recognize him in the rear car as we approached and decided to try to catch his eye by waving at him, telling the guards this was just friendliness or high spirits. If the attaché had heard of my disappearance, which was likely, he would be able to confirm to the British embassy that I was alive and well and last seen heading towards Evin. Now, with one careless answer, I had lost my chance. Our Nissan slowed down, and the distance between us and the convoy widened.

Soon we turned off the freeway to the little village of Evin, which would be a pleasant enough summer resort if it were not overshadowed by Iran's notorious political prison. There is a permanent checkpoint as you approach the huge complex, but the driver merely rolled down his window and said 'Prime Minister's Office', that misleading euphemism for the country's most feared organization.

I had been to Evin some six years earlier with Robert Fisk, then the Middle East correspondent of *The Times*. We had heard there was to be a press visit there when we were both in Tehran covering the US embassy hostage crisis, but the prison authorities had not been informed and we did not get far beyond the main gate. I think Bob made some joke about being glad we were 'Just Visiting'. Now I had picked up that hateful Monopoly card that says 'Go Directly to Jail. Do Not Pass Go'.

Having been given their body receipt my guards departed and I waited half an hour in a dingy room while enquiries were made about what to do with me. I had immediately been given a blindfold, a chic little navy blue number that I kept until the end. It was of quite stiff cloth and held in place by two elastic bands. I soon learnt to raise it for a quick look round and lower it when danger approached. With a tied blindfold of soft cloth, the standard kind, this is much more difficult to do. Finally a guard was detailed to take me to *Asayeshgah*, literally 'The Sanatorium'. It sounded ominous and I immediately thought of Soviet psychiatric hospitals and truth drugs. Would this 'sanatorium' be like that?

I was to discover that the Sanatorium was so called because of the penal philosophy of the Islamic Republic, according to which inmates were mentally sick, and were being gradually rehabilitated under the benign guidance of their interrogators. From the Sanatorium prisoners proceeded to the *Amuzeshgah* ('Training Institute'), where they would receive practical instruction in useful skills such as dressmaking and cobbling, and undergo intensive religious instruction. This would gradually qualify them for re-entry into society, providing they had not been executed in the meantime.

I trudged up a steep road through recent snow, the guard always some ten yards ahead, thus obliging me to cheat with my blindfold to avoid slipping off the edge of the road. Although I had been taking regular body exercises in the cell I had just left, my legs felt weak, and my smart black brogues kept slipping on icy patches. Finally we went through a small walled garden and the guard banged on an iron door. Once again I was signed for and, after a further wait, taken to an adjacent building. Here I was put in a corridor and given a bowl of cold greasy stew, which I was told to eat facing the wall, with the threat of a beating if I tried to see or talk to any other prisoners. I found myself, in fact, looking sideways at a rather attractive young woman, as far as one could tell beneath her black chador and blindfold, who was sitting next to me. Was it male ego or did she seem to be peeping at me with interest, or at least curiosity? She was the last woman I was to

77

see close to for many months. I took her to be a member or sympathizer of the banned Mojahedin Khalq Organization, which has always had a high proportion of bold, courageous young women in its ranks, women who do not accept the limitations imposed on their sex by Iran's official brand of Islam, and have often paid dearly for their nonconformity.

I sat there for several hours before being processed formally into the prison: 'Name, father's name, religion, date and place of birth, next of kin.' I decided to register as a Christian, fearing that otherwise I might be obliged to keep Ramadan, which now fell in the long hot summer days. A middle-aged British businessman, held on corruption charges in some ghastly hell-hole in Muscat, had recently died as a result of this enforced dehydration, and I certainly did not want to run that risk. Islam has a fine principle: 'No compulsion in religion', but I knew it was not always followed. In places like the Ministry of Oil they even turn off the water in the washrooms during Ramadan, in case anyone is tempted to take a drink. I also thought that as a Christian I would be able to request a Bible, by analogy with the Quran given to Muslim prisoners, and later I could probably get a Quran as well. Besides, if I was still inside at Easter, or, heaven forbid, Christmas, I might be allowed to attend one of the Armenian churches in Tehran.

I asked the clerk to give me a cell to myself, if possible. A cell-mate might be pleasant, but then again he might not be, and space was more important. He laughed at this and said to one of his colleagues, 'That's the first time anyone's asked to be in solitary. It's always the other way round.' Then he said to me, 'Don't worry, you'll be on your own in the Sanatorium.'

Then back I went, for a further long wait sitting on the stone staircase with a mixed bag of Kurds, Baluchis, and middle-class Tehranis, by no means all young. Just after the call for evening prayers we were led to our cells, politely enough. I was now officially a prisoner of Evin.

5

A YOUNG GUARD, aged perhaps 18 and trying to grow a beard, had been detailed to give me a body-search at the entrance to cell number 336, my home for the next two and a half years. He was an awkward village boy, with a strong Azari accent. Virtually the whole of north-west Iran, right up to the Turkish and Soviet frontiers, is peopled by Azaris, whose language is close to standard Turkish and even closer, of course, to the language spoken in what was then Soviet Azerbaijan. Iran has always been sensitive about its 'Turks', as the Persian speakers call them, indeed, their loyalty to the Iranian state has often been in doubt, especially just after World War II when a puppet regime was established under the bayonets of the Red Army. Stalin had sent his troops into Iran for strategic reasons in 1941, in co-ordination with the British invasion of the southern oilfields. When the war ended the British and US governments honoured the treaty they made with Iran after the invasion and pulled out, but Stalin was reluctant to do so. The resulting crisis can be considered the start of the Cold War. Some sources say that Stalin only withdrew when Truman threatened to use the atom bomb, which at that time the Russians did not possess, but this point is still shrouded in mystery.

Turkey has sometimes exploited the fact that many of the most fertile areas of Iran are peopled by Turkish speakers. A Turkish ambassador once told me that he could converse in his own language with everyone he met from the frontier all the way to Tehran, a distance of over 500 miles, and I could see the remark did not go down well with the Iranian officials within earshot. The Iranians can of course counter that large parts of eastern Turkey are peopled by Kurds, who speak an Iranian language and are descended from the ancient Medes, although Ankara misleadingly refers to them as 'mountain Turks'. And the Kurds, in turn, have usually been on extremely poor terms with the central governments of Turkey, Iran, Iraq, Syria and the Soviet Union, the territories between which this unfortunate nation has been forcibly divided. If those Iranian officials had really wanted to put the boot in they could also have reminded the ambassador that it would still be possible to communicate in Armenian over many thousands of square miles of eastern Turkey if the people of the oldest Christian state had not been so brutally massacred in the closing years of the Ottoman Empire. Sadly, the history and modern politics of the Middle East are bedevilled by racial, linguistic and religious intolerance.

The young man who was laboriously going through my clothes and the plastic bag containing my few personal possessions, as I stood shivering in my underpants, must have suffered countless jibes for his quaint Persian, since Azaris are the subject of numerous jokes of the Irish and Polish kind. In fact if they pulled out of the Persian-speaking parts of Iran the wholesale and retail sectors would collapse, and there would be no one to bake bread or shovel snow off the flat mud roofs in winter, for they are canny traders and hard workers.

To my surprise, I was allowed to keep my watch and cash. Prisoners in the Sanatorium apparently wore no uniform, but my belt and red silk tie were taken away, for obvious reasons. It was cold in the corridor, but when the door clanged shut behind me I found that the cell itself was grossly overheated. There were two high windows, their catches well beyond my reach, and a double loop of old-fashioned central-heating pipe that reminded me of my schooldays. I was soon banging on the door to get the guard to open the windows or turn down the heating.

This was a mistake. A tall, surly guard, also a Turk but older and aggressive, told me in no uncertain terms that banging on cell doors was a punishable offence. He would let me off this time since I had just arrived, but if it happened again I would certainly be punished. The correct way to attract a guard's attention, he said, was to turn the light on. I had noticed a light switch in the cell which did not seem to work, as it made no difference to the 60-watt bulb above the door. The switch controlled a light outside my cell, he explained, and the duty guard would then come to see what the matter was. The light in the cell could only be controlled from outside, and was usually on from dusk to dawn. He also said that the moment anyone opened the door I should turn away and squat down. The cry of 'Ru be divar' ('Face the wall') echoed down that corridor for the next two years, but gradually faded away, either because of orders from above or because the better kind of guard realized it was unnecessary and humiliating. I was later told that there had been cases of guards being attacked by desperate prisoners, people knowing that they were soon to be executed, and guards had even been killed in such attacks.

When this big guard discovered I was British he exclaimed: 'Death to Reagan', a phrase he repeated every time he opened my cell door. I tried to teach him to say 'Death to Thatcher', but perhaps because he knew she was a woman and some ancient code of chivalry lingered on, he continued to say 'Death to Reagan'. I christened him 'Reagan' in my mind, and when I knew he was on duty and he opened my cell door I used to call out 'Death to Reagan' before he could say 'Face the wall', much to his surprise. As I had suspected, the Persian-speaking guards used to laugh at him behind his back, and some of them even referred to him among themselves as 'Mr Reagan' after I told them of my attempts to teach him the difference between the two principal Western leaders of the day.

As it happened, Reagan was one of my guards for almost the entire time I was in Evin, although I was moved several times. He was not a bad man at heart, just not very bright and a typical product of Third World problems: poor education, poverty, an early marriage, and too many children. He told me later he had eight children, and it was clear he was bringing them up just as he had been brought up. Reagan, known as 'Apeman' by the Western prisoners because of his slightly simian appearance, was a fanatical Muslim and vociferous supporter of the Emam, but something told me that a few years earlier he had probably been staunchly pro-Shah, and in his youth probably a supporter of Dr Mossadegh.

Even on religious matters Reagan was quite ill-informed. He

81

made several attempts to convert me, but all he really knew about Islam was the outward rules – ritual ablutions, prostrations, dietary laws and the like. Of the substance of the religion itself, of the message of the Quran and the Hadiths, and of Islamic history, he was blissfully ignorant.

In all this he was not unique among the guards, although there were several devout ones who were willing to discuss theology without bigotry. (In fact the guards were ordered not to discuss politics or religion with me – presumably it was feared that I would indoctrinate them – but few observed the rule. Politics, religion and sex seem to be the only subjects that interest young fundamentalist Muslims, and I refused to discuss sex with them.) Several had read, with understanding, books that one might have thought beyond their grasp, and I could not help regretting that their education was so limited, for their minds were often quick and full of curiosity. I was constantly encouraging them to continue their studies beyond the primary level that was all most of them had completed, and several seemed eager to do so, or to learn English from me, but always the pressures of long hours of work, their growing families and the lack of proper opportunities made this an unrealistic goal. Many guards had three children by their mid-twenties, for that was the party line from the start of the Revolution, a reversal of the Shah's efforts to introduce family planning. When I got to know them, many of these guards regretted the lives they now knew they were condemned to, and sheepishly agreed that effectively they were as much prisoners of Evin as I was.

Eventually, on that first day, a rather jolly guard, tall, thin, and with a slight stutter, arrived carrying a long pole with a hook at one end, the only legal means of opening and closing windows in the Sanatorium. I had often heard that Evin was designed for the Shah by Israeli architects, but examples of bad design like this made me doubt the story. The guard, who I later discovered was called Majid, said he had been shutting a few windows that evening and was surprised to find me wanting mine opened.

The cell itself had several advantages over my previous one. Best of all there was a wash-basin with hot and cold taps, although the hot water was only just tepid, and a small WC, something like the ones on planes but with a tubular flushing system. It was quite filthy inside, but at least it had a cover. The carpet had long since lost its pile, but this would make it easy to keep clean and exercise on. There was a red plastic bowl holding about a pint, a plate that fitted it like a lid, a half-pint plastic mug, an aluminium spoon, and a small rubbish basket. There were two rather grubby blankets; no mattress, but I presumed the guards would be bringing me one.

Supper came. I cannot remember what it was, but Evin suppers were never much to write home about, even if one had been allowed to do so. It was usually soup, sometimes quite tasty, although like most of the food rather greasy. Later a guard came round with a cubic inch of cheese and a small pat of butter, which made up somewhat for the frugality of the main course. Only next morning did I discover I had eaten my breakfast.

With time for lights out approaching I switched on the outside light and when the guard came explained that I had no mattress.

'Nobody has a mattress here,' he replied. 'What do you think this is, a hotel?'

I said that in the prison I had come from everybody had a mattress, at which he admitted that Evin used to have them too, but the prisoners had so vandalized them that they were withdrawn on the governor's orders. So I modified my request and asked instead for an extra blanket, but he said since all the cells were full there was a shortage of blankets. He might get me another in a week or two, since there was an amnesty in the offing. When I asked him when lights out was he said one light had to be on in the cell all night and since there was a shortage of light bulbs most cells, including mine, had only one bulb anyway. So there was nothing else to do but curl up on the floor with my two blankets. The cell light, which had seemed dim, now seemed to shine like a searchlight into my eyes. Before I could get off to sleep the heating was turned down, so it was a cold and uncomfortable night.

Hosein did not send for me for a few days, and this again worried me. He had spoken about the large amount of 'work' we would have to get through before I could be released, but now he was dragging his heels again. I had not definitely decided to make a false confession, but unless I saw a glimmer of hope it looked like being the only way out. Although I was now an official prisoner of the Islamic Republic of Iran, whatever my previous status, the British government was clearly unable even to enforce its right under the Vienna Convention for consular access. The Iranians were presumably claiming that I was a spy, perhaps even that I had confessed to being a spy, and that state interest overrode any obligations under Western treaties and conventions entered into during the reign of the corrupt Pahlavis. All this, I was later to learn, is roughly what did happen.

On my first Friday in Evin a curious and unpleasant sound reached my cell. It was loud but muffled, quite close by but on the other side of the building from me, and the sound-waves reverberated around the Alborz foothills for a few seconds. It was the unmistakable sound of a firing-squad carrying out an execution. Friday is often a day for executions in the Middle East; when I was living in Riyadh some years earlier there were regular beheadings just before Friday prayers. It could not have been target practice, first because there were no further shots, and secondly because on the Muslim sabbath even soldiers usually get the day off. The knowledge that only some twenty yards away from me one or even a whole group of political prisoners had just been executed was most disturbing.

Just as disturbing in its way was the steady stream of manic cries and groans from other prisoners on my floor and from floors above and below me. One particularly persistent moaning sound seemed to come from far down, as if from a dungeon or isolated punishment cell. The guards periodically tried to stop the cacophony, but it was a losing battle and most of them turned a deaf ear to it, as I soon learned to do. Some guards would creep up to identify which cell was responsible and then burst in on the occupant, because a general 'Be Quiet' worked only until the guard passed on up the corridor. The more energetic guards like Reagan and Hosein Ainaki ('Bespectacled Hosein', to differentiate him from the other Hoseins: surnames were almost never used in Evin) would sometimes punch a prisoner into silence, but this policy tended only to make matters worse when the shift changed. What I failed to notice for a week or two was that the women prisoners on the ground floor, three down from me, almost never moaned or groaned, although they sometimes communicated by means of a code I was never able to crack, presumably one that MKO members learned during their training.

All this affected my morale considerably and when Hosein finally did send for me I was more than half-way prepared to put my confession plan into action.

It would seem reasonable to assume that counter-intelligence officers whose job includes in-depth debriefings and interrogations of captured spies would be characterized by the sharpness of their minds, complete mastery of the dossiers they are dealing with, and the ability to counter any attempts by the subject to wriggle off the hook or plant disinformation. Inevitably, I got to know Hosein quite well during the three years that my interrogation lasted and I cannot say that I would give him even an average rating by any of those criteria.It seemed unlikely that he had been professionally trained for his job, since he consistently failed to follow up any slips or inconsistencies in my statements and often did not seem to notice them. He never questioned me about the notes for a fake confession, which had been found in my first cell, and I was forced to conclude that he had not even read them: to this day they are probably in a filing cabinet somewhere in Evin. The only conclusion I can draw is that he simply did not care. He wanted a confession; how he got it and what it consisted of was immaterial.

Part of Hosein's problem was that he did not know English well, although better than he admitted. I discovered through his own carelessness that he had been to London, which he always denied. His untruths were so instinctive and transparent that he reminded me of the Cretan Liar of Greek logic, who is unable to tell the truth but can have the truth extracted from him if the right questions are asked.

At least he wanted to learn. Quite early in the interrogation, probably in my first prison, he asked me how the 'Intelligent Service' interrogated people. I said I had no idea, but understood that, in peacetime at least, interrogation was not one of its functions. That was up to Special Branch, part of the police force. I told him about the 'nice cop, nasty cop' technique: immediately after a really gruelling interview with the nasty cop, when the suspect was feeling at his lowest, the nice cop would appear with a cigarette and a cup of tea, and frequently the confession would come tumbling out.

So it was not surprising that, when the second phase of my interrogation began in Evin, Hosein was frequently joined by Mehdi, a charming colleague from Isfahan, to judge by his accent. Typically, Hosein would start in a grumpy mood, his voice rising to a slightly hysterical pitch, and would then leave the room, perhaps having punched me once or twice. A little while later Mehdi would come in, ostensibly looking for Hosein. He would chat to me in English, saying things like, 'You shouldn't annoy Hosein. He's a real nice guy, but he can get a bit excited. If you play ball with Hosein, Hosein will play ball with you.'

I would reply along the lines of, 'I know, Mehdi, I know. But you must understand that I'm telling Hosein the truth and he should realize this. The trouble is he doesn't know how the outside world really works, the way you do, and he's got all sorts of crazy ideas. Can't you get him to see that?'

I knew that even to hint that I might do a deal over a confession would imply that I had something to confess, so I was quite grateful to have Mehdi as a broker when the time came. He explained that they were not asking for every last detail of British intelligence activity in Iran, just a general outline, and they certainly did not want me to finger active agents. In fact they were mainly interested in the pre-Revolutionary period, not the present day. ('Like hell you are!' I said to myself.) Unlike Hosein, Mehdi had no objection to my seeing his face, so I looked him straight in the eye, sighed slightly, and said: 'Well, I think Hosein is going to be very disappointed. I may have some slight knowledge of British intelligence, and even some involvement, but it's nothing like what he is thinking of.' This did not seem to put Mehdi off at all. 'Don't worry about that,' he said. 'I'll take care of the details. Just tell him what you do know, no one will be any the wiser, and you can be free by Now Ruz.'

So with Mehdi's help, Hosein and I struck a deal. I would tell him what I knew of the operations of the Intelligent Service in

Iran and I would never be tortured or beaten again. I would not be brought to trial, even if I incriminated myself. There would be no publicity in the Iranian media about me. I would be quietly freed as soon as the interrogation was over. All these undertakings were agreed and sworn to by Hosein and Mehdi jointly, using the most solemn Islamic oaths, the kind that guarantee an eternity of hellfire and damnation if you break them. They must both have had their fingers crossed: every single condition was broken, some several times.

At my first meeting with Hosein in Evin he took away my watch again, but I had already noted the angles of the sun on the wall adjacent to my cell at various times of the day, so I could always tell, to within perhaps a quarter of an hour, what the time was. Even an unfriendly guard would usually tell you the time of day, so I was able to perfect this method and allow for the gradually changing position of the shadows. For one so notoriously unpunctual as I am it is curious that time has always mattered. I love chronometer watches, like the trusty Rolex Oyster that served me then and still does. When I hear a time signal I check my watch and adjust it. I joke that being born in Greenwich I have always remained on GMT, and any unpunctuality is because the only two countries I have lived in where GMT is standard all the year round are Iceland and Morocco: I was never late there.

The interrogation system in Evin was quite different from that of my previous gaol. Prisoners were typically taken in mid-morning to the office block where I was inducted into the prison, adjacent to the Sanatorium. The two buildings are in fact connected, but perhaps because of jealousies between the judiciary, which is responsible for the prisons, and the executive, which carries out the intelligence and CID work, the connecting doors are never used. This had the advantage that prisoners did at least get into the open for the short walk between the two buildings, although when the pathway was covered in snow or ice and all you had on your feet was a pair of flip-flops this was a questionable benefit. But if you cheated you could sometimes see the sun for a second.

Each prisoner is allocated to a *shobeh*, or branch, depending on the nature of the charges against him ('crimes' in Evin-speak).

Espionage comes under Shobeh 13, although the number had been 6 and confusingly became 6 again later. I never did fully understand the administrative details, which officials were naturally reluctant to talk about, but gathered that a *shobeh* is a branch of the judiciary, perhaps within the prosecutor-general's or attorney-general's department. When the investigators and interrogators have done their job, they pass the case over to the relevant *shobeh*, which prepares the indictment, almost always based on a signed confession. The case is then brought before an Islamic Revolutionary Court, presided over by a cleric, a robed and turbanned figure trained at one of the theological seminaries such as Qom, but with no particular legal qualification. (The Emam had such a high regard for the abilities of his fellow-clerics that shortly after the Revolution he was quoted as saying that mullahs could help solve the country's chronic shortage of doctors, for every Qom graduate has, after all, studied the traditional Islamic sciences, which include the rudiments of medieval medicine.)

The Islamic Revolutionary judge is in theory assisted by a lay assessor, often a 'reformed' judge from the Pahlavi era, although his influence on the verdict is minimal and he acts mainly as court clerk and stenographer. I learned this by talking to friendly guards and drivers, never thinking that I would one day be brought before an Islamic Revolutionary court myself.

When the prisoner reaches the correct interrogation section he usually waits in the corridor. The interrogations themselves take place in rooms just like government offices. Shouting and cries of pain are often heard from behind the double doors, only partially drowned out by religious chants and prayer ceremonies played endlessly on a tape recorder in the corridor. Hating loud noise, I would sometimes creep up to the recorder and gradually turn down the volume if there were no guards nearby, although this was a risky procedure.

After his personal 'interview', the prisoner would be returned to his seat and told to write his confession, or whatever he knew about a particular matter. Hosein apparently did not want me to be seen by other prisoners, so in those early days I wrote my answers in one of the empty interrogation rooms, usually unsupervised. It was tempting but dangerous to take a look at the files and papers on the desks, for the inner door had a spy-hole and I never knew when someone would come in. I had to train myself not to look round when anyone did enter, in case it was Hosein: the thought of his ballpoint remained embedded in my brain.

Hosein began by making me use carbon paper when writing my answers (photocopying was something of a luxury in Evin, because the paper has to be imported) and he expected me to finish writing before he left for the day, which was always earlier than the other interrogators. I knew that under pressure I was more likely to make mistakes, whereas in my cell, with several days to think about the answers, it would be much easier. Hosein told me prisoners were not allowed to write confessions in their cells and interrogators were not allowed to enter the accommodation block, two good features of the Evin system. I flattered him by saying I was sure he could get an exemption in my special case, particularly in response to a request from me. Perhaps because it suited him as an 'outsider', he asked me to write a formal request asking for permission to write my 'confession' in my cell.

From then on, our routine settled down to a meeting about once a week, although never on the same day and rarely on the day he said he would come. At this meeting, usually lasting about an hour, although it might be six hours before I was taken back to my cell, Hosein would go over the answers I had given him at our previous meeting and set me another dozen questions or so. He even dropped the carbon paper idea, which gave poor results, as without a table I could not press hard enough for the diacritical points, which are so important in Persian, to come through legibly.

I do not propose to describe my interrogation in detail, partly because it would fill this book and more, and much of the detail would mean very little to the average reader, and partly because I do not want to harm the people I was questioned about. Just having their names included in this account could be an embarrass-ment, but in every case where I felt the persons I was questioned about were at risk, whether foreigners or Iranians living abroad who might one day return, I have since my release told them the substance of the questions I was asked and how I replied.

To my surprise, Hosein actually started my interrogation with some very old history, showing little interest at first in any light I might throw on links between British Intelligence and post-Revolutionary Iran. He claimed that his masters – a nebulous 'they' or 'we', never a specific organization, with the implication that Hosein himself was a master himself, or at least a semi-independent operator – were simply pursuing an almost academic interest in British involvement in Iran's internal affairs. I guessed from the start that this was a ruse to get me talking (or, as had become the pattern, writing) about matters that now had little real political significance, except, and it is an important exception, in so far as they remain embedded in the Persian psyche. Once I had started the flow of information, he reasoned, the stream would gradually move forward down to the present day, whereas if he started too close to the present I might hastily erect dams or channel the flow into unproductive fields.

I had to admire this part of his strategy, with its talk of how useful it would be for Iranian scholars to evaluate some honest British testimony and help restart Irano-British relations on a sounder basis. In fact it coincided with my own attitude, although I always doubted the sincerity of such hardliners as Hosein when they spoke like this, just as I always distrusted Communist talk of 'peace'. As a student of Iranian history I had often been ashamed at the way British governments, from at least the Napoleonic era until, say, the late 1950s, had interfered in Iranian politics, partly, it is true, because with true missionary endeavour they thought they were acting for Iran's own good, but partly too from sheer arrogance, a feeling of racial superiority, with British interests, both strategic and economic, always the underlying reason. If Kuwait produced carrots instead of oil, as the British MP Tam Dalyell said, there would have been no Gulf War. Iran produced both, and the discovery and exploitation of oil, under a concession early this century, led ultimately to the creation of British Petroleum and much else. Oil from south Iran was vital to the British economy in war and peace, so much so that in both world wars the oilfields were in effect treated as British territory. Iran had also been important in geo-political terms. In the nineteenth century Britain used Persia, as it was then called, as a bulwark against Russian, German and Turkish penetration towards the so-called warm water ports of the Persian Gulf, or even the jewel in the imperial crown, India. With the start of the Cold War, Iran was regarded as a powder-keg capable of igniting the whole Middle East. That crisis was defused, but almost immediately afterwards Dr Mossadegh posed a major challenge to British interests, not only in Iran by his nationalization of the oil industry, but indirectly more widely in the region. Other nationalists saw Britain's humiliation at being unable to restore the status quo, and it became apparent that the United States had now become the major player in the Middle East, and a far less active one than Britain had been.

These events, and even earlier ones, when in the seventeenth century Britain sent ambassadors and wily traders such as the Sherley brothers to the court of the Grand Sophy, had always fascinated me, especially as there are to this day grey areas where the full light of historical analysis has not penetrated. There probably exists, in some secret Whitehall archives, documentary evidence describing in detail the role Britain played in bringing Reza Shah Pahlavi to power in 1921 and unseating him twenty years later. In his memoirs our wartime envoy to Tehran, Sir Reader Bullard, skates delicately over the latter event, perhaps because he was not privy to the decision-making process, although given Churchill's confidence in him this seems unlikely. Nor is it clear to what extent, if at all, Britain was involved in the CIA coup that overthrew Dr Mossadegh in 1953. The CIA had no permanent presence in Iran in those days and it seems evident to me that MI6 must have co-operated on the technical aspects of the coup, even though its outcome was not to prove wholly advantageous to British interests.

All these events, of course, took place either before I was born or before I arrived in Iran, and I have no secret knowledge that the Iranians have been denied access to. But I did know the published facts well, and was in my element writing long essays on individuals and topics scarcely remembered in Britain today, such as Lord Curzon; General Ironside, who commanded the British forces in Persia in 1920, in the face of the Bolshevist threat; the first Anglo-Iranian oil dispute of 1932–3 – all still of great importance to Iranians. Churchill, for example, appears in quite a different light when seen from Tehran, not as the great statesman who saved the world for democracy, but as an arrogant schemer, an anti-Iranian warlord, and it must be admitted that the Iranians do have a point.

To titillate Hosein and his masters I needed to spice my otherwise bald and unconvincing narrative with rumour and speculation. To help with this, and to justify my writing as a confession, however feeble, I introduced them to Colonel Dick Hooker, the man I claimed was my first and most influential contact in the British Intelligent Service. His name is based on Brigadier Ritchie-Hooke, a character in Evelyn Waugh's *Men at Arms* trilogy. His successor, Charles Knight, a man of about my age with some years of military experience in Germany and Oman, is named after Charles Ryder, the protagonist of *Brideshead Revisited*, while Knight's number two, Paul Penny, an academic with no military experience, is a thinly-veiled reference to Paul Pennyfeather in Waugh's *Decline and Fall*. I chose these names with care, knowing that if my confession was ever published my literary friends would spot the references, but confident that there would be few readers of Waugh's novels among Iranian intelligence officers.

Hooker, I explained, had introduced himself to me at a British embassy cocktail party in about 1964 as an official of the research department of the Foreign Office. He had heard of me as a freelance journalist with a good knowledge of Iran and commissioned some articles on contemporary Iranian affairs for his department and selected readers in Whitehall. I was to keep this to myself, as certain people were not happy with the reports coming from the British embassy. He would pay me the going rate that the *Financial Times* paid its freelance contributors, £20 per 1000 words in the early days, rising to £150 by the time he retired. Initially, I explained to Hosein, I had believed Hooker's story, but when I found by chance that his name was not in the Diplomatic List I began to suspect he was not quite what he said. At a meeting in London several months later at Wheeler's oyster bar in Swallow Street (which does not exist), he had admitted that actually he was the head of the Middle East section of the CRA, a shadowy organization set up by Churchill, on Eden's advice, when they realized that career diplomats often had their heads in the sand.

CRA stands for Country Risk Analysis, a branch of financial

expertise I first learned about when working for *Euromoney*. In the real world CRA is what bankers and financial experts do when they examine portfolios of sovereign debt, or when governments or government agencies come to the capital markets for loans. For Hosein, I turned CRA into a top secret government department with a formal organizational structure. I listed the 23 countries of the Middle East whose risks of coups, revolutions or civil wars were analysed by Colonel Hooker. The British embassies in these countries knew roughly what Hooker and his tiny staff did, and dreaded his visits because they often led to their own incompetence being exposed. That was why our Tehran embassy should never know about my involvement. Hooker had a man in the embassy, Zorik (a local employee and an old friend of mine, who had died shortly before the Revolution), but he was only an emergency link. CRA had tested the mails from Iran thoroughly and found them secure enough for most purposes. I should therefore simply post my articles to Hooker, unless they contained highly sensitive material, in which case I could use Zorik as a secure channel, or even come over to London to give a direct report, although budgets were extremely tight and I should not regard this as an excuse for a free holiday in England.

Hooker became something of a father-figure in my mind. He was a composite of several real friends and acquaintances, thus making it easy for me to believe in him myself. He had lost an eye at Alamein as a subaltern in the Royal Welch Fusiliers, a regiment known to me because my uncle Robert Graves had served in it in the First World War; his eldest son, my cousin David, followed in his footsteps in the Second World War, losing his life in heroic circumstances in Burma. I knew that the regiment had not taken part in the North African campaign. I came almost to believe in the colonel's existence myself, and when Hosein once asked me what I would do when I was released I instinctively replied that I would go and see Hooker. In an idle moment I wrote a clerihew about him:

> Brigadier Ritchie-Hooke
> Is a character in a book.
> My Colonel Dick Hooker
> Should have won me the Booker.

A useful technique in countering some of Hosein's questions was the 'need-to-know' principle. Again and again I told him: 'That's a very interesting question, one I asked Colonel Hooker myself, in fact, but his answer was always the same. "There's no need for you to know, Cooper. Somebody one day might put you under pressure to reveal the answer and that would not be good, for you or for us. It's far better if you don't know."' I explained that this principle was now established in Western intelligence circles as the 'need-to-know principle', or even the 'Hooker principle'. Hooker was proud to have originated it when Montgomery took him on his staff after his eye operation. Hosein sniffed at this and said that in Islam combatants always trusted each other and would anyway never give away secrets to the enemy, even under torture. He immediately realized this was not the most tactful thing to have said, so he added, 'I don't mean that you are giving away secrets. It is our right to know about these things and you are doing your duty as a human being in telling us.'

One of the most successful products of my imagination was the mysterious 'Iran Committee' set up in Whitehall after the Revolution to co-ordinate government policy on Iran. Even in the Shah's day, Iranians believed that foreign politicians spent most of the waking hours plotting against their country, and my Iran Committee played nicely on this paranoia. Unfortunately the Hooker principle prevented me from knowing much about its deliberations, but I listed the main organizations I believed to be represented on it. The Iran Committee reported directly to Mrs Thatcher, of course.

Hosein was also interested in the organizational structure of the 'British Intelligent Service', which from now on I got into the habit of calling the BIS. Persian has hardly any acronyms, so foreign ones like CIA and KGB provide a special frisson. Now he had two more, BIS and CRA, which were new to him. He was delighted when I offered to draw a complete organizational chart of the BIS, although I said it would take me some time. With the Now Ruz holidays about to begin, that suited him too; I was given almost three weeks to prepare my chart, which only took me a few hours.

Hosein had some business to attend to elsewhere in the prison that day and asked Mehdi to take me back to my cell. As we were leaving I told him that Hosein had forgotten to give me the extra paper I would need to do the explanatory notes for the organizational chart. As I had hoped would happen, Mehdi told me to wait in the corridor, went into an office and came out with a whole pad of the special forms that confessions were written on, telling me to give any unused sheets to Hosein after the holidays. They are printed and lined on one side only, so now I had what seemed like an unlimited supply of paper to draw and write on. Hosein had recently given me my glasses back, so I could see properly at last, and my watch: he must have decided I would not now use them to slash my wrists with. It was not going to be the best Now Ruz holiday I had ever had, but it might have been worse. I could settle down to proving Pythagoras' theorem, and trying to recall how to solve quadratic equations.

Everyone in Iran relaxes over Now Ruz, even the guards at Evin, with some of whom I was building up friendly relations. Officially the New Year festival lasts about a week, but schools are on holiday and nothing really happens for well over a fortnight. With no releases and scarcely any new intakes the guards had more time to drop in for a chat. In their eyes I was obviously a special prisoner, the only Briton, I elicited, ever to have been held in Evin. Given the special awe with which Britain is regarded in Iran, and the vituperative propaganda directed against us at every turn, at least in those days, I was something like a rare new animal at the zoo, and once they knew I spoke Persian the guards would ask me questions or just come to stare.

There was quite a turnover in guards, I soon discovered, some serving for only a few weeks before disappearing, but a hard core of old hands always remained. The younger ones, probably conscripts back from the front or waiting to go, often seemed unhappy at being in Evin. They would either insist on the 'face the wall' rule or muffle their faces, afraid of being fingered by a released prisoner and thus becoming a target of the MKO or other opposition groups. Ali Lotfi, a guard of about my age, told me he had received several anonymous death-threats, and I suspect may even have moved house once or twice for this reason. Although he always insisted, 'If it is God's will for me to be martyred in his path, then I accept it with gratitude', he would add in a slightly worried tone, 'Have I ever done you any harm?' The answer in his case was 'No,' and in fact throughout the years I knew him I received many kindnesses and small favours, which could by no means be said of all of the guards.

Some would swing back and forth between friendliness and spitefulness, reflecting perhaps their own personal problems, which they sometimes confided in me. Money was the commonest of these: they were poorly paid – although at least they earned a steady wage – they had too many mouths to feed, and they could not realistically expect that life would ever improve. Ali Lotfi told me he had had a dry-cleaning business before the Revolution and been quite wealthy, but had given it up to serve the Emam. This may have been true, but I knew that the fashion for scruffy chic which the Revolution had brought in its wake had forced many dry-cleaners and barbers to close down.

Iranians are great hypochondriacs, and most of the guards at some time or other would consult me about their medical problems. At the time I had no medicines myself, but would always try to offer common-sense advice on such matters as diet, exercise and dental care, which Iranians usually ignore until it is too late. Towards the end of my stay, when I began to receive cold remedies, spices and vitamin tablets, I was practically running a guards' clinic in the prison, in collaboration with my 'consultant' David Rabhan, who knew much more about modern medicine than I did and considered my old-fashioned remedies ineffective, if not downright dangerous. My mainstays were olive oil (for earaches and strains), salt (to make a gargle for sore throats), and cloves (for toothache); whatever a foreigner says on health matters carries special weight.

My own health was generally good throughout the five years I spent in Evin. My eyesight deteriorated considerably, especially in the first year, and I like to attribute that to the poor light I read and wrote by, although my father tells me his reading eyesight began to falter at exactly my age. One great advantage of solitary confinement is that one is not much exposed to infection. For the first three years I almost never had a cold or flu; later, in a cramped communal cell, cold symptoms lingered on for weeks. It is always other people's illnesses one catches.

Soon after my arrival in Evin I began a regular programme of exercises, working out twice a day with great vigour even in the hot summer months, and I kept this up throughout my three years of solitary confinement. In a communal cell it is considered bad manners to exercise, as it distracts people reading or trying to sleep, makes the floor shake and stirs up dust, so one is restricted to walking or jogging round the small yard for half an hour a day, or finding a quiet corner for body-building. In my little cell I gradually developed a repertoire of exercises, each with its quota or target. So as not to omit one I always did them in the same order, which I remembered by a mnemonic. It was a kind of prayer, beginning 'Jesus Christ Superstar Please . . . ', which stood for 'Jogging, Chest, Sides, Push-ups'. When I began, even a single push-up was a Herculean task, but I slowly improved until by the end I could do twenty or more without too much difficulty. Jogging, of course, had to be on the spot, although I would also stride up and down the cell to stretch my leg muscles. It was three strides and a smooth about-turn, then back again, a poor substitute for walking, but better than nothing. It made me feel like one of those lions or tigers one sometimes sees in a zoo, ranging manically up and down its cage, tail swinging angrily. Once I had my watch back I could time myself and try to improve my speed with each part of the exercise programme.

What was particularly frustrating that first spring was feeling the weather gradually turn warm, seeing patches of green sprouting on the hillside if I climbed up to the window and stole a look, and hearing the jangle of the bell-wethers as the shepherds took their flocks up into my lovely Alborz mountains, so near yet almost never seen. But although I felt deprived of physical exercise, I now see that things might have been much worse. At least I was never chained to a wall like the Beirut hostages, nor was I tortured.

Beatings were commonplace in those days in Evin and I expect they still are. They needed no special permission. Torture – or 'Islamic chastisement', since the Revolution had officially outlawed this evil practice by the Shah's secret police – required the authority of a religious judge. It was sufficient for an interrogator to tell the judge that such-and-such a prisoner was not telling the truth or was withholding information. The judge, without enquiring further, and certainly without seeing the prisoner, would then issue an order for him or her to be whipped on the soles of the feet until the truth emerged. This chastisement is officially called *falaka*, and is usually translated as 'bastinado', a sixteenth-century Spanish term, but among Evin prisoners it is called *kabl*, because thick electric cable was originally used to inflict the punishment. During my time in Evin a heavy-duty fan belt was the usual instrument, partly tied up with wire or string to make a handle. I was once left alone in an interrogation room and had the opportunity of examining a *kabl*, which was caked with dried blood. There was also a special board to which the prisoner's feet are tied while he lies on his back, which I once saw through an open door.

Later, when I was being questioned in the court building, I would sometimes return in the minibus with prisoners who had been given this treatment. Usually they could not walk, and two of us would put our arms under the man's shoulders to help him back to his cell. Apart from the pain and bleeding, *falakeh* makes the feet swell up to almost twice their normal size. Yet to an Iranian religious judge this is not torture, nor even punishment, simply an Islamic method of arriving at the truth. I was never given the *falakeh*, although Hosein occasionally threatened me with it and once showed me a piece of paper that he said was a judge's permission to inflict it on me. David Rabhan, the American I was to share a cell with for a year, had been given it. He showed me some scars on his shins that he said were inflicted at the same time. My best friend in gaol, Romeo Sabri, an Iraqi, had undergone it, and also suffered damage to his kidneys from beatings. Helmut Szimkus, a German, at the time of writing still in Evin, also told me he had been given the *kabl* treatment. What the religious judges do not consider is that a prisoner may easily make a confession, even a false one, to stop the frightful pain of *falaka*, and there seems to be no necessity for confessions to be corroborated. On a confession alone, obtained as it were through the soles of the feet, hundreds, perhaps thousands, of prisoners have been sent to the gallows at Evin prison.

One day I was taken to a part of the prison I had not yet visited, together with a score of other prisoners. We were photographed with our serial number displayed on our chests, then taken individually to a room for our personal details to be recorded on a form. When it was my turn the clerk gave me the batch of Polaroid photographs that had been taken of us and asked me to find my own. I went through them carefully and said mine was not there. He called the photographer to say one was missing, whereupon the photographer looked through them and said, 'No, here he is.' I could not believe it. Was that gaunt figure with a silvery beard really me? The Duke's lines in *Twelfth Night* came back to me:

> O thou dissembling cub! what wilt thou be
> When time hath sow'd a grizzle on thy case?

Time had certainly sown its grizzle, and I was up to my neck in the most dangerous piece of dissemblement. Had I been wise, how would it all end? Right or wrong, there was no going back now.

The Iranian plateau, on which Tehran and most of the major cities are situated, averages over 3000 feet above sea level and has an extreme continental type of climate. Foreigners sometimes assume that because the summers are hot and dry it is like that all the year round, and are surprised to learn that there is good skiing quite close to Tehran as late as April. Indeed, if you go up high enough into the Alborz, which is now served by cable car, you can ski into early summer. Having lived in Iran for so long I am quite at home in any sort of weather that arrives, except perhaps desert sandstorms, but as spring merged into summer that year I knew I would face unaccustomed problems. Spring and autumn are both short seasons in Tehran, even in the cool foothills around Evin, and in 1986 the weather seemed to change from cold to hot faster than usual. The first warm spell followed some heavy spring rains, providing ideal conditions for flies, mosquitoes, cockroaches and ants to breed. Suddenly my cell was full of flying and crawling insects, and I had nothing to fight them with except my towel and my hands. The constant battle turned into a sport, and I kept the score for each species. By bedtime I was often in the hundreds, and there were red streaks on the walls where I had flattened mosquitoes bloated with my blood. I got used to being bitten, but hated the high-pitched buzz of a mosquito when I was dropping off to sleep.

One of my cell's previous inmates had written a pathetic plea to his successors not to harm the ants. Perhaps he had derived pleasure from watching the busy little creatures at work, or he may have learnt at school the celebrated lines of the tenth-century poet Ferdowsi:

> Do not harm the ant carrying a grain.
> It too has a soul and its soul is dear to it.

Despite a few stings I found myself on the side of the Formicidae, at least provided they stayed out of my cache of sugar cubes. I would feed dead flies or cockroaches to them and watch fascinated as they devoured them or carried their carrion off to a formicary somewhere within the concrete bowels of Evin. I did not like them in my blankets, however, and quickly established some ground rules. If they crossed an invisible boundary down the centre of the cell it was a declaration of war. To my surprise they quickly accepted these conditions.

Cockroaches were another matter. Cell 336 was at the end of the first corridor, next to the shower area and close to the rubbish storage area, so when they set out on foraging missions from their homelands I was one of their first stops. Cockroaches have an instinctive intelligence, and were adept at sneaking into my cell when I was not looking, and at taking advantage of distractions such as the food-trolley. But they could not move silently enough once inside and their tell-tale rustle against plastic or paper would cause me to reach for a flip-flop, against which they stood no chance, although the hunt might last five or ten minutes.

Outside my cell window, but within the recessed frame, I had noticed a curious honeycombed structure that I took to be a wild beehive. There was no sign of life from it until well into the warm weather, when one day I noticed a pair of wasps inspecting it. They obviously liked the location but not the existing structure, and were soon building a new home next to the old one. They moved with great rapidity and purpose and the hive quickly took shape, but however closely I watched I could not fathom exactly how they did it. Were they spitting or extruding the material, or bringing it from outside? I could never be sure. A few weeks later they had bred and I had another spectacle to watch, baby wasps learning to fly. Although I did get stung once or twice I decided not to kill wasps either, and when one strayed in through the top of the window I would try to shoo it back out, not always success- fully. Wasps seemed to lack the intelligence of my other insect visitors, and would crash again and again into the window pane until stunned, when I could catch and carefully eject them using a paper tube.

I had by now discovered how to open and close my windows without calling for Majid's special tool. The trick was to climb on to the radiator pipes, when I was sure no guard was around, by placing folded blankets on my upturned trash bucket. My rapidly growing agility soon made this easy. Climbing up to the windows was another punishable offence, not that there was much to see when you got there, because the outside of the window-frame was screened by horizontal metal louvres welded into a fixed position sloping down towards the cell. All I could see from the cell floor was a patch of usually blue sky and part of the outer wall of the next corridor, since the block seemed to be built in a zig-zag. By taking timings when the trolley came round I had worked out the probable total number of cells on the floor to be 100, and when I was once taken to a more remote shower and managed to sneak a glance at the cell door numbers I was able to confirm this. The numbering sequence began confusingly in the middle of the floor, rather than at one end, and the numbers ran from 301 to 400. Iranian numbering is rarely logical and I noticed that new guards often had trouble when sent to fetch a prisoner from a particular cell, expecting, for example, to find cell number 400 on the fourth floor, not the third.

All I could see from the window ledge was the hillside across the steep Evin valley, with a strange Chinese-looking building at the top. I deduced it must be part of Tehran's National University, founded as the country's first private university in the Shah's day, and now renamed Beheshti University, after the man who would

101

have become President of the Islamic Republic of Iran had he not been killed in an MKO bomb attack on party headquarters. The pagoda-like structure I could just see was a clock-tower, but the hands on the two sides visible to me were stuck.

When not engaged in nature study and other pursuits I was steadily churning out answers to Hosein's questions and writing long essays on Iranian political history. As I had expected, we gradually reached the time of my most recent arrival in Iran, the summer of 1985, and the questions at last became personal. From the huge Savak file that he had inherited Hosein already knew a lot about my long residence in the country, although I did not know exactly what. It was safest to assume he knew the broad outlines, but never to volunteer information. I was aware that much of my life in Iran might look suspicious to people as paranoid as Hosein, and indeed his predecessors in Savak. I had been for almost twenty years either a student or a part-time lecturer at Tehran University, always a hotbed of opposition to the regime. I was a journalist, and Hosein told me that all foreign journalists were spies. I had been a speech-writer for senior government officials of the Shah's government. I had been an adviser on historical affairs to a senior general on the Shah's staff, and had worked for both the Shiraz Festival of Arts, sponsored by the Empress Farah, and the Tehran International Film Festival, sponsored by her cultural rival Princess Ashraf, the Shah's twin sister. For several years I had even been a member of the film festival's organizing committee, an unusual post for a foreigner in chauvinistic Iran.

The trouble was that all these different jobs, many of them in what might be considered sensitive areas, and my knowledge of the language, the country itself and its various social and ethnic groups, meant that I matched the profile of a successful agent of British Intelligence – or rather the British Intelligent Service. To Hosein, like Savak before him, and even some of my own acquaintances, it was obvious I was a spy.

6

FROM SEVERAL THINGS he said I could tell that Hosein was feeling complacent about obtaining a confession from a top British spy, and from time to time he would bring a VIP visitor to see, or more commonly talk to me while I sat blindfolded. On the whole he was friendly during this period, but would occasionally show a burst of temper or even hit me, although not with the vigour of early days. I tried, successfully on the whole, not to let his tactics unsettle me. I would do my best to finish answering his questions by the second or third day after his weekly visit, working at them for eight or nine hours a day. Then I would have at least three or four days entirely to myself, and did not care when he came.

Once he complained about one of my answers, saying it was incomplete and I was holding something back. It was a minor point and I told him if he gave me the pages I would add a footnote that would solve his problem. He did so, and left the room while I was writing. That was a big mistake on his part, if he valued his anonymity: there was his name, clearly written out on the first page in the space marked 'Name of Interrogator', which he always filled in after I had completed my answers. I put the first few pages upside down on the radiator and left a few words at the end of my footnote to write when I heard him return, saying, 'Just a minute, it wasn't as easy as I thought.' He must have realized the mistake he had made, for he snatched the top pages from the radiator, and doubtless felt pleased that apparently I had not seen the first page. That was how I discovered that his first name was Ali, as I had guessed at our first meeting. Knowing his identity gives me, to this day, a great sense of triumph, but I have never revealed it to anyone and probably never shall.

One week I took a calculated risk that paid off handsomely. When Hosein sent for me I handed him back his question sheets completely blank and in a tone of strain and anguish said, 'I'm very sorry, Hosein. I couldn't write anything.' He sounded more surprised than angry and asked what the problem was. I said that I was often asleep at 5.45 A M, when the guards came round with the tea kettles, so they would shout at me, and this disturbed me so much that I got depressed and then could not write. 'If you return my alarm clock,' I added, 'I can set it for five minutes before they come and all will be well.'

'What alarm clock?' he asked. 'I don't have any alarm clock of yours.'

'Yes, you do,' I said. 'It's like a calculator.'

'Oh, I know what you mean. The Casio calculator. So it's an alarm clock, is it? All right, you can have it.'

The reason for this duplicity was the certainty that Hosein would not let me have anything that might give me pleasure or take my mind off the confession. In my corridor about four prisoners out of 36 were allowed a newspaper, but even the friendliest guard would never let me have one, even to borrow. I was told that only an interrogator could authorize this, and when I asked Hosein he refused. So he would also refuse to give me my calculator, as a calculator, in case I used it for unproductive purposes, whereas as an alarm clock it would be serving his interests, according to my story.

I took particular care with the next set of questions after Hosein had returned the calculator and thanked him profusely, saying that now I could get on with writing immediately I had drunk my morning tea. I put the calculator to use at once, first on financial matters, such as trying to decide whether I had saved enough to leave McDermott if I was released soon, and what my assets would be if I was made redundant. I assumed the company would go on paying my salary while I was in gaol, since I had got here through no fault of my own while on their business, and in fact partly because of their fault. I was not quite sure what I would do after my release. If my job was still available I might stay on in Dubai for another year, as I found the work challenging, was saving most of my salary, and wanted to finish my cookery book on the seafood of the Persian Gulf. On the other hand, I did not want to become another of those expats who are mesmerized by their tax-free salaries into staying on and on in countries where they do not really belong.

I did not, of course, know quite where I belonged myself. I liked Dubai in many ways, but it was no longer the exciting place it was when I first visited it, before independence. It was comfortable, well organized, the very model of a rich little city-state in the late twentieth century, but not my idea of home, as Iran had been. England was my birthplace and where most of my friends and family lived, but I had never wanted to settle there permanently. One or two trips a year would suffice. North Wales, where my two brothers and I had a remote cottage in the Snowdonia National Park with our own river and mountains, home to a few score of wild goats and little else, is the place dearest to my heart, but impractical as somewhere to live. There is no electricity supply or telephone, and the water comes straight from the stream. I quite liked the villa in Spain, left to me and my brothers by our Uncle Christopher, but jointly-owned properties are a cause of disputes, so I should perhaps consider selling my share or buying theirs. I also liked the idea of buying a house in France, somewhere near a Channel port perhaps, or in the French Alps. Property was certainly much better value there than in Britain.

Finally I had applied to join Lloyd's, putting all my worldly wealth at risk as an underwriting Name; only my arrest had prevented me from completing the formalities (and perhaps saved me from bankruptcy, as I later discovered). All these options had financial implications and I spent many interesting hours analysing each of them with endless 'What ifs?' that with my calculator and precious stock of paper I could now rapidly answer. The calculator's time function also provided a check on my watch, a Rolex Oyster that served me faithfully throughout my years in prison. Even when the calculator batteries ran out and could not be replaced the Rolex soldiered on, towards the end badly needing a service, but even then losing a few seconds a day so regularly that I always knew exactly what the correct time was.

The calculator's greatest benefit, however, was something totally unexpected. After three weeks of effort I had finally proved

Pythagoras' theorem and relearned how to solve quadratic equations. This gave me a taste for mathematics, especially when I found a far more elegant way of proving that the square on the hypotenuse is equal to the sum of the squares on the other two sides. Pythagoras did it neatly enough by drawing lines and triangles that had nothing directly to do with the proposition. My proof was shorter and more direct, and my only doubt was whether it was quite valid. It involved similar triangles and I could no longer remember, forty years on, the rules governing these. How I wished for a battered old school copy of Euclidean geometry and an algebra text book. At school I was quite good at maths, but under the lopsided A-level system of education I had to give the subject up at fourteen to specialize in modern languages. I had remained quite numerate, and got top marks in my regiment on the technical side, which involved trigonometry and logarithms, during my training in the Royal Artillery, but in later life had rarely needed to know any maths beyond percentages, ratios and simple algebra.

One day I noticed that 1 divided by 7 was 0.142857. This seemed something of a coincidence, since the digits look like a simple geometric progression 14, 28, 56 with the addition of 1, giving a curiously circular effect. I continued playing about and was surprised to discover that each of the numbers from 1 to 6, when divided by 7, gave a recurrent decimal series consisting of the same digits but in a different order, not, I soon discovered, a random order but simply as if they were drawn around a circle, like the numbers on a clock dial: for each division by 7 you simply started at a different point on the dial or circle. This did not seem to be the case when I divided numbers by 2, 3, 5, 9 or 11, so at first I assumed that 7 was an aberration. As a divisor 13 was also strange: it resembles 7 but has two circles of 6 digits; 17 has a single circle of 16 digits, although it took a little time and trouble to work them out, since with a hand-held calculator only 7 of them appear at a time. In time I worked out the circles for all prime numbers up to about 200 and tried to find theories about the anomalies I found. All these series are, in fact, geometric progressions, but not quite as I had at first expected. It was dividing 7 by 19, which is 0.368421 . . ., that provided my first breakthrough. I guessed that this was a summarized geometric progression 1, 20, 400, 8000, 160,000, 3,200,000 ... each new number being 20 times its predecessor and the whole series then summed.

Once I had understood this it was only a matter of time and precious paper to discover that every series was the summation of a geometric progression, and then to work out the general principle. Next I learnt to calculate what the number just off the edge of the calculator was, and I also discovered that, if looked at as whole numbers, these series, at least the ones for the reciprocal, had unexpected characteristics, such as always being divisible by 27 (3^3) and often by what I called 'preferred factors'. For example, 142857, the one I started with, is 3 x 3 x 3 x 11 x 13 x 37. Here 11, 13 and 37 are all preferred factors, but I could not see why, for example, 19 and 23 never were. Unfortunately, the limited capacity of my calculator made it difficult to pursue this line of enquiry with circles larger than about 16 digits, and I could not spare the time or paper to do this manually.

Since my release I have frequently talked enthusiastically to people at dinner parties about the joys of decimal series, only to see their eyes glaze over, so I will not continue further about my discoveries lest I lose my readers' interest too. One of my party tricks, however, sometimes evokes interest. If you hand me a calculator on which you have just divided any two prime numbers up to 9999, I can quite quickly tell you what those numbers were. I published this puzzle in *The Spectator* shortly after my release, and although I received several attempted solutions none worked. The only person to have solved it so far has been the marketing manager of Casio's UK affiliate, who kindly attempted to repair my calculator. (Hosein later took it away from me and although it was returned on my release, sadly it was no longer in working order or even repairable.) He came up with a mechanical solution that does work, but is cumbersome with large numbers. I would be interested to hear from anyone else who can solve this problem, by my method or a different one.

I have no idea whether these researches have any scientific value. I liked to think that because it was not really practical to do this kind of number-crunching before computers or calculators came along it might be a neglected branch of mathematics. Later, when I got some maths books, up to first-year college level, I looked in vain for a good description of decimal series, so I would love to sit down with a top mathematician to discuss my discoveries, although since none of my gaol jottings were returned when I was released I would have to work quite hard to get back to the level I reached back in 1986. I would also like to try my theories out on numerical systems other than our decimal one, such as the binary or duodecimal systems, but I would need proper tuition to be able to do this.

Having my calculator had one amusing sequel. I did use it occasionally as an alarm clock, and Hasan Kuchulu ('Titchy' Hasan), a tiny and rather unsophisticated guard, decided it was a secret communications device. He reported it to his boss, Bespectacled Hosein, who like most young Iranians had also never seen such a device before: the technological revolution has in general passed Iran by. To cover himself, Hosein reported the matter to my interrogator, whose paranoia led to it being taken away from me for a week to be tested. He suddenly suspected that the BIS might have given me a state-of-the-art radio transmitter disguised as a calculator and that I was reporting back to Downing Street. When it was pronounced clean and returned to me I used to tease 'Titchy' by pretending to talk into it, saying in Persian things like, 'Is that the Iran Department? Cooper here. Hasan Kuchulu has just come on duty. Please tell Mrs Thatcher.' He would blush and laugh half-heartedly.

In August 1986 I was taken with a small group of other prisoners to another part of the huge Evin complex that I had not yet seen. Nobody would tell me the reason, but as we sat blindfolded and relatively unguarded I raised my eyebrows to their fullest extent and all became clear. To my left was a long corridor partitioned off into booths, the first of which I could see into. There was a similar booth on the other side of a plate glass window. Abutting the window was a narrow ledge on which stood a dialless telephone, and there was a chair on each side. We had obviously been brought here for a meeting with our families. I had no idea who I would see on the other side of the plate glass.

While the visitors were being rounded up and allotted their booths we were ordered to remove our blindfolds. I later discovered that visitors are never allowed to see blindfolded prisoners. There was actually a checkpoint: it was an offence not to wear a blindfold north of it or to wear one south of it. When a prisoner goes to court or has a visit, he must take his blindfold off as soon as he enters the room and put it back on as he steps out. Years later, when I was in a communal cell and got newspapers, we derived much sardonic amusement from a photograph on the front page of one of the hardline newspapers showing *Intifada* detainees on the West Bank wearing blindfolds as they were taken off by bus, with a caption attacking the Israelis for this breach of human rights.

I was expecting Guity, who still lived in Tehran, or possibly Gisu, who would now be on her last vacation before starting clinical training at the Royal Free Hospital in Hampstead, but it was hard to recognize faces beneath the chadors and Mother Hubbard headscarves. However careless women might be about this compulsory veiling in public in the fashionable suburbs of Tehran – and I had observed before my arrest a slight loosening up in the enforcement of *hijab* – when visiting her loved one in Evin every woman observed the rules punctiliously.

Then I saw a middle-aged European waving at me and realized it must be a consular official. Later, I was told it was indeed Victor Welborn, the British consul. At the time diplomatic relations still existed between Iran and the UK, but only at chargé d'affaires level, with skeleton staffing in both embassies. I reached for the telephone, but was told by the half-dozen guards who had gathered in my booth to witness the encounter that we were not permitted to speak to each other.

Like most Brits, I suppose, I am not naturally good at sign language, but we used to play charades as children and if I had been given even a few minutes' warning I might have thought of some way of communicating with Mr Welborn. I could easily have indicated by signs that I had been beaten up repeatedly, but did not think this would be a wise move. As it was, my mind went a complete blank and we stood there smiling at each other like idiots. From down the corridor a babble of excited voices could be heard. Iranians shout on the telephone anyway, so on an occasion like this the noise was understandably deafening. I could tell I was the only prisoner not allowed to talk.

Now Mr Welborn was mouthing something at me, but I could not lipread him. Then he was pointing at me and shrugging his shoulders and clearly asking how I was. I pulled a face that was meant to convey 'As well as can be expected', but my meaning was not clear, so he shrugged his shoulders questioningly again and gave a thumbs up, hoping perhaps that I could confirm in this way that all was well. Unfortunately, our thumbs-up is almost identical to a vulgar sign used in Iran and several other countries, to indicate 'Up yours', and this sent the guards on both sides of the plate glass into paroxysms of laughter. Soon they were all giving the thumbs up to each other and giggling uncontrollably, with poor Mr Welborn obviously unaware what the joke was. Months later guards were repeating this story and asking me if it was true that the British consul had made a rude sign at me as soon as he saw me.

I believe he reported that I seemed well, although not having seen me before he had perhaps little to judge by. Once again Hosein had wrong-footed me, although I was nevertheless grateful for the meeting, knowing it would bring solace to my friends and family, especially my 92-year-old mother, to know that at least I was alive.

One of the most intriguing aspects of the first stage of my interrogation was Hosein's persistent questioning about what I knew of a secret British radio network in Iran. According to him, when we pulled our troops out of Iran at the end of World War II we left behind an extensive network of agents in towns and villages in the north, each equipped with a radio transmitter. Their instructions were to monitor the Russian presence in their areas and especially to inform the BIS at once of any troop reinforcements or movements. Hosein seemed to believe that this network was still in place and was reporting to London on current events. He claimed that they had located some of these radios. It reminded me of Len Deighton's amusing novel *Spy Story*, in which an ageing British agent is infiltrated into East

Germany carrying a World War II transmitter, with disastrous results.

I told Hosein that this story was quite impossible, since by now the radios themselves, as well as their operators, would be beyond useful service, even if there had once been such a system, which I anyway doubted. Again and again I had to assure him that there was no British spy network in Iran. I knew the Shah had also been obsessed with this notion, although I never heard that he was worried about a wartime cache of radios. I also knew the British government had assured him that it really had wound down its direct intelligence presence. He had grudgingly accepted these assurances, it seemed, which had been a precondition for British success in one of those arms deals of the century we are always hearing about. (This one involved the sale of Chieftain tanks, which never did him or his successors much good.) When his regime began to crumble he called on Britain to reactivate its agents in his favour

'But, Your Majesty,' he was told, 'at your own request we disbanded what little presence we had. We have no current links with the opposition.'

'I know you *said* that,' the Shah reportedly replied, 'but I didn't really believe you.'

Hosein and his hardline colleagues were no different from the Shah in this respect. Again and again I tried to convince him that Britain was no longer the *éminence grise* of the Middle East, or indeed anywhere else. We were now a struggling middle-ranking power without any ambition to control Iran and certainly without the resources to do so. He wanted to believe this and could be pretty disparaging in his own way about Britain, but in his heart of hearts, just like the Shah, he saw us still as the major threat to Iranian independence.

As the interrogation moved forward and began to involve my own time in Iran, problems of memory arose. It was one thing to write essays about Iranian history, the Raj, or British policy in the Persian Gulf, quite another to remember details about where I had lived a quarter of a century ago, who my landlords had been, the different jobs I had held, the places I had visited, or the names of friends and acquaintances. Hosein had most of this information on file, since it soon became apparent that I had been under Savak surveillance as early as 1958, my first year in Iran. If the answers I gave Hosein did not tally with what he knew from my file he was convinced I was deliberately lying or holding back information, which was not, at that point, my intention.

One day I got quite angry about this and said, 'Look, Hosein, you're probably quite a lot younger than me, but the principle's the same. Can you remember in detail the sort of things you're asking me about your own life twenty-five years ago?' Typically, he said that he could, every last detail of everyone he knew. I said, 'Well perhaps you haven't had such a varied life as I have, or I'm just getting senile, but I swear I'm telling you everything as I remember it, it's just that I find it very difficult.'

My outburst had two effects. One was that he no longer harassed me quite so much if I could not remember something he wanted to know, the other was that I soon found myself able to remember things I thought I had forgotten. If he asked me for a name or an address I was often unable to provide it, but by thinking hard about it (or around it) in the privacy of my cell I could frequently hook the missing detail from deep down in my subconscious and haul it to the surface. I knew vaguely that neurologists and psychologists say we never completely forget anything, but had not really believed it. To my surprise, I found I had rather a good memory, and I put it to work on subjects other than Hosein's usually irrelevant questions.

The main result was the 'Evin Song Book', a personal collection of hymns and songs that I enjoyed singing. Often I only knew the first line or so, but by concentrating I could gradually add another line, or a rhyme, or let the tune work for me, and within a day or two I had enough to make the song complete enough for entry into the song book. Among favourites reconstructed in this way were 'Mohacs Field' and 'Shepherd, See Thy Horse's Foaming Mane', both based on Hungarian originals, and German songs like 'Muß I' Denn' (in my opinion ruined, rather than revived, by Elvis Presley's 'Wooden Heart') and 'Die Lorelei', all part of the repertoire of Amy von Ranke Graves, my German-born grandmother. There were also folksongs from the British Isles, like

112

ABOVE: Trapped by floodwaters in Persian Baluchistan, with Keith Wilson (right), April 1958. This trip subsequently led to espionage charges during my 'trial' in Evin

LEFT: Weekend climbing in the Alborz mountains of Iran, mid-1960s

BELOW: Visiting (right) an *imamzadeh*, or shrine, in central Iran in the early 1970s

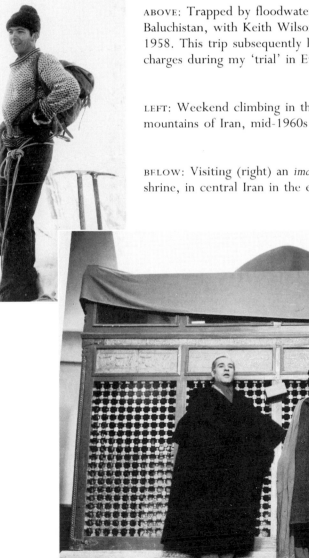

LEFT: On my wedding day with Guity, Tehran 1961

BELOW: With my daughter Gisu and brother-in-law Hamid (right)

LEFT: My mother Rosaleen visits an Isfahan mosque in 1969

BELOW: Playing backgammon with my second wife Cherlee in our Tehran house

LEFT: With our
dachshund Chopin
in the Qazvin
desert, northern
Iran, mid-1970s

BELOW: In a Persian
tea-house

'Widecombe Fair' and 'Coming through the Rye' and golden oldies like 'You Belong to Me', 'Pretty Little Black-eyed Susie', Harry Belafonte's 'Banana Boat Song', and, fast-forwarding, the Beatles' 'Yellow Submarine' and 'When I'm Sixty-Four'. Those two represented the latest pop music that I had listened to, my own taste and that of the next generation of listeners having diverged unbridgeably from then on.

Humming a selection from the song book just before going to bed often gave me musical dreams, and on at least a dozen occasions I was able to recapture these subconscious compositions next morning. Sadly, I never learned musical notation properly, so I could not retain the tunes unless they were firmly anchored by lyrics, which was rare. In grandiose moments I even wondered whether I might have become a songwriter had my education been different. My grandfather Alfred Perceval Graves, after all, was the author and composer of 'Father O'Flynn', one of the best-loved of Irish songs, while my mother had considerable musical ability and must have been one of the very few NHS doctors who was also a Fellow of the Royal College of Music. Her brother, the poet Robert Graves (who by a strange coincidence died on the day of my arrest), also had a great love of songs and music. In their Edwardian youth they had wandered the Snowdonia valleys recording Welsh songs at remote farmhouses. Uncle Robert had a good baritone voice, at its best, I thought, singing slightly bawdy songs at his home in Deya, on Mallorca, late at night, to the embarrassment of my rather old-fashioned mother.

The only song to have survived complete since my release is a regimental ditty, part-humorous, part-serious, that I wrote for the Intelligence Corps, in which I served briefly after completing the Russian interpreter's course during National Service. The tune came to me in my sleep and I spent several days writing lyrics to fit. The music is probably slightly derivative, with a nod or a bow to 'Much Binding in the Marsh', and I see it being sung as a duet in the Richard Murdoch–Kenneth Horne manner. I have not yet had the tune transcribed or sung the song with an accompanist, but here are the words:

113

The Intelligence Corps Song

A regimental ditty for two voices

If you say you're in the I Corps they say, 'Can you test my eyes?'
And if you say 'Intelligence' it causes great surprise,
As they think of cloaks and daggers and of soldiers in disguise.
So it's best to keep your mouth shut or to tell a pack of lies.

Oh, the unsung Corps, the Corps that really won the war,
The Corps that no one's heard of is the Corps that knows the score.

We're not a royal regiment, no Duke or Prince's Own,
We have no battle honours, and few heroes carved in stone,
But when you need an expert who can tap a telephone
And see what Ivan's up to, and make sure his cover's blown –

Oh, the unsung Corps . . . (*refrain*)

When it comes to learning Russian, or Bulgarian, or Greek,
Most ordinary soldiers are completely up the creek,
But the I Corps man's a polyglot, and when the blighters speak
He can listen in to what they say, the rotten little sneak.

Oh, the unsung Corps . . .

The I Corps man's a soldier, but he doesn't use a gun,
He uses his intelligence, if you'll excuse the pun.
He is no happy warrior who thinks that war is fun,
And long before the fighting starts his battle has begun.

Oh, the unsung Corps . . .

When the Argies took the Falklands we went there disguised as
    sheep:
If you listened very closely you could hear our fleeces bleep.
The I Corps man's a soldier, one who really earns his keep,
Yes, the I Corps is a menace when the enemy's asleep.

Oh, the unsung Corps . . .

Other pastimes included word games, particularly anagrams. I
would write down the names of people I knew, or public figures,
and spend hours trying to rearrange the letters into a meaningful

sentence or phrase that described them, along the lines of the most famous anagram of all FLIT ON CHEERING ANGEL (Florence Nightingale). For some reason few of my anagrams were flattering: I'M ALLAH TO KHOYENIA (Ayatollah Khomeini), a reference to one of the Emam's most hardline supporters, at that time the prosecutor-general, is practically blasphemous, and even THAT GREAT CHARMER (Margaret Thatcher) is likely to be seen as ironic. My most libellous anagrams, however, came when I turned my ballpoint on the British royal family, to reveal, perhaps, my latent republicanism. Almost none of these is printable. Assuming some royal sense of humour I suppose I might just get away with one written after I was allowed my first foreign newspaper, which reported Prince Edward as quitting the marine training depot in Topsham. Perhaps this young Royal did acquire a taste for two of Devon's finest products during his training, but to call him a CIDERED PRAWN is scarcely flattering.

Bridge was more difficult to set up than backgammon. It took a long time to obtain a piece of cardboard of the right size and quality to convert into a pack of cards, and without a knife or scissors this was not easy. Legally I could only possess a blue ballpoint, since the interrogators wrote in red. Red pens were frequently to be seen on the desks in the rooms where Hosein grilled me. One day, when I was alone in such a room, I surreptitiously put the top of one on my own blue pen, and then pocketed the red one. I had already got one or two spare blues, so the red was a bonus, and enabled me to colour the hearts and diamonds correctly.

Every bridge-player knows cut-throat, the version of the game when you cannot find a fourth player, and honeymoon bridge speaks for itself, but I doubt if bridge has often been played as a game of patience. I experimented with various formats and came up with a version of rubber bridge that was just about acceptable, if lacking in excitement at the card-playing stage. Best of all was a form of duplicate, the purest version of the game in the real world too, in which I tried to find the best contract against perfect defence, sometimes swapping the hands around to get slams, although duplicate can still be exciting when the contract is only one of a suit. Whenever I got a really interesting hand I would record it, and within a few weeks I had enough to keep a bridge columnist going for months.

There was additional excitement in knowing that cards were strictly forbidden in Iran, where even the possession of a pack had become a criminal offence. I had to assume that the older guards at least knew what a playing card looked like, even if it was only the size of a matchbox, since they were likely to have played rummy, the most popular card game in pre-Revolutionary Iran, so there was always the risk of a flogging if I was caught. Sure enough, Reagan did catch me playing one evening, after spying on me through the Judas hole.

'What are you doing?' he demanded as he burst into my cell.

'Death to Reagan,' I replied, this time with extra venom. 'I would be happy to tell you, Haji, but I am not allowed to.' I flashed him one of my tiny cards – not a court card – for a second. 'Hosein has asked me not to speak to anyone about this stage of my interrogation. All I can say is it is connected with codes, and if you want to know more you must ask Hosein.'

I knew he would never dare do this, particularly after the fiasco of my secret radio links with Downing Street, and certainly Hosein never said anything to me about the incident. Just in case he did, I prepared some phoney notes on simple codes, making some of them look like playing cards, and wrote up what little I knew of the breaking of the Enigma encryption-machine at Bletchley in World War II, then hid my cards in case Reagan was tempted to snoop around my cell while I was in the shower or being interrogated. In the early days I suspected this might happen, and sometimes left simple James Bond devices to see if my possessions had been tampered with, but as far as I could tell they never were.

One day that summer a clock struck, once only, but it had the jarring unnatural sound of electronic amplification, not the friendly chime of clapper on bell metal. Next day it struck again, several different notes this time, all equally unpleasant. Somebody was obviously trying to repair the university clock on the pagoda just across from the prison. By the third or fourth day a tune had begun to emerge. Whoever was repairing it was certainly taking his time. For a while I thought it was going to be a clone of Big Ben, but I knew that this was unlikely in the Shah's day and unthinkable today. Then I got it: it was the hymn tune 'St Anne'. Although through an oversight it was not in the 'Evin Song Book' I have always found it a rousing tune, at its best when sung by a chapelful of adolescent boys, but to hear it distorted and amplified every quarter of an hour (the repairman had got the last note wrong, so it ended on a discordant flat) would be sheer torture. By a coincidence this hymn already had an association with prison for me. In Evelyn Waugh's novel *Decline and Fall*, when Paul Penny-feather is serving time in Dartmoor, having carried the can for Lady Metroland's white-slavery, the prisoners exchange information by substituting questions and answers for lines of the hymn. I recalled:

> O God, our help in ages past,
> Where's Prendergast today?
> What, ain't you 'eard? e's been done in.
> And our eternal home.

After a few days the clock broke down again, but was soon restarted, and I knew I must do something. My complaint to the guards fell on deaf ears: most Iranians are impervious to noise. So in the end I spoke to Hosein about it, saying it was a gross example of noise pollution and was seriously interfering with the interrogation, by preventing me from concentrating. He was amused by this, but encouraged me to write a letter to the prison governor. I took particular care with this letter, drawing to his attention the facts that it struck 2076 individual notes a day, interrupted the sleep of prisoners in the Sanatorium, was musically incorrect on several notes, was based on a Christian hymn, and according to my Rolex kept very poor time.

Hosein, who was at the time in a jolly mood, made some useful changes in my draft, and took it personally to the governor's office. To my surprise and great joy, a week or so later the chimes ceased. Hosein said the governor had contacted the university and requested it be turned off, stressing the argument about the un-Islamic nature of the tune. I am not quite sure that this is what happened, partly because I was beginning to learn that almost everything Hosein said was untrue, and partly because the chimes started again several months later, now keeping slightly better time. But the mechanism was obviously in poor shape and before long it must have got on the nerves of students and professors as much as on mine, striking at quite the wrong time, or repeatedly with a single funereal note; finally it ceased altogether.

Another, friendlier sound reached my ears that summer. At first I thought it was just a truck passing on the road below the university, but noticing its regularity I realized it must be the bus that served Darakeh, a still relatively unspoilt village further up the Evin valley and a favourite starting point of mine for short climbs into the Alborz, once my own Lorna Doone valley had been put out of bounds by the Shah's security men. It was an hourly service and I began to monitor its regularity. It took passengers to Tajrish Square in north Tehran, and I had occasionally used it myself if I could not find a taxi after returning tired from a climb. Tajrish, once rather grand, had become a popular summer gathering-place for working-class families from south Tehran. I learnt to tell when the Tajrish traffic was particularly dense by the time it took the bus to turn round at the village end. On leisurely days I knew the driver had time for a tea-break, but on Fridays and holidays he would simply put down his passengers, take on new ones and start back. Then I began to notice slightly different engine sounds and gear-changing styles and realized there were two drivers, so I began to work out their schedules, giving them names and faces. Games and mental exercises like this may seem trivial and pointless, but they did help me to vault the prison walls in my imagination. By saying to myself 'I bet Ali Asghar is exhausted after three runs through thick traffic. Now he's enjoying his tea in the Darakeh café, while Ja'far takes over for a couple of hours,' I could turn my ears into eyes and escape from the reality of my hot little cell.

The worst of the summer was not the actual temperature, which rarely exceeded 90°F (32°C), but the almost total lack of moving air, which made it feel like well into the hundreds. There was a simple air cooler at the end of each corridor, but this was too far away and underpowered to affect the inside of my cell, with the door hermetically sealed on three sides. There was a slight crack at the bottom and I tried to create a cooling effect by pouring water on the tiles, but it was negligible. Again and again I asked the guards to leave the little barred window open, or at least the letter-box near the bottom, but this was almost never allowed. Sometimes I would manage to undo the catch when I came back to the cell, and then surreptitiously push it open slightly from the inside to create a draught, but all too soon a guard would notice and slam it to with his foot. I could not even sit comfortably in my underwear, since Islamic decorum demands that even in prison a man's legs, torso and even arms should be covered. A T-shirt was just about acceptable, but my British-style vest was not, and I always had to wear my pyjama trousers.

Ramadan that summer was not at first a pleasant experience. Breakfast – tea with tiny cubes of cheese and butter – was discontinued, and nothing was served between 2 AM, when *sahari*, the dawn meal, usually a rice dish, came round, and sundown, which that year occurred between 7 and 8 PM. At first I kept the rice for a kind of brunch, but by then it was cold and greasy, so I got into the habit of eating it in the early hours of the morning just like those keeping the fast, but nibbling bread and sipping water during the day. I recall that Hosein sent for me on the first day of Ramadan and the meeting developed into a huge row, with him slapping me about for no logical reason. Only later, when I saw that some of the guards were being equally foul-tempered, did I realize the effect that this enforced dehydration and starvation can have. Sexual intercourse is also banned during the daylight hours, which are meant to be spent in prayer and meditation. Most religions have similar periods of abstinence, when the flesh is supposedly mortified in order to concentrate on spiritual matters, and Ramadan can be seen as a lineal descendant of Yom Kippur and Lent. It surprises me somewhat that Islam should have such a strict version, since Muhammad was fervently against monasticism, which fasting and mortification seem to me to be associated with.

Another curious theological point occurred to me when I noticed that the radio signal marking the last permitted moment for partaking of food and drink was several hours before dawn. Ramadan is always described as a dawn-to-dusk fast, and I thought I remembered a Quranic verse to do with being able to differentiate between a black and a white thread. Later I searched the Quran until I found it and, sure enough, the Iranian Shi'ites were beginning the day earlier than the Holy Book dictates. At the end of each day, however, they were breaking their fast slightly too soon. The sun may have set, but it was still easy to tell black from white. I never did get a satisfactory explanation for this from the many people I asked, including in due course several mullahs, and no one seemed to know how the time for the dawn signal was calculated, although it is published for different cities to the nearest second. The least unsatisfactory answer I got was that the Shi'ites wanted to be sure not to offend Allah by eating and drinking too close to dawn, but by dusk they were so thirsty that they could not wait any longer. I got into long discussions with guards about whether they would fast if they were in northern latitudes in summer. How could a Muslim survive a June Ramadan in Iceland or Lapland? The best answer I got was that in such a case the Emam would advise, and if necessary abrogate or modify the fast.

One day towards the end of the holy month I decided to keep the fast myself, something I had not done for many years and only for one or two winter's days at that. I was pleasantly surprised by the result. Instead of dozing all day, or at least all afternoon, as lots of Muslims do, I found my mind particularly clear, although I became somewhat light-headed just before *eftar*, when the radio signal sounded. From then on for the next four years, with one short break, I kept Ramadan as faithfully as any ayatollah, and feel I benefited from the experience, especially once I had books to read.

Medical opinion is divided over the relative advantages and disadvantages of fasting. Some doctors say it helps purify the blood and digestive system, others say it has harmful effects. All too often, of course, the benefits of cutting down on calorific intake are nullified by excessive feasting at night. In the Arab countries, total food consumption actually increases during Ramadan by about ten per cent, contrary to one of the main purposes of the fast, which is for the rich to feel the pangs of thirst and hunger and donate the equivalent of what they do not consume to the poor, rather like the occasional charitable 'hunger lunches' in the West. All I can say is that I felt a kind of heightened spiritual awareness during Ramadan, lost a little weight healthily, and even discovered a bond of solidarity with the many millions of Muslims around the world who were also fasting, even though they might not agree on such sectarian details as when to start and stop. Certainly no cup of tea with a few dates, followed by a bowl of soup, can ever taste as good as when you have been fasting for seventeen hours.

7

SUMMER MERGED SLOWLY into a warm autumn, and all too soon winter was upon us. It could be cold at times in the cell, especially when fuel shortages or incompetent re-ordering meant that the heating was off for a few days – although I noticed this never happened in the interrogation block – but the cold weather was infinitely preferable to the six or seven hot months.

With the end of my first year in gaol approaching, I was something of an old lag. I had managed to acquire two extra blankets in the summer months, washed them during my weekly shower, and now used them as a seat by day and to provide a little extra insulation and padding between myself and the concrete floor at night. It had taken me several months to learn to sleep comfortably without a mattress. Before my arrest I used to suffer from excruciating attacks of back pain three or four times a year. This only happened twice in Evin and once since my release, so sleeping on the floor must have been good for me, as well as being a useful ability when I start travelling again in remote parts of the world.

Like many Islamic fundamentalists, in my experience, Hosein had sex on his brain. Much of his questioning was little more than prying into my personal life in a voyeuristic way. Back in 1959, when I was teaching English in Tehran University's Institute of Foreign Languages, I had two female students called, let us say, Mina and Haleh. They were cousins, Mina the plainer but more outgoing, Haleh extremely pretty but languidly shy. One evening after class they waited behind to talk to me privately. Would I be able to give them some private coaching before their exams? By then I had all the teaching I needed at the British Council and the University. I had taken on a few private students, mainly idle boys from wealthy families, but had learnt that by the time I had driven to the boy's house, given a full hour's lesson, as opposed to a fifty-minute class, and done some obligatory socializing, it was not financially a very attractive return on my time even if I charged double the university's hourly rate. Private lessons were also frequently cancelled for no good reason, and it was difficult to insist on payment in such circumstances. It also seemed wrong to put my energy into teaching one unwilling and often stupid boy when I could be helping a class of thirty enthusiastic students. There was also the ethical question of giving extra tuition to one's own students. Mrs Suratgar, the British-born director of the Institute, would certainly not have approved.

So I said to Mina, 'I'm sorry I can't help you myself, but I expect I could find you a teacher if you want,' thinking of some of my friends who were always glad to take on a private student.

Mina pouted: 'No, Mr Cooper, we only want you,' and the slight blush that came over Haleh's beautiful face made me change my mind.

'I'll tell you what,' I said. 'I'll give you a little extra help on an informal basis, and in return you can help me with my Persian.' At the time I was studying A-level Classical Persian and had not been able to find a good teacher. I knew from class discussions that they both taught part-time in primary schools, quite a common practice in those days for unmarried middle-class girls. 'I'll teach you together and you can take turns to teach me,' I added, thinking I could get Haleh on her own in this way. 'I live quite near the Institute.' They were delighted, but insisted I should first come to them.

I went and met their parents and we did a bit of work together, but I never did succeed in separating them, or even getting them to my house. They were nice girls, not particularly good teachers from my point of view, but at least they corrected the essay I wrote for them every week or so. I remember the first subject they gave me was 'Tehran'. My opening sentence was *Tehran shahr-e now ast*, my attempt at saying 'Tehran is a modern city'. This sent them into peals of giggly laughter which they would not explain, except for, 'You can't say that in Persian.' Later an Iranian friend explained that *shahr-e now*, literally 'the new city', was the red-light district of Tehran, a walled town within a town, with a police

123

checkpoint, the only place where prostitutes could legally ply their trade.

Somehow Savak had learnt of my all-too-chaste trysts with Mina and Haleh and recorded them in my file. Now Hosein was prying into this short friendship, which ended when I married Guity, whose family were distantly related to Haleh's. Through Guity's mother I discovered that it was she and not the rather pushy Mina, as I thought, who was looking at me as a potential husband. Ostensibly Hosein was trying to link these two young women with the BIS. It was obvious, he said, that I was trying to recruit them so as to get information about the Iranian school system. Trying another tack, since Haleh had later married an army officer, he suggested I was trying to get military information. 'Which one did you sleep with?' he asked. 'Or was it both of them?'

I felt disgusted by this line of interrogation, which was to repeat itself whenever he questioned me about women acquaintances. He assumed, or pretended to assume, that I had had sexual relations with all the women whose names he had found in my Savak file. I have always believed that what consenting adults of whichever sex do in private is their affair, and theirs alone, but unfortunately you cannot tell your interrogator to mind his own business, although I did try to do so in a more diplomatic way.

He soon gave up on Mina and Haleh, and several others that even he must have seen were long shots, such as a senior government official I was friendly with on a professional basis. She was a distinguished economist married to a university professor, and I had never seen her out of her office. I greatly admired her for the courageous but unpalatable advice she gave the Shah. Her career suffered as a result, but had the Shah listened to her his son might today be on the Peacock Throne.

There were two other cases, however, that Hosein stuck to tenaciously, and one of them came close to costing me my life, as will emerge later. The first concerned Alicia, a woman from one of the Christian minorities in Iran, whom I scarcely knew. She was the girlfriend of a friend of mine, but he was trying to drop her, and hoped that I might take her over. I did not find her at all interesting or attractive, so that idea fizzled out. I only saw her once or twice at my friend's flat, and years later, having forgotten her completely, at her place of work. Hosein was adamant that we had been lovers. The reason for this was obviously because she worked at the Russian Hospital, as a nurse or clerical assistant. Knowing that I had been trained as a Russian interpreter – and I would love to know which of my friends had told Savak that – Hosein was sure that I had used her to make contact with some of the Soviet staff there, or even to recruit them for the BIS. He claimed he had a tape recording of a telephone call between Alicia and me, in which I said I had a parcel for her to look after for me and asked to meet her. Again and again I told Hosein I had never telephoned her, had never known her telephone number or address or even her surname, but he refused to believe me. Even the word for parcel was not one I used, although I understood it. Hosein simply would not accept any of this. Losing his temper, he tore up the two or three pages I had written in reply to 'Write everything you know about Alicia Gowharian' and started punching me wildly from behind. Eventually he calmed down somewhat, wrote out the same question again and sent me back to my cell with the words: 'Right, you'll do it again and this time I want the truth.'

I felt sick with anxiety at the situation I was now in. Hosein had returned answers to me before demanding a more detailed or truthful account, but he had never torn one up like that, and he had not been in such a foul temper with me for months. He could be stubborn, I knew, but he had never been quite so insistent. He obviously felt he had found a chink in my armour and was not going to let me escape. His beatings were always unpleasant but had become much less frequent, and they were not so bad if they came out of the blue. Knowing that if I did not satisfy him next week he would start punching me again was almost as bad as the punches themselves.

I began to consider alternatives. Should I admit the parcel and make it something innocent like a present I had bought her? Should I even admit to some sexual hanky-panky? But no, it was out of the question. She was a woman, an Iranian, quite possibly in Evin at that very moment undergoing interrogation herself. If I started lying about her to save myself it could lead to her being tortured, and so it would go on. She would obviously be denying any links with me of an intelligence or indeed any other nature, and Hosein must just accept that his theory was wrong. So after much thought I wrote out much the same answer as the first time, easily done since I always kept an English draft. Then I added a note saying I was very sorry Hosein had not accepted my earlier answer, but I could not change it because it was the truth: however much he put pressure on me (avoiding words like 'beat me' because this might embarrass him on an official document) my answer would always be the same. To placate him I said that if he let me hear the tape of the mysterious phone call, or even read the full transcript of it, I might be able to identify the speaker, but it was certainly not me. I did not entirely believe that such a tape existed, but if it did it might possibly have been my friend's voice wrongly identified by Savak as mine.

I handed the answer in and Hosein read it immediately, sitting behind me. I heard him put the papers down and tensed my body for the first punch, but it never came. I had won that round.

The second case concerning a woman, one that Hosein was even more tenacious about, was my brief friendship with a law student whose real name I did not learn until I was in Evin. If this sounds strange I should explain that in the Shah's day girls, and to a lesser extent boys, were often given an official 'religious' name, always an Arabic one such as Fatima or Khadija, which appeared on their identity cards, but were actually known by a more poetic, usually Persian, name. A friend of mine, for example, is officially Seyyed Ahmad, but is known as Shaida – literally, 'one intoxicated with love'. A girl might have Akram ('The Most Merciful') on her identity card but be called Zhaleh ('Dewdrop') or Fereshteh ('Angel') by her friends and family, many of whom might not even know her real name.

After Guity and I got divorced and before I met my second wife, Cherlee, I was very short of money. For a while I slept on a couch in the downtown office of an English friend, John. He had a girlfriend called Pari ('Fairy'), but already had an Iranian wife. He had rashly promised to marry Pari, meaning once he was divorced: polygamous marriages were becoming much less common among Iranians and were actually illegal if the husband was a foreigner. Doubtless my friend knew that, but he had not reckoned on Pari having an uncle who was the chief notary public of a provincial city. His daughter Nilufar ('Waterlily'), whom I had met once, was working for her doctorate in law at Tehran University, and had promised her cousin that daddy would be glad to bend the rules to 'legitimize' his niece's position by marrying them. John, in a weak moment, had agreed to this arrangement, but soon returned to his senses. What should he do? he asked me. I replied that he must get out of it at all costs. For a start such a marriage would be a serious breach of Iranian law and if his foreign employer got wind of it he would undoubtedly lose a well-paid job, with a pension not far off. (In those halcyon days time spent in Iran actually counted double in terms of years of service. Many of us thought half would have been fair.) The story of a bigamous Englishman would undoubtedly go the rounds of Tehran's gossipy expatriates, perhaps even be picked up by Fleet Street, and John would be ostracized by polite society, besides putting his much-respected Western-educated wife in an invidious position, to say the least.

I proposed a solution. He should give me the uncle's address and I would go there at once and tell the cousin, who was making the arrangements, that I had come without his knowledge to implore her to stop the marriage after my own efforts to do so had failed. I would tell her that in England bigamy was such a serious offence that if he ever went back there he risked a stiff prison sentence. In addition, he would be dismissed from his job, and then what would he and Pari live on, with alimony to pay as well? The sensible thing was for him to divorce his present wife; then they could get married.

John agreed with great relief, and early next day I set off for the town in my VW Beetle, a ten-hour drive from Tehran. The address was simplicity itself: just the uncle's name, since everybody there knew him. In the early evening I checked into the best hotel in town, a modest one-star affair. The first person I stopped in the street pointed out the house to me, and I rang the bell rather nervously. A maidservant told me that Nilufar had gone to the cinema with friends. I walked to the cinema, waited till the end of the performance, but could not see anyone like Nilufar in the crowd. I went back to her house and was told she might be going

127

to the next performance. So I returned to my hotel and had supper.

Back I went to the cinema, but failed to see Nilufar in the crowd. The maid laughed to see me again and said, 'She may not come back till very late now, or not at all.' I said I would be in my hotel waiting up for her till midnight, but if that failed I would appreciate it if she came to see me early the next morning as I had important business to discuss and had to get back to Tehran.

I was fast asleep when the door of my room opened at about seven next morning and in came Nilufar. In those distant days I never locked hotel bedroom doors, nor wore pyjamas, so I was at something of a disadvantage. Nilufar asked me my business in none too friendly a tone, and from under the sheets I said my piece. 'On no account,' I concluded, 'must John or Pari know I have come here. You must say your father has discovered it would be a serious offence for him to marry them, which is true. Once the divorce goes through they can get married openly and legally.' She agreed to this, rather reluctantly I thought, and left.

I was getting dressed when the chambermaid came in, like Nilufar without knocking. She gave me a roguish look and said, 'Sir, you came to our city last night and already you have found a pretty friend.' I began to protest: 'No, it's not like that at all. It was a business discussion,' but I could see it was useless. Oddly enough, that city had something of a reputation for fast ladies, which seemed to be confirmed by the maid's remark.

I drove back to Tehran feeling that I had more than repaid John's hospitality, so I stayed on at his office, sleeping on the couch, for a few more weeks. During this time Pari and Nilufar came to see John several times, and I felt sure that Nilufar had kept her promise. She and I became quite friendly and agreed to exchange lessons. I helped her with her studies of English contract and agency law, since her thesis was a comparison of the Iranian Commercial Code with its European counterparts. In return she helped me to appreciate the *ghazals* of Hafez, Iran's greatest lyric poet, explaining the subtle use of carnal metaphors to express mystic love much more effectively than my doddering professor of poetry at the Faculty of Letters, where I was now studying for a doctorate in Persian literature and philosophy. Nilufar communicated a deep love and understanding of Hafez. In return, I did my best to explain such concepts as 'estoppel' and 'warranty'. Coming as I do from a litigious family and having won my first case in the High Court, acting in person, in my mid-twenties I flatter myself that it was a fair exchange.

In Iran most old-fashioned notaries come from religious families and Nilufar was quite a strict Muslim in her way. At our first meeting alone, excluding the hotel visit, she said it was not proper for us to see each other tête à tête unless we were at least technically man and wife. I was at first astonished at this, but then remembered the case of Guity's great-aunt Khanom-e Amiri. When we were first married and living in part of the huge family home in central Tehran whenever I came into the courtyard from the street I had to shout *'Yallah!'* ('O God!') in a loud voice so that she could pull on her chador. Apparently Guity was not a close enough relative for our marriage to make me *mahram*, a term indicating a degree of kinship close enough for her to appear in front of me unveiled. Everyone else in the family compound was *mahram*.

One afternoon I came back from teaching at the university to find her smiling hideously at me and saying I was now *mahram*. 'How can this be?' I asked, thinking she looked much better with the chador on. 'Because you have just married Soheila,' she replied. I was baffled until Guity explained that she had gone to the local mullah, and paid him some money to 'marry' me to her nine-year-old granddaughter. I laughed and asked what the dowry was. 'A bag of sweets,' said the aged crone. 'Well, let me at least pay my dues,' I said, and went out to buy Soheila the best bag of sweets I could find. Years later when I saw her again as a nubile young woman I considered telling her that she was legally my wife, but I thought her solidly-built fiancé might not appreciate the joke.

So when Nilufar asked me to repeat the Arabic formula for entering into a contract of *sigheh*, as the great-aunt had once done on my behalf, I laughingly agreed. If it made her happy why not? *Sigheh* is a term used by Shi'a Muslims for a temporary marriage or a temporary wife. Given Islam's hatred of fornication and adultery it really is a practical solution to a variety of problems. In the old days pilgrims and merchants might be away from home for months or even years and feel the need for a companion, not necessarily a sexual partner. In some cases *sigheh* is the Islamic equivalent of a morganatic marriage, where the temporary wife has no permanent rights to her husband's estate, although in this case if a child is born it can inherit. It is also seen as a sensible way of avoiding prostitution, although in the Shah's day, I believe, pilgrims to large shrines such as Qom and Mashhad could get a mullah to arrange a *sigheh* for them for as short a time as half an hour. There were, however, and perhaps still are, respectable widows in Karbala and Najaf prepared to enter into *sigheh* contracts of six months or a year with gentlemen pilgrims or merchants. They do the shopping and cooking and cleaning, but do not necessarily share their husband's bed. *Sigheh* contracts can be entered into for as long as 99 years, and few 'permanent' marriages last that long.

Early in the Revolution, when two persons of the opposite sex found in compromising circumstances risked 72 lashes or even stoning to death, careful Romeos armed themselves in advance with a *sigheh* contract signed – for a fee – by a mullah, the name of the wife sometimes left blank until shortly before the 'marriage' was consummated, but this loophole has now been closed, I gather. At all events, *sigheh* is a recognized doctrine of the Shi'a, scorned by Sunnis and feminists, but which I personally do not find repugnant.

A *sigheh* marriage must be for a fixed time and a fixed dowry, specified and normally paid at the time it is entered into. A woman can only have one temporary spouse at a time, but a man of course can have several. I cannot remember what arrangements Nilufar made with me, perhaps six months' duration and I expect she waived the dowry. The *sigheh* lapsed when I met Cherlee.

When Hosein began to question me about a woman called Batoul with an equally unfamiliar surname I told him I had never known or heard of such a person. This was quite common in my interrogation and as a rule Hosein quickly accepted my word. He was usually just trying to link me to some other real or imagined spy network, I assumed. But in this case he pressed on despite my denials, finally supplying some biographical detail that enabled me to identify Batoul as my old friend Nilufar. Batoul is such a

130

joke name in Iran, although (or perhaps because) it was Mrs Khomeini's name, that no Iranian girl except the humblest maid-of-all-work would admit to having it. An English equivalent might be Agatha or Matilda, although even these names might in time return to favour. I had forgotten Nilufar's surname after all these years, as the only time I had ever used it was when I went to her home town. Now it all came flooding back.

Hosein badgered me and badgered me about Nilufar and flatly refused to believe that my relationship with her was purely pedagogical. I cannot altogether blame him, for she was an attractive woman and doubtless her photograph was in my file, but I certainly was not going to give him any additional ammunition by telling him about our *sigheh* contract.

He left the matter for a while, but came back to it more strongly than ever a few weeks later when he suddenly announced that cross-checking other information had revealed that Nilufar was an Israeli agent. This was so preposterous that I daresay I laughed out loud. What a crude try-on, I thought. On and on he went, insisting that correspondence between Nilufar and someone in Israel had been found in the files. This slimmed down to her having sent a letter to Israel in the Shah's day. I said, 'Really, Hosein, would an Israeli agent write a letter to Israel?' and he countered cleverly by reminding me that I communicated with Colonel Hooker by post. I then suggested that one of her relatives or friends might have gone to Israel for medical treatment, not an uncommon event in the Shah's day even for non-Jewish Iranians. The medical treatment there was probably just as good for most conditions as in London and Paris, and the cost much lower. I did not of course know whether such a letter existed, but given the Shah's paranoia and Savak's ubiquity it was not impossible that records were kept of people writing to Israel. Certainly letters to or from communist countries were investigated.

Hosein refused to accept my theory. To him, Nilufar just had to be, however implausibly, an Israeli agent, with whom I was somehow involved, perhaps trying to recruit her as a double agent, or simply as an up-and-coming barrister who could keep the BIS informed of what was happening in the judiciary. After many hours of interrogation, in person and by written answers, with me firmly

131

denying any intelligence links whatsoever, he seemed to weary of the subject.

'All right then, Mr Cooper,' he said, 'what was she then, just your girlfriend?' Equally weary, I replied, 'Yes, if you like.' This was to prove an almost fatal mistake.

As someone often regarded as disorganized and unpunctual I surprised myself in gaol by my detailed record-keeping and consciousness of time. This was partly the result, no doubt, of having nothing to read for so long, but I later discovered that the passage of time is something close to the hearts and minds of all prisoners. The phrases 'doing time' or 'serving time' are apt. Prisoners are also essentially creatures of habit, ultra-conservatives inherently suspicious of change, even if ostensibly made to improve their conditions. I wanted to know everything about the routines of Evin, not only to be prepared for what might happen but also just for its own sake. 'They' did not want me to see other prisoners or learn the layout of the prison, and this made me determined to see and learn all I could, even though the information was of little practical value to me. So if it moved or made a noise I listened, timed and recorded it.

The first problem was to crack the guards' roster. Quite early on I had asked a friendly guard when he went off duty, and when he would return. He reddened and said he was not allowed to tell me. Within a week I had worked out an approximate timetable, quickly discovering that the guards worked alternate days, regardless of holidays, with a changeover soon after breakfast. Each day the nine duty guards, with one or two in reserve, were divided into three groups, one for each of the three men's floors – the 'sisters' were on the ground floor – and each guard worked three shifts, two daytime shifts of two and a half hours and a night shift of three hours. Between shifts they could eat, watch television or catch up on their sleep, but they were expected to help the duty guard at busy times such as serving tea or lunch.

After each meal the guard coming on duty would go round with a spirit burner to light cigarettes, since matches and lighters were strictly forbidden. The ration was a packet a week, so smokers could have a cigarette after every meal. Many chain-smoked at the start of the week and could be heard begging for a cigarette when they had used up their ration. I often heard a sympathetic guard give a prisoner a cigarette, such is the camaraderie of smokers, but usually with a stern warning that next week they must smoke more prudently. Fortunately I had never been an committed nicotine addict; I did not smoke a single cigarette for over four years and would not allow guards to smoke in my cell if they dropped in for a chat.

To make my draft roster I first had to name each guard. I began, as in the case of Reagan, with a nickname, but I gradually discovered their real names: his was Allahqoli. One or two told me theirs, although they often gave me a false one. Usually only one guard was on duty at a time, but if he was summoned to the office another guard might shout his name down the corridor, so if I knew who was on duty I could then assign a real name to him. This could later be confirmed by bringing it into conversation with him and watching his reaction. 'Good morning, Reza, how are you today?' might be answered by, 'Fine, thanks,' or a suspicious 'Who's Reza?' and I would have to judge if this was genuine or not. Another trick would be to ask a guard some simple question and then say to the next one 'Majid told me such and such.' Guards usually protected their own anonymity better than a colleague's, especially if it seemed that I already knew his name.

Once I had all the names, or nicknames, and knew whether they served on odd or even days I soon realized that the floor they were assigned to was a random decision taken by the day boss, Bespectacled Hosein or Seyyed Satari, and it was equally random whether they got first, second or third shift. This was good security practice since it would make any escape plan more difficult. In theory, since the cell doors were locked not by keys but simply by not having a door knob on the inside, it would have been quite easy to overpower a guard as he opened the door, lock him in and then quickly open the doors of other cells. The guards were not armed at all, and a group of determined prisoners could conceivably have rushed the office, grabbed the front door key, and escaped from the block. Not that this would have done them much good because there were a dozen or more watchtowers constantly manned by armed guards, high perimeter walls, and,

133

reportedly, minefields. Only two men are reputed ever to have escaped from Evin, one in a dustcart – rubbish is now disposed of internally – the other by bluffing his way out on a visitor's pass, although it is not recorded what happened to the visitor.

The random assignment of duty meant that I might see a guard on three or four successive odd (or even) days, or not at all for over a week if he was assigned to a floor other than mine during this period. There were further factors such as sickness, leave or day-swopping. I might see a guard three days running, on the middle day covering for someone else. It was quite a challenge to work out whom he had swopped a day with. They tended, like Westminster MPs, to have a 'pair' that they regularly exchanged duty with, and once I had worked these pairs out it was fun to see a guard on an unscheduled day and say casually: 'I suppose you're standing in for Mahmud today.' The commonest answer to such remarks was 'How on earth did you know?' Depending on who it was I might reply: 'The Intelligent Service knows everything.' By the second year I had worked out their leave entitlements and could surprise a guard by saying: 'You must be due for leave soon. Are you going away anywhere?'

The meal schedule was harder to crack, being slightly more variable, especially as dishes changed to some extent with the seasons. But in time I could predict with over seventy per cent accuracy what we were going to have for lunch or supper. (Breakfast was easy: in my first year it was cheese and butter every day, in year two it was just cheese, and, from then on, as dairy imports dwindled, it was cheese one day, runny carrot jam the next.) I used to test my forecasts by telling the guard as he came to collect my little bowl what he was about to dish out, and my reputation grew to the extent that guards would come and ask me in mid-morning what we were going to have for lunch. They usually ate the same food as us, doubtless making sure they got plenty of any meat content, but in addition they had good supplies of eggs and cheese, which were strictly rationed for prisoners. The supreme accolade was when one guard told another: 'The cook at Evin doesn't know what the next meal is going to be, but Cooper does.'

I also monitored the distribution of soap (coarse, but free) and detergent (a tiny ration and paid for). Sometimes the duty boss would say, 'When did we last issue soap, Cooper? Is it time for another ration?' and I would say, 'Issues are averaging twice a month, so there's still two days to go, but there's no harm in giving it out now.' All this helped the time pass and added to my status among the guards. If a new guard was rude or tricky with me I now had enough clout to get the others to tell him privately not to annoy me. There might even be a reference to the long arm of the Intelligent Service, I was told.

Every Friday morning the guard on first shift came round offering nail clippers and sewing materials. The more literate ones wrote down the cell numbers they had given these to, the others relied on their memory; it was many weeks before I was able to keep a needle, and over two years before I managed to get a pair of nail clippers. Nothing that cuts or could be used as a weapon or means of suicide could be kept in a solitary cell. It annoyed me to have to cut my nails when somebody told me, especially as I soon discovered that my nails needed cutting on the sixth, not the seventh day. Something always seemed to need sewing on Saturday morning, and most of the needles were blunt, having doubtless been used to scratch messages on cell walls rather than sew buttons on, so I was determined to get one of my own, even though it would be risky to use it except on Friday morning.

There were not enough needles for every cell to get one at the same time, so the guard would do about a dozen cells at a time and then collect them up half an hour later, the whole floor taking his entire shift. Unfortunately, because of the position of my cell I was always in the first group and the guard never forgot to collect mine. One Friday, however, Ali Lotfi, who always liked to do things efficiently but differently, began at the far end of the floor so I was for once in the last group. When he came to collect my needle I let him see I was still working on a big stitching job and got him to agree that I could finish it off and return the needle to the next guard who would soon be on duty. When I had finished I put the needle on the floor and slid it under the crack, so that it was just outside the cell, having made sure I could pull it back in with a piece of paper. If the next guard insisted hard enough I would say I had put it on the ledge of the little window in the door. Then I could 'find' it on the floor

135

outside the cell, the assumption being that the guard had knocked it off in opening the window.

The next guard, luckily for me, was rather inexperienced, and when he came to collect the needle I said I had put it on the ledge and if it was not there Ali Lotfi must have collected it himself. He seemed surprised, but accepted my story and went away. I left the needle where it was until next day when Ali Lotfi went off duty, and then pulled it back into the cell and kept it in a secure place. For the next few Fridays I asked for a needle, gradually trading upwards until I got one of the few sharp ones, and I kept this with me the whole time I was in the Sanatorium.

Try as I might, I could not get nail clippers in the same way. In my third year, however, when I was finally allowed an occasional stroll in the garden, closely accompanied by a guard, I spotted a rusty pair near the rubbish dump. I picked them up, but saw at once they did not work. My guard looked as well and said, 'They're no good', so I threw them away, carefully marking the spot where they landed. Later, with a different guard, I surreptitiously undid a shoe-lace, then stopped at the spot as if to do it up, and pocketed the clippers as I resumed my walk. Back in the cell I buffed them up as well as I could, and having taken a working pair I returned the useless ones. Again, I gradually traded upwards until I had the best pair in the block for my own personal use.

It seems incredible that I went to such lengths to beat the system and get a slight advantage for myself. My behaviour may even have been antisocial, inasmuch as some prisoners had presumably been given a pair of dud clippers, while I had a working pair to myself. But I also knew that even in Evin needles and clippers were replaced from time to time, so all I was doing was accelerating the system. I had complained often enough about the bad condition of these implements and had even offered to pay for some new ones, since I had quite a large amount of cash and little to spend it on. Once my offer was refused I felt justified in taking alternative action.

Islam sets great store by actual, as well as ritual, cleanliness, the strict rules for the latter presumably having been established to reinforce the former, just as Mosaic dietary laws – many of which, such as the prohibition of pork, were incorporated into Islam –

must originally have been practical rules of hygiene in a hot climate. As I was to discover when I left solitary, most prisoners, whether Muslims or not, had an obsession about cleanliness, and I was no exception. Never before or since have I spent so much time and effort trying to keep myself, my clothes and my habitat clean.

Every day I washed myself all over at the little basin, whether the water was warm or not, and once I had acquired extra pyjama trousers and T-shirts I changed my clothes every day, and twice a day in summer. My cell walls were a dark coffee colour when I arrived, the result of years of cigarette smoke. Bespectacled Hosein gave me an extra ration of detergent and I set about cleaning this off, and once I had degrimed the windows my cell became a much brighter place. The WC was the most difficult cleaning job, but I had that sparkling in time. Guards who had not seen me at work thought when I had finished that my cell had been repainted, and even the governor was favourably impressed when he came round.

We had a shower only once a week, with a curious exception, which I discovered one morning when I heard the man in the next cell being taken for an unscheduled shower. It was a hot and sticky day and I demanded equal treatment. The guard said that the man was having *ghosl*, a technical Islamic word meaning total immersion in water. When I asked why I could not have *ghosl* also he explained in embarrassingly graphic detail that this was because he had had *mani*, a nocturnal emission, which like sexual intercourse should be followed by *ghosl*. Masturbation was a punishable offence, the guard said, but *mani* was surprisingly common. One hot afternoon I demanded *ghosl* from a different guard, but was told that as a non-Muslim I was not entitled to it.

Having a shower in the Sanatorium was in fact a stressful experience. My cell and the five adjacent to it had a Thursday afternoon shower schedule, convenient for me as Hosein hardly ever kept me after lunch on Thursday, the equivalent of Saturday in the Islamic week. The guard on duty would take six of us, blindfolded and in single file, each prisoner with a hand on the shoulder of the man in front, and put us one by one into a cubicle, which was about the size of a walk-in wardrobe, and lock the door. There was no window, just a light, well-protected against a suicide attempt, and a hook for one's pyjamas and towel. Iranians love long showers and we were allowed to stay for twenty minutes, but I found I suffered from claustrophobia and begged the guards to let me out after ten minutes. Sometimes they forgot or just did not bother, or had no watch or sense of time; this could induce a sense of panic in me and I would beat on the door to be let out. More than a year after my arrival I was once taken by a friendly guard to a normal-sized shower room with a window, which I had not known existed. From then on I always pleaded to be taken to that one, even going so far as to decline a shower if a guard insisted on putting me in the windowless one. Mashti, the janitor, a tough old tribesman from Lurestan, lent me a plastic washtub and at last I was able to wash my clothes, and even my blankets, properly, treading them in hot soapy water like grapes.

'Mashti' is the colloquial title of someone who has been on pilgrimage to Mashhad, the holiest shrine in Iran, where the Eighth Imam is buried, murdered, according to the Shi'ites, by the son of the Caliph Harun-al-Rashid, although the Sunnis say he died of a surfeit of grapes. The first eleven of the twelve Imams recognized by mainstream Shi'ites – there are in addition several break-away sects, including the Druzes and the Aga Khan's Ismailis, each with its own chain of Imams – are all said to have been martyred, while the Twelfth, the Imam of the Age, is believed to be still alive, living in occultation at the ripe old age of 1120. He may even wander among us today, some say, without revealing his identity, and once a year he travels to Mecca, where he looks into the hearts of the pilgrims. In popular belief one sure way of recognizing him would be to see if his body casts a shadow: the twelve Imams lacked shadows. One day he will reveal himself to usher in an age of perfect justice, as a prelude to the Day of Resurrection. Saintly figures like Khomeini are in spiritual communion with the Imam of the Age, and he may appear to believers in dreams commanding action or offering advice. These are difficult concepts to understand and accept, and most of the guards became almost embarrassed if I asked them for clarification.

The janitor was about my age and had presumably earned his title when the journey to the Imam's shrine was more arduous than it is today, with adequate road, rail and air links. Mashti was a good-hearted man, almost never ill or on leave ('What would I do if I didn't come here?'). He would come round punctually every day except Friday with his bins and trolley to collect our rubbish. If any of the guards made jokes about him, which sometimes happened, he would challenge them to a fight, an offer which was never taken up, for Lurs have a reputation as tough guys. I once complained to him about the cockroaches and asked if he could spray the area where I thought they were breeding. He looked genuinely puzzled. 'Several people have complained to me about cockroaches,' he said. 'I don't know why. We've got plenty at home and they've never done me any harm.' I was always offering to work as his assistant collecting rubbish; although he was willing enough to take me on, I knew my offer would never be approved.

Another character I sometimes saw was Haji the barber. 'Haji' is the title given to someone who has made the pilgrimage to Mecca, but it is often used in Iran simply as a title of respect, especially since the Revolution, replacing the traditional word Agha ('Sir') which has feudal or servile overtones. The chambermaid in my hotel before I was arrested called me Haji, for example. The barber, however, really had been to Mecca, several times it seems. The Iranian 'caravans' were as self-sufficient as possible, and he had been going almost every year to shave the pilgrims and trim their hair in the Islamic way. He was a jolly little man and once I had got to know him he was a good source of information about the holy city of Qom, where he lived. He came all the way to Evin twice a month, as a religious duty he said, but I calculated he also made a pretty good income out of it, as he got his customers in and out of the chair in about ninety seconds and the going rate was 100 rials, 50p at the admittedly unrealistic official rate. He was worried that under a new rule he would, at the age of sixty, be too old to go to Mecca any more. He never cut my hair as short as I asked him to, presumably to ensure I would have another trim on his next visit, which I always did. One of the bonuses was being allowed to see my face briefly in his pocket mirror. He trimmed my beard in the style some journalists call 'designer stubble'. True Muslims apparently do not use razors, though hand clippers are allowed, and the effect is as if one has not shaved for about three or four days.

By the end of my first year in gaol I found I was settling in quite well, though still believing that it could not possibly be much longer before diplomatic pressure on Iran would bring my release. Had I known then how long this process would take my spirit might have broken. As it was, despite all the deprivations, I was surprisingly cheerful.

8

As the first anniversary of my arrest approached Hosein began to renege on further aspects of our deal. Already, on over a dozen occasions, he had broken the non-aggression pact. Now he was trying to impose a new condition: if I made a confession on camera it would be broadcast on the national television network and I would be freed immediately after. I rejected this out of hand, and for a while he did not pursue the matter.

That autumn he started to tell me that one of my brothers was very ill, but without saying which one, or what the illness was. Each time he saw me the prognosis seemed grimmer, until one day he said that my elder brother Dan had died of a brain tumour. I could write a letter of condolence.

Dan was always a difficult person. Physically and in terms of character he was a giant of a man, with many loyal friends, but recently he had become quarrelsome and irrational. I had last seen him, in fact, in the High Court, where he was representing himself in an action against my younger brother Paul and myself, concerning the villa in Spain which we had jointly inherited from our Uncle Christopher.

Despite this sorry incident I was deeply fond of what I considered to be the real Dan, and when I heard he had died of a brain tumour I could not help thinking that this might have explained his odd behaviour in recent years. For a long time he had complained of migraine-type headaches, and I later discovered that it was their increasing severity that had finally persuaded him to have a brain scan. There had been an exploratory operation, but it was far too late for surgery to be effective. He died on 22 August 1986, two months before I was told.

I wrote a one-page letter of condolence to his widow Pat, whom

I have always loved dearly, and was told I must supply a Persian translation of my letter. Years later I discovered that only the Persian translation had been sent, another of Hosein's dirty tricks.

Almost exactly on my first anniversary Hosein unexpectedly took me himself for a meeting in the visitors' block, although he took care to stay out of my line of sight. This time it was with Guity and her mother Touran, and we were allowed to use the telephone. After five or ten minutes the phone went dead and Hosein went to see what had happened, so for a few minutes we were alone, face to face through the plate glass. We used this opportunity for some sign-language and I tried to convey that I had been beaten into making a false confession. Hosein said nothing when he returned, but next day he gave me quite a beating for holding an illegal sign conversation. He wanted to know what I had indicated, adding that the whole scene had been recorded on a secret video camera and that he had left me alone deliberately to see what I would do. 'You must know, then,' I replied, 'that the only signs I made were to indicate I was well,' a remark which earned me some more slaps and punches. 'Why don't you ask Guity?' I said, knowing that she would deny that I had signalled any adverse comments about my condition. 'We have already warned her not to say anything about your signs,' said Hosein. Presumably a guard had seen us gesturing and reported it.

He used this vulnerability on my part to revive the question of a televised confession. I still resisted, telling him frankly that I no longer trusted him. How could I know that he would really let me go if I did agree to his proposal, which was in any case specifically excluded from our original agreement as brokered by Mehdi.

A few days later I was summoned by Hosein once again, this time, he said, for a meeting with a judge of the Supreme Court, who was on his way to Evin to meet me. I was put into rather a grand room I had never been in before, where I waited a good half-hour, blindfolded, until the judge arrived. I had no way of telling, of course, whether he was really a judge, and I soon decided he was not. A real judge would not have objected to my seeing his face, as this man did. Like Mehdi he had an Isfahani accent and sounded not more than in his mid-thirties. Whoever he was, though, he made quite a convincing story. He understood, he said, that my interrogator had given an undertaking that if I made a televised confession I would be released without trial. Although it was unusual to release a confessed spy without trial, he went on, the higher interests of the Islamic Republic made my co-operation important and he was authorized, on behalf of the Supreme Court and in the name of the Islamic Republic, to confirm the promises made by my interrogator.

'Is that a formal assurance that once this confession is broadcast I will be allowed to leave Iran?' I asked, and he gave me a categorical 'yes'. 'May I know your name?' I asked, but he refused, merely saying he was an authorized spokesman for the Supreme Court. 'So you are not a judge of the Supreme Court, then, as my interrogator told me?' I continued. 'No, I am not a judge, but what I say is authorized by the Supreme Court,' he replied. By now I was decidedly sceptical about his status, so I said I would like to think about it overnight and give my interrogator the answer the next day. I was sent back to my cell without seeing Hosein.

He did not send for me for a few days, doubtless to put me under further pressure, and when he did I told him I was not prepared to accept the offer. I told him my main objections were that it would harm Irano-British relations and make it impossible for me or my daughter ever to come back to Iran, as well as creating serious embarrassment for her Iranian relatives, particularly her uncle Mohsen, who was more than half-way through a ten-year sentence (reduced by an amnesty from a sentence of life imprison-ment) for allegedly plotting against the regime.

Mohsen had been a high-flying regular army officer, a major in the Special Forces, Iran's crack Green Berets, having trained in the Shah's day on commando courses in Germany and the United States, and speaking good German and English. He had been impli-cated in one of several attempted army coups against the regime early in the Revolution, after being denounced by one of his best friends, who was soon after promoted colonel. I was sure he had not been involved in any plots or coups. By chance, I had been with him the day before his arrest and, having known him since he was a teenager, I would immediately have sensed something was in the air. Rumours of impending coups were rife at the time, fanned I thought by Abolqassem Bani-Sadr, the first president of the republic, a foolish and insecure politician who eventually fled the country for France after losing the Emam's confidence.

Mohsen actually asked me what coup rumours I, as a journalist, had heard, but in a tone of general curiosity, not that of a plotter. As I understand it, there was no evidence against him, except his friend's word, yet together with a dozen or so of his colleagues he was arrested, tried live on television, and but for the testimony of some of his soldiers would have been executed that very day, as several of his co-defendants were. The prosecutor was the well-known activist cleric Mohammad Mohammadi-Reyshahri, who had subsequently become Minister of Intelligence, and so the man chiefly responsible for my detention. I was afraid that if I was publicly identified as a British spy it could harm Mohsen's chances of amnesty. As it was, he stood a good chance of going free soon. I had always thought his main 'crime' was his training in the West, plus the fact that he was descended from the Qajar shahs.

Hosein kept the pressure on me for the next few weeks, alternately threatening and cajoling me. Mohsen was already free, he said, although when I had asked Touran how he was she had merely said, 'All right'. If he had been freed she would certainly have replied differently. He also argued that my confession on television, followed by my immediate release, would show goodwill on Iran's part and actually improve bilateral relations. On another occasion he said that although he had given his undertaking to me in good faith he was to some extent in danger of being overruled, and if I did not co-operate over the televised confession I was running the risk simply of being tried on the evidence of my written confession. It would then be impossible to release me.

To cut a long story short, I finally agreed to do a confession to camera. I did not really believe the Supreme Court story, but did not think they would ever bring me to trial, naïvely assuming that this would have to be in public, with foreign journalists and diplomats present, and I would be able to explain that my confession was false and made under duress. Perhaps the television idea was simply a face-saving gesture on Iran's part, the domestic

144

propaganda value of the confession outweighing my denials of its authenticity once safely back in Britain. I could probably lace the television confession with misinformation, as I had done with the written confession, and the Iranians would end up looking foolish internationally, although there would always be a question-mark over me personally.

In truth I did not really know what my best course of action was, but there seemed to be some chance that if I went through with Hosein's plan I might be freed, whereas if I did not all sorts of nasty things might happen to me, among them simply being left to rot in gaol. If they could keep me for over a year without proper consular access and virtually incommunicado, God knows how long I might be kept without anyone able to get me out. The British government seemed curiously powerless, and I cynically thought MI6 might even be glad that suspicion had fallen on me instead of their actual intelligence network in Iran, if they had one. So I gave in and we began to prepare my public confession.

It was a joint effort from the start, with each of us suggesting questions to the other and arguing about them, then doing the same with the answers. I made it as vague as possible so that, if carefully studied, it was not a true confession at all, especially since I referred to having contact with the BIS (for British Intelligent Service), which anyone familiar with security matters would know to be incorrect.

I had to do the interview in both English and Persian, and I spent many sessions rehearsing with Hosein. He obviously saw himself as a talented scriptwriter, but many of his sentences were long and awkward, in a style altogether different from the way I spoke, which made it difficult for me to learn them. I did not mind this, as the more stilted it sounded the less credible it would seem. At the last minute he said I could have the script in front of me, adding that this was normal practice with televised confessions from Evin. Later, when I had access to television and found these confessions a regular feature, I noticed that in nearly every case the interviewee's eyes would drop down in front of him, although the camera angle never allowed the script to come into view.

The first time round we used Evin's in-house film unit, but Hosein did not like their wooden style and decided to send out for a professional crew, so we did it again a few days later. The curious thing was that there was no interviewer present. Hosein, in his mask once again, read the questions from near the camera and I was filmed replying. Later I discovered why. In the broadcast version a well-known presenter asked me questions and my answers were slotted in as if we were having a real interview, although it would have been obvious to a sophisticated viewer what was happening. Another twist was that the questions had been completely rewritten. They were now much more loaded and hard-hitting. In the original script my answers sometimes confirmed innocuous suggestions and implications, whereas in the broadcast session I was apparently agreeing to much more incriminating statements by the presenter.

When we finished filming Hosein became quite excited. 'This is going to be the most interesting programme on television for a long time,' he said. 'You were very good. Now I have a surprise for you. Let's go to the interrogation block.' It was late now and when we got there almost everybody had left. I could not guess what his surprise was, and almost fell off my chair when he told me I was about to have a visit from my brother Paul, accompanied by the British consul. As usual, Hosein had given me no advance warning.

Paul was sporting a colourful bow-tie and bearing gifts of chocolate, books and newspapers. He was determined to be jolly, which was probably a good idea, and of course I was delighted to see him and get some family news at last. One of the books he had brought was the English translation of Gabriel García Márquez's *One Hundred Years of Solitude*, and he apologized for the pessimism implied in the title. There was also a Spanish translation of a collection of tales by Edgar Allan Poe. Paul told me that there was an error in one of the stories involving a coded message used by a pirate. He had noticed it reading the book on an all-night train journey from Madrid to Barcelona, and thought it would exercise my mind to try to spot it. I did, although I doubt if I would have noticed it had I not been advised. He gave me details of our brother Dan's death and of our uncle Robert Graves's memorial service in London, which had been a huge family reunion, attended by Graveses from all over the world. My mother was quite well, he said, but rather frail, and her one wish was to see me again before she died.

Hosein did not of course attend the meeting himself, as I would then have seen his face. He was represented by Mohammad, another of the interrogators, who spoke good English and with whom I was later to form a reasonably good friendship. Tea was served and I passed round the chocolates I had been given. Despite the thousands of pounds and great trouble this trip had cost the family we were allowed only about half an hour together and were under pressure to end the visit as soon as possible. It seemed unfair to have combined Paul's visit with that of the consul, who could just as easily have come on another day. Just before the meeting started Hosein had told me that on no account was I to discuss my case or prison conditions, except to say they were good. If I tried to say anything forbidden the meeting would be broken up and I would be in deep trouble. I suspect he was listening from outside the room.

Nor could I tell Paul about the confession, which was to be broadcast soon. He said he would stay on for a few more days and try to arrange another visit, which Mohammad said was quite possible. Paul had brought his camera, but was not allowed to take any pictures. Mohammad arranged for a picture of us all to be taken by one of the Evin staff and said it would be given to Paul to take to our mother, but needless to say no picture was ever provided.

In the confusion as they left the room I managed to indicate to Paul that I thought the best strategy was not to make too much of a fuss about my detention just yet, but if I was still in gaol in a few months' time then he should organize a strong publicity campaign, which as a television journalist with TVS I knew he could easily do. I had given Paul the names of books which he should send me – inevitably the Bible and Shakespeare, but also a good English dictionary and some A-level maths books. I was not allowed to take the ones he had brought back to my cell. 'They must be checked first,' said Mohammad. Nevertheless I went back to the Sanatorium in excellent spirits. Perhaps after all I might be freed soon. Who knows? Perhaps Paul had been invited for just such a purpose. It would be a very Iranian way of doing

147

things and provide a good human-interest story, which would go far to counteract any adverse publicity my imprisonment might already have caused. Since such questions would clearly have been out of order I had no way of knowing how much publicity had already been generated on my behalf, or even whether anyone knew or cared. But as a journalist I knew for certain that my confession would cause ripples.

For my first two years in gaol I was almost completely in the dark about what was going on in the outside world, but from time to time Hosein or a guard would give me a snippet of news, usually in order to taunt me or to test my reaction. When the price of oil dropped dramatically in 1986, for example, Hosein got extremely angry with me, almost as if I were to blame. He certainly blamed Britain, claiming this was another example of our anti-Iranian policy. I could not let him get away with that.

'Hosein, you're out of touch. Britain has been a net exporter of oil for some time. If the price goes up we gain, almost alone amongst the industrialized countries.'

'I know that,' he replied petulantly, 'but I still say it is a British plot against us. And anyway lower oil prices are good for your industry.'

'There's some truth in that,' I conceded, 'but we'll also lose because the OPEC countries are among our most important markets. They're already worried about their import bills, so they'll have to cut them even further.'

Privately I was worried about my own job, still naïvely thinking I would be free to return to it before long. As oil prices decline it becomes less attractive to develop offshore oilfields, on which McDermott largely depended. Large-scale redundancies were being made before my arrest, and the new oil prices would not improve the situation. At the same time I had a feeling of professional pride. Part of my job was to manage the Middle East end of MMS, our head office's Market Monitoring System, which had been introduced shortly before I was hired. I had managed to expose some wildly over-optimistic forecasts in the MMS which were leading to exaggerated expectations; I had also warned my superiors that insufficient allowance had been made for fluctuations in the price of crude oil, as they were doubtless about to discover.

Early in 1987, before Paul's visit and the television broadcast, Hosein told me something else of interest. The Archbishop of Canterbury's personal envoy Terry Waite, who had been trying to negotiate the release of American hostages in Beirut, had himself been kidnapped. Hosein asked me what I knew about him. The answer was 'not very much'. I had seen some brief reports about his work before my arrest, but at the time I had other things on my mind and it was anyway not until 1986 that he became widely known.

Hosein then surprised me by claiming that Terry Waite was a CIA agent. This is such a common allegation against Americans in insecure countries that I did not take it seriously, and I said so. Apart from Waite's not being an American, I said it was most unlikely that a representative of the Church of England would compromise his position by working for the CIA. But Hosein persisted, saying he had evidence to support his claim. 'We already knew he had close connections with the Black House [Khomeini's amusing expression]' he said, 'and when our friends' – a reference to the Lebanese Shi'ites – 'searched him they found a parasite in his beard.' This puzzled me until he explained that in Persian a bugging device is known as a parasite. He said it was a highly sophisticated parasite that sent a signal to a satellite or AWACS, enabling its position to be monitored at any time to within ten metres. He went on to say that Terry Waite had dismissed his Druze bodyguards and was expecting to be taken to where some Western hostages were being held. He would obviously be blind-folded and unaware of the location, but the Americans would be able to pinpoint it exactly, enabling them to stage an Entebbe-style raid soon afterwards, according to Hosein. I could not help think-ing that such a raid would more probably end like Jimmy Carter's fiasco in the Iranian desert in 1980.

There was nothing I could say except, 'Well, if that is true it was both foolish and wrong of him to have co-operated with the CIA, but I can't really believe it.' As far as I know, the alleged parasite was never produced as evidence of the claim and Terry Waite later denied the story. After my own release I came in for much criticism merely for repeating what Hosein had said. I have no way of knowing whether his allegations had any foundation, although it emerged that he was right about Waite's links with the White House. I told him at the time that I thought kidnapping a person who has come to negotiate with you, especially when he represents a major branch of one of the world's great religions, was a despicable and treacherous thing to do, something that was against Islamic and Persian codes of behaviour, although certainly with ample precedents in this unscrupulous part of the world. He countered by saying that it was despicable for the CIA to use the Church of England for its own nefarious purposes.

The newspapers that Paul had brought began to reach me a few days later. I would certainly have expected suggestive pictures to be blacked out, as happened to the few foreign magazines allowed into Iran, but Paul had gone one further, scissoring out all pictures of women, regardless of whether this meant cutting into an article on the next page. Even Hosein was surprised by this, although he was more interested in any mentions of Iran and made me translate all such items for him.

When I asked why I had not received any of the books, Hosein said they were still being 'read', clearly a euphemism for censorship. Several years later I discovered, when a book reached me with the 'reader's report' still inside the cover, that this work was carried out by trusties. From the comments I could guess that the reader was one of the many members of the Tudeh Party or other communist groups then being held in Evin. The book was *Memoirs of a Bengal Civilian*, an autobiography by John Beames, a nineteenth-century East India Company official who had worked hard for the people in his charge and not been at all well treated by his masters, ending his life in genteel poverty and broken health back in England. According to the reader, however, the book was an account of how the greedy imperialists had enslaved and exploited the suffering natives. This meant, of course, that it was politically acceptable and so reached me promptly.

Eventually I got my first English book, a translation of Umberto Eco's *The Name of the Rose*, a thoroughly satisfying novel in every way that I did not want to put down. Not knowing when, or even if, I would get any more books, I had to ration myself strictly to

150

a chapter a day. Next came *One Hundred Years of Solitude*; it seemed surprising that it had reached me in view of its erotic content. Perhaps being set in a Third World country with references to the 'pirate Francis Drake' made it acceptable to a communist-trained censor. The third, Lisa St Aubin de Teran's *Keepers of the House*, also set in a dirt-poor South American country, was politically correct, too. After a slight gap I received Salman Rushdie's *Midnight's Children* and Poe's short stories in Spanish.

These were not the first books I had in Evin. A few months earlier Hosein had lent me a copy of some of Ayatollah Khomeini's sermons, which I had read with great interest but found intellectually disappointing. The Emam was addressing groups of theological students at Qom soon after his return from France, where early in 1979 I had interviewed him at length for the *Financial Times*. Some of my questions had inevitably been about his plans for the country he was soon to rule over and I found him completely uninformed about Iran's economic problems and potential. He simply was not interested. Industry to him meant carpet-weaving and handicrafts, oil was a devilish commodity from which Iran had never benefited – I secretly agreed with him there – and petrochemicals and telecommunications were like unknown territory.

In his Qom sermons he was preaching to the converted. Simply to see and hear the Emam must have been pure bliss to his audience, but on the printed page he rambled and said little of substance. Shi'ite preachers are usually master-rhetoricians, trained at the seminary to speak for hours on end and hypnotize their audiences with sonorous phrases and skilful repetitions, but what they say does not always stand up factually or logically. In the first sermon, I recall, he launched a bitter attack on people who used the Quran to promote their own political ideology. Here he was probably getting at the MKO, who try to reconcile Islam with Communism or at least radical left-wing views. The Emam stated categorically that only people like himself and his audience, the traditional Shi'ite clergy, had the right to pronounce on what the Quran means, disregarding completely the fact that the Quran describes itself as being written simply so that everyone can understand it. The Shi'ites themselves make quite biased commentaries on Quranic verses, claiming that they contain many half-veiled references to Ali and Fatima, the progenitors of the line of Imams, although independent Quranic scholars and plain common sense do not often agree with these interpretations.

In another sermon the Emam was trying to prove a theological point by means of a scientific analogy, claiming that water everywhere always boils at 100 degrees. From where he was speaking, on a clear day, he could have seen a massive example of a place where this is not true, the 19,000-foot peak of Mount Damavand; indeed, an accurate measurement of the samovar that made his tea that morning would reveal that even this did not quite reach the 100-degree mark, for Qom, like most of Iran, is some 3000 feet above sea level. The Emam often digressed from his argument with a sudden attack on a rival point of view, but would then fail to return to what he had been saying. In the end this series of sermons or lectures petered out after only three or four sessions. Although he had told me in Neauphle-le-Château that on his return to Iran he had no plans to become involved in politics, and would devote himself to preaching and teaching in Qom, affairs of state and a gradual decline in his physical and mental health forced him to change these plans.

I managed to keep the book of sermons for several weeks and read it at least three times. Without a dictionary there were a few words or phrases I could not understand, but Seyyed Ahmad, one of the kindest and best educated of the guards, who was intending to try for the university entrance exam the following year, helped me and by the end I could understand everything. I told Hosein I would like to translate the book into English if this had not already been done, and he promised to find out. A week or so later he said that for various reasons I would not be allowed to translate the sermons, but there might be an interesting alternative.

Seyyed Ahmad meanwhile, on his own initiative, brought me a book by Martyr Ayatollah Professor Motahari, as he is formally styled. Motahari was one of the most scholarly of clerics, and after the Revolution taught at my old alma mater, Tehran University, until on 1 May 1978 he was gunned down by a member of the fanatical Forghan group. The book was well written, quite logical and convincing, and although it took the conventional Shi'ite

152

standpoint it did consider other views fairly as well. I discussed it afterwards at length with Ahmad, and he agreed to bring me another. By the time I got my first English book I had read at least a dozen of Motahari's works, which can be described as popular theology and often deal with Islamic attitudes to particular issues like marriage or education. This reading led to a dramatic improvement in my own written Persian. I began using some of Motahari's turns of phrase and Hosein commented with surprise that my Persian was improving. Another bonus from this clandestine reading was that the books often contained quotations from the classic poets, such as Hafez and Sa'di, which I copied out and learned by heart. I surprised Hosein one day by quoting a couplet or two from Hafez which I told him Nilufar had taught me. He might have allowed me to read Motahari if I had pressed him, but he was so unpredictable that I did not risk it. I was definitely not on the list of prisoners allowed to take books out of the Sanatorium's library, which I never even saw during my three years there. I heard it was about the size of a broom cupboard and few inmates were allowed access to it.

One day Hosein announced that in order to get the translation job, for which I would be paid, I must write an application setting out my credentials. This was easily done, as I had translated over the years perhaps five million words of Persian into English, including the official texts of the Third, Fourth and Fifth Five-Year Plans and numerous documentary film scripts, as well as the Shah's second book (the first was ghosted for him in English). In addition I had been the first person to pass with distinction the Institute of Linguists' final examination in Persian.

A few days later I was told the job was mine. The title was hardly inspirational – *Principles of Islamic Ideology* – but the author's name was a bombshell. It was none other than Ayatollah Mohammad Mohammadi-Reyshahri, currently the Minister for Intelligence, the man who must have signed or approved the warrant for my arrest, Hosein's boss and the person responsible, as the former chief military prosecutor, for my brother-in-law Mohsen's sentence of life imprisonment and many a hasty death sentence.

*

153

I started translating *Principles of Islamic Ideology* about the time that my 'confession' was broadcast on Iran's main television channel. I did not of course see the programme: no prisoner in the Sanatorium had access to television, but all the guards on duty were glued to the set in their common-room, as were those who were off duty, and for the next few days I received many comments. There is a mystique about seeing someone you know on television, and although the guards were quite used to chatting to the 'British spy' there was from now on a new aura about me: I was a TV personality as well. Several of the guards described the pride with which they told their family and friends that they knew Roger Cooper. Some of them went as far as to describe me as a friend of theirs, a rash remark to make about a man who was depicted as a major enemy of the Islamic Republic, even though he was now safely behind the bars of Evin prison. Such is the power of television, in Iran and elsewhere.

A week or so later Hosein came to see me, bringing a videotape of the programme. It was an elaborate presentation, running for half an hour of prime time, and had clearly done wonders for Hosein's personal prestige. 'The whole country has seen it,' he boasted. 'It was a huge success.' I was not quite happy with the word 'success', and complained to him of the distortion that had resulted from the alterations to the questions. He pooh-poohed that, ascribing the changes to the nature of television itself, an argument I could not accept. 'So when do I go free, Hosein?' I asked. 'That was the deal, wasn't it?'

His mood changed. First, he said I had caused him embarrassment by referring to the BIS. This deliberate solecism had been spotted by journalists covering intelligence matters in Britain, as I had intended, but I had not foreseen that one newspaper, *The Guardian*, would point it out in print, with the comment that this proved Cooper was not making a genuine confession. I had also said 'I must say', in reply to one or two questions, hoping that subtle viewers would notice the implications of the remark, which I later learned was the case. The *Guardian* comment put me in a vulnerable position, which Hosein was quick to exploit.

'What we must do now,' he said, 'is to have another television programme correcting this and going more into Irano-British relations in history.'

I argued strongly that this was not necessary, that despite what *The Guardian* had written it was perfectly correct to refer to the British Intelligent Service, and BIS was just the initials of that name. 'Moreover,' I added disarmingly, 'you yourself refer to it as the BIS.' Certainly there were specialized names for branches of the BIS, I said, of which MI5 and MI6 were the best known, and the CRA one of the least known, but all of these collectively were the BIS.

Hosein seemed relieved by this explanation, but insisted that I should make the point in a follow-up television interview, and then I could be freed. Although I now no longer believed anything he said, there was little choice but to agree, so once again we began preparing questions and answers. He also sprang it on me that although my interrogation was now formally completed, 'there were still a few points they needed me to clarify'. These, he said, could best be summarized in a single long essay by me on the history of the BIS (I was glad that he had slipped back into that name). There was also the translation: the minister would obviously expect me to finish his book before signing my release papers. For the next few weeks I worked like a demon, doing three or four hours of translation every day, as well as an hour or so learning the script that Hosein and I were putting together, and also reading and studying.

Paul had despatched promptly most of the books I wanted, and since even the strictest censor could scarcely complain about the Bible, Shakespeare, Chaucer and half a dozen maths text books these reached me quickly. From then on until my last few months in Evin I always had a choice of books to read – fiction, poetry, religion, Persian and other foreign languages, mathematics, and later history, philosophy and science. I could now embark on a serious reading programme, spending between half an hour and two hours a day on each category, so as not to overdo any single one. Sometimes I would become obsessed by a single topic and I might break my own rule and devote an entire day to mathematics or a particularly gripping novel. In my entire life, including school and university, I had never followed such a dedicated programme of study, and I am sorry to admit that it ended the day I was released.

I have always enjoyed translating – into my native English that is – and I enjoyed the challenge of the minister's book. Frankly, it will never be a bestseller in English, or, I suspect, in its Persian original. Many of the ideas, and even quotations, were already familiar to me from the works of Motahari that Seyyed Ahmad had brought me. Reyshahri had studied under the martyred professor. and it showed. It was nevertheless interesting for me to get into the mind of a leading member of the Iranian establishment, the man in whose hands my destiny chiefly lay. Whether or not he believed the pious thoughts he expressed was impossible to say.

It was also my intention to give his book the best possible translation. *Traduttore, traditore,* as the Italians say, 'The translator is a traitor', and all too often this is true, but I was determined that Ayatollah Reyshahri would never be able to accuse me of selling him short. I even took pains to provide good verse translations for his frequent quotations from the Arabic and Persian poets, and it often took several hours to do justice to a few lines. As I went along I also checked his footnotes and other references as best I could. This is not strictly a translator's duty, and of course it should not have been necessary, but in fact the research and proof-reading had all been careless and I discovered scores of misprints, incorrect Quranic references, repetitions and the like, which I noted and submitted with my translation. I also made comments on where I thought his arguments were false. Like the Emam, he too felt it necessary to insert a few analogies with modern science, but usually got them wrong. From my years of experience with Iranian publishing I also foresaw the problems that would arise if my manuscript translation was given straight to the printers for typesetting, so I stressed to Hosein the need to put the text on to a word-processor or, if this was not available – he did not seem quite sure what a word-processor was – to let me have the portable typewriter I had with me when I was arrested. I would gladly type the whole manuscript, I said, thinking how useful it would be to have a typewriter in my cell. But he did not rise to that particular bait.

By midsummer 1987 I had finished translating the 500-page book, slightly worried that it was described as Volume I, with no indication of whether there were more volumes to come. Might I have to stay in Evin until the completion of some vast encyclopaedia of Islam, like the hero of Waugh's *A Handful of Dust*, who spends his final years reading Dickens to a madman in the Amazonian jungle when his family have given him up for dead?

The second interview was broadcast with less fanfare, but apparently received a favourable reception: Hosein indicated that I could shortly be on my way back home. Despite my scepticism of anything he said I began to believe that it might really happen. Surely even the Iranians could see they had got their money's worth from me and it was time to end the whole silly business.

Then, in mid-May, an event occurred in Manchester which was to blight my hopes of early release. Hosein summoned me one day to say that an official in the Iranian consulate there had been falsely accused of shoplifting, arrested, despite having diplomatic immunity, and beaten up by the police. He was to be put on trial shortly. How, Hosein asked, should the Iranian government react? I stated categorically that whatever the alleged offence and whatever the police may have done there could be no question of his being put on trial provided he was an accredited diplomat. Under the terms of the Vienna Convention, I said, to which both Britain and Iran were signatories, diplomatic immunity was absolute. An ambassador or one of his accredited staff could in effect commit murder and be immune from prosecution unless the ambassador or his government lifted the immunity. The British police or prosecution service would never institute criminal proceedings against a diplomat. Was Hosein sure that the official, whom he named as Qasemi, was really a diplomat, or was he perhaps a non-accredited employee of the consulate travelling on an ordinary or service passport, rather than a diplomatic one? What was his job title?

Hosein then backtracked somewhat and said that Qasemi was the consulate's cipher clerk, or perhaps telex operator, and so someone scarcely likely to be recognized as a diplomat by the Foreign Office. It was nevertheless an outrageous provocation, he said, for the police to charge him falsely with stealing a pair of socks. I told him that this altered the situation completely, and the man almost certainly could be put on trial, although I thought it possible that he might be allowed to leave the country quietly; it was hardly in the interests of already extremely fragile Irano-British relations to make too much fuss over such a minor charge. Hosein did not seem satisfied with my reply, so I asked for time to think about it and said I would give my detailed recommendations the next day.

I quickly prepared a legal strategy that I hoped might limit the potential damage and possibly help me. If the British authorities were determined to press charges the Iranians should immediately instruct a good solicitor, and possibly obtain counsel's opinion, gathering all the evidence they could, especially medical evidence, in support of the claim that Mr Qasemi had been assaulted in police custody. This was known to happen, after all, although I thought it doubtful that the police really had behaved improperly towards an employee of a foreign embassy. It might be best, I wrote, to apply for an adjournment in order to buy time for some kind of political settlement, while doing everything possible to avoid publicity.

Privately I felt rather sorry for Mr Qasemi, a minor official probably on a tiny salary, since Iran was by now desperately short of foreign exchange, who had perhaps been tempted to pocket, of all things, a pair of socks. If he was brought to trial it would be an embarrassment to the Islamic Republic. Doubtless the popular press would pick it up, making the point that if he was found guilty in his own country he might have risked amputation of his right hand. If properly handled by the Foreign Office, I thought, it might be enough for a deal to be brokered whereby Mr Qasemi would not be charged and I would be released after a decent interval. The danger, from my point of view, was if he appeared too soon in a magistrate's court, which would rule out my chance of a deal, regardless of the verdict.

Hosein read my report with interest and left me for several hours, blindfolded in the corridor, while he went off somewhere, presumably to discuss my recommendations with his superiors. When he came back his mood had changed. The pitch of his voice rose, a sure sign that he was becoming angry. He ranted on about our fascist police and the hostile elements within the British establishment, whose aim was to sabotage relations with Iran. They must be taught a firm lesson. I did not like the sound of this at all, especially as I thought he might start taking his revenge on me, and I sat dumbly, expecting a shower of blows.

Instead, Hosein began to calm down and asked me what I thought of a plan he had: the British chargé d'affaires would be stopped in the street by *pasdars*, the Revolutionary Guards that exist in parallel with the regular police force but are far more loyal to the regime, often fanatically so. He would be charged with some offence such as black-marketeering, and then beaten up publicly. That would teach the *pir-e estesmar* (literally 'the old colonialist', one of the many terms of abuse for Britain) not to show disrespect for the Islamic Republic.

I was appalled at this proposal. Christopher MacRae, the head of mission, was a senior British diplomat who undoubtedly did enjoy diplomatic immunity, unlike Mr Qasemi. Such an act would almost certainly force Mrs Thatcher, no lover of Iran in the first place, to break off relations with Iran, as she had done with Libya in April 1984, after WPC Yvonne Fletcher was shot dead in St James's Square. In addition, such an act would be viewed with revulsion by the entire diplomatic community in Iran, who would see themselves suddenly hostages to what might be considered insults to the Islamic Republic emanating from their own country. There might be mass breaks in relations or at least withdrawals of ambassadors and downgradings from embassy status, especially among the European Community states. In addition, the British authorities would undoubtedly close down the Iranian consulate in Manchester. It could in any case hardly be justified in view of the decline in the number of Iranian students and trainees in Britain after the Revolution, especially given that Britain's only consulate outside Tehran, in the southern port of Khorramshahr, had been closed in 1979.

Hosein seemed surprised at my vehemence. 'All right then,' he said, 'suppose we choose another of your people, Chaplin, for example?'

I knew Edward Chaplin, head of chancery and number two in the British embassy. Early in 1985, soon after his arrival, he had invited me to dinner together with some visiting British journalists, and we spent an enjoyable evening with his wife and their New Zealand nanny, discussing Iranian politics and economics. From the questions he had asked I was sure that by now, almost three years later, he was playing an important part in improving relations between Britain and Iran. It seemed almost unbelievable that an Iranian official was cold-bloodedly suggesting a plan to assault this talented young diplomat in public. I told Hosein that although this might be considered marginally less serious than action against a head of mission it would still be totally unacceptable behaviour in Western eyes, and would probably also lead to a break in relations.

By now I knew enough of Hosein's character, I thought, not to take this conversation seriously. However much he and his hardline colleagues might like to tweak the British lion's tail and sabotage the almost imperceptible improvement in relations that had been seen in the years before my arrest, and which I assumed was still continuing, I could not imagine that they would dare carry out such a provocation. So it was with dismay and near-incredulity that a day or two later, when Bespectacled Hosein delivered my morning newspaper, the hardline *Jomhuri-ye Eslami*, he gleefully pointed to the main news story of the day. On 28 May, Edward Chaplin had been driving home with his wife and young children when he was stopped by a group of *pasdars* who pulled him from his car and punched and kicked him when he resisted arrest. He was accused of black-marketeering and trading in pornographic magazines. The news item clearly linked this action to the 'brutality perpetrated by the fascist British police on the Iranian diplomat Qasemi'.

Hosein sent for me soon afterwards and solemnly told me that pornographic material had been found in Edward Chaplin's car. The *pasdars* were only doing their duty and had not known of his diplomatic immunity. He added that they had been keeping Chaplin under surveillance for some time and had evidence that he was engaged in illegal currency dealings. I told Hosein that I knew Chaplin personally and considered this charge ridiculous. It was true that many foreign diplomats changed dollars on the free market – and who could blame them when the official rate was set at only one-eighth of its true value? – but I was sure that a British diplomat would never do such a thing. I recalled how gratefully Mrs Chaplin had received a box of pistachios when I dined with them, mentioning how they could rarely afford this local delicacy, although at the free market rate they were one of Iran's great bargains, like caviar. She said that they could get meat at a reasonable price through the Ministry of Foreign Affairs commissary, whereas potatoes had to be bought in the open market and so were actually more expensive for her. So it was unthinkable that Edward Chaplin was selling foreign exchange for rials. This was obviously a crude tit-for-tat action that would convince nobody and merely discredit the Islamic Republic further. Hosein made no direct reply but confirmed my prediction that the British government was to withdraw all but one of its embassy staff from Tehran. Diplomatic relations would not be formally severed but the embassy would now be headed by a Swedish diplomat, as the British interests section of the Swedish embassy.

Apart from the disgust I felt at what had happened to Edward Chaplin, particularly the fact that his family had witnessed the appalling incident, I suffered some feelings of guilt myself. Perhaps I should have tried harder to dissuade Hosein from what he had done or been party to. I also realized that the chances of my being released were becoming slender in the acrimonious climate that must now exist between Britain and Iran.

Hosein was by now showing signs of contrition, which told me that a major row was probably going on behind the scenes between the hawks and the doves in the Iranian establishment. In a surprisingly friendly tone he told me my release would inevitably be delayed now. 'I have another plan which I hope will work, although it may take a few more months,' he added. 'So continue with your work and don't be discouraged.'

9

IT WAS NOT long before Hosein explained his so-called plan for my release. A few weeks after the Qasemi–Chaplin affair he sent for me to say that he hoped Mrs Thatcher would agree to 'trade' me for a young Iranian named Kurosh Fuladi, who was imprisoned in Britain.

Hosein almost always said 'Mrs Thatcher' when referring to the British government, and like all Iranian extremists he had a particular loathing for her. I had perhaps unwittingly fostered this 'L'état, c'est elle' attitude in some of the many briefing papers on British politics and social affairs I began writing for Iranian intelligence and/or the Ministry of Foreign Affairs as my formal interrogation drew to a close.

It was never my policy to mislead my captors about such matters, rather the contrary, for I have always felt that only if regimes such as Iran's and Libya's start to understand the real world, and see that their fantasies and irrational phobias have led them nowhere, will they be able to make any progress. In painting a broad-brush picture of British politics in the mid-1980s I had therefore to say that Thatcherism, despite its successes in liberating the economy, had by now probably run its course. I sensed a danger that Mrs Thatcher's dominant personality was becoming counterproductive, seriously harming the tradition of government by Cabinet consensus. She had just won her third general election, and I was convinced that her strident style of leadership would become even more intense, driving independent-minded colleagues out of office and bringing in yes-men.

There may have been a touch of self-interest in this analysis, because I was far from confident that Mrs Thatcher would condone any deal with Iran over my case, whereas with a new Labour government gestures of goodwill on both sides might have been possible. I was fairly certain that despite having got some useful mileage out of me in propaganda terms, at least domestically, the Iranians would want some tangible quid pro quo before releasing me. Although such matters were usually shrouded in secrecy, it was common knowledge that Western agents captured behind the Iron Curtain were from time to time exchanged for Soviet counterparts. I could not, however, see Mrs Thatcher agreeing to trade me for an Iranian terrorist.

Hosein had mentioned the case of Fuladi before, but I knew little about it then. I was later to discover the details from a clandestine conversation with an Iranian prisoner shortly before his execution, and his version was partly confirmed when a Persian-language newspaper reproduced part of the coverage of the case in a British newspaper. It seems that Fuladi – literally 'the man of steel', though whether this was an assumed name based on Stalin's, or just that his grandfather had been a metal-worker, I do not know – had gone to London shortly after the Revolution. Ostensibly he was a student, although he is not known to have attended any regular course of studies, and this was presumably a cover for his real mission as a semi-official heavy. He lived in the embassy, where he sometimes acted as doorman or security guard. He was big and strong, a Lur like our janitor Mashti, but twice his size. On Sundays he would go to Speaker's Corner in Hyde Park, a popular meeting-place for Iranian and Iraqi dissidents, where anyone who spoke against the Emam was likely to receive a sharp physical response from Fuladi. One day he was driving up Park Lane and as he approached Marble Arch an explosion demolished his car, killing his two backseat passengers outright. Fuladi himself lost an eye and the use of one arm. It appeared that the two passengers were putting the finishing touches to a bomb, destined, it was assumed, for MKO headquarters near Marble Arch, when it detonated; their hands were blown off in the blast.

At his trial Fuladi pleaded not guilty of involvement in the botched bombing and claimed the MKO must have planted the bomb in his car, although the missing hands made the jury discount this story and he was sentenced to ten years, plus two years to be served consecutively for assault and battery at Speaker's Corner, a total of twelve years. The fact that he owned a car, unusual among Iranian students, especially those from deprived backgrounds like his, and lived at the embassy, indicated that he had links with the regime, but the embassy was quick to disown him after his arrest.

By the summer of 1987 Fuladi had served seven years, in some forty different prisons, each governor arranging for him to be moved on because of his insubordinate behaviour and attempts to stir up unrest among other prisoners. Hosein seemed to know him personally and I could not help wondering whether he had perhaps been Fuladi's controller. The fact that Hosein was not a regular Evin interrogator, never showed me his face, and from one careless remark revealed that he had himself visited the Iranian embassy in London – although he always denied having been to Britain – made this seem quite probable. A desire to secure the release of his former agent might well have been Hosein's main motive in having me arrested.

When the question of trading me for Fuladi had first arisen I told Hosein that the British government would never agree unless I had first been sentenced. Although Iranian justice has never been widely respected, there is an international principle of respecting sovereignty and hence sentences imposed with due process of law, however unjust. Hosein could not expect the British government to release a convicted terrorist (to Hosein, a wrongfully imprisoned follower of the Emam) for one of its nationals who had merely been arrested and detained in custody. Otherwise a Briton might be arrested every time an Iranian was convicted of an offence in the UK. Since my deal with Hosein specified I would never be brought to trial, I thought there was no way he could get round this problem.

Hosein had obviously taken a second opinion, which confirmed what I had said, and now he was proposing that I should after all be tried. He even implied that the British government had agreed to such an arrangement, although I doubted this. The trial would be a pure formality, he said. I would get, say, a five-year sentence, which would nicely match the period Fuladi still had to serve, so 'honour' would be satisfied on both sides. The Iranian government did not want to see their innocent student Fuladi linger in gaol, and the British wanted to see their spy freed, as Hosein put it.

The idea made me feel distinctly uncomfortable. I might get a five-year sentence and then if Mrs Thatcher did not like the idea of a swop I would serve my five years and so would Fuladi. Honour would certainly be satisfied on both sides, but five years of my life would be destroyed, on top the time I had already served, since I had learnt from the guards that in Islamic Iran pre-trial detention did not count towards sentence. But as always with Hosein's betrayals there was nothing I could do except hope that this time he would keep his word.

Although I had by no means seen the last of Hosein, at this point my case passed formally out of his hands, in other words from the Ministry of Intelligence, part of the executive branch, into those of the prosecutor-general, part of the judiciary. Within a few days I was taken by minibus to a building in Evin I had never been to before, a large and imposing one that housed the various Shobehs, or branches of the Islamic Revolutionary Courts, with their corresponding prosecutors, and, I soon learnt, the courts themselves. Until then I had assumed that the courts were somewhere in central Tehran and that the public had access to them.

For the rest of the summer and well into the autumn I went once a week to Shobeh 13, the branch dealing with foreign spies and terrorists, spending many hours in a corridor, blindfolded in principle but in practice allowed to read a newspaper or do the crossword provided I kept my eyes down. The head of Shobeh 13 never introduced himself, but once he answered the telephone while I was in his office and automatically gave his family name, Hoseini. He seemed better educated than Hosein, and I think had a law degree, whereas Hosein only claimed a diploma in electrical engineering, but he was far from intelligent. He had inherited all Hosein's files, I gathered, and his job was to prepare the indictment against me and select papers from the file as evidence for the judge to peruse.

This task should not have taken him more than a day or two, nor should it have required my presence more than once or twice, but Mr Hoseini seemed baffled by the complications of the dossier and repeatedly asked me questions that showed he had not digested all the material. This may partly have been Hosein's fault, of course.

In some ways I found these visits to the court building welcome.

Although blindfolded, there were moments when I could sneak a view of the trees, the flowers and the mountains, and occasionally even exchange a few words with other prisoners. I remember one day listening to a woman with an Arabic accent being questioned in a room with the door ajar, while her two children ran playfully up and down the corridor. The boy had bright red hair and I played some games with him as he passed, like pretending to trip him up. On another occasion I found myself alone in the minibus with a tall, redhaired young man who said he was an Iraqi refugee imprisoned on charges of trying to get a visa for Germany. He thought his wife and children were also in Evin. I said, 'I think I have seen them.' He was greatly excited at this, not having had any news of them since his arrest, but before I could give him details a guard appeared and we had to stop the conversation. This was my first meeting with Romeo, who was to become my closest friend in Evin.

It must have been around then that I was allowed for the first time to go for a stroll in the prison grounds without a blindfold. It was about twenty-one months since the single such outing in my first prison. Late on a Thursday afternoon, to my great surprise, since Hosein never came at such a time, I was summoned to the interrogation block. After a while an interrogator I had spoken to once or twice and who had always seemed friendly asked me if I would like to go for a walk with him in the garden. He said he knew I had never been allowed such a privilege and thought he would take a short stroll himself before going home. I did not know his name, but he said I could call him Jalal.

As we walked out into the gardens, I was allowed to remove my blindfold, which gave me a wonderful sense of freedom and joy. We passed an Olympic-sized swimming pool, which he said prisoners sometimes used. Behind the diving board was a large calligraphic panel giving one of the Hadiths, or traditional sayings of the Prophet, which in Islam are second in importance only to the Quran itself. This one was the injunction that Muslims should teach their sons to swim, ride and use the bow. I have sometimes wondered how useful swimming could have been in the Arabian desert in the Prophet's lifetime, which makes me doubt the authenticity of this much-quoted Hadith, especially since it echoes a pre-Islamic Persian adage that young nobles should be taught archery and to speak the truth. In even larger letters painted on a wall was a saying of Emam Khomeini, a rather obscure aphorism claiming that 'these high walls' were not a prisoner's main problem, rather it was his evil instincts that he should concern himself with, and imprisonment was to help him overcome them. How this was to be achieved through sensory deprivation was not explained. Accompanying these words of wisdom was an excruciating English translation, presumably for the benefit of foreign journalists and VIPs who were sometimes given sanitized tours of Evin.

I tried not to let these cynical thoughts blight the magic of the evening. It was warm, without a trace of humidity, and a light breeze wafted the scent of blossoms across what seemed the most beautiful garden I had ever seen. Iranians are superb gardeners and the rose bushes and herbaceous borders were faultlessly maintained by prisoners, I was told, working under a professional horticulturist. We looked into his greenhouse, full of exotic tropical plants.

Jalal led me to a vantage-point and we stood gazing over the city, which for once looked beautiful. The sky was absolutely clear and I could see the flames of the refinery some twenty-five miles to the south. A full moon was rising over Mount Damavand, a view usually obscured by urban pollution. As I drank in the balmy air Jalal asked me if I would like some herbs, and pointed out lush beds of parsley, mint and basil. I picked a modest handful and he joined in until my arms were full. I had not eaten a green vegetable or herb for almost two years and the scent was so powerful that I threw hygiene to the wind and began nibbling at them. All too soon Jalal took me back to the Sanatorium, telling me not to say anything to the guards about the outing or where the herbs came from, and especially not to Hosein when I next saw him. As I had suspected, then, this was a humanitarian gesture that Hosein might not approve of. Jalal was to repeat it once every two or three weeks, and I remain to this day deeply grateful. I never got to know him at all well, but he always had a kind word for me when he saw me. As far as I know, he never beat his interviewees, unlike most of his colleagues. While waiting in the corridor I sometimes

167

heard him conducting an interrogation, but always in a gentle tone of voice. How different my life might have been, I often thought, if he had been my interrogator and not Hosein.

Paul's second visit took place in September 1987 and was much more relaxed than the first. Once again he was accompanied by Victor Welborn, one of the few remaining British diplomats in Tehran, presumably so that the Iranians could claim it as a consular visit, although it was nothing of the sort. Before the meeting began, as in fact before all such meetings, I was firmly told that if I spoke critically about my conditions or gave any details about the case or my interrogation the meeting would be summarily ended and no more allowed in future. Such conditions make a consular visit pointless, particularly if the official does not know the prisoner personally.

Two other factors militate against the effectiveness of meetings censored like this. The first is that the prisoner is in any case likely not to want to add to the anxiety of his family and friends by telling them the truth about conditions in gaol, the second is that the visitor is also likely to report good news rather than bad, hoping in this way to ingratiate himself with the authorities and make the prisoner's release more likely. That is why in my televised 'confession' I said how good conditions were in Evin, and why I told Paul that there was always plenty to eat, true enough in terms of calories but misleading in terms of protein and green vegetables, both of which, while basic to Persian cuisine, are rarely provided in Evin. I obviously could not mention being 'banged up' twenty-four hours a day except for interrogation, nor the compulsory wearing of a blindfold every time I was taken out of my cell, the inadequate medical care, the stifling atmosphere of the cells for half the year, let alone the brutality of many interrogators. It may have comforted my family to think that 'things might be worse for Roger', but if the reality had been known more pressure might have been put on the Iranians to secure my release. At the end of my meeting with Paul I managed to convey in family shorthand that although things might be about to take a turn for the better he should not wait indefinitely before starting a campaign on my behalf. I left it to his judgement when the cut-off point should be, but tried to indicate that the start of my third year in gaol should be the latest date.

As the autumn of 1987 progressed I found myself getting quite used to my surroundings. Now that I had books, paper and a calculator there was a vast range of things to occupy my time. I was slowly working my way through the Bible, Shakespeare and Chaucer, although I was frequently frustrated by not having reference books or critical editions. Because of all the writing I was doing, pen and paper were no longer a problem, and I could make notes on my reading. I recorded, for example, all the words in Shakespeare that had oriental etymologies (from Persian, Arabic, Turkish or Hebrew) and all references to the sea or sailing. I found these surprisingly frequent for a man who grew up as far away from the coast as is possible in England. Perhaps in his 'missing' years, I thought, he had gone to sea. I also noticed how concerned Shakespeare was with medical and health matters, and planned a study of these, perhaps with the help of my daughter. I thought between us we might be able to surmise the illnesses Shakespeare suffered from. I had no idea whether any of these ideas were of real value or whether similar research had been carried out. In any case, the many hours of labour that went into them were wasted, unless, against all probability, the authorities decide to return my prison papers.

The Bible came as a terrible shock. Although in my youth I had read, or had read to me, large parts of the Torah – I prefer this name, used in Islam for the whole of the Old Testament, a term which I feel shows Christian prejudice – and most of the Gospels and Epistles, I had never read the whole text from cover to cover before, and large parts of it were quite new to me. I soon began to wonder why the Bible is called 'Holy', when much of it is anything but. Nor could I accept any universal relevance in Judaism, with its emphasis on a chosen people, a promised land and a jealous God, although admittedly it is not – at least now – a proselytizing religion and has many other attractive features. My copy was the King James's Version, with which I was of course familiar, but I began to see how impractical this was for an understanding of the text today, however fine the words sound to my ears.

When I came to the Psalms and the Song of Solomon I was in a different world, however, the world of poetry and mysticism, one in which I felt much more at home than among the chronicles of incest, rape, genocide, murder and deceit which the earlier books of the Torah seemed to consist of. As I read the Psalms, and, less frequently, other books, I began to notice ideas and phrases that reminded me of the Quran.

I soon developed a theory about these frequent similarities, although I realize I could be treading on delicate ground even to suggest that Muhammad might have been inspired by knowledge of the Psalms. To a conventional Muslim the Quran is the Word of God, revealed to the Prophet by the Angel Gabriel, so it is blasphemous to suggest that there might be any human input or literary antecedents in the text, even though it was 'revealed' in Muhammad's own language, that of seventh-century south Arabia. It is, however, known that the Prophet travelled extensively from his birthplace Mecca, as far even as Syria, trading on behalf of the wealthy Khadija, who in time became his wife and first convert to Islam. It is almost certain that, given his own spiritual nature and subconscious yearnings for a true religion to replace the idolatry and corruption of his own tribe and city, he would have met and conversed with Jewish and Christian clerics and monks, possibly even Zoroastrians, such as his boon companion Salman the Persian.

My thesis involved correlating linguistic and semantic similarities between the Torah and the Quran, having first tried to arrange the surahs, or chapters, of the Quran chronologically: in the standard version they are ordered primarily by length. I would not be surprised if these Torah 'echoes' occur more frequently in the earlier Mecca surahs than in the later Medina ones, by which time Islam was firmly established and the revelations tended to be more political and social in content. It is perhaps significant that there are no such similarities between the Quran and the Gospels, which may explain why Islam is much closer to Judaism than to Christianity. If I am right, this may, curiously, help to explain both the intractability of the Arab-Israeli conflict and the historic suspicion between Western society and Islamic fundamentalism.

There is of course a danger that such ideas might be misconstrued by fundamentalist Muslims, but I think it is only a slight risk. At the time of the *Satanic Verses* crisis several leading *ulema*, Shi'ite as well as Sunni, including some quite close to the Emam himself, stressed that there was no objection to genuine scholarly enquiry into Islamic doctrines or history. What affronted them was Salman Rushdie's apparently gratuitous slandering of the Prophet and his family, particularly the fictional portrayal of his wives as prostitutes.

I also developed a theory about Holy Writ. It seemed to me that religious innovators do not as a rule claim divine status for their words, even assuming that they are written down in their lifetime. It is only later, sometimes centuries later, that such a claim is made by their followers. Muslims lay particular stress, however, on what they call 'celestial books', or revealed scripture. Both parts of the Bible, which sadly not many of them have ever glanced at, are considered 'celestial' by Islam. It is quite possible that by the seventh century whichever Jewish rabbis or proselytizers Muhammad may have met on his travels were actually claiming the Torah to be in its entirety the revealed word of God. There are still fundamentalist Christians who hold such views today, and the belief must have been common in medieval Europe. Muhammad could easily have felt that if his religion were true, then the inspired utterances that came bubbling up from his subconscious were likewise direct revelations from God. The doctrine that the Quran is the Word of God – many Muslims would even say co-eternal with Creation, with the original preserved in tablets in heaven – became important when sceptics scorned Muhammad's claims to prophethood. Prophets should perform miracles, they said, and where were his? The reply was the Quran, and a challenge was issued for any man to produce even one verse as beautiful as any verse of the Quran. The challenge was taken up by several poets and reciters, but by common consent none could match the original.

Apart from these literary and religious ponderings my life had a practical side to it. I finished my translation of Mohammadi-Reyshari's book and collected several thousand rials as my fee. Outside the amount would have been derisory, not even up to the rate paid by government agencies before the Revolution when the rial could look the dollar in the face without flinching. Now

171

the rial was worth in real purchasing power somewhere between a tenth and a twentieth of its former value, although the money went a lot further than that in gaol, if only because there was so little to buy. It meant, for example, that I would never have to worry about the price of fruit, as I could hear some prisoners did. I offered Bespectacled Hosein the basis of a slush fund to enable such prisoners to buy fruit or cigarettes, but he shook his head and said the prison authorities gave money to the destitute. I later discovered that in communal blocks a meagre allowance was paid if a prisoner was in dire straits, and unable or not allowed to work, but I do not believe such payments were made in the Sanatorium, and to my certain knowledge many prisoners could not afford to buy fruit.

My half-dozen outings with Jalal gave me a taste for more, and having accidentally discovered that a few long-term Sanatorium inmates did have exercise privileges I badgered any prison official who came round into giving me this right, especially now that my interrogation was technically over. Eventually they gave in and several times a week that autumn I was taken out into the Sana- torium's tiny garden, usually by grumpy off-duty guards who did their best to cut the allotted fifteen or twenty minutes to the very minimum. Then an old man from Hamadan, seventy if he was a day, was recruited just for this purpose. He did it, he told me, from a sense of religious duty, and on the whole I believed him, but I also gathered that he had fallen on hard times, so I daresay the small salary and permission to buy from the prison co-op were additional attractions. Haji Me'mar, as he was called, had not in fact been to Mecca, nor was he an architect as the title Me'mar implied, but he had spent several years in Karbala, the holiest of the Shi'ite shrine-cities in Iraq, working as a jobbing builder. He was half-deaf, with a severe stoop, and none too literate, although he could just manage the list of cells he was given. Instead of fighting with me over the time, as his predecessors had done, he trusted me to tell him when the time was up. Knowing that he had a fixed number of prisoners to escort in a fixed amount of time, I never 'stole' a minute from him, and to judge by his punctuality neither did the other lucky prisoners.

Haji Me'mar had a delightful personality, and would often tell

172

me jokes and anecdotes as we walked or sat chatting in the shade. He knew about Persian traditional medicine and explained the therapeutic qualities of various weeds. I should harvest the seeds of the plantain, he said, which was a better cure for colds and coughs than anything the prison clinic might have. One day, before my translation fee arrived and when I was completely out of cash, I had to decline some beautiful pears on sale to prisoners. I tried to buy on credit, knowing I would soon be in funds, but the duty guard, a relative newcomer, refused. Haji Me'mar was most upset when I told him, saying what wonderful fruit pears were, especially if they came from Hamadan, his birthplace, as he believed these ones did. The next time I saw him he waited until he was sure we were alone, then slipped me 5000 rials, a fortune for me at the time and probably at least two or three days' salary to him. I refused, but he insisted so hard that I gave in. When I got paid shortly afterwards I tried to return the sum, on the grounds that it had been a charitable loan, not a gift, but he refused point-blank.

Not long afterwards Haji Me'mar was telling me about his plans to provide a feast at the end of the days of deep mourning in the month of Muharram. The mourning period commemorates the massacre at Karbala, where on 10 October 680 Husain, the Prophet's grandson and Third Imam of the Shi'ites, was butchered with his 72 followers on the orders of the evil Caliph Yazid. The ten days leading up to Ashura, the actual anniversary, are marked by anguished, almost hysterical, wailing, and on the last two days men parade through the streets flagellating themselves with chains and metal scourges. I saw my chance and offered to contribute to the feast out of my respect for Husain's martyrdom, and this enabled Haji Me'mar to take the 5000 rials back.

Within a week or two of this incident all exercise privileges – known in gaol Persian as *havakhori*, literally 'eating the air' – were cancelled. Unconvincing reasons were given, such as, 'The weather is bad', 'Haji Me'mar is ill', 'The sisters' block [on the ground floor] is being rebuilt', and it was four or five months before I could eat the air again, once again with grumpy guards. From time to time I used to see Haji Me'mar, who told me he had never been ill and did not know why he had been transferred to other duties. I never discovered what caused the cancellation.

173

On one of our outings there had been a large new influx of prisoners who were held for some hours in the garden, so instead we went to the larger garden by the swimming pool, where Jalal had taken me. The greenhouse was now shut, but I saw some old broken flower pots lying about and easy-going Haji Me'mar let me take one back, as a waste basket, I said. On another outing I took a plastic bag and filled it with earth, and on a third I uprooted some quite ordinary plant, a marigold I think; thus began my horticultural career in Evin. I did not want it to be seen, which meant it got no sun and ultimately died. But Majid had spotted it and offered to bring me something better. It was a poor specimen of an attractive leafy plant called simply *avizan*, 'the hanger', because of its preference for downward growth, and I put it openly on my high window-ledge, which got a few hours of direct sunshine for part of the year, and natural light all year round. A few guards queried its presence but I brazenly claimed the governor had approved, on the tenuous grounds that when he had last visited me he must have seen it but did not say anything. I had also managed to pocket some manure from the rose-beds, which I fed successfully to my hanger. I had heard that talking to plants promoted their well-being, so I often gave it some friendly words of encouragement. Soon I acquired a reputation for green fingers and the final accolade came when Majid himself asked me for a cutting of the plant he had given me, which he said was the best one he had ever seen. He also brought me another pot with a straggly *hosn-e Yusef* ('Beauty of Joseph', a reference to the story of Potiphar's wife, which is one of the best known in the Quran). I soon had this one in good shape too, and for the rest of my time in the Sanatorium the window-ledge of Cell 336 was a pretty sight, and gave me much pleasure.

My interest in gardening was matched by an interest in food. Before I had any books I made a sort of 'Desert Island Discs' of the culinary world. I would ask myself if I could only take with me, or ensure the survival of, ten vegetables or ten fruit, or ten fish, which ones would they be, and then spend hours agonizing between, say, carrots and parsnips, or mussels and oysters. It would make an amusing party-game for foodies, I thought, although I am sure that any list reached by consensus would be rather boring.

After hours of consideration I would finish up with a prosaic list of such items as potato, onion, tomato and cabbage, having reluctantly rejected more exotic candidates like artichokes and aubergines.

I could not of course do any cooking in the normal sense of the word while in the Sanatorium, since I had no access to a stove, but from the earliest days I was engaged in other forms of food-processing and preservation. The first thing was to buy as much fruit as possible and this meant learning to keep it in good condition. Much of the fruit we got was already far from being of merchandizable quality, but beggars can't be choosers, so I was never fussy. Some of the guards would even offer me leftovers free or at a reduced price. It was some too-far-gone apples that gave me the idea of making cider, since an apple should be brown all over before being crushed for juice. Having grown up in the cider belt of south Devon it was the first alcoholic drink I ever had and replete with genial adolescent memories.

Like wine, and unlike beer, cider is easy to make, but timing is critical or one ends up with vinegar. All that is required is to let the apples go completely brown, crush and strain them – a handkerchief will do – and put the juice in a covered container. Nature does the rest. In the warm autumn days or on the radiator pipes in winter fermentation only took a few days, although I sometimes fed some sugar to the brew to give it added strength. I knew I was taking a risk with this, and the penalty might well be 72 lashes, but I was confident I could talk my way out of it. If found it could simply be a cup of apple juice that had 'gone off'. Fermentation and storage vessels were my biggest problem. In the early days I could only use a spare mug I had acquired, so consumption had to be immediate. Glass is forbidden in the Sanatorium cells, and when in my third year I was at last allowed to buy food items like pickles and jam, the jars were kept on a shelf in the corridor. But I did manage to buy some plastic containers and gradually smuggled glass jars into the cell. I never got enough grapes to make wine, but I did have reasonable success with watermelon, which produced a powerful pink sparkler. Best of all, and certainly the strongest, was the slivovitz I made from tiny yellow Iranian prunes, which I soaked and fed sugar to. I do not suppose that I manufactured more than a few litres of pure alcohol in my entire five years in Evin, but the knowledge that I had a little bottle of something special tucked away was a wonderful morale-booster.

I also made a kind of marmalade. I once got some oranges that were so fresh and juicy that I started eating the peel. Next I scraped the pith off with the edge of my spoon and soaked the zest in heavy syrup, made by dissolving my sugar ration in water, to produce something not a million miles away from Cooper's Oxford Marmalade (no relation, unfortunately). Another form of food preservation was my 'haybox'. Meals were often served too early for my appetite, yet unless eaten promptly the food became cold and greasy. So I would cover my plastic dish with its lid and put it into a cardboard container well insulated with bits of old blanket and my sweater. This was so efficient that I could eat my stew or soup hours later at close to the original serving temperature. Much later, in a communal cell, with access to a stove, a refrigerator, herbs and spices, there were far greater opportunities, and I was to meet a master of the art of gaolhouse cooking, David Rabhan, whom I succeeded as cell chef.

By now I was getting local Persian-language newspapers quite regularly and devouring every word, despite the censorship and editorialization of both local and foreign news. I guessed that this was mainly due to self-censorship, since the only papers allowed into Evin were *Jomhuri-ye Eslami* ('Islamic Republic'), *Kayhan* ('World') and *Ettela'at* ('Information'), all of which took a hardline stance on political events. *Jomhuri-ye Eslami* in particular was the mouthpiece of the hawkish faction of the regime, having begun as the organ of the Islamic Republic Party. In effect this was the only party permitted in Iran after the crushing of the MKO in 1981, the banning of the Tudeh Party and other communist groups in 1983, and the muzzling of the few parties that might be called liberal or centrist (although the use of Western terms to describe Iranian politics can be misleading). With the demise of all formal opposition Iran then became technically a totalitarian state, just as it had been in the last few years of the Shah's reign, after he disbanded even the sycophantic pro-monarchy parties he had earlier sponsored. The Shah created from thin air the Rastakhiz

176

('Resurrection') Party, a cross between the Communist Party of the Soviet Union and Hitler's National Socialists, which every single Iranian, from teenagers onwards, was pressured into joining, either individually or on an affiliated basis through employers, schools and co-operatives.

Advisers to the Islamic leadership must have noticed this embarrassing similarity with the Shah's regime – not the only one, incidentally – and so the Emam, never a lover of party politics, announced in 1987 that the Islamic Republic Party was also dissolved, even though most senior politicians were members of it. In theory Iran thus became a country with no legal political parties, although it could be argued that the Emam never dissolved the Hezbollah ('Party of God'). In Iran the Hezbollah has never had a formal organization. It first came into prominence in 1979, during the US embassy hostage crisis, and seemed to me at the time to be composed of angry, not-so-young men from the south of Tehran, the slum areas of the city, who formed a kind of militia reminiscent of the Nazi Brownshirts. They turned up in force at public meetings and political demonstrations, disrupting anything that was not to their liking. Their activities reminded me of the rent-a-thug tactics used by Savak to break up any anti-Shah demonstrations: factory workers, often armed with clubs or staves, were bussed in to potential trouble-spots, and doubtless well rewarded for their efforts. It is not too cynical to suggest that the early Hezbollah activists were the same people – they certainly looked and spoke as if they were.

Soon after the victory of the Revolution the Iranian ambassador to Syria, Hojatalislam Ali Akbar Mohtashami, had the brainwave of establishing a similar organization in Lebanon. The result was Hizbullah, as it is spelled and pronounced in Arabic, the extremist militia of Lebanese Shi'ites responsible for most of the terrorist and kidnapping activity in that country. In Iran, however, the movement went rather upmarket: many a top politician would claim to be a Hezbollahi, a term which in Iran meant little more than having a working-class background. My interrogator Hosein and most of the more fundamentalist guards would often claim to be Hezbollahis. I have the impression that the authorities had by then decided to discourage any overt practical role for excitable men in dirty shirts. The Revolutionary Guards (*pasdars*) and local vigilantes (*komitehs*), both organized through government ministries, were more reliable, although whenever serious unrest occurred, as it did in mid-1992, Hezbollah thugs could be unleashed again.

Kayhan and *Ettela'at* were much older newspapers than *Jomhuri-ye Eslami*: I had written for both of their English-language stablemates before the Revolution. Needless to say, under clerical control they had changed their political stance dramatically, but at least in terms of news presentation they were streets ahead of the *Jomhuri-ye Eslami*, which had a provincial, almost amateurish feel.

All three papers were vehemently anglophobic, and any news they published about Britain was invariably hostile, several degrees more so than, say, *Pravda*'s coverage of the United States at the height of the Cold War. If a picture of Mrs Thatcher was used it was the most unflattering available, and there were regular editorials and feature articles attacking all things British. *Jomhuri-ye Eslami* even went so far as to coin a new name for the United Kingdom, referring to it as the 'Island of England'. The more bizarre of the articles appealed to my sense of humour, like the one on an archeological discovery which indicated that neolithic Britons practised cannibalism. *Jomhuri-ye Eslami*'s headline implied that the British were still cannibals, so I stuck it on my wall as a warning to the guards, until an embarrassed official made me remove it.

I also put up a picture of Mrs Thatcher, to the annoyance of some guards and the amusement of others. I already had a picture of the Queen – a postage stamp soaked off an envelope containing a Christmas card from a complete stranger, received in May 1987 – but that was too small to cause offence. I argued that whatever they thought of Mrs Thatcher, indeed whatever I thought of her myself, she was my 'leader'. They had pictures everywhere of their leader: from peeking under my blindfold into open doors I knew that some prisoners had pictures of the Emam in their cells, so I too should be entitled to have a picture of my leader on display. This point was surprisingly conceded by both Bespectacled Hosein and Seyyed Satari, provided I did not display the picture too prominently, so for the rest of my time in Evin Mrs Thatcher, in full handbag mode at a European summit, gazed down at me with haughty disdain, and indeed at any visitor to my cell who caught her beady eye.

About this time I took up Persian crosswords. I had almost never attempted a crossword in a language other than English, and at first I could not get the hang of them at all. What was annoying was that I rarely received the same newspaper two days in succession, so could not compare my effort with the solution. I saw at once, however, that they were not sophisticated puzzles, more like American ones or the quick ones of the popular press, and lacked the wit and subtlety of, say, a classic *Times* or *Daily Telegraph* crossword. The occasional pun would appear, but the clues were mainly straightforward synonyms. Surprisingly, *Jomhuri-ye Eslami* was the only one to use a symmetrical grid, the others merely scattered black squares as required.

One guard, Reza, was quite good at crosswords and helped me in the early days, but I worked hard at the challenge, taking notes which in time formed the basis of a crossword-solving Persian dictionary, finally becoming the crossword champion of the Sanatorium. Guards would drop by to ask for help when they got stuck and I even introduced one or two beginners to the pastime. Most of the guards, however, were too uneducated to try, or indeed even to want to try.

This interest in crosswords had several advantages. To begin with, it was an entertaining way of learning new Persian vocabulary. It also increased my knowledge of Islam: the *Jomhuri-ye Eslami* puzzle was clearly written by a mullah or someone with a detailed knowledge of the faith. I recorded all this information by subject, like the names and nicknames of the Twelve Imams, the surahs of the Quran, major works of Quranic exegesis and Islamic jurisprudence, place names and battles important in early Islamic history, thus building up a kind of pocket encyclopaedia of Islam. My reputation for crosswords also won the respect of those I helped, and led to jokes along the lines of: 'Naturally the representative of the Intelligent Service can solve crosswords better than we can!' In prison, respect is a valuable asset.

There was another interesting spin-off. Hosein had told me that a CIA agent, an American, had been captured in Iran, having arrived on an Italian passport. He would not give me any more details and when I asked him what was going to happen to him he said, 'We've already executed him.' I tried to find out from the guards about this case, but they were either afraid to tell me or did not know. When I was still a beginner at crosswords, one clue in *Kayhan* read, 'The American spy now held in Evin prison.' I worked out that his name was John, but could not solve enough vertical clues to discover his surname. Unfortunately I could not get next day's paper, but I kept the puzzle to work on later. A few weeks later I managed to finish it off and found that the American's name was John Pattis – actually his first name is Jon, but the Persian transliteration is the same. Reza told me that about the time of my televised confession I had also featured in a similar clue, although that was before I was allowed newspapers. Next day I asked a visiting official why I could not take exercise with Jon Pattis before we both forgot our native language. He laughed and said, 'Pattis's case has been completed and he is serving his sentence in a communal part of the gaol. You have not yet been tried. Perhaps when you have been sentenced you can be together.' He said he did not know what Pattis's sentence was, but thought it was 'at least ten years'.

As usual in such conversations, the possibility that I might be acquitted was not even mentioned, the principle of 'You wouldn't have been brought here if you were innocent' pervading every level of Evin staff. It was good to know that Pattis was at least alive. Hosein's claim that he had been executed was simply an attempt to unsettle me, and one that had worked.

Meanwhile, Mr Hoseini had almost finished preparing the indictment and organizing the prosecution's case. About a week before the day set for the trial to begin he summoned me to his office and said it was time to prepare my 'final defence'. 'How can I do that,' I replied, 'when I have not yet seen the indictment, or the law or regulation I am being charged under?' He seemed baffled by this reply. 'But surely your interrogator has told you what the charges are?' I said this was not so, and anyway I understood it was the task of the prosecutor's office, to which Mr Hoseini belonged, to draw up the charges, while the interrogator's job was to gather the evidence. He admitted that this was the case, but began to show signs of irritation. Directing me to a small cubicle in a corner of his office, he gave me some sheets of paper. On the first page he had written: 'Mr Cooper, what is your final defence to the charges against you?' I filled two or three pages on this subject, mainly to avoid a further confrontation with him, but the gist of my answer was as before: I could not reply to the charges until I knew what they were. He glanced at my answer and said it did not look very satisfactory, to which I replied, 'Well, that is the only defence I can make at present. Please consider it only as an interim defence, and do what you want with it. I will make my final defence when I have seen the indictment and heard the evidence against me.' I did not see him again until we met in the courtroom.

The trial was set to start on Saturday 31 October, and two days before I was summoned to the court office, which was in the same building as the prosecutor's office, and so within the prison precincts. I had to fill in various forms, including, ominously, my next of kin, and was asked whether I wanted an interpreter to attend. I had foreseen this question and declined the offer on the grounds that it would not help me. I did not imagine that any translator working for the Revolutionary Court inside Evin would have much knowledge of English, and it would delay the proceedings and confuse the judge if I had to correct the interpreter's version of what I had said. I was not yet sure what I would be saying, but I felt it would be more effective if I spoke directly to the judge, looking him in the eye. I did remember that Anthony Eden always used an interpreter in talks with foreign statesmen, even when he knew the language, saying it gave him time to consider what had been said and how he should reply, but I thought the circumstances were different in my case. Another factor was that the judge would know from the file that I was fluent in Persian, so speaking through an interpreter might look like evasiveness.

What I did ask for, however, was the services of a lawyer. I assumed this was an automatic right, and seemed to recall from skimming through the new Constitution at the time of the referendum in December 1979 that this right, as well as other legal safeguards, was inalienable. I went so far as to tell the chief clerk that I did not just want any old lawyer, the Iranian equivalent of

181

a dock brief, but a lawyer of my own choice. I had a barrister friend whom I trusted implicitly, but if he was unwilling to represent me I wanted someone recommended by the British embassy. If this meant a delay in the court hearing, so be it, I would request an adjournment.

The clerk became rather evasive at this point. He did not exactly say no, but neither did he ask me for my friend's telephone number or offer to call the embassy. 'You must speak to the judge on Saturday,' was as far as he would commit himself.

When I asked him to give me a copy of the indictment he was most unhelpful. 'It will be read in the court on Saturday,' he said. I got quite cross at this and told him to talk to the judge immediately, and if he was not there to any other judge in the building, who would doubtless confirm that an accused person should be allowed to hear the charges before, and not after, the start of his trial. This is one of the most elementary principles of natural justice, I said. And while he was seeing the judge he could tell him that I had declined the services of an interpreter, but was insisting on being represented by a lawyer of my own choice. He came back suspiciously soon, saying he would give me a copy of the indictment and I could speak to the judge on Saturday about legal representation.

It took a good half-hour to get a fuzzy copy of the indictment – each sheet of photocopying paper had to be formally requisitioned and signed for, he told me – and he then tried to shoo me out of his office. I continued firmly sitting there and told him I wanted to read through the whole document to make sure I understood everything.

It was a muddled compilation. Many of the 'facts' were simply wrong: even Hosein's files were more accurate. There were three or four pages of closely-spaced typing listing some thirty or forty vague charges, although some of them were not really charges. Most of them were 'supported' by phrases like 'See p.236 of File 37' and obviously it would be impossible for me to answer them without seeing the references. The last sentence went something like: 'The Prosecutor General's Office requests the honourable Court to consider these charges and the corresponding evidence and issue an Islamic sentence in accordance with Articles 2 and 3 of the Code of Criminal Penalty'. Naturally I asked for copies of these articles and naturally he replied, 'You must ask the judge on Saturday.' One surprising charge tucked away in a document that was otherwise devoted mainly to accusations of spying was on the lines of 'the accused had illicit relations (see p.97 of File 23)'. The phrase was ambiguous, but seemed to imply sexual, not intelligence, relations, and the chief clerk confirmed that this was also his understanding. 'What's the penalty for that?' I asked, expecting him to say '72 lashes'. He replied '*Rajm*', an Arabic word that rang a bell from my crosswords, though I could not immediately place it. Seeing me look a bit puzzled he then used the Persian word for the penalty. It came as a nasty shock: 'Death by stoning'.

10

EARLY ON SATURDAY 31 October 1987 I was taken to the court building where I sat blindfolded in a corridor waiting for the judge to arrive. I had spent Thursday afternoon and all day Friday writing comments on the vague charges against me, and pointing out factual errors. In some cases, my comment was a simple request for what English lawyers call 'further and better particulars'. On the question of my alleged 'illicit relations', for example, I wrote: 'I cannot respond to this charge without knowing what relations the prosecution is referring to. Please explain and inform me of the evidence against me.' I wrote these notes in English, intending to make each point to the court by translating it directly into spoken Persian.

I had another plan up my sleeve. If I felt that the judge was really impartial I would explain the whole story of how I had been cajoled into making a confession, and that I had never had any links with British intelligence or any other espionage organization. Because I knew Russian, Hosein had for a while entertained a crackpot theory that I was a KGB double agent, and he once offered to release me to the Soviet Union in exchange for a 'full' confession. Here he was not alone: a former British ambassador had also once implied to a colleague that I was a Communist sympathizer and might have links with Soviet intelligence; and he was not the only person who over the years had assumed that anyone who knew Russian must be suspect, regardless of how or why he had learnt the language.

I realized that such an appeal to the judge would be an extremely dangerous step, as it might spoil a genuine attempt to trade me for the gaoled terrorist Fuladi, and the judge might simply send me back for further interrogation. The Iranians had held me virtually incommunicado for nearly two years and might feel they could continue to do so with impunity for a great deal longer, simply to avoid embarrassment. Alternatively the judge might decide that my confession was true and I was now lying to protect myself. Everything would depend on how I judged the judge.

Suddenly I was ordered by the chief clerk to take off my blindfold and enter the court. I found myself in a small office, of the kind that in most Iranian government ministries would have housed at most three or four desks for minor officials. I was told to sit in the usual wooden chair with a writing armrest. It was placed a few feet away from the table where the judge would sit, and I was instructed to face the judge at all times. If the door opened and somebody entered I was on no account to look round. To my left was a table at which sat the minute-taker and lay assessor, a man I came to know reasonably well over the next two weeks. His name was Mir-Fenderevski and he was from a distinguished family of philosophers and writers going back to Safavid times. He himself had studied abroad – in Paris, I believe – and had been a judge before the Revolution. He obviously had a good knowledge of Iran's pre-Revolutionary law, much of which was still in force, particularly the Civil Code, and one of his functions was to advise the judge. Revolutionary Court judges have no formal legal training although *fiqh*, Islamic jurisprudence, forms a major part of the curriculum at Qom and other theological colleges. Mr Mir-Fenderevski never revealed what it felt like to be demoted in this way, always showing complete respect for the judge and not openly resenting that the other part of his job was to write down everything that was said in court. He did this with great skill and efficiency, not like a court stenographer taking down every word verbatim, but making an instant summary, which I had to sign at the end of each session. This was so accurate that after the second day I only did spot checks before signing. Between us was a large old-fashioned tape recorder which Mr Mir-Fenderevski also had to control. In the corner of the room to the judge's right was a table for the prosecutor.

Then the judge swept in. He was a tall and handsome figure, wearing quite the smartest clerical robes I had ever seen in Iran. His outer garment, or *aba*, was of the finest camel hair, and the

185

long blue *qaba* under it was immaculately pressed. His beard was neatly combed, and I detected a whiff of attar of roses as he passed. I had already discovered that his name was Nayyeri, a word meaning something like 'fiery brilliance', and my initial impression was favourable. Mr Mir-Fenderevski and I stood up without being told as he entered, followed by the prosecutor Mr Hoseini. While we were still standing the judge began chanting verses from the Quran in a melodious voice; I would have liked to know which ones they were, but although I asked afterwards no one could or would tell me.

Mr Justice Nayyeri then told the prosecutor to read the indictment, but before he could begin I asked if I could say something. He gave me an indulgent look that had something of a smile in it and told me to speak. I made a formal request for the session to be adjourned until I had obtained a lawyer and briefed him properly. I also asked to be shown the law under which I was to be tried and the evidence against me. He replied that it 'would not be necessary' for me to have a lawyer. He was there, as was Mr Mir-Fenderevski, to explain anything that was not clear, and it would be sufficient for me to answer his questions truthfully. Lawyers were all liars, he said, and the more you paid them the bigger the lies they told. At this point I decided to risk a joke. 'In that case, Your Honour, in view of the serious nature of the charges I need the services of the most expensive lawyer in town.' My joke fell extremely flat. Mr Justice Nayyeri frowned and made a note on the pad in front of him. Regarding the evidence, he said that would come out in the trial, but anyway I must know the evidence myself. Details of the law I was being tried under concerned him rather than me, as it was up to him to judge me according to the law. Unless I had any more questions he would now like to get on with the trial.

I said I did have some more questions and it seemed better to ask them now, rather than once the trial began. I wanted to know how long the proceedings would last and when the verdict would be delivered. I was beginning to think Mr Justice Nayyeri was not the fine upstanding judge he looked, and his reply confirmed this. 'The length of this trial is entirely up to you. If you want, it can last one day, one week or one month. I am here to listen to whatever you have to say. As regards the verdict, that is obvious from the start, but it has to be typed out and that can take time, usually about a week.'

I could scarcely believe my ears. Was the learned judge telling me, even before the indictment was read out, that he considered me guilty? It seemed to me improper that he should even know, at any rate in detail, what I was charged with, let alone tell me in advance that he knew what his verdict would be. I looked at Mr Hoseini and Mr Mir-Fenderevski, but they showed no sign of surprise or emotion. So I simply said as politely as possible that his words surprised me, and I would like it to be entered into the court record that I had requested the services of a lawyer and been refused. He said that Mr Mir-Fenderevski would undoubtedly record this, and now the trial would begin.

Mr Hoseini read the indictment – a formality, as both the judge and I had a copy. His duty done, he then, to my great surprise, left the court and did not return until the last day. His assistant Mr Shirazi attended occasionally, but for the rest of the trial only the judge, Mr Mir-Fenderevski and myself were invariably present. Once or twice during the first two days I heard the door behind me open, and remembered only just in time not to turn round to see who had entered. There was another door behind the prosecutor's desk which was usually ajar. The room it led to was dark, either because it had no window or because the curtains were drawn, but I occasionally heard a slight movement from inside. Hosein told me later that he had sometimes sat there to listen to the proceedings. He clearly did not wish to run the risk of my seeing his face. I have no idea who the other people were who came into the court.

The judge's attitude from the start had made me realize that it would be a waste of time to tell him the background to my so-called confession. In case things went seriously wrong, however, I did write a short note, in English, explaining how my interrogation had been conducted, the reasons for my confession and my complete lack of confidence in the judge, which I hid one day on the way to court, somewhere I was fairly certain it would not be found, at least for a long time: in fact, I believe that as I write it is still there. I am not quite sure why I did this, but I think I had

187

some idea that I might one day be able to use this document as evidence that I had not been given a fair trial, should there be any doubt.

The procedure was for the judge to read out each part of the indictment, or simply say, 'Let's go to the next item', and ask me what my defence was. I began by saying I would first like to hear the evidence against me, but the judge usually said that this evidence was confidential. The only exceptions were when the evidence was one of my own written statements during interrogation, which he would read out or sometimes let me study, rather reluctantly – presumably because of the annotations added in red ink on the sheet.

One of the charges against me was that in the spring of 1959, aged twenty-four, I had gone on a spying mission to south-east Iran. The facts were that on my first long holiday in Iran – universities and schools close for about two weeks for Now Ruz, the Persian New Year festival – I went on an ambitious trip across the Dasht-e Lut desert to Baluchistan, returning to Tehran via Zahedan, Zabol, Birjand and Mashhad. My travelling companion was Keith Wilson, a close friend who lectured at Tehran University. I had mentioned my plans to one of my classes at the Institute of Foreign Languages, where I taught English, and Jafar Bitaraf, a Kurdish army officer and one of the best students, asked if he could join us. I introduced him to Keith and they got on well, so it was agreed. We were going to remote parts of the country, and only a year or two earlier Baluchistan had been terrorized by a notorious bandit named Dadfar, so it seemed prudent to take Jafar along, especially as my Persian was still rather basic and Keith's even more so. The trip proved arduous, with such adventures as our car breaking down in the middle of the desert, trying to cross a flash flood and getting stuck, and endless worries over whether we would reach the next dot on the map and if so find food and petrol there. Jafar's presence was invaluable. He had been top cadet at the officer training school and in presenting him with the sword of honour the Shah had joked, 'I hope you don't live up to your family name, Lieutenant. I don't want neutral officers in my army.' Bitaraf means 'neutral', a reference to his family's refusing to take sides in some Kurdish dispute at the turn of the century.

There were, and still are, strict rules against Iranian military personnel fraternizing with foreigners, so Jafar must have obtained special permission to accompany us, unless he was prepared to risk a promising army career. He did not wear army uniform or otherwise 'pull rank' when we dealt with officialdom, and told us he wanted to come to practise his English, which was almost certainly true, but may not have been the whole story. A friend of Keith's told him later that Jafar might well have been planted on us by Savak or army intelligence, since we were going quite off the beaten track and the authorities might have wanted to keep an eye on us.

Naturally we gathered useful information about roads, accommodation and the availability of fuel and supplies, and on our return to Tehran I thought I should put my travel notes into order and produce a report for other travellers. Part of our journey, after all, was along the main route between Europe and the Indian sub-continent, although one would not have thought so crossing the Dasht-e Lut, which is said to contain the largest area on the surface of the world completely devoid of life. In those days the only road signs were the tracks of other vehicles in the sand.

I therefore put together a two-page report, and the British Council, where I also taught, ran off a few dozen copies, which I distributed to European motoring organizations, the Touring Club of Iran, some Western embassies and friends who were thinking of following in our tracks one day. I think I even sent a copy to the Ministry of Roads, which at the time appeared to have no interest in that part of the country. There was of course nothing secret or confidential about the report, yet the very fact that I had written it was to haunt me. Savak had brought it up during one of their grillings, and it had featured prominently in the early stages of my interrogation. I knew that a copy of it almost certainly existed in the file, so I told the judge, as I had told Savak and Hosein, to study it and see if there was anything suspicious in it. Judge Nayyeri replied that it was unnecessary for him to do so, since it was obvious that the Intelligent Service had required information on remote parts of Iran for military planning purposes. We had invaded Iran several times before, he said, and might wish to do so again one day. I suggested that Jafar be summoned as a

189

witness to describe exactly what we had done on that trip. It was extremely unlikely that I would be making trouble for him, as he must have been questioned about this trip both before the Revolution and possibly since my arrest.

My so-called intelligence mission to the deserts of south-east Iran was the first substantive item on the indictment, and I was still discussing it when the muezzin's call came over the Tannoy system and the court rose. Since nobody told me to put on my blindfold I wandered about the third floor for a while. In the toilet area clerks were busy splashing water on their arms and feet before praying, and once they had gone I spent several minutes examining myself in the large mirror, the first time I had been able to do this since my arrest.

Looking into a mirror and recording what one sees is something of a family failing, although hardly a sign of narcissism. My mother, a good traditional poet, if overshadowed by her celebrated brother, wrote a poem called 'Crumpled Old Face', and as I looked at myself I remembered the second verse:

> Crumpled old face, with sagging cheek and chin,
> How felt you, raised to the morning's wet hill wind
> The sea, a breath in your nostrils, out of sight,
> With rapture of gulls?

I could tell that when she wrote that she was thinking of the hills behind Harlech, where she spent much of her early life, and nostalgia for that magical land welled up inside me now.

My Uncle Robert's self-description in 'The Face in the Mirror' is also unflattering:

> Grey haunted eyes, absent-mindedly glaring
> From wide, uneven orbits . . .
> Cheeks, furrowed; coarse grey hair, flying frenetic;
> Forehead, wrinkled and high;
> Jowls, prominent; ears, large; jaw, pugilistic . . .

What I saw was just as unprepossessing. It seemed to me that as I grew older I was beginning to look more like my mother – not the beautiful young woman she had been in the First World War, as a nurse in France, but as she had looked when I had last seen her, aged 91. I certainly had her green eyes, as my passports used to confirm until one day a consular official in Iran had exclaimed, 'Green eyes? Nobody has green eyes.' Then, looking up, he said firmly, 'They're brown,' and altered my application accordingly. They have been officially brown ever since.

Whatever their colour, my eyes now had Uncle Robert's haunted look and I saw I was developing his prominent jowls and furrowed cheeks, even though my face had not taken the battering from boxing, rugby and shell-splinters that his had. My skin was pallid from lack of sunshine and my teeth were decidedly yellow, hardly surprising when I had been deprived of proper dental care for two years. My hair was thinner and going grey at the temples, as was my unwelcome stubbly beard. I had certainly lost weight, but in an unhealthy way, and despite my exercise programme my shoulders seemed to sag. Not reflected in the mirror was a sensation almost of choking at the back of my throat, and the natural position of my teeth was clenched. I looked tired and worried, in a word haggard. Before a wave of self-pity could engulf me, however, I pulled back my shoulders, gave a wan smile and in my most Pollyannaish mood went down the marble stairway to see what was for lunch. Being a Saturday in winter it would almost certainly be *khoresh-e qeimeh* – split peas and gristly meat – but the rice was always good. Things could be worse, I told myself.

We resumed at 2 PM and wrangled over that trip to the desert almost thirty years before, until even the judge began to show signs of fatigue. After two hours in the morning and three in the afternoon the court adjourned. I signed Mr Mir-Fenderevski's impeccable minutes and was sent to join a crocodile of prisoners on its way to the 'prison office'.

This was a large waiting-room with bench seating, so called because of its location in the administration area. Here, grumpy guards jumped on inmates for the most minor breach of regulations, often slapping them from behind, as they waited to be taken back to their block. It was an interesting place as a rule. There were often 'sisters' – female prisoners, blindfolded and enveloped in black chadors, but female just the same and so to be surreptitiously observed. Sometimes there would be inmates returning from leave with their little bundles of goodies, one of the few humane aspects of Evin, and even the occasional foreigner.

But this time I was not in the mood to appreciate such variety in my routine. I just wanted to get back to my cell as soon as possible, unwind a little, then plan for tomorrow. It was almost certainly a waste of time, but I was stubbornly determined to make the most of my 'day in court'. At least I would go down fighting.

The trial lasted for almost two weeks, moving ponderously forward as each of the thirty-odd items in the indictment came under Judge Nayyeri's review. Somehow I managed to keep the bill of indictment; as a rule prisoners had to return papers relating to their trial once it was over. My efforts to smuggle this intriguing document out of the prison during my last year in Evin backfired, however, and the Iranian government always refused to publish it or give a copy to the British or UN authorities. After the trial I only glanced at it occasionally, and now, five years later, I cannot remember all the details.

I do nevertheless recall that many of the so-called charges were not crimes at all, such as 'the accused wrote speeches and translated books etc. for high officials of the defunct former regime'. This was perfectly true, I told the judge, but what was wrong in that? Many other people had done such work; were they all criminals? A translator or a speech-writer is a literary technician, I argued, and demanded to know what law I had broken in carrying out such work. While in gaol I had translated a book by a high official of the present regime, I said. If the regime changed would that make me a criminal? The judge frowned at this analogy and made a note on his pad, probably to the effect that I was advocating the overthrow of the Islamic Republic.

Another charge was that 'the accused entered the Islamic Republic with two passports'. I had already explained to Hosein that there is nothing sinister about a British subject having more than one passport: any businessman or journalist, for example, can apply for a second passport if he or she is likely to have to go abroad at short notice while the first passport is with a foreign consulate awaiting a visa. At the risk of further offending the judge, I added that unfortunately it was nowadays extremely difficult to travel freely in the Middle East with an Iranian visa in one's passport, just as having an Israeli stamp was enough to get one banned from most Arab countries. (Another frown from the judge at this comment.) I explained that I therefore had a second passport specifically for travelling to Iran, which meant leaving Dubai on my main passport and arriving in Tehran on the second. Why, I argued, would I keep both my passports in the safe of a govern-ment-owned hotel, against a receipt, if this were somehow related to espionage? A passport, I told him, at least a British passport, was simply a document to enable the bearer to travel freely and if this meant having more than one, so what? Again, would the learned judge please tell me what law I had broken?

In respect of most of the charges against me, I told the judge, there would be no case to answer in any normal system of justice; he merely replied, 'But this is an official accusation. You must answer it', completely missing the point. In others, I was not shown the evidence against me because the judge said it was confidential, so all I could say was, 'In that case it is impossible for me to answer the charge. I simply deny it.'

On one of the rare occasions when Deputy Prosecutor Shirazi was in court I was telling the judge about my doctoral studies at Tehran University, and started a sentence with the words, 'When I was a student'. But it had been a long day, and by mistake I said, 'When I was a spy'. I corrected myself at once, but not before noticing a knowing look that passed between the judge and Mr Shirazi. It was perhaps a minor point, but it shocked me nevertheless that a judge and a prosecutor could be so much in collusion as to exchange significant glances.

Every day I began by reminding the judge that I wished to study the law under which I was being tried. Finally he gave in and said that on Thursday, when there would be no hearing, I could come to the court where Mr Mir-Fenderevski would inform me. At first he wanted just to read out the relevant extracts from the Code of Criminal Penalties, but eventually he did let me study the articles and take notes. What I read was quite encouraging. Article 2 dealt with terrorist activities, such as hijacking and other serious offences, and carried a maximum sentence of ten years' imprisonment. There seemed no way it could be stretched to cover the charges against me. Article 3 was for less serious offences and carried a maximum sentence of five years. This made me wonder whether the judge's bark was worse than his bite. He might wish to adopt, on the record, a tough anti-British stance, and then sentence me to, say, three years, which with remission for good behaviour could see me free by Christmas. At least there was no mention of a death penalty in the articles I was being tried under, and that was something of a relief. Then I remembered the clerk's remark about stoning. I nearly raised this with Mr Mir-Fenderevski, but it seemed too ludicrous, and might just stir up trouble. If the prosecution wanted to ask for a death sentence, I presumed, surely this would have to be mentioned in the formal request to the court with which the indictment ended. The clerk was probably just being sadistic; now I was in the real world.

We finally reached the 'illicit relations' charge. I asked, as usual, for the judge to give me details, and as usual he declined, saying the charge arose from my confession and I must know perfectly well what it was about, unless there were other cases I had not confessed to. So I knew this was a reference to Nilufar. My general knowledge of Islam and recent extensive reading of Motahari's works gave me an advantage here. I explained to the judge that far from my relations with Nilufar being illicit they had been purely scholarly. Since she came from a religious family, I told him, she was concerned that it was un-Islamic to be alone in a room with me, and her cousin could not always accompany her. She had therefore entered into a *sigheh* contract with me and I had repeated after her the Islamic formula making her technically my wife. Since she was a law graduate there could be no doubt that the ceremony had been perfectly lawful, although I could not remember the details after all these years. The *sigheh* was for formality's sake and never sexually consummated. I mentioned that I had also entered into a *sigheh* contract several years earlier with a young cousin of my wife's. I stressed that if he had any doubts on this he could simply summon Nilufar as a witness and she would confirm what I had said. I knew, of course, that he would not do that.

194

For good measure, I questioned whether the laws of the Islamic Republic could be applied retroactively, especially to a foreigner, to which he replied chillingly that the laws of Islam applied from their revelation to all eternity. In cases of fornication or adultery, however, Islamic jurisprudence demands four male witnesses to the actual act of penetration, not a likely occurrence, or else a confession. In the event that my weary agreement with Hosein's suggestion that Nilufar was my girlfriend were construed as a confession, I had a back-up defence that she was in any case my legal wife. I could not see how the most devious Qom-trained jurist could make any mileage out of that. Judge Nayyeri did his best, all the same. He asked me a lot of personal questions, but I stood my ground and after an hour or so he passed on to the next charge, much to my relief.

One of the many aspects of Iranian justice, at least as practised in the Revolutionary Courts, that is contrary to natural justice and human rights is the fact that an accused person is not allowed to call a witness or produce evidence in his defence. On the question of my passports, for example, I asked the judge to order their production so that he could see clearly how I had used them, and that the photograph and personal details were exactly the same in each. The passports had been taken from the hotel safe by Hosein or his colleagues, so it would be quite easy to obtain them. All the judge would say, however, was that this was unnecessary. The charge that I had used Alicia Gowharian to gain access to Soviet doctors working in Iran was also on the indictment, and of course the judge refused to call her as a witness in refutation, or to order the production of the tape recording of my alleged telephone conversation with her.

Another ridiculous charge was that a month before my arrest the Intelligent Service had telexed me a shopping list of secret information that I was to gather. Hosein had mentioned this early in my interrogation, and not knowing what he was talking about I asked to see the telex. He never produced it, but from what he said I realized that he was referring to the synopsis of a forthcoming survey on Iran, which the *Financial Times* correspondent for the Gulf region had sent me, asking me to check it out with my contacts in the Ministry of Islamic Guidance, the body responsible for foreign press relations, and the Ministry of Foreign Affairs. It consisted of a summary of each of the articles which the newspaper intended to publish as a special supplement, and was a necessary first step to get the government's blessing and the visas for the team of journalists who would write the survey. I simply retyped it and gave copies to officials I knew in both Ministries, and got a generally favourable response.

I had told Hosein that it was scarcely conceivable that a foreign spymaster would send instructions to one of his agents by open telex to a government hotel; anyway, I had been in London not long before so any 'instructions' could have been given to me then. He seemed to accept this argument and did not pursue the matter. Now it was brought forward as evidence that I was a British spy. More in sorrow at Mr Hoseini's stupidity than in anger, I asked Judge Nayyeri to send for a copy of the telex and request the Ministry officials I had contacted to state whether or not I had given them this proposed editorial synopsis or not. 'This will not be necessary,' he said predictably. 'The matter is quite clear.' By now I knew what he meant by that.

Another technique that I objected to was my televised 'confession' being used against me. Several times the judge read extracts from it and they rarely sounded as I remembered the script at all, so I asked to see the text. I discovered that he was quoting not from the actual script that Hosein and I had written but from Jomhuri-ye Eslami's coverage, which included considerable editorial comment. I explained that not only was this just a piece of propaganda written as much by my interrogator as by me, under an agreement whereby I was promised freedom in exchange for the broadcast, but subsequently the questions had been changed by the television 'interviewer', whom I had never met, and there had been further distortion by the newspaper. I said I thought the whole broadcast was inadmissible as evidence, but that if he ruled otherwise he should at least use the original script. His reply was to the effect that I was slandering a reputable newspaper.

Towards the end of the second week the judge asked me to prepare my final defence, after which, he said, the prosecution would make their comments and the trial would end. I argued that this was not the right order of events. The prosecution should make their comments first – although since they rarely attended it was difficult to know what they could add to the indictment – and then I should have the last word. He said he could not see the difference, but finally seemed to agree to my proposal. In the end, however, he made me give my final defence first and then allowed the prosecution to comment on what I said.

My defence was irrefutable, I thought. In most instances, I argued, there was simply no case to answer. I had read the law and it did not cover, even indirectly, the vague charges against me. In others I had not seen any evidence to support the charges, so it would be unjust to convict me without my being able to refute such evidence by producing counter-evidence or witnesses. The prosecution had not attended the court regularly and since the judge was impartial – how I said that with a straight face I do not know – he should accept my version of the facts, which had not been challenged by the prosecution. It was too late for them to do so now because they had not bothered to hear my detailed defence.

Furthermore it was wrong to invoke Article 2, which covered far more serious cases than any of the charges against me. Another strong argument, I thought, was that no evidence had been produced or referred to showing that I had access to classified or secret information, nor was I accused of this. In many countries, my own included, spying or espionage is defined as the misuse of classified information, and our counter-espionage legislation is appropriately named 'The Official Secrets Act'. One could hardly be accused of espionage, I argued, without access to such secrets, and although the law I had been charged under did not define espionage it is obvious that this is what it means. If it did not, then the use of information that was public knowledge could be classified as espionage, which would be absurd. Any journalist could be classified as a spy, or even two ordinary citizens discussing something they had read in the paper. I had written about Iran's political, economic and cultural affairs for many years, drawing on facts that were public knowledge, never hiding behind a nom de plume. It is a foreign correspondent's duty to report facts as he sees them, and analyse them objectively, I told the judge. Such activity is good for the whole world, since ignorance can give rise to distrust and suspicion, which are breeding grounds for aggression. Provided he sticks to the rules of impartiality and fair comment, as I had always tried to do, a journalist's output is beneficial to all concerned and has nothing to do with spying.

I could tell from Mr Justice Nayyeri's expression that my words were falling on deaf ears. Knowing that the judge almost certainly believed in the principle 'You wouldn't have been brought here if you were innocent', I finally threw him a sop. 'In the unlikely event that Your Honour feels that any guilt attaches to me, I would suggest that in view of the long time I have already spent in detention he should not consider passing a sentence in excess of that period. Although political questions are not properly speaking relevant, it would be wrong to let the poor state of Irano-British relations adversely affect my fate; and Your Honour might bear in mind that a generous verdict from him would do much to raise the image of the Islamic Republic in Britain, and would be likely to have beneficial effects.'

While I was making this peroration I heard the sound of a page being turned and looked up from my desk to see Judge Nayyeri sipping tea and reading the evening paper. From time to time he would offer me a glass of tea, an unusual gesture in Evin, when both tea and sugar are severely rationed, but on this occasion he had not done so when the teaman came round. I paused, greatly put out, until he asked me to continue. 'I would prefer to wait until Your Honour has finished perusing his documents,' I said, as icily as I could. 'No, go on,' he said. 'It's only the newspaper. I'm listening.'

Mr Hoseini had appeared for this part of the trial and he spoke for a few minutes after I had finished. He rambled and waffled and when I looked at my notes, so that I could have the last word as promised, I saw that he had really said nothing new. I deliberately asked the judge to summarize his speech for me. The judge seemed unable to do so and instead asked Mr Hoseini to repeat it. Basically his argument seemed to be that the charges were correct and my defence was false, so in my concluding words I asked sarcastically how he knew what my defence was since he had not heard it.

By now I was past caring. From beginning to end the trial was such a parody of justice that it would be insulting to marsupials even to call it a kangaroo court. It was obvious that the judge would find me guilty, but even then I could not see how he could sentence me to more than five years in gaol. If this happened, and happened quickly, the British government might agree to release Kurosh Fuladi, who had about five years to serve, in exchange for my freedom. This was obviously the deal that Hosein was after, and although Mrs Thatcher might be unwilling at first to agree to it, the principle of respect for the courts of a sovereign state would leave her with little option. She could hardly let me rot in gaol for several more years if all that was necessary was to let Fuladi go.

A day or two after the trial ended I was recalled to the court. From what Judge Nayyeri had said on the first day I did not expect to hear his verdict quite so soon, and sure enough the purpose of the summons was to question me about my links with the 'accursed Baha'i sect', as the five million adherents of this faith worldwide are always termed in Iran. No representative of the prosecution was present; once again it was just the judge, the lay-assessor and myself.

Back in 1982, at the request of my old friend Ben Whitaker, former MP for Hampstead and founding director of the Minority Rights Group, I had written a briefing paper on the Iranian Baha'is, who had suffered great persecution since the Revolution. Indeed the Baha'is, and their predecessors the Babis, have since their earliest days been persecuted in Iran, often horribly so. I knew a number of Baha'i families in Iran before the Revolution and always admired them for their high moral standards, hard work and devotion to education and good works. The Shah did not exactly support them, never, for example, permitting them to rebuild their temple in central Tehran or establish their own schools, but they were at least tolerated by the regime, whereas in the early years of the Islamic Republic they were treated appallingly. In 1980 the entire eleven-person National Spiritual Assembly – the leadership body – was arrested and presumably executed. In all, more than 200 Baha'is have been killed for their beliefs, mainly by summary execution but also by being beaten or stoned to death by mobs.

Baha'i property and businesses have been illegally confiscated and they have suffered from widespread administrative discrimination: Baha'is who worked in the public sector before the Revolution, such as civil servants and most doctors, nurses and teachers, were not only dismissed from office but ordered to repay in full the salaries and benefits received during their careers.

I had been reluctant to take on the task, knowing that anything I wrote about the Baha'is, no matter how impartial, would be a black mark against me in Tehran. Baha'ism is a particularly sensitive subject since the Revolution, for its roots are in early nineteenth-century Iran. Although it has developed away from Islam to become a faith with universal appeal it can still be regarded to some extent as a breakaway Shi'ite sect, or even a reformed version of Shi'ism, although Baha'is do not like to be reminded of this. Ben argued that I was well qualified to write on the subject and he did not want the author to be a Baha'i himself. There was an urgent need, he said, for such a paper to inform the public about the Baha'is and what was happening to them in Iran. So I agreed to do it.

Delving into the history of Baha'ism and its predecessor-sects Shaikhism and Babism had been academically fascinating. I unearthed a few skeletons in the Baha'i cupboard, such as the question of polygamy, which was acceptable to the early Baha'is, who had also been less pacific than their successors, and I included these in my text. Ben sent a copy of the first draft to the UN office of the Baha'i International Community in New York asking for comments. They kindly corrected some factual errors I had made and expressed mild objection to some of the skeletons, but did not contradict them, so I left them in. The paper, part of MRG's comprehensive series on minorities of every kind, became something of a bestseller, and has gone through four editions. For the third of these the Baha'is asked for certain passages they did not like to be removed. I objected, on the grounds that they showed my lack of bias, and in the summer before my arrest I told Ben that if the cuts were made I did not wish my name to appear as sole author, since I felt my impartiality compromised.

I had been somewhat surprised that my involvement with Baha'ism had not formed part of my indictment, nor been raised by the judge at the trial, since Hosein had questioned me intensively on the subject and I had seen a photocopy of my pamphlet in his briefcase soon after my arrest. The story of how it got there is a sorry one. In January 1985 I had been in Tehran lobbying on behalf of McDermott's bid for the Kharg pipeline. I was tipped off that our rival, the Singaporean firm, was playing the Islam card; their Malaysian chairman had visited Tehran and gone so far as to produce his prayer rug at a meeting with the Chairman of the National Iranian Oil Company and ask which way Mecca lay. I tried to counter this by stressing that McDermott was the second largest employer of Muslims in Dubai (after the city council), that we had a score of experienced Iranian workers and foremen and were willing to train or employ more. I thought that if my *Euromoney* article on Islamic economics and banking, which had been read with interest by officials in Iran's Central Bank, had a wider public it might help improve our Islamic image, so I phoned my secretary in Dubai and asked her to send me a copy, which I would translate into Persian and give to selected oil industry officials. I was told the Central Bank would also like to publish it in their quarterly bulletin.

Unfortunately she also came across my Minority Rights Group booklet *Baha'is of Iran* and thought, 'He'll probably want that as well' – a disastrous assumption. The package reached me by courier the next day, and my heart sank when I saw the Baha'i booklet inside, with its purple cover, since Iranian customs check all courier mail and they could hardly have missed it. I considered tearing it into small pieces and flushing it down the lavatory, but in the end I gave it to the Reuter's correspondent, who had asked me what I knew about the Baha'is one evening, urging him to keep it in a safe place.

Hosein told me later that customs had indeed seen it and his office had given instructions for the package to be resealed. He had expected me to contact Baha'is and pass the booklet on to them for secret distribution, since such a publication was of course banned in Iran, and had ordered me to be kept under twenty-four-hour surveillance. He was quite amused when I explained that it was sent to me in error, an error which must have been a major factor in my arrest.

Judge Nayyeri had before him a copy of the third edition, which the Ministry of Intelligence had had translated into Persian, and I was now being accused – though without being formally indicted – of being a Baha'i, a supporter of Baha'ism, perhaps even a Baha'i proselytizer. Any of these charges was likely to aggravate my sentence, and the last could carry the death penalty. I explained at length to Judge Nayyeri why I had written this paper and how the Baha'is themselves had not been altogether happy about it. Unfortunately the passages I would have liked to draw his attention to – the ones the Baha'is had not liked – were no longer there, and he clearly did not believe me when I told him I had received a number of critical letters from members of the faith. I added that in researching the paper I had asked the Iranian embassy in London for assistance, either in disputing facts given to me by the Baha'i community or in justifying their government's actions against this minority. They declined to co-operate, but I nevertheless stood by what I had written as an impartial account and put my name on it as author. I pointed to the phrase on the title page of the third edition, 'by Roger Cooper, with revisions by the Minority Rights Group', and asked him to study the first edition, which I knew Hosein had. Predictably, he said this would not be necessary.

A week or so later I was again summoned to court, this time expecting to learn my fate, but the judge only asked for clarification on the *sigheh* question. I had mentioned having had a *sigheh* contract with a young cousin of my wife's. Would I provide details? I told him the story of Khanom-e Amiri arranging for me to marry her granddaughter so as to be able to unveil herself in front of me. He listened without comment, asked if I had any other *sighehs* and, apparently disappointed, sent me back to my cell. I felt distinctly uncomfortable that since his mind was clearly made up on the spying question he was so concerned with Baha'ism, *sighehs* and illicit relations one week after the trial had ended.

11

T HE SECOND ANNIVERSARY of my arrest passed without incident, and Christmas 1987, New Year, my birthday, Now Ruz, Ramadan are now just a blur in my mind. There were no visits, but a sprinkling of Christmas cards arrived, and a letter from each of my parents. For the first half of this period newspapers and exercise privileges were cut off. I continued to read extensively, however, and worked my maths up to A-level standard.

This was in many ways the best period of my imprisonment. Despite having almost no contact with the outside world I had a great deal to keep my mind busy. I recalled Milton's moving lines from *Paradise Lost*, which became my inspiration in Evin:

> The mind is its own place, and in itself
> Can make a heav'n of hell, a hell of heav'n.

Milton was blind when he wrote that, whereas I still had my sight, however blinkered. So I decided to make the most of the opportunities I had and not to brood too much. Richard II's famous prison speech also came frequently to mind:

> I have been studying how I may compare
> This prison where I live unto the world...

although I found quite a different set of answers to those Shakespeare provided his sad but noble king.

It was becoming difficult to fit in all this reading and studying, to say nothing of the crossword dictionary project when newspaper delivery resumed, and my keep-fit programme. Besides, there were always one or two briefing papers on the go for mysterious people who came to see me from I knew not where. Some were clearly from Iran's intelligence fraternity, others were perhaps connected with the Foreign Ministry, others again graduate students needing ideas or material for their doctoral theses. Their questions usually indicated which category they belonged to, and I rarely turned anyone down, believing that in this way I was helping people to understand the real world, people who were, or might become, opinion-formers. By now I had a dictionary, and my written Persian had become fairly good. I could write it about as fast as I write, say, French and faster than German or Russian. All this occupied more hours a day than seemed to be available, so I trained myself to cut back on sleep. The duty guard would usually agree to leave both my lights on – by now I had wangled two 100-watt bulbs – until two or three in the morning if I said I had 'urgent work for the ministry', and I got used to starting again soon after breakfast. How I wish I could rediscover this discipline today and fit more into my life, but maybe I am repaying my sleep debt now, as I am with my dream-life.

By pressing hard on the metal hatch in my cell door I had developed a small crack, not noticeable to any guard, which enabled me to see the doors of the two cells diagonally opposite mine, and keep records of the occupancy of each. Frequently, a prisoner was put in a cell during the day, but without an elaborate body search, as if he had been moved from another part of the prison: a newcomer was always thoroughly searched. I hypothesized that these were prisoners moved back to the Sanatorium on the eve of their execution. I say back because some of them seemed to know the duty guard and I assumed that all Evin inmates spent their early days in the Sanatorium. Sometimes there would be four or five such overnight occupants of a single cell in a week. They might of course have been brought back to the Sanatorium before release, but the only people I ever knew that left Evin alive went straight out from communal cells, either on completion of sentence or on the basis of an amnesty. If my theory was correct this implied an extremely high rate of execution, given that the two cells I could see must have represented a random sample of the 300-odd in the male section of the Sanatorium. A horrifying thought, but difficult to prove, because well before my arrest Iran had stopped publishing statistics on executions in order to minimize criticism from abroad. I later learned that more people were executed in Iran in 1988 than in the entire rest of the world, at least 2500 according to Amnesty International.

My busyness was perhaps what some psychologists call displacement activity. It certainly helped take my mind off my own fate, but in the spring of 1988 I received a letter from my father saying that according to the *Daily Telegraph* I had been tried and sentenced to death. This letter reached me quite promptly and I imagine the only reason I got it at all was because few people can read his handwriting. My first reaction was anger. How dare the *Telegraph* print such baseless rubbish, which would obviously upset my family and friends? I even wondered whether I could sue them for libel when I was released, which I hoped would be within the next few months. There must be some difficulties in Irano-British negotiations over the exchange, I thought, that would explain the delay in sentencing me. I never saw Hosein in those days, nor anyone else who could tell me what was going on, but that seemed the most likely explanation. Then a horrible thought occurred to me. I had grown up with the *Telegraph* as the family newspaper, and although I did not always see eye to eye with it on domestic politics the foreign coverage was first-class and its reputation for accuracy well known. Suppose its report was correct?

At first it seemed impossible. Surely an accused person would be the first to hear his sentence, so how could the *Telegraph* know my sentence before me? But this is Iran, I remembered, and things are almost always done differently here. Besides, Judge Nayyeri had talked about the delay in typing my sentence. Judges everywhere normally give their verdicts and sentences in open court, from notes perhaps, but not from a typed document. So prisoners condemned to death in Iran might not be told their sentence until shortly before it is carried out, which would explain the relaxed attitude of the men who spent a night in the cells opposite me. *They probably did not know what was about to happen to them.* Then there was the worrying aspect of *rajm*, the Islamic penalty for adultery, to die buried to the waist in sand, slowly bleeding to death as a frenzied mob helped themselves from a truckload of

205

stone chippings; that is how it is done in Iran. Surely this fear was absurd, though, because even if Judge Nayyeri disbelieved my *sigheh* story, which might well be so, the penalty for fornication was only 72 lashes. But then Nilufar might have been married, or not yet divorced, and failed to tell me: that would make my offence adultery. Suppose they suddenly led me away to be executed? Who would do the stoning? Probably the guards and those trusties in brown uniforms I sometimes caught a glimpse of weeding or watering the garden. Doubtless they would be only too happy to oblige the authorities and earn extra points towards remission. And after what he had said about the happiest day of his life I would expect Hosein to be there, casting the first stone.

As these disjointed thoughts raced through my mind I felt quite wobbly. I reread my father's letter sitting on my folded blanket with my back to the wall, seeking further clues. When I stood up my legs were weak, my mouth was dry and my stomach knotted. But I managed to overcome these fears using the old 'Why worry?' technique: the thing you fear may never happen, there is probably nothing you can do to prevent it, so why worry?

I never saw the *Daily Telegraph* article, but it must have been based on something in the local media – from time to time I would be told they had run out of newspapers and I guessed this was because a particular issue contained something about me or relations with Britain – because from about that time certain of the nastier guards began to make remarks about my being executed. One or two of them said, laughingly perhaps but with hidden malice, things like, 'If we ever get the order to release you, Cooper, we'll hang you in the cell and say we carried out your sentence.' I would look Reagan or whoever it was in the eye and say sardonically, 'Do you really think you could do that to a member of the Intelligent Service? Do you have the courage?' It was best to take such remarks as sick jokes, but they were unsettling all the same.

In the first half of 1988 I became friendly with the prison governor. He was a lively and intelligent person and used to enjoy dropping in to discuss politics or the war with Iraq which now seemed to be entering its final round. In March the papers were full of an Iranian breakthrough in Kurdistan, until Iraq responded with a devastating poison gas counterattack in which some 5000 civilians died. In April, Iraq recaptured the Fao peninsula, again using chemical weapons, and in June I read that 'the combatants of Islam have been deployed in new defensive positions' in the strategic Majmun area that included a 30-billion-barrel oilfield, a sure sign that things were not going well. I felt ambivalent about the outcome, feeling that if either side won an outright victory it could destabilize the region. Yet Iran still showed no signs of accepting the cease-fire proposals of UN Security Council Resolution 598.

The governor used to visit the Sanatorium every week and spoke with about one prisoner in four or five, according to my observations through the crack and counting the number of cell doors opened in my corridor. He always included me on his rounds, however, usually shooing away the guards accompanying him and almost closing the door so that we could speak frankly without being overheard. It was through him that I got permission to have all three local newspapers every day, an unprecedented privilege. I had said that it was difficult for me to have proper political discussions with him without knowing what was going on, and I repaid the favour by feeding him titbits from the papers every time he came, since he was too busy to do more than glance at them, he said.

He often asked me about the elections that were to be held in April and what sort of candidates I thought would win, but when the election campaign began he stopped coming. I put two and two together and guessed he might be running for election himself. Knowing he was a 'Turk' I read everything I could on the Azarbaijan constituencies until I found his name – or a name identical to his – standing for Zanjan. He had just one mention, however, whereas other candidates for this important seat were often quoted or featured in advertisements paid for by their supporters. I asked several guards where the governor was, but they did not seem to know. On leave, they thought. He did not win, and in Iran they only list the winner and one or two runners-up, presumably so as not to embarrass the less successful candidates.

When he dropped by a few days after the results were published he seemed in more of a hurry than usual, but I said I had something

207

important to tell him. He closed the door and I said, 'Governor, do you know why you lost in Zanjan?'

He was flabbergasted. 'How did you know?' he asked. 'Almost no one in Evin knows. Have you told anyone?' I assured him I had not, but repeated my question. 'You tell me,' he replied.

'You lost, Governor, because you made no effort to publicize yourself. Your name appeared only once, in one newspaper. You seemed to have no supporters. If you had a policy no one knew what it was.'

'You are right, Cooper,' he said. 'I thought an election in the Islamic Republic should be just the public voting for the best candidate, but frankly it's just like in the old days. You spend money, bribe people, tell lies.'

'Governor, don't be surprised,' I said. 'It's like that all over the world, even in the communist countries. But if you had let me out of prison for a week to act as your press agent I could have got you elected.' This was meant as a joke, but he looked at me earnestly and said, 'Cooper, I wish I had done that.'

He then told me that he was leaving Evin shortly to take up a new post (I never discovered what it was), but before going he wanted to tell me something I should know, although he was not supposed to do so. I had received two sentences: one was death, the other ten years' imprisonment. I was distinctly shaken by this news, but the surprising double sentence gave me a curious kind of hope. Without pausing, and half-way between flippancy and seriousness, I asked him, 'Which comes first?'

He looked puzzled for a moment, then said, 'Ah, I see, yes, a good question. I will recommend they keep you here for ten years and then hang you!'

I replied, 'Please don't make it the other way round.'

One day in the summer of 1988 the Evin postman arrived with a book he said a friend had sent me. He rarely came to the Sanatorium because so few inmates were allowed mail: I had never seen him before my trial, and only rarely since. His name was Seyyed Masih, and he was one of the kindest men in Evin. He told me that a lot of mail came for me but he was not allowed

208

to deliver it. Even knowing that people were writing to me was a morale-booster. The book was by an American economics professor and turned out to be a kind of academic *Crash of '79*, but without the excitement. The inscription on the flyleaf told me at once that it must have been meant for Pattis, not me: in American handwriting 'Joanna' had sent a short note with her love to 'Jon'. The mistake had occurred because the first name on my passport, which I rarely use, is John. When I came to the Sanatorium I was called 'Jan' (with a long a), which in Persian means 'soul' and is a common term of endearment, or 'Jani', which means 'murderer' or 'wild beast', by less friendly guards. Instead of giving the book back I put it aside, while I chatted with Seyyed Masih, who I had heard was a crossword fan, and told him about my dictionary plan, which interested him.

I skimmed through the book that day, noting dozens of errors or predictions that were already proving wrong, and imagining how I would have slated it if it had been sent to me for review. It was nevertheless a heaven-sent opportunity to establish communications with Jon Pattis. I knew he would read it thoroughly because the note indicated he had requested such a book. I wrote several tiny pointers in faint pencil on the inner margin close to the spine, starting about the fourth chapter, simply saying 'See p.274', which I picked as being three pages into a 16-page signature. The pointers themselves were on similar pages. I felt confident Jon would see at least one of them. When I had written the message I forced the book open at each signature division so that it opened naturally there and the next page could only be turned over with some difficulty. I had learned this trick years before when I wanted officials to see only a particular page in my passport, usually the one with their country's visa on it, instead of leafing through pages containing visas or entry stamps I might not wish them to see. It was unlikely that my note to Jon would be spotted unless a thorough check were made. Next day I explained to Bespectacled Hosein that the postman had brought me someone else's book in error, so Seyyed Masih came back to collect it. I pretended not to know of the existence of Jon Pattis, or to have had any interest in the book, but just said that I knew no one called Joanna and my name had an H in it. He quickly realized he had made a mistake, one he would obviously not draw attention to.

I had kept the message short, just my name, nationality, block and cell number, charge and sentence, and proposed that if he was ever taken to the main garden he should leave a message in a crumpled ball in the small unused fountain. When I next went there myself with an expanded message for Jon I found that the fountain was unsuitable for a letter-drop. It was the highest point in the garden, clearly visible from the interrogation block windows, and since I had sent my message the basin was suddenly full of water. Worse still, the elderly guard who had recently taken over exercise duty had decided to sit on the stone bench by the fountain while the prisoners walked around below him.

I codenamed Jon 'Jay Pee' or 'Japer' and wrote my messages in verse on a corner of newspaper. The first one went something like this:

> Japer, Japer, cuts a merry caper,
> But inside the fountain's no place for a paper.
> Down by the poolside while the keeper dozes
> In among the onions and close to the roses
> Seems to Will far better
> As a place to leave a letter.

I signed it boldly 'William Shakespeare' in case it fell into the wrong hands. In early spring I had cheekily planted some onions in the rose beds and these had now grown into fine plants, which I hoped to harvest soon for their green tops, having failed to persuade any of the guards to take me back to the herb garden of blessed memory and being consumed by a craving for green vegetables.

Then I crumpled the paper into a ball and left it under the fountain basin. Every time I came out I checked whether it was still there. When it was not I substituted a new one in both places, but had no way of knowing if it had been picked up by Jon, or a gardener, or had simply blown away. There was the worrying possibility that it had been intercepted. It later emerged that Jon did indeed see my message in the book, but his block took their exercise in a different part of the prison and he never found a way of replying.

That February, Saddam Hussein had ordered extensive missile attacks on Tehran and other Iranian cities. Since the start of the Iran–Iraq war there had been regular bombardments by aircraft, artillery and ground-to-ground missiles of border towns, the effects of which I had witnessed on my journeys to the oil province of Khuzistan. Now, by adding fuel tanks and reducing the payload of the Soviet-built Scud-B missile, following weapons development work sponsored by Iraq at Egyptian research establishments, Saddam's batteries could easily reach Tehran and other targets previously safe from attack. I used to keep the score, since explosions even in downtown Tehran ten miles away were clearly audible, while some were much nearer. On many days I recorded over a dozen. Once or twice my cell would shake when a missile landed close to Evin. There were no obvious targets close to the prison so I supposed they were aiming at the Emam's house a mile or two further east, and falling short. One afternoon an Iraqi MIG screamed past only a hundred yards or so from my window and dropped its bomb before hurrying back to Iraq. It went off in the valley just above the prison, causing no damage, the guards told me, although the blast knocked one of the plants off my window-ledge.

On the whole I felt fairly safe myself. Evin is solidly built and the thick cell windows did not even crack from close explosions. A stray missile might hit the gaol, but I could not imagine it would be targeted deliberately, with so many of the regime's enemies inside. It was an unnerving experience, all the same. It was bad enough to be unfairly tried and sentenced to death in a country that was undergoing both a war and a revolution, without finding oneself also in the firing line of that war. What else could happen? I wondered.

During the missile bombardment, which continued for almost two months, I was taken out for exercise several times and always took the precaution of looking for the best place to hide if I saw a Scud approaching. The swimming pool was empty and the shallow end looked like a good place to shelter from the blast. I did occasionally see Scuds approaching Tehran, but always the city centre. They reminded me of the World War II doodlebug or

211

flying bomb, although I understand they are in fact ballistic missiles rather than rockets. Their trajectory changed over the city as if the motor had cut out, although it was difficult to believe that they were accurately targetable. The local media, however, insisted that they were and that the Iraqis were deliberately bombing schools and hospitals. They did not give precise information on where the missiles landed, but foreign journalists were accused of helping the Iraqis by giving details of damage. The newspapers even stopped printing weather forecasts in case meteorological information was helpful to the enemy.

At the end of April, and after considerable international pressure on Iraq to stop attacking non-military targets, the bombardment ceased. It made me realize how vulnerable Iran was to aerial attack. There seemed to be no real anti-missile defences, and Iraqi pilots were able to strike with impunity. They even did serious damage to one of the country's main power stations, Neka, on the south-east corner of the Caspian Sea and returned safely to base. The Iranian air force was desperately short of planes, and many of the existing aircraft, which the Shah had been criticized for buying in such large quantities, were grounded for lack of spares. Anti-aircraft defences were clearly quite primitive, as I had seen on my visit to Kharg Island, despite its being one of the country's vital locations.

It was difficult to discover what was actually happening at the front, a straggly line 500 miles long stretching from where Turkey, Iraq and Iran meet to the north all the way to the Shatt-al-Arab and out into the Persian Gulf. The most active sector was in the south, where Iran had until quite recently been reportedly on the brink of capturing Basra, Iraq's second most important city. Saddam's weaponry and Soviet-engineered defences seemed able to withstand Iran's 'human-wave' attacks, however. In July 1987 the UN Security Council had passed Resolution 598 requiring both belligerents to cease fighting and return to internationally recognized borders. Iran neither accepted nor rejected the resolution, thus in effect prolonging the war for a further unnecessary year in the hope of an outright victory. In the spring the papers were full of glorious advances across difficult terrain, but before long the tide seemed to turn. On 3 June, Ali Akbar Rafsanjani, the

Majlis Speaker and it seemed to me already the most powerful politician in the country, was appointed by the Emam overall military commander, which indicated something was wrong. He quickly installed a unified command structure designed to overcome inter-service bickering. About this time there were mass departures of Evin guards for the front, a sure sign of manpower shortages, and the situation apparently continued to deteriorate until on 20 July a very depressed Emam announced that he had reluctantly 'drunk the cup of poison' and agreed to abide by Resolution 598.

A month later the ceasefire agreement was signed. My hopes soared again that the ending of the war would mean an improvement in Iran's relations with the West, from which I would be likely to benefit. The guards came back, not apparently having seen any action and full of stories of desert scorpions, but did not seem as happy as I would have expected. In fact, they looked distinctly edgy and gloomy. Something was clearly up, but nobody would tell me what it was, and once again my newspapers had been cut off.

In June 1988 there was an unexpected visit to Iran by a British parliamentary mission led by John Lyttle, secretary for public affairs to the Archbishop of Canterbury. Hosein sent for me and said I could write a letter to the mission suggesting ways of improving Irano-British relations – no easy task if I wanted my letter to be delivered. In it I analysed the outstanding differences, delving frankly into Britain's colonial past and Iran's own mistakes. The letter was approved, to the credit of Hosein and his masters, and I was allowed to hand it personally to Mr Lyttle the next day, together with a message wishing my daughter luck with her medical finals, which were about to start. I gathered that John Lyttle had been appointed to supervise Terry Waite, who had been exceeding his mandate: this must have been good news to the Iranians, who understandably had become suspicious of emissaries from Lambeth Palace. My letter was later reprinted in *The Spectator*.

This was one of the last times I saw Hosein, and I took advantage of the opportunity to raise the question of my sentence. He was embarrassed to discover that I already knew what it was and half-apologized, saying that it was not what he had expected and that it could be reduced on appeal. He sounded extremely depressed and I was not totally surprised when a year or so later I heard on the grapevine that he had had a nervous breakdown and left the Ministry. Although he had treated me shamefully in many ways, I actually found myself feeling sorry for him.

Meanwhile it was clear that I had been grossly deceived. Once the prison governor had confirmed that I was under sentence of death I decided I must find a way of telling the outside world, or at least an independent Iranian authority, how I had been treated. Obviously I had nothing more to lose. The problem was how to get the message out.

After much thought I wrote out in two copies a summary of what had happened to me, and always carried one copy with me every time I left my cell, even for a shower or exercise, since there was never any advance notice of a visit. For months no suitable opportunity occurred. I considered giving a copy to the prison governor, requesting him as a personal favour to get it to the highest judicial authorities. But something told me that he might simply shred it in case our quasi-friendship proved an embarrassment to his political career, and fob me off with promises that he had passed it on.

A better bet would be if I got a visit from Paul or another family member and could slip my statement to them. My mother, now in her 95th year, had applied for a visa to visit me, and although I had written telling her not to come I knew my letter would not be sent if the Iranian government's policy was that she should come. Neither of my parents had travelled abroad for many years; on his last trip my father had somehow found himself in Spain having left his passport at home, managing nevertheless to complete his holiday and return to the UK, still without a passport. He also decided to visit me, but was annoyed to find that his passport was no longer valid and it would take some time to get a new one. If either of them did turn up suddenly I might be able to slip the statement into a pocket or bag while greeting them, although this would be a big risk.

Finally Paul arrived. He brought me a kilo of black mulberries – still called king mulberries (*shah-toot*) as opposed to ordinary white *toot*. (My joke to the guards about them now being *emam-toot* fell a little flat.) They were already oozing out of their flimsy wrapping and in the confusion of mopping up the dark juice with a newspaper Paul had brought I could have slipped the paper into his pocket, but I funked it at the last minute.

After catching up with family news I noticed Mohammad, the friendly English-speaking interrogator, was deep in conversation with the man from the Ministry of Foreign Affairs, so I quietly pulled my message out and in the same tone of voice as the one I had been talking to Paul in, I read it into the tape recorder that was always running during a visit. The two officials took at least a minute to realize what I was doing and immediately interrupted me, for some reason turning the tape recorder off as they did so. The visit was declared at an end and Paul was told to leave. I appealed to Mohammad, saying that it was my right to tell my brother the circumstances of my trial and the sentence I had received, and I was openly recording the statement into the tape recorder. His colleague seized the paper and when I tried to slip Paul my back-up copy this too was taken away from him with a weak promise that it would be sent on to him. I continued to say that all I was doing was to report an official act of the Islamic government, and what could possibly be wrong with that?

Of course, I was hustled back to the Sanatorium in disgrace, although surprisingly they let me keep the mulberry-stained news-paper and what was left of the fruit itself. Before we parted I managed to indicate to Paul that he should report what he had heard of my statement, so I was sure that my story would now get the publicity it needed if the deadlock were to be broken. If the news of my death sentence were known in Britain I hoped it would cause such an uproar that the Iranians would not dare carry it out. It might of course go the other way and tip them into executing me, but I felt on balance that publicity would work in my favour. The most likely response to Paul's announcing my death sentence would be for the Iranians to deny it officially, especially at this delicate time of negotiations with the United Nations over the cease-fire. I returned to my cell feeling reasonably pleased with the outcome, although regretting I had not succeeded in slipping Paul my back-up copy undetected.

For some months there had been talk of moving me out of solitary to a communal block, but having quizzed various guards about conditions there I resisted the move. I felt that the advantages of company, perhaps even Jon Pattis's, and unlimited exercise in the corridors, besides several hours outside, would be outweighed by living in a smoky cell with twenty or more prisoners and the television on all day. Better the devil I knew, I decided. Iranians cannot stand solitude, so both guards and officials thought I was mad. Luckily the governor supported my choice, and as long as he was in charge I remained in the Sanatorium, but the pressure on me to move became so great I assumed that the British press or the Foreign Office were complaining that I had been in solitary detention for nearly three years. Finally orders were given to move me, and the only concession was a promise that I would be in a no-smoking cell.

The move was a mere hundred yards or so, to the block known as the *Amuzeshgah* ('Training Institute'), where I found myself mobbed by hundreds of curious prisoners. I soon learnt that there had been many comments about my case in the papers and on television which I knew nothing about, so my name was already familiar to them, but it was my insistence on a non-smoking cell that had chiefly intrigued them. There were many non-smokers, and when my future cell was so nominated there were scores of requests for a place there. It seemed I had really started something and won considerable kudos for changing the system.

Among the inmates of the Training Institute were two Americans, Jon Pattis and David Rabhan. Jon was shortish, with a neatly trimmed beard, a few years younger than me, and reticent in the extreme. He was highly self-contained and seemed in quite good mental shape, although polio as a child had damaged his foot muscles. Despite this disability he had taken up sky-diving, only to break his back after his parachute became entangled in a high tree. A telecommunications engineer, he had come to Iran to supervise the installation of a giant new dish-antenna at the Asadabad earth-satellite station in west Iran, on which almost all the country's international telecommunications depended. He was one of only a handful of experts in the world capable of getting such a project exactly right, but the national telecommunications

216

company realized there would be a scandal if it were known that such a sensitive assignment had been entrusted to an American. The company had therefore asked another foreign contractor, a Milan firm, to arrange an Italian passport for Jon, although his birthplace was given as South Carolina and there was no attempt to give him an Italian name or otherwise disguise his nationality. Like all such stations Asadabad is visible from many miles away and is close to the border, so it was surprising that the Iraqis had never attacked it. One day they did so, by bad luck (since there were no casualties) while Jon was on leave in Tehran.

Naturally a scapegoat had to be found. Among the charges against him were arriving in Iran on a false passport and secreting a homing device in the antenna, although as the attack was in broad daylight a pilot who needed anything other than normal vision to locate such a huge target should not have been flying in Saddam Hussein's air force. Like me, Jon had made a confession and appeared before Judge Nayyeri, who had sentenced him to ten years' imprisonment. He had been arrested about a year after me, and only spent one year in pre-trial detention, so he still had some eight years to serve. Iran and the United States have had no diplomatic relations since the US embassy hostage crisis; Jon's wellbeing was therefore in the hands of a US Interests Section at the Swiss embassy, which had been denied proper consular access and not been of much help to him.

David was quite a different kind of person. About five foot ten in height, he was extremely muscular and fit, especially for a 63-year-old. His most striking feature was his large head, which he kept completely shaved, earning from the older guards the nickname Yul Brynner. Everyone knew and was intrigued by David – even the guards seemed somewhat in awe of him. He had the presence of a natural leader and when he spoke, whether in English or his confident, if grammatically non-standard, Persian, people listened. David was first arrested some eight years earlier, but had been freed and then rearrested at least once. Before coming to Evin he had been in Qasr, another Tehran prison used mostly to house prisoners charged with less serious offences than those in Evin, such as theft, fraud and what was quaintly called 'ordinary' murder. The original charges against David were of a complicated financial nature. When espionage was added to the list he was transferred to Evin, where in due course Judge Nayyeri had sentenced him in the spring of 1988 to two years' imprisonment, a sentence so lenient that other prisoners said it proved he was innocent.

David had come to Iran shortly before the Revolution to set up a factory to make 'Mother's Milk Replacement', a non-dairy product that he said was much better for babies than regular powdered milk, though nothing was as good as mother's milk. Problems of various kinds culminated in accusations that he had defrauded the state on the foreign exchange allocations covering the importation of machinery.

But his real 'crime' was threefold. First, he was a personal friend of Iran's bugbear Jimmy Carter, whom he had known since his youth. Secondly, he had been a subaltern in an armoured unit in Germany at the end of World War II, flown in combat in the Korean War, served as a major with the Special Forces in Vietnam and was still a pilot in Georgia's National Guard, which made him an American warmonger. His third crime was being Jewish, his grandparents having arrived in the United States in the early 1900s. One of David's aunts had emigrated to Israel, and a letter from her, written before or early in the Revolution had been found among David's papers, together with a copy of his typed reply. These 'links' with President Carter, American imperialism, and Israel were all Mr Justice Nayyeri required to find him guilty.

I at once decided I would become great friends with David, who had an outgoing personality and was interested in many of the same things as I was, including food and drink, having trained as a nutritionist and being an unusually adventurous cook by American standards. Despite his experiences, he also had a real love for Iran. Jon was much more withdrawn, taciturn almost, but I felt we would make a good trio. I began to wish I had moved to the Training Institute sooner.

12

TOWARDS THE END of my time in the Sanatorium I had received a visit that gave my flagging morale a boost. It was from my friend David Reddaway, a rising young diplomat who had been awarded an MBE for his work as press attaché in Tehran during the early days of the Revolution. He knew Persian well, having done a one-year course at London University soon after joining the Foreign Office. At the end of his tour in Iran he had married Rowshan Firouz, whose parents became good friends of mine after the Revolution. Narsi Firouz, of an aristocratic Shirazi family, is an American-educated civil engineer and one of the most cultivated Iranians I know. His wife Louise Laylin, an American from Virginia, is a remarkable woman with a deep interest in the evolution of the horse. Almost single-handedly she resurrected the Caspian Pony from near-extinction by re-breeding this most beautiful of the miniature equines, relying on such evidence as the friezes at Persepolis for her genetic programme. By the time of the Revolution the Caspian Pony was well established in Europe, North America and Australasia as an ideal children's mount. She also started a successful equestrian centre near Tehran, which sadly had to be sold when her husband's company ran into financial difficulties by undercosting a large urban development programme.

During the early years of the Revolution, Louise did much to save horses from starvation and pointless slaughter, but the Caspian Pony breeding stock in Iran, which had been taken over by the Imperial Horse Society, was effectively wiped out. Since then, against all the odds, she has reinstated the breeding programme and started a second equestrian centre an hour's drive from Tehran, which is where I had last seen David, Rowshan and their son Alexander, whose godfather I am.

Louise wrote a book about the development of the Caspian Pony and at the time of my arrest I had just finished reading the manuscript and writing my comments at her request. This was found among my papers and translated into Persian, including the foreword by Prince Philip. Several sessions of my interrogation were devoted to the Firouzes, who had both been arrested and detained for short periods in 1979. Louise went on a hunger strike and was as thin as a rake when released. In my early days in gaol I remembered her advising me to do the same if I was ever arrested, although at the time this advice had seemed purely hypothetical. I do not think in my case it would have done much good.

David Reddaway, who had gone on to serve in Madrid and on the Falklands desk, had unexpectedly been given a visa to visit Iran in late August before the Tehran International Fair. It seemed that for the first time in years individual British firms would be allowed to exhibit, although without having national day ceremonies or a pavilion. In discussing the arrangements he was also able to talk to the Foreign Ministry about ways of improving Irano-British relations, including my case. Even more surprisingly he was allowed to visit me and Nicolas Nicola, a young Cypriot-born Londoner who had been arrested in possession of firearms in 1988 on the Pakistan-Iran border. Our meeting went quite smoothly and David subtly indicated that I should not mention my godfatherly links with his family. He could not give me grounds for optimism beyond his own presence, but that in itself was something. At one point David compared the process of normalizing relations with Iran to building a wall. 'How many bricks have been laid so far, do you think?' I asked. 'About two,' he replied wryly. He brought as gifts a piece of Cheddar cheese, a wonderful treat, and a bar of chocolate. I do not dislike chocolate, but it is not something I am particularly fond of, and as prison regulations forbade prisoners giving other prisoners or guards presents I decided, after David had gone, to try to send it to Nicolas, who was somewhere in Evin and would probably appreciate it more than I would.

David Rabhan and Jon Pattis had been in the same block as Nicolas, but, in one of the regular moves that Evin subjects its inmates to, he had been left behind, and they were now the only

Westerners in my part of the Training Institute. I soon began to get to know other prisoners as well. My no-smoking cell slept about fifteen, including Jon; although not a smoker himself, for some reason David preferred to stay where he was next door. There was a pleasant former Iranian air force colonel awaiting sentence on some political charges and two or three other interesting and well-educated people. I asked the colonel if by any chance he knew my former brother-in-law Mohsen Jalali Qajar, who had been a major in the Special Forces. He did indeed, both before his arrest and in gaol, and this helped establish the confidence that is often slow in coming among newly acquainted prisoners, particularly those not yet sentenced, who are always fearful that a new friend may turn out to be a dreaded *antenna*, Evin slang for an informer. The colonel thought Mohsen might recently have been released after serving eight years of his ten-year sentence as an alleged coup plotter. The colonel told me there was no doubt in his mind that I was now a political pawn. If relations with Britain improved I would be freed, otherwise I would stay put. He thought Reddaway's visit, which had been highlighted in the press, was a good sign, and said he expected me to be released within six months.

I told him that as a journalist I would like him to introduce me to some members of the MKO, the Mojahedin Khalq Organization, in the block, as I had always had difficulty in understanding what they stood for. He laughed sardonically and said I was a little late. There had been thousands of them in Evin and other prisons, but most had been executed recently. After Iran had agreed to the UN cease-fire plan in July the MKO's so-called National Liberation Army, not being a party to it, had launched an attack across the border with Iraq, where many of them had been based in recent years. The Iranian army was so demoralized at the time that these forces, using equipment supplied by the Iraqis, had advanced almost unopposed several hundred kilometres into Iran, to a point only a few hours' drive from the capital. I had heard nothing of this, but now understood why my newspapers had been cut off and why the guards had been so despondent after the cease-fire.

'What happened?' I asked, in great excitement.

'From the military point of view,' said the colonel, 'they had hopelessly extended their lines of communication. They began to run short of supplies, and a counterattack by the Iranian army devastated their column. You'll see it on television tonight, I expect. They show the pictures most evenings now that the danger is over. With different tactics, however, they could still be in control of large parts of the country.'

When I told the colonel I thought I was under a death sentence, he asked me who my judge had been. I said 'Mr Nayyeri', and then he asked me a curious question: 'Did he offer you tea?' 'Yes,' I replied, 'several times, in fact.' 'Then you did get a death sentence,' said the colonel. 'Judge Nayyeri only offers tea to those whom he intends to sentence to death.'

Life in the Training Institute was quite different from the Sanatorium routine. The doors of the cells were always open and throughout the day prisoners were free to walk up and down the corridor or visit other cells. There was a large tea urn, refilled two or three times a day. Iranians consume large quantities of sugar with their tea, preferably sucking it through a hard cube chipped from a sugar loaf, so the small sugar ration limited their consumption. This meant that I could now in practice get as much tea as I wanted, drinking it with little or no sugar, an unbelievable luxury. In addition to the corridor we had access to a small yard for three hours a day. It was used at different periods by each section of the block, and we had it from two o'clock to five every afternoon. Each cell had a black-and-white television set. At first I watched with interest, but quickly realized that it was a liability rather than an asset, since the quality of the programmes was so poor, although it was good practice to listen to a higher standard of spoken Persian than that of the guards. Luckily most of my cell-mates were not TV addicts either, and we reached an agreement to turn the sound off unless someone particularly wanted to watch a programme, in which case the others could go for a stroll in the corridor. It was not easy to concentrate on any serious reading in the cell with so much to-ing and fro-ing, but there was a small room used as a mosque or prayer-room and I was told that nobody would mind if I sat there reading unobtrusively.

The colonel noticed that although I had been given two blankets I was forced to sleep on the floor, whereas everyone else had his own mattress, made by folding and sewing three blankets together. I knew I would never master this Evin art form, even if I could get three extra blankets, but to my great delight the colonel presented me with a well-made mattress on my second day there. 'A friend had a spare one,' was all he would say about it. Although I had by now got used to sleeping on the floor it seemed the height of luxury to have this palliasse between me and the thin carpeting over the concrete. The colonel also introduced me to two former MKO members, warning me that the only reason they were still alive was that they had renounced their allegiance, so I could not expect to get a favourable report on MKO policies, 'if there could be such a thing': he was no lover of the MKO himself. He said they were almost certainly *antennas*. I walked round the yard with each of them in turn, but as the colonel had predicted they were not forthcoming, and obviously scared of me, too scared even to denounce their old organization in case the attempt backfired.

Just as I was settling into this exciting new life my world was once again turned upside down. Orders came for all foreigners to assemble in one room with their possessions, and there was great speculation about what was going to happen to us. Some said we were to be freed, and one or two prisoners asked me to pass on messages to their families, but did not want to put anything in writing. I memorized a few telephone numbers but had little confidence in being able to use them. Then came the question of who was a foreigner, and the order was amended to non-Muslim foreigners, which left only David, Jon and me. We were taken out of the section and after long delays and discussions among the guards we were told to go to the third floor of the same block. There we were put in an empty cell just like the ones downstairs, about six metres by four. There were prisoners walking up and down the corridor but our cell was separated from the others by a small barrier. Soon we were joined by two other non-Iranians, Nicolas Nicola and a Ghanaian, Ibrahim Pasha, or Aswell to use his Hausa name. The door was slammed and we began to organize ourselves. I recognized Aswell as the young black who had once whispered his cell number to me on the prison minibus and asked me to try and get some books or newspapers to him; it had proved impossible, even through the friendliest of guards.

The cell had no water or toilet facilities. To get to them we had to press a button to turn on a light outside. After a long wait a grumpy guard would open the door and, if he felt like it, allow us to go to the ablutions area as a group, or simply tell us he was too busy. We were given strict orders never to talk to any other prisoners. These new conditions were most unsatisfactory and for the next month or so it was a constant battle to get out of the cell. We could not exercise properly because even walking up and down stirred up the dust and upset the others. There was no one in authority to complain to.

For several weeks we had no outside exercise, but our protests eventually led to our being allowed half an hour a day in a small concrete yard. On no account were we to talk to the other prisoners who passed through it from time to time on their way to the workshop. This was a dark Satanic mill that I never actually entered, although I did manage to peep through its windows a few months later while on snow-clearing duty. It was a basement hall containing perhaps 200 workbenches, each with what looked like an industrial sewing machine. The so-called Training Institute was in effect a sweatshop where poor-quality plastic luggage, shoes and, surprisingly, women's clothes were produced.

At first I was glad to be with Nicolas. David and Jon had been together now for over a year and being Americans naturally formed a closely-knit duo. With Nicolas it would be more balanced, I thought. In fact he was extremely disappointing as a cell-mate. His education had been minimal and he could only read haltingly: in practice he rarely even tried. He was a loner, with a passion for firearms which had finally landed him in Evin. After various attempts to become a mercenary, in South America, the Guineas and the Middle East, he had got himself to Pakistan. He had no visa for Iran, but persuaded a taxi driver to take him to the border post. On the way he produced a pistol, ordered the driver out and attempted to drive the car himself across the frontier into the Baluchistan desert, where some Revolutionary Guards disarmed him and took him into custody. We never understood whether he had been tried, and if so what his sentence was.

Nicolas had been turned down by the British army because

ABOVE: Trial by television in Tehran: my first television 'confession', January 1987

BELOW: Press conference at Heathrow, 2 April 1991

ABOVE: Being met at Heathrow airport by my daughter Gisu and brother Paul

LEFT: With Gisu at Heathrow

ABOVE: With Jill Morrell and Brian Keenan delivering a petition to Number 10, Downing Street, in support of John McCarthy in April 1991

RIGHT: Family reunion at Wardington with my father, daughter Gisu and stepmother Anne

ABOVE: Reunion at Wardington with David Rabhan, my American cell-mate, in the summer of 1991

BELOW: With General Sir Peter de la Billière, Brian Clough, John Parrott and John Simpson at the November 1991 Men of the Year Awards. Parrott has just declined my challenge

of his low educational level and poor physique: he was clearly underweight, despite a certain wiry strength. Although he had grown up in London he was liable for military service in Cyprus if he returned there. Whether to go back or not was his major dilemma. On the one hand he would be a soldier at last, but on the other he spoke almost no Greek and could not expect to see much real military action during his service.

While I could not help feeling sorry for Nicolas his case was a serious embarrassment for the British government in its efforts to free me, since there would obviously be requests for his release on humanitarian grounds based on diminished responsibility. This would involve a favour on the part of the Iranians and inevitably delay my own release. Quite soon after we met I remembered the chocolate bar David Reddaway had brought me and asked Nicolas if he had got it. Instead of a smile or a word of thanks he turned on me.

'So you're the bastard who did that?'

'Did what?'

'Sent me that chocolate.'

'I'm sorry, Nicolas, I thought you would like it, or your cell-mates might. What was the matter?'

'I got sent for and I had to hang around this office for an hour until they found this half-melted chocolate bar. I could have done without all that.'

I vowed never again to send a bar of chocolate to a prisoner, especially in hot weather to someone who does not know how to resolidify it in cold water.

Despite his prickly nature both David and I tried to help Nicolas improve his reading skills, but he was not really interested and we soon gave up. What he liked best was to listen to stories of the unusual and mysterious, preferably with hidden treasure or supernatural events, and I racked my brains to think of tales that would entertain him, recycling and embellishing some of Poe's stories from the collection which Paul had brought me. When we finally got permission to go out for exercise Nicolas declined to come, preferring to do body-building exercises in the privacy of the cell while we were outside.

The fifth member of our group was quite a different character.

225

Aswell or Ibrahim – we called him both – was the eldest son of a wealthy landowner in north Ghana, who was also the Friday prayer leader of the main mosque in Accra, an important position in a country where Muslims form a substantial minority, even if politically they are not so influential as the Christians. Ever since the Revolution the Iranians had been looking for Third World countries where they could extend their influence; Ghana was an obvious candidate, and Ibrahim's father was a man to have on their side. When they heard that Ibrahim was studying theology at Al-Azhar university in Cairo they proposed that he should come to Qom to continue his studies at their expense.

In Iran he found himself the target of racial abuse for the first time in his life: Cairo is, after all, an African city, while Iran's legitimate protestations that under Islam all men are brothers has not yet affected popular attitudes. One day he simply left Qom and moved to Tehran. He made friends in the Nigerian embassy, and they looked after him and gave him an office job. His own country did not have any diplomatic representation in Tehran, although Iran had a large embassy in Accra. In due course he started a small business exporting to West Africa such unlikely items as rock salt, with the help of an Iranian partner. He fell in love with an Iranian schoolteacher and even married her, using his knowledge of Islamic law to perform the *sigheh* ceremony himself, since her family would have strongly disapproved. Soon she was pregnant, but money became tight when his export business went through a lean spell. His father had asked him to buy a pair of carpets for the Accra mosque. Ibrahim, seeing a chance to make some money, foolishly altered the export certificate from 2 to 12 carpets and was arrested on fraud charges.

His real crime, however, was almost certainly his frequent criticisms of Iranian influence in Ghana and corruption in Qom. Instead of simply being fined and losing the carpets, followed perhaps by expulsion from the country, which would have been a fair result, he was taken to Evin and interrogated for several months on vague charges of spying for the Nigerians. His marriage was declared unlawful, for which in due course he received 72 lashes, and worse he was simply left to rot in Evin, with an indeterminate sentence. His father, who was invited to Iran every year to take part in an international seminar on the anniversary of the Revolution, declined to plead for his release, and there was no embassy or consulate to help him.

Some of his stories about Qom were appalling. He told us about an Australian woman, an attractive blonde, who had converted to Islam and been invited to Qom to study, with her French husband. A senior cleric had taken a fancy to her and virtually forced her into becoming his concubine under the guise of acting as her spiritual mentor. Many of the older clerics, according to Ibrahim, seduced young boys sent by their parents to study in Qom, and he had received sexual propositions himself. He told us that many followers of Grand Ayatollah Kazem Shariatmadari, who outranked even the Emam in terms of spiritual seniority and was opposed to Iran's becoming a theocracy, believed he had been poisoned. He certainly looked in fine health when I had last interviewed him in 1980. There seemed to be good reasons why the religious authorities in Qom were anxious to keep Ibrahim incommunicado in Evin.

We naturally discussed why we were being segregated from the Iranian prisoners. The most likely reason, which earned me some bitter reproaches, was that the former MKO members had reported my attempts at discussing politics with them, since Jon, David and Nicolas had been mixing freely with Iranian prisoners. David applied to work in the textile factory, and Jon asked for a transfer to Raja'ishahr, a much more pleasant prison some fifty miles west of Tehran, but both requests were refused. It reminded me of when I was studying for my doctorate at Tehran University. We foreign students were segregated in special classes and discouraged from talking to Iranian students, even though both groups would have benefited. We understood that Savak felt such contacts might have adverse political effects.

When Seyyed Mehdi, the newly appointed block commandant, came to see us he claimed our isolation was due to Iran's respect for foreigners. It was felt that we would be more comfortable together in a cell with fewer occupants. We said that this slight advantage was cancelled out by being locked in all day, and we would much prefer to return to where we had been. Mehdi was a decent man, who I think genuinely tried to improve things for

227

us, but was obviously under orders from the new hardline governor. He did eventually get permission from above for our door to be unlocked, but even then we were not allowed to talk to the other prisoners on the same floor.

I heard that an old acquaintance was also in Evin. Maurice Leroux, who was born in South Africa, came to Iran about the same time as I did, married an Armenian, took Iranian nationality, and stayed on after the Revolution. We had both worked years earlier for Homayoun Beklik, the man who recruited me for McDermott as his assistant. Maurice was an engineer and had always worked in and around the oil industry, in recent years representing foreign manufacturers. I kept in touch with him, thinking he might be helpful to me in understanding the politics of the Oil Ministry and the various Iranian oil companies I had to deal with. A few years after the Revolution, Maurice's marriage broke down and his wife emigrated to California, but he had fallen in love with a pretty Muslim divorcée, converted to Islam, and was about to re-marry when he was arrested. At one stage of my interrogation I had been questioned intensively about Maurice. He spoke good Afrikaans, which is close to Dutch, so it was not unreasonable for him to have friends in the Netherlands embassy and he also knew people in the British embassy. That made him a spy in Hosein's view. I did my best to pour cold water on this idea, but soon afterwards I saw some Iranian-made luggage with fresh Amsterdam airport labels in a room used by Hosein to interrogate me and guessed, correctly as it turned out, that Maurice had been arrested on his return from a trip to Europe. He was not in our cell because he insisted on being treated as a Muslim, performing his ablutions and saying his prayers, although according to Ibrahim, who had shared a cell with him, never getting the rituals quite right.

I was keen to communicate with Maurice and learn how his interrogation had gone and what sort of questions they had asked about me, but I could not see a safe way of doing so. I was also worried that he might blame his arrest on his friendship with me. Once Mehdi allowed our cell door to be opened we were given the use of a washroom shared only with a dozen Baha'is, three prisoners in their mid-teens, and occasionally the guards. The youngsters were in gaol on armed robbery charges, and were allowed to use our washroom for their own protection as, whatever else we were, we were not considered pederasts. The Baha'is used it because strict Shi'ites considered them unclean, and prisoners in Evin are often more Catholic than the Pope in such matters, hoping to prove their Islamic credentials. I had exchanged a few words with the teenagers, and finding one of them alone in the washroom one day, I asked him if he knew Maurice. He said he did.

'He's a friend of mine,' I said, 'and I'd like to send him a letter. Would you give it to him? Don't if you don't want to, but if you do please don't tell anyone, even your friends. Perhaps you could just put it on his bed-roll or something. Think about it and let me know.'

The next time I saw him I had my message prepared and he agreed to take it. I am not sure exactly what went wrong, but an *antenna* got wind of it and I was hauled off to the interrogation centre and given a grilling. Luckily my note was an innocuous opening-round, so I simply said that Maurice was an old friend of mine and I could see no good reason why I could not send him greetings. If he wanted, he could be with us in the foreigners' cell. It was nevertheless an awkward situation for me, and I hoped it would not cause trouble for Maurice, who I discovered had been sentenced to six months' gaol for 'having illegal contacts with foreign embassies'. He had already spent eighteen months or so in Evin. Maurice never attempted to contact me after that and I cannot say I blame him. The teenager was embarrassed, especially as I gathered one of his own friends had denounced him.

We were soon joined by an elderly Korean, Mr Song. He had worked in Tehran for several years as a fish exporter, buying species the Iranians did not appreciate, such as needlefish and ribbonfish, which he could market as delicacies in the Far East. He had been arrested when his Iranian partner absconded shortly after shipping a large consignment of caviar to Europe. Mr Song, unable to pay the foreign exchange commitment of several hundred thousand dollars which his partner had left him with, was put into Evin, where he was even less able to sort out his financial affairs. Two more Koreans soon joined us, sea captains in their mid-thirties, also arrested on fishery matters, while their trawlers, modern vessels owned by a Seoul company and worth several million dollars, were impounded. Although the Iranians had close political links and military contracts with North Korea they could not afford to upset South Korea, a major trading partner, and I believe after a year or so Captains Chang and Hong, together with Mr Song, and the trawlers, were all released. South Korea provided Iran with a multi-million-dollar fisheries training scheme in a totally unrelated gesture of goodwill.

The last person to join the foreigners' cell was the red-haired Iraqi whose family I had once encountered in the court building. Romeo Sabri was a flamboyant character, about six foot six tall and red-haired, unlike any Iraqi I had ever met. He came from a well-to-do Assyrian Christian family who owned land in the Kurdish north of Iraq as well as businesses and property in Baghdad. Like all young Iraqis, Romeo had spent years in the army, chiefly as a radio operator, and had been part of the initial invasion of south Iran back in 1980, subsequently serving in various sectors of the front until the mid-80s. Seeing no end to what he thought was an unjust war he finally deserted to Iraqi Kurdistan and then over the border into Iran.

As with many prisoners I met in Evin, Romeo's story was somewhat fluid, with slight variations each time he told it, but it seems he had a passionate affair in Orumiyeh, in north-west Iran, with an ayatollah's daughter, who was herself the commander of a women's combat unit in the area. He must have kept quiet about having a wife and two children in Baghdad, because for a time he lived in the ayatollah's house and several times took phone calls from Majlis Speaker Rafsanjani, he said. His prospective father-in-law, who would not have considered an Iraqi Christian refugee an ideal match for his daughter, might well have had him investigated in an attempt to break up the affair. Whatever the cause, Romeo and the girl eloped across the border to Iraqi Kurdistan, but the ayatollah's arm was long and within days they were caught and brought back. Romeo was accused of abduction, but walked free, despite the ayatollah's objections, when they were married in the courtroom. (Parts of this story, I must say, seem unlikely.)

The next episode in the saga has Romeo sending for his Iraqi

230

wife and children and living in a primitive refugee camp near Tehran, where he organizes a demonstration against conditions. He then obtains some kind of travel document and begins applying for visas to Western countries. A priest offers to intercede on his behalf, provided Romeo spends the weekend with him, an offer which he declines. Somewhere he meets a visa broker, who promises to get German visas, for a price, but the visas he is selling turn out to be forgeries and when the ring is broken up Romeo, his wife and children, together with a number of other refugees trying to leave Iran, are rounded up and taken to Evin for questioning. Not a serious charge, one would think, but the authorities begin to wonder where he got the money to stay in a suite in the former Sheraton Hotel – he claims his Iraqi brother-in-law sent them dollars. Things go from bad to worse and Romeo is soon accused of spying, too.

After being transferred to our cell Romeo caught one or two glimpses of his family as they trooped between the prayer hall and the women's block, but he was never allowed a visit. For his wife's birthday he succeeded in sending a few gifts from the prison shop, and David, the master-cook, somehow managed to concoct a cake for her, which a friendly medic delivered. As I got to know Romeo I worried about his espionage charges, but they seemed so vague I could not take them seriously and felt sure he and his family would soon be freed.

Our courtyard had crude facilities for volleyball and basketball, but we rarely managed to make a quorum for a proper game. I had only played volleyball once before, at the American embassy in Baghdad of all places, when I dislocated a finger and swore I would never play the game again; but with few other sporting opportunities I gradually developed a crafty service and when teamed with either David or Romeo, who were both good players, we could usually beat the trawler captains.

About this time, my relations with David began to deteriorate sharply. He often made deliberately provocative remarks, to which I over-reacted. He called me wishy-washy and a bleeding-heart liberal and I accused him of racism, unjustly I am sure. He may also have disliked the media attention I got from time to time, however hostile it was. What capped it was when a representative had to be chosen for the cell so that officials could deal with just one person when issuing regulations or filling in the endless questionnaires. David had proposed himself, and we all agreed, but Seyyed Mehdi overruled the choice and insisted on my becoming 'cell sheriff' as the post is called in Evin slang, largely I think because I could speak and read Persian better than the others. David objected, and told Mehdi that he would be sheriff, with me as interpreter, but Mehdi disliked his tone and said bluntly that he made the decisions and he wanted me.

The job was not the most exciting I have ever had, the highlight being working out the ablutions cleaning schedule with the Baha'i representative. I needed the co-operation of all my cell-mates, especially David's, given his strong personality and ability to influence others, to make the schedule work and keep the toilets, showers and basins clean. Far from being unclean in the literal sense, the Baha'is were spotlessly hygienic and we soon got the washroom sparkling, despite the poor quality of the fittings and the shortage of cleaning materials. Initially there were about a dozen Baha'is, but several were too elderly for cleaning work and they were successively released, so constant changes in the schedule were required, which led to grumbling on the part of some of my cell-mates. My frequent summonses to the interrogation block on political matters led to rumours that I was an *antenna*, and if I did not condemn everything about Iran, Evin and the guards hurtful innuendoes were made that I was a collaborator, just as though we were prisoners of war. I did not see things in that light.

One of the big advantages of our new cell was that we had a small Valor stove and could obtain limited supplies of spices and canned goods. The only dietary concession in Evin was a dish called 'invalid's food', a salt- and fat-free meat broth containing potatoes and carrots. As served, it was unappetizing and always exactly the same, and by declaring two of us to be invalids we were able to get quite generous quantities. By means of closely guarded techniques and ingredients, which certainly included heavy amounts of chilli and garlic powder, David turned this dreary broth into tasty soups, which transformed our rather scanty suppers into proper two-course meals, although at the cost of losing two portions of regular prison fare. This in turn meant less rice, the only really good food to come from the Evin kitchens.

Because I was now taking regular outdoor exercise I was almost always hungry in the Training Institute. So were the others, of course, and this led to occasionally acrimonious disputes over the division of food. My earnings from translation and, later, money sent to me by Guity made me easily the wealthiest in our cell, but when I tried to give or even 'lend' cash to some of the others resentment arose in some quarters, although the 3000 rials which non-working prisoners in the Teaching Institute receive each month – workers got at least twice that – was inadequate for such items as fruit, writing materials, cigarettes, clothing and toiletries. Mr Song had broken his glasses and when I gave him money for new ones I was criticized on the grounds that the prison would have been obliged to give him free ones since he was destitute. This may have been true, but it would have taken months. Cash was certainly king in Evin, but in the communal blocks, just like food, it caused endless bickerings and even accusations of theft, which I had been spared in the Sanatorium.

Nicolas, wisely in some ways, opted out of our food arrangements, bought almost nothing from the shop and retreated into his own world, while the rest of us divided into two camps, David and Jon in one, the Koreans, Ibrahim and me in the other, with Romeo floating between the two. The Koreans had been insulted by disparaging remarks David had made about their country, and there was soon trouble between Ibrahim and David, who objected to the fact that Ibrahim stayed up most of the night and then slept till noon, which was tolerated by the guards although against prison regulations. A row broke out one day between them over the ownership of a small table, and when Jon intervened on David's side Ibrahim, who was young, tall and vigorous, hit him, not David, which I found unforgivable, given Jon's physique. As cell sheriff and a witness to the incident I had to give Mehdi a written report, in which I strongly criticized Ibrahim, but had to say he had been provoked by David, whose claim that he had also been hit I could not confirm. There was talk of Ibrahim being tried for assault, but luckily Jon was not seriously hurt and in the end Ibrahim was moved back with the Iranians, against his will. These are the kind of things that can happen when otherwise charming and sensible people are thrust together in over-crowded conditions without proper facilities, often suffering from legitimate grievances and under intolerable pressures.

On Boxing Day 1988, Nicolas was suddenly told to pack his things. That autumn there had been painfully slow negotiations between Iranian and British diplomats culminating in a Memorandum of Understanding signed in Vienna under which they would reopen their respective embassies. As a goodwill gesture the Iranians released Nicolas, having known for some time that far from being a British agent he was a mentally disturbed young man obsessed with guns. Mohammad told me a week or two later that when Nicolas had been taken by the British consul to the Ministry of Foreign Affairs to complete the paperwork for his repatriation he had suddenly flared up over nothing in particular and started punching the consul, and had to be restrained by officials. In one of the few letters that reached my daughter I asked her to try and see Nicolas and arrange for him to have some proper counselling, but her attempts to help were rejected.

The man sent out to reopen the British embassy was another Persian-speaking former press attaché, Gordon Pirie, whom I had known from his previous posting there. Gordon was intelligent and knowledgeable about Iran, especially Persian art, but perhaps lacked the toughness required for his new task. He agreed to be interviewed by the hardline *Kayhan* newspaper soon after his arrival, but did not handle the aggressive probings of the interviewer too skilfully and was badly mauled. A month or two later Nicholas Browne, whom I also knew well, a flamboyant character and potential high-flyer, was sent out as chargé d'affaires.

Although I could not help feeling resentful at the Nicolas Nicola business, his release had at least cleared the decks, and I should now be the beneficiary of any further gestures of goodwill. There was, however, a new potential threat to improved Irano-British relations. Back in November I had received a copy of the *Financial Times* containing a long review of a new book by Salman Rushdie, *The Satanic Verses*. The *FT* had reached me several weeks after publication and by then we had already heard rumblings of displeasure over this book, which was seen as a slur on the Prophet Muhammad by a turncoat Muslim. Having read two of Rushdie's previous books, *Shame* and *Midnight's Children*, I was not totally surprised to find him writing about the early years of Islam, however enigmatically, but it was equally clear to me that Rushdie had not written the book as a plot against Islam, as was now being claimed by hotheads in Iran and elsewhere. For a start, a literary novel in English could hardly have much effect on Muslims in the Middle East and elsewhere, and there is no doubt in my mind that, but for the fuss made over it by the Iranians, *The Satanic Verses* would have been consigned to the oblivion many consider it deserves.

It was nevertheless a useful stick to beat the British with. Things became more worrying when demonstrations in Pakistan against its publication threatened to destabilize Benazir Bhutto's government, while in India there was also violence and a number of deaths. It seemed unlikely, however, that this problem would jeopardize relations between Iran and Britain. At heart the Iranians have always been pragmatists, and they must have seen that if the Islamic Republic was to prosper it would have to rebuild the economic ravages of war and revolution. This could realistically only be done with Western, above all European, technical and financial assistance, and willy-nilly this meant improving links with Britain, whose influence in Europe could not be ignored. The *Satanic Verses* affair was a storm in a teacup, I thought, that would blow over in the euphoria generated by the tenth anniversary of the Revolution in early February 1989.

Months before the anniversary excitement began building up among the Iranian prisoners about the prospects of a massive amnesty to mark the occasion, and this spilled over into our little group. We celebrated the New Year with a few glasses of the white wine David and I had produced from a crate of grapes that autumn. We may have argued a bit about the technicalities of fermentation and bottling, but between us, with Jon's help, we had produced an excellent vintage, dry, fruity, with quite a kick, and that is what mattered. We drank each other's health, confident that 1989 was the year when we would all go home.

13

It was the coldest winter for years, with heavy falls of snow almost every week. To prevent our yard icing over after a thaw we attacked the snow as soon as it stopped falling, clearing pathways before it was trodden in and piling it into the centre, where the Koreans created a beautiful and unusual snowman, called simply 'Man', much admired by guards and prisoners alike. Without proper shovels it was slow going, but it was the first real physical work I had done for years, and I loved it. David would criticize our methods from the sidelines, while Jon walked up and down by himself, lost in thought and discouraging company. Romeo worried constantly about his family and forthcoming trial, rehearsing his six-point defence aloud during the exercise period or practising German with me.

Despite our often stormy relationship I usually walked with David; he taught me about clouds and navigation and weather prediction, or discussed his latest business idea, and I gave him French lessons. He had a proper French course book, but was impatient with grammar, especially irregular verbs. 'When I take over as World President I'll abolish irregular verbs,' he used to say. 'What's the *point* of them?' He had no patience with anything old, either. 'All houses should be torn down and rebuilt every thirty years,' he would say, probably to annoy me as much as anything. 'Design and technology are advancing all the time, and houses should keep up.' David insisted on controlling the French lessons, and got quite cross if I used a word from the next chapter, even though he had worked his way through the book once already. This meant I had to read the lesson he was currently studying and structure the conversation accordingly, leading to such exchanges as:

'What is that, David?'

'It is a wall.'

'What colour is the wall?'

'The wall is grey.'

'Is the wall tall?'

'Yes, it is tall.'

'How many people are in the courtyard?'

'We haven't done courtyard yet!'

'Sorry, how many people are in the garden, David?'

'There are six people in the garden.'

We often got into religious discussions with our guards. At Christmas one of the local newspapers printed a large portrait of Jesus, looking distinctly Iranian, which David cut out and pinned up. The guards were interested in this as they see Jesus as a major prophet and precursor of Muhammad. They even consider Jesus a Muslim, along with all the prophets recognized by Islam, starting with Adam and including Abraham, Moses and John the Baptist, much as Russian Communists used to consider Tolstoy as 'one of them'. David would say casually, 'You know Jesus was Jewish, I suppose?' This was considered a joke in extremely poor taste, but I would confirm it, adding that every single prophet before Muhammad was Jewish. I would ask innocently why, since they do not accept the great sixth-century BC Persian prophet Zoroaster as a divine prophet, God never sent the Iranians, or indeed the Romans or Greeks, a prophet of their own.

We were occasionally visited by the chaplain of Evin, a young mullah whose brother, Asadollah Bayat, was deputy speaker of the Majlis. He was no match for our polemical skills, never having debated with anyone who was not already a Muslim. When we trapped him into some untenable position he would get confused and embarrassed, and say, 'That's a very interesting point. I'll think about it and let you know next week.' He never did, and if we reopened the discussion he simply made further excuses. David had a good knowledge of the Quran and would sometimes quote a verse that contradicted the chaplain, who would temporize, 'The Quran's too difficult for you. Don't read it yet. I'll explain it bit by bit,' to which David would say, with me translating, 'But in Sura xii.2 God says, "We have sent this Quran down as a clear

237

discourse so that you may understand"',' causing the mullah even more embarrassment. He was fair game, having studied for half a dozen years at a Qom theological college, while the guards, most of whom had only five years of primary education, were not usually worth debating with, as they knew little about Islam beyond the basic rituals and a few legends.

The Koreans mainly walked and talked by themselves, but sometimes Captain Chang would give me a Korean lesson. I learned quite a few words and phrases, and was told I had a good accent, though I think this was chiefly oriental politeness. We had seen a little of the Seoul Olympic games on television – female and American athletes were never shown – and this whetted my appetite to visit Korea one day. The guards were also interested in Korea. 'Is it true you eat dogs?' they asked, never getting a straight answer.

Before the snow came I had become friendly with the prisoner responsible for our block's garden, and helped him sweep up litter and leaves. The garden was so small that there was really almost nothing to do once summer was over. His name was Abbas Tabakhi, an Iranian of about my age, who to my surprise said he was a British subject. He had settled in London after the Revolution and married a girl called Maureen. We exchanged our London phone numbers and promised that whoever got out first would contact the other's family. These conversations were illegal, but in winter the guards were less strict and we could chat as we shook snow off the trees or stacked it around the dozen rose bushes. Abbas told me that he was charged with being a supporter of one of the opposition groups in Paris, the monarchists I believe. The truth was, he said, he had stopped off in Paris on his way to Iran – he had come to see his aged mother, probably for the last time – and had met a few acquaintances there who were opposed to the regime, but he himself was not interested in politics and was not a member of any group.

As the tenth anniversary approached and it was officially announced that preparations were being made for the largest ever amnesty, Abbas became quite excited. The first group of amnestees in his corridor had already been informed, but he was not among them. 'There are two more groups still to come, so I am sure to be on one of the lists, don't you think? What have you heard?' I had heard even less than Abbas, but if his story was true it did seem likely that he would soon be freed. To give him some encouragement I said that there must be a lot of paperwork involved with such a large amnesty, because every prisoner released had to provide a guarantee of future good behaviour, unserved time being technically suspended rather than cancelled. 'I'm sure the process will be over by Now Ruz, Abbas, despite these delays,' I said.

Meanwhile the *Satanic Verses* affair dragged on. British politicians were being as conciliatory as possible, but it was not enough for the extremists, who persuaded the Emam to issue his famous *fatwa* against Salman Rushdie and the book's publishers, ironically on Valentine's Day. Nicholas Browne, the British chargé, asked for clarification from the Foreign Ministry and was assured by Dr Javad Larijani, the California-educated deputy foreign minister, that the *fatwa* should not be a barrier to better relations 'because the Emam is not part of the government'. That day I was summoned to the interrogation centre and asked what I thought about the affair, and what Mrs Thatcher's reaction might be if it escalated. I analysed it from the beginning and explained that however much the British government deplored the book – which they clearly did – there was nothing they could do to ban its publication, and they would be obliged to give Rushdie full protection against the danger he now faced.

I concluded by saying that I thought Dr Larijani would almost certainly be forced to resign for the implications of his remark about the Emam, and I thought it possible that even Foreign Minister Velayati might be forced out of office. A man I judged to be from the Foreign Ministry was astonished and angry at this, but I simply said, 'You asked my opinion and that's what it is.' Two days later Larijani's resignation was announced and Dr Velayati found himself under such pressure from the Majlis hardliners that when a bill was rushed through giving Britain an unacceptable ultimatum over the issue he actually supported it, although he must have been totally opposed to the break in relations that inevitably followed. My hopes of release collapsed, and I resigned myself to a further two years in Evin, at the very least.

The only consolation for me in all this was the glee felt by the interrogators when my prediction over Dr Larijani proved correct. I had already received some plaudits for forecasting that Sir Geoffrey Howe would be replaced as Foreign Secretary, having read an article in the *Financial Times* on the subject, although I did not get that quite right. Howe certainly went, but when I was asked what I knew about his successor, John Major, I said there was no such person; they must have got the name wrong. Douglas Hurd would be the new Foreign Secretary. I had to eat my words when I found that Mrs Thatcher had appointed the Chief Secretary to the Treasury, whose name was unknown to me, to run Britain's diplomacy. I said it was a strange appointment, and probably indicated that Mrs Thatcher wanted to control foreign policy herself. When Hurd did take over a few months later and Major became Chancellor of the Exchequer one of the interrogators said, 'You see, Cooper knows better than Mrs Thatcher.' It was even more of a coup to predict a major unexpected change in Iranian political circles, and the interrogators, who considered me an asset of theirs, were delighted that the Ministry of Intelligence had thus scored over the Foreign Ministry. It was from leakages about such incidents that the rumour started in Tehran that I was secretly advising the Iranian government, and that my detention in Evin was a cover. After my release I was sent a cartoon from a Tehran satirical magazine which showed a reporter asking the Foreign Minister, 'Why was Roger Cooper freed?' Dr Velayati replies, 'Was he in prison?'

Meanwhile David too had suffered a set-back. Out of the blue Jimmy Carter had sent two letters to Tehran, one addressed to the Emam and the other to Majlis Speaker Rafsanjani. The letters were identical, asking for help to secure the release of the US hostages in Lebanon and start to heal the political rift between the two countries, but the one to Rafsanjani had a postscript asking for the release of 'my friend David Rabhan'. If Carter had written to only one of them, particularly if he had written secretly to Rafsanjani, some good might have come of it, but it was a serious breach of protocol – and even good business practice – to send identical letters to the two most influential men in Iran. The texts were published in the local press, and even the guards were convinced David would soon be freed. David himself did not think so, and I was also dubious. The initiative fizzled out as Rafsanjani could do nothing once the Emam's hardline son had rejected the olive branch.

Our block began to empty rapidly. All the Baha'is were released except one, who had been 'charged with a real crime', as one of the guards amusingly put it, and so was our friendly doctor, possibly a Tudeh supporter. His surgery was on the ground floor by our exercise yard and he would give us what he could in the way of relief from cold symptoms: living cheek by jowl in such conditions we had coughs and sore throats constantly. We saw the doctor on television taking part in the anniversary march-past in front of the Majlis building. Like other amnestied prisoners he was holding up a banner that proclaimed remorse for past crimes and confidence in the way the Revolution was going.

Some other departures were not so cheerful, however. Suddenly Farhad the shopkeeper, Akbar the barber and one or two other prisoners I knew slightly were no longer around. The Training Institute shop never had much stock, but Farhad had always been fair to us, and Akbar, like most barbers, was a mine of information, except about his own case. It was often difficult to get confirmation, but we soon heard on the grapevine that they had been executed. The terms of the amnesty and sentence reductions looked good, until we read the fine print. Spies and armed robbers, plus various other categories, including prisoners not yet sentenced, were all excluded under its terms, so not one of us benefited.

One day I came down to the yard, having arranged to do some work for Abbas. There was no sign of him, and when I asked a guard his air of slight embarrassment made me assume the worst. Another prisoner on his corridor, whom I knew by sight, confirmed my fears. I asked in sign language across the yard if he knew where Abbas was and he replied by drawing a finger across his throat indicating, Evin-style, that he had been executed. When I met Maureen Tabakhi after my release she confirmed that her husband had indeed been executed early in the spring of that year, according to an official statement months later. He probably spent those last few weeks in the Sanatorium.

*

The weeks and months following the tenth anniversary celebrations were depressing for all of us. Evin was emptying, but none of us could see any progress in our individual cases, or even find out what was going on. Incredible though it seems, Iran and Iraq had never broken diplomatic links despite being in a state of full-scale war for almost eight years. Now that a shaky peace had come they finally did so, dashing Romeo's slender hopes that better relations would result in repatriation, although he still said he was afraid to return to his country. Even the question of prisoners of war remained unsettled, despite Red Cross efforts to effect a complete exchange. The sea-captains, although not Mr Song, had a consular visit, during which they received a Korean Bible but little else. Ibrahim's country, Ghana, had no diplomatic presence in Iran. He thought that Britain was probably responsible for the welfare of Ghanaian citizens, so he was in the same boat as me. David and Jon were visited by a Swiss official, who offered no hope beyond saying he would try to see that any food parcels sent by their families via Bern were delivered. Shortly after Christmas, Gordon Pirie had brought gifts from my family, but although I saw them few reached me. After the *fatwa* I knew it would be a long time before another British official visited me.

Suddenly it was Ramadan again. I decided not to fast that year because the atmosphere was not right. With our stove we could reheat the rice at normal meal-times, but following complaints from fasters down the corridor about the cooking smells our stove was confiscated, and we took to eating the main meal when it arrived about 2 AM and snacking on bread, fruit and water till sundown. David and Jon had turned an old blanket into a snug-fitting tea-cosy that kept our large tea-kettle warm for several hours, since we had no access to the corridor's urns, but during Ramadan there was no tea for seventeen hours.

About this time Ayatollah Mohammadi-Reyshahri, the Minister for Intelligence, made what I believe was the only detailed official statement about my case during my imprisonment. At a televised news conference he answered an obviously planted question – an Iranian reporter never asks the country's top intelligence official a question without prior clearance – by describing me as a 'notori-ous spy who must undergo his Islamic punishment'. As proof of my guilt he said that he had evidence that I had spied against the Russians during World War II. He did not of course mention that I had recently finished translating a book of his, or that when the war ended I was ten years old. It was frustrating, to say the least, having to watch this conference from a prison cell without the right of reply and with the British government not taking the trouble to reply on my behalf.

About a week after the start of Ramadan one of the most frightening experiences of my time in Evin occurred. Without warning, late in the day, David, Romeo and I were ordered to pack our possessions. *Kolliye vasa'el* ('all your things') is the most chilling command a prisoner at Evin ever hears, because these words normally precede an execution. If Jon or one of the others had been included we would not have been so afraid, but there seemed no good reason why we three should be taken away. We sat for hours in the entrance hall of the block awaiting instructions, then we were moved outside in the dark and told to sit on the roadway between the Training Institute and the Sanatorium. Romeo and I were the most worried. David had an official gaol sentence with just under a year to run. In view of his age, years of pre-sentence detention and Jimmy Carter's letter, there was a chance that he was going to be granted an 'early' release. On the other hand, I was under a death sentence and Ayatollah Reyshahri's remarks could mean it was now going to be carried out. Abbas Tabakhi, after all, was technically a British subject and there had been no outcry in the UK over his death. Romeo also admitted, for the first time, that he thought he might have received a death sentence as a spy: he was not quite sure whether he had been tried or not. We hoped against hope that we were being moved to another communal cell, but when orders came for us to proceed to the Sanatorium, we feared the worst. Expecting to be put in solitary cells we embraced each other, knowing that we might never see each other again.

To our surprise we were put together in No. 345, a cell slightly larger than the one I had been in for almost three years, No. 336, although we were still quite cramped. Bespectacled Hosein was on duty and asked me why I had returned. I joked that I preferred it here, but had to admit I had no idea. We slept badly that night, but by mid-morning when no summons came we began to feel better. That evening Jon joined us, and despite the further pressure on space we were overjoyed to see him. He himself had no idea why his transfer had been delayed.

We remained about ten days in cell 345, without shower or exercise privileges, or even space to move around. It was bad enough by day, but at night my bedding and feet got wet from the leaking WC, which the guards said could not be repaired. One night two more prisoners joined us, despite our protests. Luckily they were both slightly built and by moving all our possessions into the corridor it was just possible for the six of us to stretch out on the floor, although turning over was a problem. They were both merchants, well-dressed and educated, and had been arrested that day, without being told why, they said. Despite the space problem we welcomed their arrival as our first contact with the outside world, although they were extremely cautious of what they said in case we were *antennas*. In the morning they were taken away and we never saw or heard of them again.

Meanwhile the prisoner in cell 344 had been knocking on our wall. There is a way of communicating with an adjacent cell by talking into the plughole of the washbasin, but it can be picked up by an *antenna* down the line. I found that if I climbed up to the window and one of the others listened by the door for an approaching guard I could converse with our neighbour fairly safely. Bahram told me he had been arrested as part of a so-called 'American network' that we had read about briefly in the Training Institute – our newspapers had once again been cut off, so there was not much we could tell him about the case. The network was said to include members of the armed forces, particularly the navy, and the oil industry, where Bahram worked. 'My only crime is that I studied in the United States and I don't hate the Great Satan,' he told me. There was a note of slight panic in his voice, and I did my best to reassure him, although without much confidence. The combination of espionage charges, defence and oil secrets, the United States and Iranian nationality was not promising. A year or so later it was announced that the members of this alleged American spy ring had all been executed.

Our complaints about the conditions finally bore fruit and we were moved to number 468, a large cell at the far end of the top floor. Leading off it was a tiny room containing a washbasin, WC in the floor and shower above. There was even a door that shut, a great relief after the all-too-public toilet arrangements of number 345.

To my surprise, Romeo asked me if I would fast for the remaining two weeks of Ramadan. Although born a Christian, he had apparently converted to Islam at the time of his mysterious marriage to the ayatollah's daughter, but without being circumcised. He even sent a message to the clinic that he wanted to have this operation done, despite my warnings that Evin was not a suitable place for such delicate surgery. Whether he thought it would impress the authorities if he practised Islam, or whether he really had converted, I never discovered. I noticed that several times a day he disappeared into the toilet for a long time, and there was a slight smell of cigarette smoke when he came out. Smoking, of course, like eating or drinking, invalidates a fast, though I was too polite to remind Romeo of this piece of Islamic law which he may have overlooked.

My relations with David continued to deteriorate, and we constantly bickered over trivialities. Luckily, just as things were becoming intolerable I was sent a copy of the printed version of the book I had translated for Ayatollah Mohammadi-Reyshahri. It had been published in London, by what looked like a vanity publisher, but printed in Iran, presumably to save foreign exchange, and the result was disastrous: there must have been 20 or 30 typographic and other errors on each page. My name was not given as the translator, I was glad to see, but if it was widely distributed someone would sooner or later point out how poor it was, and I might be accused of sabotage. So I wrote an urgent letter suggesting it should be withdrawn and offering to correct the text. I could not help reminding the author that I had warned what would happen if I did not personally correct the typescript and galley proofs. My offer was accepted, so I imposed a condition. I could not do this sensitive work in a communal cell, and should be given a solitary cell nearby to work in. Bespectacled Hosein co-operated; the prisoner next door in cell 469 was moved and I was allowed to spend mornings and afternoons in what became known as 'the translation bureau'. Gradually I moved my possessions until, despite a few arguments with guards, I spent most of my time there, only returning to 468 for my morning shower and the occasional meal, or to watch the evening news on television, which the others liked me to translate for them.

Exercise privileges were resumed, although only for about half an hour, and not every day, and it was on one of these outings that Romeo was suddenly taken away. When we got back from the yard he and his belongings had gone, causing us considerable anxiety. A friendly guard assured us, however, that this was only for the duration of his trial, and that afterwards he would return. I even managed to send him some money for cigarettes and fruit, because I knew he was broke and our monthly allowance had been stopped. Within a week he was back, looking more relaxed and saying the trial had gone well.

We never discovered why we had been moved back to the Sanatorium. The theory that it was because of our cooking during Ramadan seemed implausible once the holy month was over. More probably it was because in the Training Institute it was much easier for us to find out what was going on in the prison and the outside world. Here we were really cut off. A good example of our incommunicado state occurred one day in early June. When Javad came round at 7.30 AM to light the first of the day's three cigarettes with his spirit lamp, I noticed a look of grief on his face. I almost said something, but decided it was better to wait until I had spoken to another guard. Obviously Javad had lost a close relative and I should offer my condolences. When the next guard, Vali, came on duty he had the same expression. This could only mean one thing, I thought: the Emam must be dead. We had heard from a guard that he had recently undergone a minor operation successfully, but perhaps this had only been put out to prepare public opinion, as when my brother had died. So I asked Vali what the matter was. He pulled himself together and said, 'Nothing.'

Meanwhile, we were discussing my theory in the cell. David inevitably disagreed with me, as did Jon, with Romeo uncertain, so when Reza came round with supper that night I put on my most mournful face and said, 'On behalf of myself and the others,

Reza, I offer you sincere condolences on the demise of the Emam, Khomeini the Great.' He looked surprised and said, 'How did you know?' I replied, 'I knew in my heart and saw it in your face.' Reza knew I had slightly tricked him, and said, 'We were told not to tell the prisoners, but you'll find out sooner or later. Just don't say I told you.'

We had speculated about this event for months, having realized from occasional glimpses of the Emam on television that he could not live for much longer. The only time he had spoken publicly in recent months, and then only a few halting words, was when Soviet Foreign Minister Eduard Shevardnadze came to Iran and had an audience with the great man, becoming the first foreign statesman to be so honoured in years. The visit was the result of a letter the Emam had sent to President Gorbachev informing him that Communism was dead and he should look to Islam as a successor ideology. When Communism did collapse a year or two later this initiative was hailed as proof of the Emam's mystic prescience, and it certainly can be seen in that light, but I believe he was really echoing the semi-mythical story that Muhammad wrote to the rulers of his day inviting them to embrace Islam, and the Emam was determined to do the same thing himself before it was too late. Gorbachev was reportedly furious when this letter was read out to him by the robed envoy from the Islamic Republic, but he put on a brave face and cleverly sent his foreign minister to Tehran to make polite noises and obtain some trade concessions. There were even plans for some young Soviet citizens to study Shi'a Islam in Qom.

Now the Emam was dead and we would soon learn – but only indirectly and from unreliable sources – whether the power struggle between contenders for his mantle would actually take place, and if so whether we would be caught in the cross-fire. We were all a little apprehensive, for whatever his faults the Emam had kept a rough balance between the hardliners and the moderates. We were already in a sector controlled by the hardliners, and if they seized total power we would obviously be in a much worse position.

Soon after the Emam's death we lost Romeo. I was in my private cell, but with summer now in full blaze, the little south-facing room became intolerably hot, too hot for translation work, I insisted, and I had got permission to keep the 'letterbox' in the cell door open. I could hear a guard telling Romeo the dreaded words, '*Kolliye vasa'el*'. Only a few days earlier he had received a visit from his wife (his Iraqi wife, that is), and she had brought him a light jacket as a present. Sewn into the lining was a short message written in numerically coded Assyrian, which I thought was odd, saying how much she loved him and was looking forward to their being united. She had finished her six-month sentence for illegal border crossing and was back in a refugee camp with the children. Romeo was overjoyed and thought the visit was an omen that things would soon be better for him. He might go free, or at the worst have only six months to serve himself.

Now I saw the visit in another light. I had heard that prisoners to be executed often received a family visit beforehand. That must have been why he had at last been allowed to see his wife. I knocked on the door and asked the guard to let me into the big cell. I could see at once that Romeo knew what was in store. He took his bedding and small bag, but waved to his books and said to me, 'I won't need those.' We embraced him in turn and muttered that it looked as if he was going to be released, but none of us believed it. Romeo himself looked ashen. The guard told him to hurry and he went out, closing the door behind him.

We tried hard to discover what had happened. The guards began by saying they did not know, or that he had been moved back to the Training Institute. Ali Lotfi even said he had been freed. 'That's good news,' I said, 'we were afraid he had been executed.' 'Executed? Nobody is executed in Evin any more,' he replied unconvincingly. By chance the new head of Shobeh 13 passed through the yard while we were at exercise a few days later and we asked where Romeo was. 'Romeo Sabri? Yes, I remember, he's been moved to Raja'ishahr prison. It's near to the camp where his family are living, so they can visit him more easily than in Evin.' It sounded convincing, and our hopes were raised for a while. David refused to believe it, though. 'If that guy said "Good morning" to me I'd look at my watch to see what time it was,' he said.

During my next session of questioning about internal politics I asked one of the interrogators, 'Why was Romeo executed? He told me all he did wrong was to try and get a visa from a dodgy middleman.'

'Romeo? Oh yes, the tall Iraqi redhead. He would say that, wouldn't he? No, he was a dangerous terrorist. He was caught with explosives near Ahwaz. He was a top Iraqi agent.'

Truth is a rare commodity in Evin, and we never did learn the full story, but once they knew that we knew the guards gradually confirmed that Romeo was dead. Even before his execution I had been demoralized. Now my spirits sank even lower. What made his death particularly hard to bear was that the day before he was taken away we had quarrelled.

Romeo was a heavy smoker, and the ration of three cigarettes a day was not nearly enough for him, so when we moved back to the Sanatorium he asked me to declare myself a smoker and give him my ration. The guards were naturally surprised at this request, remembering my insistence at being put into a no-smoking cell when I was moved to the Training Institute. Evin policy, to its credit, was to discourage smoking, so to help Romeo I claimed that I had been driven to cigarettes by the uncertainty of my fate. To overcome any possible scepticism I would often light a cigarette from the spirit lamp when the guard came round, and once he had gone pass it to Romeo. This ensured him six cigarettes a day, and in addition, because of my good relations with the guards I could often get him a third or even fourth pack of Oshnu, the coarse oriental-leaf cigarette sold to prisoners.

Although I did not smoke myself and strongly disliked a smoky atmosphere I often thought it would be useful to have a pack on me when I went to the interrogation block, so as to be able to offer one to a desperate smoker on the bus coming back or in the Prison Office waiting-room. The quarrel occurred when I made the mistake of telling Romeo that I intended to keep one of the two packs of cigarettes I had just received for this purpose. He nearly hit the roof, so important to him was his ration of nicotine, although I told him that the pack would probably last me one or two months. His reaction annoyed me and I refused to back off, reminding him that the cigarettes in question were mine, even paid for by me, like all those he smoked, because he had no cash. He sulked for the rest of the day and I had almost decided to give him the pack and replace it next week without telling him, but before I could do this he was taken away. Our last embrace had been as warm as possible in the circumstances, but I could not help blaming myself, however illogically, that the last time we had spoken properly had been a silly disagreement over a pack of cigarettes.

The next time a guard came round with the spirit lamp I instinctively lit one. Without Romeo to take it from me I smoked it myself. It made me think what a good companion he had been, how he had always supported me, with infinite tact, in my arguments with David, and what good advice he had given me, after lights out in whispered Persian, about how to handle our disagreements. He was also good at crosswords, especially, of course, when obscure Arabic words were involved. Luckily I still had a large stack of unsolved ones from my stay in the Training Institute. I had received three daily newspapers there, but because of the distractions of a communal cell had only solved one or two crosswords a day, clipping the others and keeping them for a rainy day. Romeo's English was not good enough to read any of my books, but he loved to work at what he called a 'fabriki', or virgin, crossword, usually getting bored half-way through and giving it back to me for completion.

Virgins, in fact, were often on his mind. In Iraq he had had many girlfriends, the best of whom were virgins, he said. His face would light up and he would kiss the fingers of his right hand, like a stage Frenchman, as he remembered a particular 'fabriki' he had picked up outside a Baghdad high school. 'Fabriki', a Franco-Persian word meaning 'straight from the factory', was his highest compliment for a woman or a crossword. David would argue with him on this subject, saying that no 'fabriki' could compare with an experienced and loving woman, while I secretly thought that many of Romeo's romantic encounters were the product of his imagination. I even wondered whether he felt under pressure to live up to the popular image of his unusual Christian name. Romeo's romantic streak came through strongly in his poems, which were technically first-class, according to the rules

250

of classical Arabic prosody, although it is difficult to be sure about poetry in a language other than one's own. I translated several quatrains of his, spending hours matching the sense and images of the Arabic with non-stilted contemporary English. Several were about his wife, and one in particular described how when she first came on the scene, as his true princess, all her predecessors faded into nothingness. That poem rang so true that I would not have been totally surprised to learn that the affair with the ayatollah's daughter never happened. The more I thought about it, in fact, the less probable it seemed. None of this, however, prevented Romeo from being a good companion at the time, my best friend in gaol, and his execution affected me deeply.

It was followed some two months later by news of my mother's death. She kept her intelligent mind and strong will to the end, but her body simply wore out and on 3 August 1989 she died peacefully in her sleep, at the age of 95. From the reports I had received and the sheer number of years she had lived I should not have been surprised, I suppose, but I somehow assumed that her determination to see me again would enable her to hang on until my release. The news of her death, conveyed to me over a crackly telephone line by my daughter, therefore came as an unexpected blow. The guards, who must have known what the news was, as I half did myself, watched me dispassionately to see if I would burst into tears, which is what they consider the proper reaction. Being British I did not, but could feel a numb coldness inside and a tingling in the eyes. I sat in the prison office for a while after the brief phone call – the prison was paying for the only call I was ever allowed to receive – and went back to cell 468, where David and Jon, who both had widowed mothers, gave me comforting condolences. Although I have always tried to avoid bitterness at the way the Islamic Republic treated me, I could not resist cursing inwardly those responsible for my continued detention and the uncertainty of my fate even after almost four years in gaol. I had now lost my mother, a brother and my last uncle. Who would be next?

The combination of these two deaths must have exacerbated the depression I was already sinking into, and that in turn triggered off a recurrence of the hiatus hernia I had suffered from briefly ten years earlier. The symptoms were more severe this time, with unpleasant acid reflux whenever I lay down, and bouts of indigestion. At least I knew what it was, however, since the chances of getting a proper diagnosis from Evin's inadequate medical services were slight and I might have feared stomach cancer. Gastric disorders are common in Evin and peeping under my blindfold after a shower or exercise I could see that almost every cell in the Sanatorium had a bottle of the white aluminium liquid that is the only medicine available.

The next few months were in many ways the worst I went through in Evin. I lost the will to read or study and spent almost all my time alone in cell 469, sweltering in one of the hottest summers for years and feeling sorry for myself. There were disappointments on the political front, too. The power vacuum created by the Emam's death was filled in a compromise when the hardline President Ali Khamene'i, only a *hojatalislam* ('proof of Islam') and barely 50, was unexpectedly chosen as Supreme Leader – although without the title Emam. He was hurriedly promoted to Ayatollah ('token of Allah'), but his relative youth and lack of clerical seniority forced the authorities to state that the aged and almost moribund Grand Ayatollah Eraqi was now the supreme arbiter on theological matters, for Grand Ayatollah Montazeri, elected by the clergy as the Emam's destined successor, had been unceremoniously ousted (apparently at the instigation of Ahmad Khomeini) only months before the Emam died, and was now virtually under house arrest in a small village south of Qom. Montazeri was particularly popular in Evin since he had made strongly worded remarks in favour of prisoners' rights.

It became clear that after the ousting of Montazeri the Emam had not nominated a successor, which meant that those provisions of the Constitution should have been invoked whereby the leadership should pass to three or five senior clerics if no single *faqih*, or supreme jurist, commanded universal acclaim. It reminded me of the death of the Prophet Muhammad in 632, when the absence of clear guidelines about the succession led to the Sunni–Shi'a divide that has plagued Islam ever since. Inevitably statements were put out that the Emam had wanted President Khamene'i to succeed him, but they lacked conviction. The only good news from our point of view was that Majlis Speaker Ali Akbar Hashemi Rafsanjani, a pragmatist or moderate in Iranian terms, was duly elected President with the additional executive powers the post now carried after the Constitution was revised at his behest. It was becoming increasingly clear, however, that he could do nothing until the economy began to pick up, while the hardliners in the Majlis and many other key positions were determined to block the structural reforms that economic revival depended on. Iran was therefore doomed to muddle along indefinitely, or at least until President Rafsanjani, or some other leader, could get a mandate for real change.

My depression, or at least its intensity, lifted somewhat dramatically on 22 September 1989, when without advance warning I suddenly found myself face to face with my sister-in-law Lili Lion, Paul's wife. I did not know Lili well because I had rarely even been in the same country as her, and I often felt that the antipathy between Dan and Paul had made her wary of further contacts with our family other than her mother-in-law, who treated her like a daughter. Lili is of German-Jewish origins, but grew up, luckily for her, in Italy. She is a talented artist, of a somewhat dreamy and impractical nature, and my first thought was a selfish one: 'It's a bad sign that Paul couldn't get a visa. Lili's a woman, and she's never been to Iran before. What possible good can her visit do?' I was soon to be proved wrong.

Typically, Lili had brought me something splendidly impractical that was exactly right: a large bunch of English country-house flowers picked that morning in the gardens of the British embassy, where she was staying as the guest of Carl Akesson, the Swedish head of the British Interests Section. 'Flowers grown on what is technically British soil,' I thought, and they immediately seemed extra-special. She told me about my mother's funeral in Wimbledon, not far from Red Branch House, on the edge of the Common, where she was born and Collin and Torr House, the nursing home where she died. They had sung her father's best-known song 'Father O'Flynn', despite the objections of the officiating deacon, though whether these reservations were because the song immortalizes a Catholic priest or because it is not a hymn Lili did not say. Paul sent with her a long letter about the funeral which was

253

never handed over, nor did I get the two or three copies of it he sent later.

Lili also told me about the 'Friends of Roger Cooper Society' that had recently been formed. It started with a small group of close friends, mainly journalists and people I had known in Iran, but gradually expanded to include friends from the more distant past with whom I had lost touch. The initials FRCS, which members were supposed to add to their names, were designed to amuse, or more probably annoy, Harley Street. It was never a large lobby group like the 'Friends of John McCarthy', whose advertisements occasionally got past the Evin censor, but it served as a clearing-house when I was able to write letters relatively freely – roughly from the end of 1989 to mid-1990 – and the FRCS also did its best to send me books and other items I wanted. The first organizer was Emma, a former girlfriend, which I found almost as moving as Guity's efforts to visit me, accompanied by her mother, when her brother Mohsen was still in gaol and she knew that any contact with the notorious British spy was politically most incorrect. John Hatt FRCS, founder of the enterprising travel publishing firm Eland Books, wrote to me enviously, convinced that there was a Society for the Enemies of John Hatt, and that it was planning to hold its annual general meeting in the Albert Hall.

When Lili got back to London she wrote a report for FRCS members about her visit, which is worth quoting, especially since I never knew or in some cases had forgotten much of what she described or else had seen it in a different light.

Lili was accompanied by Carl Akesson, the Swedish diplomat. The Swedish Ambassador, Hakan Granqvist, had come to see me in April that year, within a few days of his arrival *en poste*, together with his consul, Rolf Wiktor. When presenting his credentials to President Khamene'i the ambassador had cut through the diplomatic small talk and asked if he could visit me at once. The President obviously felt obliged to agree to this unusual request and the next day the two Swedish diplomats had turned up at Evin with a presidential order to see me. The ambassador promised to follow my case up and arrange consular meetings, but the authorities failed to co-operate and I never did receive the formal consular meeting I had demanded throughout my imprisonment. I remain deeply grateful to Ambassador Granqvist for going so far out of his way to protect my interests, when most diplomats would have put bilateral relations, whether political or commercial, ahead of the embarrassing case of a third-party national accused of espionage.

Apparently I told Lili that I had 'lost concentration' in my studies and had recently 'looked at the maths papers of a year ago, and could not make head or tail of them'. I asked her for books, saying I had not received any for a long time. Describing my appearance Lili wrote 'Roger did not look well. He was very pale. The skin around his eyes was thin, and he had a very strained expression. He had a short stubble, but looked clean.' She added that I was vomiting a lot and thought I 'had a stomach ulcer as a result of depression and anxiety', contradicting my memory that I had diagnosed the problem as hiatus hernia.

She goes on to say that I 'had been given a bad time recently because of Fuladi. In saying this he got quite agitated, gesticulating and pointing at the guards . . . I had a feeling they had said they would get revenge for Fuladi on him . . . Roger repeated twice that they had given him a hard time . . . and they responded with slightly devilish laughter. They looked pleased with themselves for what they had done, whatever it may have been.' Three years later I simply cannot recall this part of the meeting.

While Carl was talking to the officials (whom Lili calls guards) I apparently told her about my death sentence. She commented in her report, 'Since he told Mr Granqvist nothing about this in April I imagine it was fairly recent. He clearly believed they were capable of carrying it out, saying, "I know it would create a great scandal in London and Tehran, but that wouldn't stop them doing it." He had a fatalistic expression on his face, making it clear that he saw this as a real possibility. I felt that Roger was so desperate that he had to say all these things to me. He needed to let us know what was going on. He was desperate and very angry. Accusing his guards, with whom he has to establish some modus vivendi, of giving him a bad time was a measure of how bad things were and how he felt.'

I have completely forgotten this and am puzzled that Lili was unaware of my death sentence, about which I had told Paul a year earlier. Perhaps he had not wished the family to know.

I had also forgotten that she brought me a copy of the *Tehran Times* with my translation of a poem by the Emam, published soon after his death. I had heard, third- or fourth-hand via the guards, that something had appeared in my name, but I was stunned at the two-page spread that Lili gave me, which being a local newspaper I was allowed to keep.

The poem was a *ghazal*, an Arabic-Persian verse-form that is possibly the ancestor of the sonnet. It was written in the style of the 14th-century Shirazi poet Hafez, and published in all the local media by his son Ahmad within weeks of the Emam's death. It contains the traditional references to wine and taverns that lovers of Omar Khayyam are familiar with. I imagine Ahmad Khomeini was worried that the opposition might have made some satirical mileage out of the suggestion that his father had really been a wine-women-and-song person, so when I finished my translation I added a 2000-word commentary explaining the symbolism of wine as the intoxicating power of divine love, the *saki* (or barmaid) being the neophyte mystic's guru, and so on, and I added a word-for-word translation so that the English-speaking reader could understand the problems of translating classical Persian poetry meaningfully into English.

Extracts were quoted in the London *Times* of 11 August 1989. Christopher Walker wrote from Nicosia, 'The *Tehran Times* is regarded as the mouthpiece of the newly-elected President Rafsan-jani,' adding that my article reached the newspaper 'after slicing by the prison censor at Evin where the author is now incarcerated'. *The Times* quoted the editor as saying that my article and translation 'bore the stamp of a highly brilliant, gifted and inspired poet and scholar'. I had heard that the *Tehran Times* often reflected the President's views and when I read this piece of hyperbole I hoped it was so. My unsolicited contribution had in fact bypassed the Evin censor – I do not propose to say exactly how – and I did know one or two people on the paper, but the editor would clearly not have allowed 'the notorious British spy' to write about the Emam's literary talents and spiritual insights without a nod from the Presidential palace. The exaggerated compliments seemed a coded message of reassurance. Even the hardliners would think twice before executing a 'poet and scholar' who had translated and explained the Emam's mystic poetry to a wide international audience.

My explanation of the alcoholic references, which were potentially shocking to some ordinary Iranians, may also have helped clear the path for further such poems to be published, and before long I was given a pre-publication copy of a small collection of the Emam's poems, with a strong hint that I might like to continue my translation efforts. I did one or two more, but they seemed to lack the force and beauty of the first one, or else I had lost my inspiration. Doubt had also seeped into my mind as to whether the Emam really had written these and if he had, when. The claim that he jotted down one of them on the back of a letter from the commander of the air force – which was produced as evidence – in a fine strong hand and without a single second thought, when already in his late eighties, strains belief. In the year before his death, when he was already finding it difficult to talk coherently, long political treatises in classical script were regularly published, claimed to have been composed and written by him. The too-perfect handwriting, the occasional use of terminology that did not match the Emam's vocabulary – having interviewed him in Persian in France I feel I know how he expressed himself politically – made me suspect that there were experts in his office capable of turning out the ideas, *fatwas,* addresses, anathemas and political testaments that the theocracy thrived on. So why not in-house poets and calligraphers as well? On the poems I hope I am wrong; it is certainly possible that the Emam wrote them earlier in life, but my literary nose tells me that you do not suddenly start writing high-quality classical Persian in your mid-eighties. To accept these late *ghazals* as genuine one would like to see the products of his youth and middle-age, which should be even more remarkable, whether scribbled on the backs of letters or on more conventional paper.

The visit, timed by Carl Akesson, lasted 32 minutes. As she left Lili said she would try to come again before she flew back to London. I replied, 'That's highly unlikely. You're never allowed more than one visit.' As I was taken back to my cell I remember thinking how mean this was. A visit from a member of my family

257

involved a long wait for a visa, a journey of several thousand miles, one or two weeks hanging around in Tehran for the formalities to be completed, in other words a considerable expenditure of time for busy people, not to mention money, and at the end of it half an hour of strictly controlled conversation. Hardly a generous concession on the part of the prison authorities, who always publicized such visits as a proof of Iran's humanitarian ways.

What I had not expected was that at Paul's urging Lili wrote asking to meet Ayatollah Yazdi, who as head of the judiciary was one of the country's very top officials. She delivered the letter personally on Sunday morning and the next afternoon was summoned to the Marble Palace, the magnificent seat of the short-lived Pahlavi dynasty. She wore, of course, the Islamic head-covering which even foreign non-Muslim women must wear in public, and was accompanied by Mr Akesson and his interpreter. In her report she wrote: 'When we reached the corridor outside his palatial office, we took off our shoes and were offered tea and waited 5–6 minutes. Several minor officials went in and out. I also saw the chief prosecutor Mohammed Reyshahri, the former Minister for Intelligence, who is deeply implicated in Roger's detention, coming out of the room. It was he who volunteered a very hostile statement about Roger in February when he was still minister. He said Roger had been given a "heavy sentence".

'Mr Reyshahri had his head down, and I felt he was deliberately avoiding looking in my direction, as we were fairly close to him. We went in and sat down. Yazdi was an elderly man with a long white beard and mullah outfit. He had a gentle face. I opened the meeting by thanking him for allowing me to visit him. That was translated, and then I asked him directly how much longer Roger was to be in prison. He did not answer this immediately, but told me that when he had been in prison under the Shah his wife was not allowed to see him or meet any judicial officials to discuss his case. He was determined to give prisoners' relatives access.'

The ayatollah went on to tell Lili that I was not under a death sentence, that my case was not political or connected with Irano-British relations, but was simply an Iranian judicial case. She was not to ask him how long my sentence was.

Lili then asked him when my trial had been held. 'He had been speaking up to this point with great eloquence. But there was a moment of hesitation and he looked at one of the officials, then said it had taken place recently. I had the impression he had not been briefed on this point and did not know the answer. He added that as a human being he wished Roger to be freed as soon as possible, but only the spiritual leader (Khamene'i) could make that decision. Again I bowed and thanked him very much. By this time I became aware of the official importance of the meeting, as I saw the Foreign Ministry representative making frantic notes of what was being said. Opposite me sat a rather frowning mullah, seemingly displeased with what was happening.

'I then asked Mr Yazdi if I could bring the good news to Roger myself, and see him once more. He said there should be no problem.' Lili also asked if I could have regular consular visits, at which point one of the officials told him I already had such visits, which of course was quite untrue. She did not ask any more questions, feeling that the visit had lasted a long time. She was told afterwards that the ayatollah had made a sign ten minutes earlier to bring the meeting to a close, but she had not noticed and went on asking questions. His closing remark was that the case was going on and he was dealing with it himself, but 'some aspects were complicated'. She thanked him, bowed and left.

Two days later, against all the odds, Lili was back at Evin giving me the news, although the prison authorities had tried to prevent her seeing me and only allow Mr Akesson in. 'Roger had read the news about my visit in the Iranian press,' she wrote, 'including criticisms of Yazdi's reference to a pardon. On this visit Roger was a changed person, looking as if a great burden had been lifted from him. He was excited about the news and seemed quite his old self, charming, confident, talkative and humorous ... Roger talked with Mr A about his case, saying he wanted a fair trial, complaining that he had not been allowed to have a lawyer, as was his right. He did not want to be pardoned, but if a clemency was to free him he would want to insist on clearing his name, even if it meant staying on longer in Iran. I said surely if he were to be pardoned he would be glad to leave, but Roger quite seriously said that he would not want to leave with a tarnished reputation in Iranian eyes. He asked Mr A to find him a lawyer. On this visit we were told in advance we would only be allowed 15 minutes, so it soon came to an end.'

I was puzzled, as well as elated, by what Ayatollah Yazdi had told Lili. For a start I had been tried two years earlier, which is hardly 'recently', and at that time, despite his statement, I was still under sentence of death. It seemed unlikely he had been so badly briefed as to have got such details wrong when agreeing to see Lili, so it looked strongly to me as if the head of the judiciary was after all in the moderates' camp and was sending a signal to the hardliners that the death sentence they had imposed was not going to be carried out while he was in charge of Iran's courts and prisons. Powerful though his post is, he was right to point out that the power of clemency lay with Ayatollah Khamene'i, although individual recommendations were his prerogative. His denial that my case had a political dimension was also strange, when everyone in Iran, whether hawk or dove, knew perfectly well that it had. There was obviously considerable confusion in high places, and even pressure on the leader to overrule the head of the judiciary, as the hardline newspaper editorials made clear.

But, as Lili noticed, I did feel that a burden had been lifted from me. I was not sure how the authorities were going to sort it all out, and it sounded as if I might have to face a new trial, but at least I knew that the threat of execution no longer hung over me, and I shall for ever be grateful to Lili for having helped establish that point.

14

THE CASE OF Kurosh Fuladi began to be publicly linked with mine in the Iranian press that summer. Fuladi had been sentenced at the Old Bailey to twelve years' imprisonment in 1981, so with one-third remission for good behaviour he would become eligible for parole in 1989; but just then the news came that a quantity of a 'prohibited substance', presumably drugs of some kind, had been found in a search of his cell. If proved, this would obviously have led to a fresh sentence or at least a loss of remission, which would increase the chances of my being exchanged with him. My spirits rose slightly. There were charges that he had been tortured by 'fascist police' in 'Britain's medieval dungeons' and that drugs had been planted on him in order to secure the release of 'the notorious British spy Roger Cooper', as I was usually called in the media. Fuladi did not even smoke cigarettes, it was said, so the charges were obviously untrue.

I never did hear the full story, but apparently the 'substance' was not a drug and soon after Lili's visit Fuladi was released, returning to Iran as a national hero. This was another setback for me, especially as his stories of ill treatment in gaol led to a new outburst of anti-British hysteria in the press, fanned by the extremely radical Labour Minister Abolqasem Sarhadizadeh, who had himself served fourteen years in gaol under the Shah as an Islamic militant, the best of credentials after the Revolution. Before his cabinet appointment he had risen to become head of the council controlling Iran's prisons. While Fuladi was still in gaol the Minister wrote an impassioned account of the tortures and indignities which 'this valiant combatant of Islam' was undergoing, without saying how he knew this. A few days after his release I was surprised to be asked to meet Fuladi in the governor's office. I was not ordered

261

to meet the valiant combatant, and David warned me it was probably a propaganda trap, but curiosity got the better of me and I went.

One of the newspapers covering Fuladi's homecoming had reproduced, much reduced, an article from a British paper covering the incident that led to his imprisonment. With my magnifying glass I could just read the report, from which it was clear that Fuladi had lost the sight of one eye and partial use of an arm when the bomb he was transporting went off prematurely. Now he was claiming to have received these injuries while in gaol. We shook hands, and I said I was glad for his sake that he had been freed. I spoke in English, which I assumed he now spoke fluently, but he replied in Persian, which I found strange for someone who had supposedly been sent to London on a government scholarship more than ten years ago. Throughout the meeting I only heard him use one word of English, prison slang for a punishment cell, I think. I asked why he had come. He said it was because he felt sorry for me and wanted to help in any way he could, although he knew conditions in an Islamic prison were far better than the medieval tortures he had been subjected to in Britain. I asked him if he had any plans to write or give an interview about our meeting. He said absolutely not: his motives were purely humanitarian.

I took his remarks at face value and went on to ask if he had been allowed a radio in prison. Looking puzzled, he said he had, so I asked him if he would ask the governor for our cell to be allowed a radio. The newspapers said that he had been able to take a Spanish course, and he confirmed this. Would he therefore ask the governor if we could be allowed to do correspondence courses? I had spent some time in the so-called Training Institute, yet no instruction of any kind was provided. He did not like the turn the conversation was taking, nor did the governor. Without replying to my requests he launched into an obviously rehearsed speech in which he listed the terrible things that had been done to him in prison, such as being blinded, paralysed in one arm, assaulted by homosexuals and having urine poured over him. When he mentioned his injuries I looked surprised and said I had read in *Kayhan*, in a reproduction of a British press report at the time, that he had received these injuries when the bomb went off. He

262

got quite angry at this and denied it, but quickly passed on to other complaints. He said he had been in more than forty different prisons. When I asked why he said it was for practising and preaching Islam. He mentioned being punished for spreading his prayer-mat in the governor's office, at which I asked innocently, 'Could you just walk into the governor's office, then? We're not allowed out of our cells here. And if we were I don't think you would like me to come into your office uninvited, would you, Governor?' The governor said nothing.

I could not help feeling from his own account of what he had done in gaol that the British authorities had taken an extremely broad interpretation of the term 'good behaviour' in giving him a four-year reduction in sentence, but I listened attentively and when he had finished I said that I was most distressed at his tale and would like to help. How could I? he asked. I said we should sit down on our own and I would put everything he said into a formal complaint. There were several organizations in Britain involved in protecting prisoners' rights, I told him, and I would ensure that through them his complaints were investigated. If what he said could be substantiated, I said, there would certainly be an enquiry and he would probably be awarded substantial damages. What he must do immediately, I went on, was to get expert medical reports on his eye and arm, which would form the linch-pin of his case. He began to bluster. 'It's too late now, this happened in the early part of my imprisonment.' I assured him that Iranian doctors could still state what had probably caused these injuries, and since he must have had a medical of some sort when he began his sentence it would be difficult for the prison authorities to deny that his injuries had been caused by brutality inflicted in gaol. He fell silent.

I then offered to tell him some of the injustices I had suffered in the past four years. With a thin smile at the governor I said that no guard had ever struck me, but that I had been subject to regular beatings during interrogation. Worse than that, though, was the totally unjust trial I had received, denied a lawyer, not allowed to call witnesses or evidence, without a representative of my embassy or the public being allowed to attend, and with a judge who told me before the trial started that he knew what the verdict was. Could he bring this grave miscarriage of justice to the attention of the senior officials who had given him a hero's welcome at the airport? That would be the best way of helping me.

As I expected, the meeting quickly drew to a close at this point and I said goodbye to Kurosh Fuladi, who barely shook hands with me. 'When can we meet again, Kurosh?' I asked. 'I'm very busy, but soon, I hope,' he replied, with total lack of conviction. Early in the meeting he had asked me if I had any letters he could post for me and foolishly I gave him two quite important ones, which he promised to send at once. The governor gave his approval and he took them away. They never arrived.

I suppose I should not have been surprised to read his account of our meeting in one of the hardline papers a few days later. According to this, he had told me of the terrible experiences he had suffered in gaol while I confessed that I was extremely well treated in Evin and had no complaints whatsoever. David had been right, and I should have known better than to meet him. Fuladi was given a high-ranking, or high-sounding, position in one of the ministries controlled by the hardliners and gradually faded into oblivion. I never saw or heard from him again.

Early one Thursday morning in November, before I had even had my tea, I was told to get dressed at once. Normally in the cells we wore pyjama trousers and a T-shirt, with perhaps a sweater on top during the cold months. If I thought I had a visitor I used to dress up, putting on the white shirt, silk tie, pin-stripe suit and shiny black shoes that I was wearing at the time of my arrest. Knowing that visits never took place in the morning, and expecting to be taken to the interrogation block, I wore trousers and a sweater. This time, however, I was taken to the prison office, where I was kept waiting, blindfolded, for an hour or more before being handed over to two guards I had never seen before. I was led to an unmarked Paykan, the locally assembled Hillman saloon, and told to sit in the back seat and remove my blindfold. There was a civilian, or plain-clothes, driver, and one guard sat in the front, the other next to me. We drove to the main gate. Could I possibly be going free, I wondered? It seemed unlikely, but my spirits soared as the gates swung open and we drove out of Evin.

The guards were an odd pair, cracking jokes but with a sinister tone in all they said. In reply to my questions they said we were going for a picnic in one of the city's parks. We drove fast, but as we approached central Tehran the traffic thickened and I could see ordinary people going about their business for the first time in years. The first thing I noticed was dozens of attractive women, just about covered in Islamic *hijab*, but on nothing like the scale I remembered from four years ago. They seemed to stride with confidence, wearing make-up that enhanced their natural glamour, subtly rather than boldly, as in the Shah's day. But perhaps I was just carried away by the sight of women not totally encased in black chadors.

It dawned on me that we were heading towards the former British embassy, and the whole world suddenly seemed brighter. I guessed I was about to be handed over to the Swedes and would soon be free. But the car did not slow down, and the huge statues of lion and unicorn flanking the gateway flashed by. On we went towards the bazaar, said to be the biggest covered market in the world, stopping just on its northern edge in Citadel Square where I was handcuffed to one of the guards and ordered out of the car. I knew the building we were about to enter well. It had been the HQ of the former Ministry of Information, where I had gone each year to renew my press credentials, and now, the plaque told me, it had become Tehran's main civil courthouse. A few passers-by spotted the handcuffs, but looked away quickly.

The guard took me up the stairs, asking directions for a numbered office where I sat handcuffed to him, feeling a mixture of anxiety and elation. The second, more senior, guard soon caught up with us and said I was about to appear before a judge and would soon be joined by my lawyer. At once I protested, saying I did not have a lawyer, had not been notified, had not brought my notes and papers, and refused to appear in court thus unprepared. He laughed at me and said, 'Tell the judge.' 'Some picnic,' I said bitterly. 'Why didn't you tell me the truth?'

A few minutes later an elderly gentleman entered the room and sat down in the corner opposite me. He introduced himself as my lawyer and began discussing the trial that was about to begin. I said I refused to discuss my legal affairs with anyone in a public

265

place while handcuffed. He saw my point and asked the guards to release me and leave us alone. They reluctantly took the handcuffs off, but refused to leave the room. A compromise was reached when the guard I had been handcuffed to changed places with the lawyer. As he sat down he said, 'I don't know English, but if you speak French we would have some privacy.' I began to warm to the man and decided to listen to what he had to say.

He told me, in formal, old-fashioned French, that he did not know the details of my case but understood I was being tried on charges of having had illicit sexual relations some years ago. Had I confessed to this? I said no. Had the woman? I said I was sure she had not. 'In that case,' he said, 'the legal position is clear. You simply deny the charges, and unless they have evidence of a nature which is almost impossible for them to have, such as four male witnesses to the act of penetration, there is no case to answer. I will say that on your behalf, but you must also say it yourself.'

I began to think that perhaps the whole trial was a charade set up by Ayatollah Yazdi. According to this lawyer I would be acquitted for lack of evidence, which would automatically quash my death sentence. It would then be easy for me to be given early release at the next amnesty, due in about two months' time, by which time I would be in my fifth year of imprisonment. Nevertheless I smelled a rat. I thought for a few moments, then told the lawyer that while I was most grateful for his advice I could not agree to be tried at such short notice. According to the Constitution I was entitled to a lawyer of my own choice, and it was clearly a grave breach of natural justice for a person to be put on trial, or to have his appeal heard, without prior notice, without seeing the charges or evidence against him, and without even being allowed to have his breakfast. I demanded to be allowed to contact the Swedish embassy and have them find me a lawyer. 'With regret and respect, monsieur,' I concluded, 'I cannot accept you as my lawyer in these circumstances, but I would be most grateful if you would ask the judge, on my behalf, for an adjournment of a few days.'

'There's no time for that,' he said. 'Your trial is about to begin. Bonne chance.' As he spoke, an official entered and told the guards to bring me to the courtroom.

I found myself in a spacious room with a raised dais in the centre, opposite which I was told to sit in the first of several rows of wooden chairs. Behind me, in a section apparently open to the public, sat the two guards and a few excited bystanders, obviously invited to create the illusion of an open trial. The lawyer sat, like me, in the front row but some distance away to my right.

The judge appeared and I stood up out of respect. When he had sat down I made to do so myself, but he motioned me to stay on my feet and kept me so throughout the trial, despite my feeling rather unsteady as time passed and hunger and unfitness took their toll. I was never told the name of the court or the judge, who at once started to ask me questions about my early days in Iran, referring as he did so to a file in front of him. Before answering I asked him to tell me exactly what this trial was about. I had not been given any papers, did not have a lawyer, and objected strongly to the whole procedure.

He pointed to the elderly barrister: 'There is your lawyer.'

I replied, 'He is not my lawyer. I wish to see the charges and brief a lawyer of my own choice, as required by natural justice and the Constitution of the Islamic Republic of Iran.'

The judge ignored this remark and declined to tell me exactly what the charges against me were, but did confirm that he was there to 'review' the death sentence against me. He added that he could endorse it, annul it, substitute a sentence of Islamic lashing, or take what he called 'other measures'. And now he would like to ask me some questions. I asked if I might sit down and take notes, but he replied that this would not be necessary, a phrase unpleasantly reminiscent of Judge Nayyeri. There was no prosecutor and the only other court official was a note-taker.

I stood there for at least an hour, having decided that refusing to answer his questions would serve little purpose and might be counterproductive, especially if the whole thing was being staged in my favour, as I at first believed. The judge delved into matters that had not even been raised at my first trial, asking about women friends of mine from twenty years or more before, which showed me that he had access to my interrogation file, and not just the records of the previous trial. In each case he asked explicitly, 'Did you have sexual relations with her?' Remembering the elderly

267

lawyer's advice I replied each time with a firm 'No'.

He seemed rather cross at the results of his questioning and after a while changed tack, asking me about my conversion to Islam. I was on dangerous ground here, since I had registered in Evin as a Christian and the penalty for apostasy in Islam is death. I parried his questions by saying that I had been deeply impressed by my exposure to Islam as a young man, and as I had progressed in my studies of Persian literature this respect had deepened, so that I really did consider myself a Muslim, one tending towards the Sufi persuasion, but did not currently observe the obligatory rituals except that I always fasted in Ramadan. He frowned at this and asked me further questions, finally getting round to my relationship with Nilufar, which I could tell he had been keeping up his sleeve. 'I have decided that you are not a Muslim and that therefore your *sigheh* with her was not lawful. Yet you had sexual relations with her.' It was a statement rather than a question, but one that clearly needed answering, so I replied firmly: 'That is not true and I deny it.'

At that moment a ridiculous aspect of the case occurred to me. If I was not a Muslim, as he claimed, then my marriage to Guity was null and void and therefore my relations with her 'illicit'. I could hardly deny these in view of my daughter's existence. For a moment, I considered pointing this out to him, but it might easily have backfired so I kept quiet.

Abruptly he indicated that the trial was over, but as he stood up so did the elderly lawyer, whose name I had not even asked. He launched into a short but passionate speech on my behalf, making the point that I was a foreigner and knew little about Iran or Islam, therefore the judge should show mercy on me. Apart from being untrue this was contrary to the argument I was advancing. The judge made a note, whereupon I entered into the fray and said, 'As I have already made clear to Your Honour, this gentleman does not represent me and I would like it to be entered on the court record that despite my request for a lawyer of my own choice I was unrepresented at this hearing. Please ignore the representations he has just made on my behalf.' The judge frowned, said nothing, and swept out of the courtroom.

I was immediately handcuffed to one of the guards and taken

268

to the car. On the way, we passed a barrow-boy selling cauli-
flowers, which I had not seen for four years. I asked my Siamese
twin if I could buy one, but he only jerked my wrist painfully
without answering, put me in the car and handcuffed my left wrist
to the rear left door. Their mood had changed, the jocularity of
the way down replaced by open hostility. They attacked Britain
in general and Mrs Thatcher and myself in particular. One of them
told me gratuitously that the Islamic penalty for spies was death.

'Maybe,' I said, 'but Islam is also a religion of justice, and I have
not yet had a fair trial, either in the Revolutionary Court two
years ago or in this civil court just now. You did not even have
the courtesy to tell me you were taking me to court.' I lapsed
into silence and for the rest of the journey looked out of the
window at the streets and buildings I knew so well.

As we neared Evin on one of Tehran's major highways we had
to turn left across the oncoming traffic. The traffic lights were not
working and we were waiting for a gap in the traffic, when the
guard in the front passenger seat turned round.

'You see this gun?' he asked, producing from a holster what
David Rabhan later told me from my description was a Colt. 'You
see this bullet?' he continued, sliding one into the chamber and
cocking the gun. 'You see the safety catch is off.' I did not at first
understand what this was all about. 'Now I am going to carry out
the death sentence I just heard the judge say you have been given.'

Everything went quiet in the car, and I felt panic rising inside
me, as if I were about to vomit. I fought back the feeling and
managed to stammer out, 'Yes, but you also heard him say that
the purpose of the trial was to review that sentence. You may
also have heard Ayatollah Yazdi's statment that I am not going to
be executed.'

'Correct,' replied the guard, 'but I will say you were shot trying
to escape, as we were stuck in the traffic. The penalty for spies
like you is death.'

'How could I escape while handcuffed to the car door?' I said.

'Naturally I will unlock you afterwards,' he replied.

The gun was now pointing at the top of my head less than two
feet away. The sense of panic returned. So this was it. I made one
last attempt to save myself.

'How will you account for the bullet entering the front of my head if I'm supposed to be escaping?' I asked, looking straight into the barrel. The guard seemed about to say something and the gun moved, but then I saw his index finger curl and he pulled the trigger.

There was a slight click, and I realized it was just another trick by a sadistic guard to frighten a prisoner. Mock executions had been quite common in the earlier stages of the Revolution, I learned later, but the authorities had banned the practice. Verbal death threats still persisted and I had received my share from Hosein and unfriendly guards over the years. The guard's intention was obviously to scare the daylights out of me, and I must say he succeeded admirably. I still do not understand what he did to the gun to prevent it from firing and even David, a firearms expert, could not explain it.

I was taken to a part of the prison I had not visited before and made to wait a good hour for no clear reason. While I was there the other guard tried the same trick on me, but by now it had lost its novelty and I simply stared at him in silence as he pulled the trigger. Eventually I got back to my cell, still shaken, but also with a sense of burning indignation. I was not going to let those guards get away with it if I could possibly help it.

When I learned from a friendly guard that mock executions were now illegal I decided to write a formal letter of protest to the prison governor, and also to tell the interrogators and any other officials I met. I wrote the letter despite warnings from David that I would simply be stirring up trouble for myself, that it was not really something to make a fuss about, that it had happened to him several times, and so on. Bespectacled Hosein promised my letter would at least reach the governor's office, although he too thought it would have little effect.

Nothing happened for over a month and then one day I was summoned to the old interrogation building, which now housed various prison departments such as *ejra-ye ahkam*, the 'execution of sentences office', the one where prisoners are informed of their fate. Although one of the most feared departments in Evin it was said that if you went there at least you were going to live, since death sentences were supposedly notified to prisoners only in solitary confinement, the evening before being carried out. The office I was taken to had no sign on the door, but from telephone conversations I overheard I guessed it was the internal security office of Evin, which is where one would expect misdemeanours by guards to be investigated. The two guards had been interviewed already and denied my story, claiming that the gun had been produced because I had tried to jump out of the car while it was held up in traffic and that they then handcuffed me to the door. I came under strong pressure to agree to this version of events, whereupon the case would be closed and no action or reprisals taken against me.

'It's their word against yours,' said the investigator, 'and there's two of them.'

'Not so,' I replied. 'You've forgotten the civilian driver. Why not question him? He witnessed the whole incident and something tells me he did not like it.'

The investigator seemed unhappy at my response, but gave me a sheet of paper to write out a formal complaint on oath. I did so and was returned to my cell, after receiving a promise that I would be informed of the outcome of the investigation. Officially I never heard what happened, but I did get some harsh criticism from one of the unfriendly guards for 'having got some colleagues into trouble over a joke'. I said it did not seem a very funny joke to me. I also had the satisfaction of hearing that one of the guards had been suspended from duty.

15

THE YEAR 1989 drew to a close with our spirits much lower than when it began. We had not managed to get any grapes for wine, although David and I both made substitutes. He had produced an excellent dry vintage from dried figs, while I continued on a small scale with my 'slivovitz', really just plum wine heavily doctored with sugar at the fermentation stage, which Romeo had greatly enjoyed. But with no signs of a breakthrough in any of our cases, and deteriorating living conditions, we had little to celebrate. Making wine was something we both did in dangerous defiance of the system rather than for the alcohol produced.

Just before Christmas we were joined by Helmut Szimkus, a German from near Frankfurt. His English was poor at first, so I took the opportunity of speaking German to him whenever I came to the big cell, to the annoyance of David, who said only English should be used. To avoid conflict Helmut and I would restrict our conversations to the exercise period, walking up and down the small yard and getting to know each other.

Prisoners in Evin rarely volunteer information about their cases until confidence has been established, and all that Helmut told us at first was that he was charged with entering Iran illegally from Iraq in Kurdish costume, horribly reminiscent of what Romeo originally told us about his charges. We could not see why a West German, who was neither a journalist nor an aid worker, would do such a thing, since it was relatively easy for Germans to obtain visas. But we made no comment.

Soon after his arrival Helmut said something in English about the Emam as if he were still alive. I thought he might have just got his tenses wrong, but just to be sure I said in German, 'You know he's dead, don't you?' He looked at me as if I were joking

272

and said, 'Do you think I wouldn't know if Khomeini were dead?' It took us some time to convince him that he had died more than six months earlier. By now there was a television set in the big cell and it was not long before we could point to pictures of the Emam's mausoleum and flashbacks to the funeral.

Helmut had been in Evin for about eighteen months and during the course of his interrogation, which had recently ended, he had been taken out of prison to towns he had lived in – Kermanshah in the west, Arak, an important industrial town in central Iran, and Ahwaz, the chief town of the southern oil province of Khuzistan. He was only a few months older than me, but gaunt and somewhat battered. He blamed this, and the frequent cramps in his legs and back, on his apprenticeship in a metal works. Handling lead had caused him to lose most of his teeth and hair and had weakened his bones. He was an expert installer of heavy machinery, and worked for a manufacturer of metal-shearing equipment, for whom he had frequently travelled to the Middle East, including Iran and Iraq. His father was an ethnic Lithuanian and he had spent much of the war in what became Kaliningrad in the Soviet Union, although as Königsberg it had been an important part of East Prussia, connected to Germany proper by the Polish Corridor. To Helmut it was still German territory, just like Austria, Danzig, Sudetenland, and probably Alsace and the Volga Basin as well. For amusement, I used to get him to sing old Nazi songs like 'Wir fahren gegen England' and the 'Horstwessellied', finding it interesting that German expansionism was alive in someone who was only ten years old at the end of the war. In his mid-twenties he had gone to a university or polytechnic in Aachen and completed a degree. To my surprise he was not interested in the three or four modern German novels my cousin Ulrich had sent me, nor in the quality German newspapers his embassy occasionally sent, preferring sports magazines if he could get them.

One day Helmut was summoned to his Shobeh to be officially charged. He spoke colloquial Persian quite well, having married, for the second time, the pretty daughter of the chief accountant at a factory in Arak, where he worked for a few years after the Revolution, but like most foreigners he could not read or write it, so as we strolled in the yard that afternoon he asked me if I would translate the indictment for him. I was shocked at what I read. Helmut was accused of a number of extremely serious offences, such as supplying Iraqi intelligence with information about Iranian army movements, by means of a radio that he had smuggled into Iran from northern Iraq. The charges were specific, with names, dates and references to his own confession statements and those of Iranians allegedly working with him, most of whom had already been executed. The money he was said to have received from the Iraqis for this work was also mentioned. It was not a large sum: 20,000 Deutschmarks as I recall. I completed the translation that evening and slipped it to him during next day's exercise period, promising not to mention it to David and Jon. He said nothing.

I had translated the charges into English, which was easier for me, and Helmut said he would be able to understand. A few weeks later, after I had received a German dictionary and was speaking quite fluently again, I asked him if he would now like me to translate it into German. He told me not to bother, but then asked me some questions about it, saying he had not read my translation. I found this almost unbelievable, as his very life was at stake. If, like me, he had made a confession, for whatever reason, I would have expected him to study the charges and start to plan his defence. Helmut just seemed to ignore it in total apathy, which made me fear the worst.

As his English improved, his mood would sometimes change and without ever telling the others details of the charges – I had also kept my promise about this – he fantasized about what would happen at his trial. He assumed he would have a lawyer and that a representative of the German embassy would be present, and he was going to launch such a blistering attack on his interrogator that the man would soon be behind bars while he himself walked free. He told us he had been badly beaten and, knowing his interrogator to be a particularly nasty individual with whom I had once quarrelled myself, I could well believe it. On more than one occasion he had received *falaka*, the bastinado, although his feet had now healed. We listened in amazement to his fantasies, at first saying, 'Helmut, trials in Evin are not like that. You will not even get a chance to raise points, and if you have a lawyer or consular representative you will be the first ever in a Revolutionary Court.' But he was in a world of his own at such times.

Early in the New Year we were moved out of our cell for a day while it was being redecorated. The whole building was being painted and whitewashed, for the first time since its construction shortly before the Revolution. We surmised that this must have something to do with a forthcoming visit by a UN official. Trusties in brown pyjama-style uniforms did the work, and we were advised by the guards to move all our stuff into an empty cell in case items went missing, since their trustworthiness was only relative. David and I in particular had quite a lot of gear by now, in my case mainly books, while he had acquired cooking equipment from freed prisoners in previous blocks, as well as a series of marvellous sculptures he had made from bread while in solitary. The hurried move aggravated my old back problem; next day I was in such agony that I could hardly stand up, and for a week I could only lie in my cell. Bespectacled Hosein was most helpful and as soon as I could hobble about got me to a doctor, who gave me some pain-killers but said there was nothing else he could do.

While I was still recovering I was summoned to the 'execution of sentences office' to be told of my fate. First I was shown Judge Nayyeri's verdict, which, as I already knew, was 'death plus ten years', the death sentence for alleged fornication some 25 years ago, the ten years for 'espionage on behalf of the British Intelligent Service'. It made interesting reading and I asked if I could keep a copy. The answer was no, nor could I make notes. Then I was given the verdict of the second trial, presided over by the judge whose name I never knew and whose signature was illegible. As I had expected, the document claimed that I was represented by legal counsel, also unnamed, while my demand to have a lawyer of my own choice was not recorded. The judge spent some paragraphs discussing the death sentence that had been imposed, before con-cluding that it was not Islamically correct since no confession or evidence had been produced. I was overjoyed: all had come out as I had hoped. Now I 'only' had a ten-year sentence for espionage, which would be relatively easy for the authorities to commute now that I was in my fifth year of detention. Perhaps the forthcoming amnesty to mark the eleventh anniversary of the Revolution would be an appropriate moment. If so, it meant just one more month. Good old Yazdi, I thought. But, hang on, I said to myself, I haven't got to the end of the verdict. There's still one more paragraph to go.

My heart sank as I read it, for the learned judge, in spite of having decided that there was no evidence against me and striking down my death sentence, now substituted a prison term. He wrote that I must serve six years in prison, to run consecutively with my existing ten-year sentence, making a total of sixteen years. The appropriate authorities were instructed to calculate the release date and inform the condemned party accordingly.

I expected to be allowed to keep a copy of this verdict, even if the possible embarrassing earlier one was now to be lost in the judicial filing system, but again the 'execution of sentences' chief clerk refused. I asked for more time to study it and when he left the room for a few minutes I quickly wrote down key phrases on the piece of paper I always carried. I did this before he returned, but he suspected something, ordered me to empty my pockets and took away my notes. I realized too late I should have slipped the paper into my underpants. My protest that I needed these notes to file an appeal against an unjustifiable verdict went unheeded, but when he ordered me to sign that I had been duly informed of my sentence I added that the verdict was unjust and I wished to appeal against it.

The chief clerk then began calculating the date of my release, insisting at first that the six years was a substitute for the death sentence and should therefore begin at the date of the second trial, to be followed by the ten-year sentence. The two years between the two trials, and the three years between my arrest and the first trial, were all pre-trial detention, which did not count towards sentence. Eventually he conceded the point, and after the deduction of about eight religious holidays per year over the sixteen-year period he arrived at a release date of 14 July 2003, the first time I had seen a date in the 21st century that applied to me. He wrote this out on a slip of paper and without a touch of humour told me, 'Don't lose this or there will be trouble when you're due for release.' I returned to my cell decidedly shaken, but at least knowing that I was officially no longer under sentence of death, even if I would be in my 69th year when released.

My relationship with David had improved slightly. We still got into frequent arguments, but at least this was better than cold silences. With hindsight I can see that perhaps we both needed someone to vent our frustrations on, and there was nobody else around. Neither Jon nor Helmut was a suitable candidate for this role, so we gravitated together in outward antipathy, although we often needed each other's advice or support, and it is worth recording that we never withheld this. David used to quarrel with some of the guards, and occasionally, under strong provocation, I would too, never forgetting, however, the importance of their goodwill.

The first half of 1990 was the only period of my detention when I was able to correspond freely with friends and relations. The rules were supposedly strict: letters should not exceed seven lines, not be addressed to members of the opposite sex unless blood-relatives, and had to be written in simple language and block letters. Seyyed Masih, the crossword whizz, was replaced as mail-man by an out-and-out crook, who gouged extra payment from us by claiming that our letters had to be sent by registered airmail, whereas he actually sent them by unregistered surface mail. Our complaints bore fruit, however, and in due course we got Ali, a delightfully simple and honest man, whom we got to know and like better than almost anyone in Evin. He brought us stamps and turned a blind eye to the frequency and length of our letters: I was able to write almost one letter a day. The year before, I had started to receive cards and letters from friends and strangers without being able to answer them. Now I was gradually able to catch up with my correspondence and establish contact with many old and new friends who had heard about my plight. This was one of the good things to come out of my Evin experience.

David suddenly found he was a multiple grandfather. His son and two daughters had all married while he was in gaol and they had already produced some seven or eight children between them. One of his daughters practised strict Orthodox Judaism and had married a bearded fundamentalist. Their four children had unusual biblical names which David had trouble remembering, while letters from his mother and aunts were full of references to family members only half-remembered. We used to show each other most of our letters and as a result I began to construct a family tree for the huge Rabhan clan, adding information as it came in, which David found useful when replying. He also wrote numerous business letters, mostly trying to get the information he needed on, say, the migratory habits of South Atlantic krill, or the landed price of New England menhaden (a type of herring), since he was determined to carve out a new career as a fish and fish-processing tycoon. Having always had people to take care of his correspondence, even his personal letters, he found me a useful secretary.

Our cell buzzed with excitement as the day set for David's release approached. He promised to stop off in England to tell my family how I was, and he would soon be seeing Jon's mother and sisters, as the two families had become quite close. I had told him that my brother Paul was now a financial journalist and David wanted his advice on how to set up a public company in the UK; having read a few copies of the *Financial Times* he had decided it was a better place than Georgia to raise capital for his projects.

The great day came. Nothing had been said beforehand, so we were surprised and overjoyed when in mid-morning a guard arrived to tell David he was to be released. He put on a smart jacket we had never seen, with a pair of flamboyant leather boots, and carried an expensive hide briefcase. We gave him bear-hugs and he promised to write, having agreed in advance on certain codes to cover such subjects as the degree to which he was searched on departure. I was particularly keen, if released, to take with me my indictment and release date slip, as well as the manuscript of my crossword dictionary, my annotated Persian dictionary, various poems, songs and other papers, although our exclusion once again from the provisions of the 11th anniversary amnesty in February had made early release unlikely. I had always said that even in the uncertain world of Iranian justice David would not be kept even one day after he had completed his sentence. I countered his pessimism by saying that there would be an immediate outcry from the State Department, via the Swiss embassy, if he were not released promptly, and the regime would lose credibility

278

internationally at a time when the UN was turning the spotlight on human rights abuses in Iran.

An hour later David was back in the cell, having been told that he must find a 'guarantor' for his future good behaviour, a rule that apparently applied to all released prisoners in Iran, not just amnestied ones. It was a Catch-22 situation, since it was obviously impossible for him to arrange a guarantor from inside a maximum security prison without even being allowed to telephone. Off went a letter to the Swiss embassy requesting an urgent visit from a representative of the US Interests Section, and weeks later someone came to see him. David explained that all the official had to do was to sign the guarantee form, but with what I think it is not unfair to call a typically Swiss, or perhaps typically consular, attitude he refused, on the grounds that he had not received instructions from Washington or Bern.

So David was brought back to the cell for another long hot summer. During this time, he was occasionally allowed out of Evin, under armed guard, for meetings with his lawyer in an attempt to sort out his complicated financial affairs and arrange a guarantor. Little progress was made on either front, but in late summer some senior Iranian politicians must have realized that there could be no justification for keeping a man in gaol longer than seven or eight years once he had completed his two-year sentence. Whatever the reason, one day David really did leave Evin for good, bundled on to a Swissair flight to the United States. A gourmet to the last, he answered a reporter's questions on arrival at Atlanta airport by saying, 'I would not recommend Evin gaol for its food.' In the euphoria of his release he must have forgotten our code, but some weeks later we did receive a brief letter from him, addressed to us all as 'Dear Spies'. I would not have been surprised to learn that Judge Nayyeri used this as evidence against Helmut.

With the build-up to the 'Second Gulf War', the West versus Saddam Hussein, conditions began to deteriorate. Senior Iranian politicians like President Rafsanjani can have had few illusions about the outcome of the 'mother of all battles'; during the Iran–Iraq war they had watched in impotent rage as the US Navy captured and sank one of their vessels in the act of laying mines in international waters, blasted an Iranian offshore oil platform out of the water in retaliation for the mining of a US-flagged Kuwaiti tanker, and finally shot down, albeit in error, an Iranian airliner. They feared (wrongly I was sure, but how could they tell?) that, having dealt with Baghdad, the Americans, aided by the British, planned to turn eastward to settle scores with Tehran. So while the moderates' policy of strict neutrality prevailed, the hardliners seethed inwardly.

Inevitably, we bore the brunt of their frustrations. A new governor, called Pishva, had been appointed earlier in the year; he was gradually tightening his hold on the prison and making life hard for us. The first time he visited our cell he sat cross-legged on the floor, wearing scruffy clothes and grizzled stubble, saying nothing and eyeing us dolefully: we took him for the bodyguard of the English-speaking official accompanying him. He was old in comparison with most hardline officials, and his appointment was almost certainly a reward for having been a prisoner in Evin himself in the Shah's day. We speculated that his open hostility to us arose from a feeling that our three governments had turned a blind eye to the Shah's human rights abuses. Now he seemed to be taking his revenge.

Our mail was stopped, we were kept in our cells for all but two hours a week, and the quality of our already poor food declined. From September 1990 onwards we rarely saw meat, cheese, yoghurt or eggs, and even vegetable proteins such as beans and lentils, which had been plentiful, were now severely reduced. Ordinary Iranian households were also suffering from food shortages at this time, as Ali the postman told us. Iran's reasonable expectation that the Gulf War, by removing Iraqi and Kuwaiti oil from world markets, would result in a massive rise in oil prices failed to materialize. President Rafsanjani, like his counterparts in the collapsing communist world, was allowing market forces to replace subsidies, so people like Ali on small government salaries simply could not afford meat or chicken, and even pulses were now expensive. Bread was still cheap, but he or his son had to be up by 4 AM to get a place in the baker's queue before supplies ran out.

That summer we began to hear of plans to move the foreign prisoners to a new block. We were told it would be an attractive place, but we were suspicious, and pleaded to stay put in the Sanatorium. Nearly every move we had made in recent years had been for the worse. Here we did at least have our own washroom and the use of a stove, even though getting kerosene was becoming difficult. But we were powerless to resist, and one day in mid-September we were ordered out with all our gear. To Jon's disgust we were moved to a place he had been in before, 'Section 4 of Block 325', a self-contained two-storey building. The three of us were put in a largeish cell on the upper floor, segregated from the other foreigners, who were chiefly Pakistanis, Indian Muslims, Iraqis and Bengalis. They numbered about 120 in all, and had been gathered together from prisons all over the country. Jon said the cell we were now in and the ones next to it had housed literally hundreds of MKO supporters in 1988. Day after day they had been taken out in groups to be executed, then the rooms filled up again and the process was repeated. Given the wall of secrecy Iran built around such matters estimates of the numbers executed are conjectural, but Jon thought at least 3000 young people died in three bloody weeks. Many of them had spent their last night on earth in our cell.

A serious drawback of our new home was that there were no toilet facilities in the cell. We were taken to the washing area three times a day for ten or fifteen minutes, but if we needed to go to the lavatory outside those times we had to slide a thin metal plate under the door and wait for a guard to see it and allow us out. Banging on the door only got us into trouble, and the guards spent little time in our corridor. We knew most of them already, and sadly not one of them was among our favourites. Allahqoli, alias Reagan, was there, smouldering inside about what the Great Satan was about to do and taking it out on us in his ignorant and sanctimonious way.

Earlier that year, when mail and parcels had been flowing smoothly, I had asked for a thermometer, claiming that David was teaching me meteorology. To my surprise it reached me, so from then on I was able to record the cell temperature. That summer it had been in the mid-30°s Celsius, aggravated by an almost complete absence of breeze. When we arrived in Block 325 our south-facing cell with its thin walls and broken cooler was like a furnace, and we were worse off than in the solidly-built Sanatorium. The door was always shut and the large unshaded windows scarcely opened, so it was not until about midnight that the temperature dropped to a tolerable level. As summer ended this poor insulation began to work in the opposite direction, and the mercury fell rapidly. The new governor was a determined penny-pincher and the guards grumbled even to us about the economies he was imposing. He refused to allow the heating to be turned on until winter was almost there, and then the thermostat was set so low that sometimes we were not sure if the radiators were on or off. The wintry sun took some of the chill off the room by midday, but soon afterwards it set behind the bleak ridge of hills that formed the western flank of the prison, and the cell temperature then stayed at a maximum of 12°C until mid-morning next day. I was reading Irina Ratushinskaya's prison memoirs at the time and was amused to see that in Soviet prisons the minimum temperature is not supposed to drop below 15°C, although that principle was not always observed.

The block boss, Qasem, seemed at first sight a reasonable person. He spoke some English and wanted me to give him lessons, but like all my students in Evin apart from the friendly interrogator Mohammad, who was studying for a master's degree in linguistics, he lost interest after the first few lessons (saying he was 'too busy') and the idea fizzled out. Although he was to prove two-faced and unhelpful, to his credit he did allow us to exercise regularly in the ugly concrete yard, devoid of all vegetation. There were no facilities for volleyball here, but the other cells often played 'small-goal football', the major street game of the urban Third World, which I feel deserves Olympic recognition. Their shouts and laughter and the reverberations of the ball made it difficult to concentrate, but it did enable us to steal glances out of the window and see who else was in our block, although we got into serious trouble if we were spotted doing this. The duty guard usually sat in the yard during football games, only occasionally looking up at our cell.

We had already heard Ibrahim's unmistakable African accent,

speaking mainly in Arabic with prisoners we took to be Iraqis, and there was also a tall Westerner who walked silently up and down whatever the weather. We guessed he was John Bowden, an Englishman arrested on vague economic charges, as reported in the papers, at a time when the British government was rounding up and expelling Iranian students allegedly involved in the rash of fire-bombings of bookshops selling *The Satanic Verses*. Iranians have always gone in for tit-for-tat diplomacy and by then Bowden was one of the few Britons still living in Iran. We got confirmation when I gave Ali a couple of newspapers and asked him if he would pass them on to John Bowden. Instead of saying, 'Who is he?' Ali naïvely asked how we knew he was there; I said that one of the guards had mentioned it and I had accidentally seen him in the courtyard when I was hanging my towel up to dry.

At that time two Afghan prisoners brought us our tea and food, and occasionally washed the corridor. We were not supposed to talk to them, but supervision was slack and I was soon able to win their confidence. They told us Ibrahim had a morning job in a small café that served sandwiches and soft drinks to off-duty guards and through them I began to communicate with him. When the Afghans told me they had been arrested for possession of firearms I had a feeling they might not be around for much longer. Sure enough, they were both executed within weeks of our arrival in Block 325, but by then I had set up a letter-drop system with Ibrahim. In a corner of the courtyard, out of sight except from the watchtower and two of the downstairs cells, was a crude washing area with half a dozen taps and basins where the Afghans washed out the cooking pots in cold water. During our exercise period, particularly when the weather was bad, the duty guard would sometimes go inside, and with two of us covering him the third would dart into the corner to collect or leave a letter hidden in a disused pipe. To reduce the risk of being caught, we established a code by hanging different coloured towels from our cell windows whenever we had dropped or received a letter, or if we felt we should temporarily suspend the system for any reason.

This exchange of letters worked well for almost six months and proved invaluable as a way of exchanging information. Ibrahim soon lost his job, apparently over misappropriating a packet of the better-quality Tir cigarettes that the guards smoked. (They were made from imported leaf as a counter to the Winstons and Marlboros which continued somehow to be smuggled into the country, war or no war.) Even without such a useful source of information as the guards' café Ibrahim seemed to know what was going on. He delivered a note from me to John Bowden, who indicated he did not want to run risks by communicating with his 'spy' compatriot, especially as he could not trust all his cell-mates. Ibrahim also told us about a new arrival, Captain Manuel Rosales, who was in our block but in a downstairs cell by himself.

Captain Rosales, a Spaniard, was serving as first mate under a German master on an Iranian oil products tanker when a serious accident occurred. While he was supervising the discharge of a load of gasoline in Bandar Abbas harbour the connecting hose broke and fuel leaked into the sea. Nearby were a dozen or more wooden dhows, and on the inner berths three or four of the Swedish-built Boghammer patrol boats manned by Revolutionary Guards during the war with Iraq. Somehow the gasoline caught fire, turning the basin into an inferno. Captain Rosales succeeded in manoeuvring the tanker out into open sea, as did the foreign crew of the ship next to his, which was unloading – of all things – dynamite. He was initially praised for his prompt action, which prevented an even worse disaster. But most of the Iranian vessels in the basin were destroyed or damaged and the loss of life must have been high. We were astonished not to have heard of this disaster, which had occurred a year or so earlier, but in a country like Iran it is easy enough to impose a blackout on unfavourable domestic news. The German captain, who had been asleep in his cabin at the time, realized he might be held responsible, and embarked at once for Dubai in a lifeboat, leaving Captain Rosales to face the music. There had been a brief trial and he had been ordered to pay personally millions of dollars in compensation. When he could not do so he was sent to Evin.

A disaster of such dimensions should clearly have been subject to a full enquiry by marine safety experts, who, it is reasonable to assume, would have found numerous contributory factors, such as the reckless proximity of vessels unloading dangerous cargoes to native dhows, where cooking takes place on deck and smoking is permitted. A cigarette stub thrown into the water may in fact have triggered the blaze. The tanker itself was no longer in its first youth and maintenance had been virtually non-existent. It had not been insured at Lloyd's by the owners, the National Iranian Oil Company, and Iran presumably hoped to squeeze some damages from the Spanish government by holding Rosales in Evin. Because the case was in no way political, or even criminal in the ordinary sense, Rosales was treated better than the other prisoners. Every day he was allowed a hot shower in the guards' quarters and we could see instant coffee and cartons of imported cigarettes on the shelf in his cell, together with other luxuries brought by the Spanish consul. He was allowed a radio, and when the World Service news bulletins came on he obligingly turned up the volume if we were in the courtyard, enabling Jon or me to lounge outside his window and glean titbits of uncensored news about the war that was clearly about to start. Unfortunately a guard twigged what we were up to and he was ordered not to use his radio during exercise periods.

By early October the whole block was becoming excited by press reports of another visit by Professor Reynaldo Galindo Pohl, a Salvadorean jurist and Special Representative of the UN Commission on Human Rights. He had already visited Iran in January that year, and it was that visit which had led to the hasty redecoration of the Sanatorium, although as far as we could discover he only visited the Training Institute and perhaps the women's section of the Sanatorium, so the new paintwork went unnoticed. The mandate for his investigation went back to 1984, but he had not been allowed to visit Iran until 1990, so this was already something of a breakthrough. His report on that visit was condemned from two sides: the hardliners objected to any impartial investigation, let alone any criticism, of human rights in Iran, while the opposition groups, from outside the country of course, claimed it was a whitewash. I saw it as a confidence-building measure. By listening to the Islamic Republic's inadequate replies to allegations of serious abuses of human rights the Special Representative had at least started a dialogue, and was reminding Iran that the world was watching it. The blustering remarks trotted out routinely by the Tehran press that the human rights issue was simply an imperialist stick to beat Islam with looked absurd when this highly experienced, patient lawyer, himself from a troubled Third World country, arrived with detailed questions about specific individuals and practices. His report concluded that the Commission 'should continue to monitor the situation . . . and that another visit seems desirable'. Only nine months later he was back, having apparently persuaded the regime that he was not biased, and that they did have some serious allegations to answer.

I felt sure that Galindo Pohl would have heard of my case from the British government, or at least from my brother Paul's lobbying efforts on my behalf, and while I was disappointed not to have been one of the prisoners he interviewed in January I felt my chances were better after Ayatollah Yazdi's remarks to Lili. I updated the letter I had constantly carried with me at the time of his first visit, so that I could simply give him the facts of my case in writing and spend the rest of the time telling him about people such as Jon, Helmut, Ibrahim and John Bowden. Ibrahim had also asked me, if I saw the Special Representative, to raise the question of Iraqi prisoners of war who were being held in Evin long after the war had ended without visits from the Red Cross, contrary to the provisions of the Geneva Convention. Once again, however, he was not allowed to see me.

Since my release, I have read Mr Galindo Pohl's two reports on his visits to Iran and the various statements made by Governor Pishva about my case seem worth recording. Regarding the visit in January 1990 the Report states:

> While visiting the cells, the Special Representative asked for permission to visit Mr Roger Cooper, a British citizen who has been in prison since December 1985. His request was turned down by the Director of Evin on the grounds that the prisoner was a self-confessed spy who was in solitary confinement and whose sentence had been handed down a month earlier and was currently being translated from Farsi into English. In reply to the Special Representative's question concerning the penalty to which the prisoner had been sentenced, one of the prison officials said that he had been given ten years in prison, but the Director said that he was not sure exactly how many years he had received.

Mr Galindo Pohl gave the names of twelve other persons who according to his information were in Evin and asked to see them. The name of only one was in the governor's card file, so he ordered the main files to be consulted. After some delay the message came that the person in charge of the files was not available since it was Thursday afternoon.

On 13 October 1990, Mr Galindo Pohl again asked to see me. Mr Pishva refused on the grounds that my trial was still pending. The UN Report goes on:

The Special Representative recalled that, on his first visit, he had been told that Mr Cooper had been sentenced to ten years in prison and that his sentence was being translated into English. The Director said that the trial was not over because the sentence had been appealed. The Special Representative said he did not consider this a valid reason for refusing to let Mr Cooper see him, for the interviews were neutral and had nothing to do with the status of trials. Moreover, some of the other prisoners he was going to interview had appealed their sentences and he did not see why Mr Cooper's case should be handled any differently. The Director replied that a new accusation had been made against Mr Cooper and another trial had begun. He then confirmed that Mr Cooper had been sentenced to ten years of imprisonment.

Although Mr Galindo Pohl was refused permission to see me he was allowed to see Jon. During the investigations, the report said,

(Pattis) had never been presented with formal charges and was held for three months in solitary confinement. In September 1986, he made a public confession on Iranian television. His trial before a revolutionary court took place in March 1987 before one judge, one representative of the prosecutor and one interpreter. There were three witnesses for the prosecution and the court session lasted approximately four hours. He had not benefited from legal counsel and the sentence was passed with the annotation that it could not be reduced. He had received three consular visits, in

287

1987, 1988 and 1989, from the United States Interest Section at the Swiss Embassy. He had not been tortured but had received threats.

Jon also told the Special Representative that he was in a cell with Helmut and me. Mr Galindo Pohl noted Helmut's name and said he had tried unsuccessfully to see me. Other prisoners told the Special Representative that they had been tried two years ago and were still waiting to hear their verdict, had never been formally charged, or had not been allowed defence counsel. One said his trial had lasted only fifteen minutes. A leading political dissident awaiting trial described the treatment as 'satisfactory' and the food as 'superb', which as the Special Representative stated drily 'contrasted sharply with statements by others'.

The Special Representative also asked to be allowed to attend an Islamic Revolutionary Court at which capital punishment might be awarded. Somewhat surprisingly his request was granted. The case he was permitted to attend was for armed robbery and banditry which, as is pointed out in the UN Report, does not fall into the competence of Revolutionary Courts. There were witnesses, a defence lawyer, and the nine accused were asked whether they were ready to apologize to the victims after they had admitted robbery, while denying carrying weapons; the implication was that an apology would lead to an acquittal. Although armed robbery does carry the death penalty in Iran, this was not a typical Revolutionary Court trial, as Mr Galindo Pohl makes clear.

Although I received no direct benefit from the visits I remain grateful to Mr Galindo Pohl for having tried to see me and perhaps for making the Iranian authorities realize that my case was being monitored not only by the hated British government but by the United Nations as well.

The main event of this period for me, however, was a visit from my daughter in March. I had not seen her for almost five years, and had not been allowed to receive any photographs of her. She had blossomed into a beautiful and confident young woman, despite her strict *hijab* and the hostile atmosphere of Governor Pishva's office. We were not allowed to embrace, although as she left Gisu gave me a quick illegal kiss. The governor not only refused to shake hands with her but never once looked in her direction. The visit ended strictly after thirty minutes, much of which was wasted by Pishva's interruptions.

16

IN AUGUST 1990, I read in the *Tehran Times* that Douglas Hurd, the Foreign Secretary, was insisting on my freedom as a precondition for re-establishing diplomatic relations. This worried me, as Iranians merely dig their heels in when faced with ultimatums, so I at once wrote to Mr Moussavian, the senior Iranian negotiator, saying I did not wish my case to be a stumbling-block to improved ties. I wrote in English so that my letter could be shown to the Foreign Office, and I heard later that it had helped pave the way for the reopening of the embassies that autumn, after the British government dropped its second precondition regarding the *fatwa* against Salman Rushdie.

To my great pleasure David Reddaway was transferred from the British High Commission in New Delhi, where he had been head of chancery, back to Tehran as chargé d'affaires with a staff of four British nationals. Iran reopened its embassy in London at the same time. It was announced that staffing levels would gradually be built up to sixteen diplomats in each capital, possibly headed by an ambassador, although the Foreign Office made it clear that this would depend on 'developments in the relationship'. This was interpreted as meaning Iran's help in freeing the four British hostages in Beirut and my own release. We read the details in the *Tehran Times*, which we now had a subscription to. Although it reached us several days late it relied heavily on foreign news agencies and was relatively uncensored. We could see that neither side was particularly optimistic about the rapid normalization of relations, but at least it was a step forward. I was confident that David Reddaway would fight hard for me, and he certainly did.

His first success was establishing the right to visit me once a month. Although the month sometimes stretched to five or six weeks, and the meetings were never smooth, this was a major breakthrough. He usually came himself, but once or twice Phil Ambrose, a tough young man who had served in Beirut, stood in for him. The main trouble was that Governor Pishva insisted on all my meetings taking place in his office, so that he could control the conversation. At the first one with David Reddaway he began by demanding that we spoke Persian. I objected, and David stated firmly that as the representative of the British government he was clearly entitled to speak to a British subject in English, especially when he was accompanied by a Foreign Ministry official who knew the language well and was prepared to act as translator. The governor reluctantly agreed. He insisted on having everything either of us said translated before the other could reply, but we were able to get things across by subtle use of slang and literary allusions that the translator did not always fully understand.

The next trick up the authorities' sleeve was when a hostile young man, almost certainly the representative of the Ministry of Intelligence, claimed at the second of these meetings that I was an Iranian national and therefore had no right to consular visits. I told him in no uncertain terms that this was quite untrue. I had in fact applied for Iranian nationality some twenty years earlier, partly to avoid the constant battle to get my residence permit renewed, partly to be able to own land in my name, a right in practice denied to foreigners, and partly because I had already acquired what is called a 'domicile of choice' in Iran, that is to say it was the country where I intended to spend the rest of my life. Soon afterwards I was summoned to Savak, the Shah's secret police, and told bluntly that if I 'co-operated' my application would be granted. This caused me to have second thoughts; I certainly did not want to be beholden to Savak, so I simply let my application lapse and heard no more about it. Now they were claiming I had been granted Iranian nationality, though without saying when this had happened. David was on to the matter at once. Putting on his firmest diplomatic tone he told the officials that this claim raised important questions and he must insist on seeing the documentation about my Iranian nationality, since I myself clearly knew nothing about it. And why had they waited five years before making

291

such a claim? Needless to say, no evidence was ever produced and the claim soon fizzled out.

David also told me that both Paul and my daughter had applied for visas and were likely to visit me before Christmas. Much as I would have liked to see them in ordinary circumstances, I was now against their coming. With Governor Pishva in control the visits would be pointless and perhaps even painful. Although it had been wonderful to see Gisu on her first visit earlier that year, after such a long time, I felt that unless she was coming anyway to see her relatives it was simply not worth the trouble and expense. As for Paul, I knew that he was unpopular with many Iranian officials; if they would not even let us correspond regularly, what were the chances of our being allowed to converse freely in the governor's office? The visits would simply be used for propaganda purposes.

Both visits did take place, however, and my expectations proved correct. Paul came first, just before Christmas. I naturally asked about Gisu's current work, not having received any letters from her for several months, but the governor said this topic was not allowed. I had already prepared a list of items we wanted. From my attempts to give such a list to David I knew that there would probably be objections, but I had hoped that he might be less strict with my brother than with the official representative of the British government. If I asked David for something, he always said, 'That's unnecessary. We probably have it in the prison shop and if not I will order it for him,' and then of course do nothing about it. So the list was carefully prepared with the most important items put first.

Paul was not on good form, tired and suffering from a heavy cold. When I read the items off, instead of writing them down he asked questions about each one, especially number six, a hair sieve. This was much more important to us than could be imagined. With David Rabhan's departure I had become cell cook and one of my main problems was to degrease the prison food. By now the meat content was negligible, but the grease content was rising in inverse proportion. It was easy enough to strain and rinse what we were given in a makeshift colander, remove the potatoes, which, contrary to preconceived ideas about Germans, Helmut

292

could not abide, and later lift off the solidified grease. Helmut, who knew nothing about cooking, having always had a mother, sister, wife or bartender to provide his food, once caught me throwing this away, 'the best part', as he called it. Jon and I, however, were trying to reduce our fat intake, on David Rabhan's advice, and fat-free 'invalid's food' was no longer available. Jon had some kind of heart problem and fat was bad for him. From then on I followed the old Jack Sprat routine. Having separated out as much fat as I could I used it to sauté the non-potato elements of whatever we got in the fat for Helmut, while Jon and I ate the potatoes, sometimes heated up, sometimes as a salad with ersatz French dressing. Once degreased, the stock could be turned into tasty and nutritious soups, but to do a proper job I needed a fine sieve to catch the fat particles.

Paul puzzled over this request. What was a hair sieve? Why did I need it? I explained that a fine nylon sieve would do, and I could not explain exactly what it was for. Meanwhile valuable time was being lost and just at this point the governor banned the rest of my list, saying everything would be provided through the prison shop.

Cooking in gaol is a subject that could fill a book. In the sense of food preservation and processes not involving heat, I had been cooking since my first days in Evin, even using the radiator pipes to dry slices of apple as a way of preserving them and varying the flavour. Now I had inherited David's mantle and the use of our small kerosene stove. Getting fuel was always a problem, but luckily the guards sometimes borrowed the stove and part of the deal was that if they did so they filled it up. For a time I was allowed to cook in a disused shower cubicle, but when the governor discovered he stopped the practice for no good reason, insisting that I cooked in the corridor near the main door and only for restricted time periods. This certainly honed my culinary skills: not a moment could be wasted if I had only twenty minutes to produce a meal over a single small flame which was almost imposs-ible to regulate.

As a result of executions and amnesties the numbers of foreign prisoners began to decline and Qasem kindly moved the last few prisoners in our corridor to cells downstairs and allowed us to have our cell door open. This was a wonderful boost as we could now for the first time walk up and down the L-shaped corridor, some 40 metres in each direction, as much as we liked. Some of the guards even let me sit in the corridor after lights out under a fluorescent lamp. They knew I had translated the Emam's first published poem and was working on some more. In practice I could read anything I liked, but I always took care to have a copy of one of his *ghazals* at hand. If I sat round the corner I could always hear the guard on his rounds, whereupon I would pick up the poem and a ballpoint, and adopt a poetic expression. Unfortunately Governor Pishva discovered these arrangements and cancelled them and we were once again banged up in our cell.

Jon's food parcels from home via the Swiss embassy had been coming through well, and the German embassy occasionally sent Helmut some luxuries, while Guity kept me well supplied with Iranian spices. This was just as well, for by now the prison food had become really poor in both nutritional terms and variety. It was potatoes, potatoes, potatoes in various kinds of grease, and the frequency and portion-size of the rice, our favourite food, rapidly diminishing. Mail had by now been virtually cut off and food parcels were fewer, so I had to ration our stocks strictly. Once a week I prepared a sort of spaghetti milanese, making a 500-gram packet of pasta last a fortnight. Helmut adored spaghetti and would have eaten our entire stock in a week if I had let him. My sauce was quite heavy on onions, which I sliced with our *tizi* (literally a 'sharp one', a knife made by rubbing an aluminium spoon handle against metal or concrete). *Tizis* were highly illegal, but never totally eradicated. Islam does, I think, respect privacy more than Western societies and even in Evin cell searches were most unusual, although body searches were common when a prisoner returned to his cell, even from interrogation. Above all, transfers from one block to another were used as an excuse to search prisoners' possessions. Any *tizi* found would be confiscated, and the owner or cell punished, but a replacement could be made provided metal spoons were available, as they usually were for communal prisoners. Once a week or so we would open a can of tomato puree and flavour it heavily with up to a dozen spices and condiments, including some vegetable oil as a preservative. A dollop of this hot sauce did wonders for any dish, especially my spaghetti sauce.

To save kerosene we boiled the pasta water by means of another piece of illicit Evin gadgetry, an immersion heater. This consisted of two stainless steel spoons set in a wooden frame connected by wires and plugged into the television socket that every communal cell has. Jon and David had fabricated this from bits and pieces scavenged during exercise periods, something I could never have done myself. The danger was its being discovered. We used it on the window ledge covered by Helmut's towel, as if he had put it there to dry, with one of us ready to pull the wires out if a guard came in. Once Ali the postman dropped in unexpectedly just as the water came to the boil. He saw the steam rising, but luckily thought it was condensation from a damp towel over the radiator, not realizing that the radiators never got hot enough for this to happen. By starting to heat the water half an hour before I was allowed to start using the stove, I could just get the pasta and sauce ready in the permitted time. Getting food to the table punctually is something I have never been much good at in a normal kitchen. The governor's spiteful regulations made it essential.

Jon's health began to decline seriously that winter, perhaps because of the cold and malnutrition. His face took on a bluish look, he had palpitations and his ankles began to swell ominously. He thought these symptoms were heart-related. We knew there was one good doctor in Evin, a former member of the Politburo of the communist Tudeh Party called Dr Baqa'i. He had been under sentence of death for several years, but intervention by Mr Galindo Pohl and the German government – he had trained in Germany, worked there, and his wife was German – led to this sentence ultimately being reduced to life imprisonment. I was determined to ensure that Jon got to see Dr Baqa'i, for although he was a prisoner and primarily a gynaecologist, we felt that he would be able to diagnose the problem and perhaps prescribe some effective medication or, better still, press for Jon to get an appointment with a heart specialist. Somehow I got into a huge row with Qasem when the guards refused to let Jon go to the prison clinic, and from then on relations with him declined rapidly.

As my sixth Christmas in gaol approached I thought of ways of celebrating it that might at the same time cheer up Jon and Helmut, who were by now both suffering from depression, as I had been the previous year. I enlisted the help of Vali, a moody young guard but one often sympathetic to Western ideas. Late on Christmas Eve he came to our cell with the news that I had a visitor. 'Who is it?' I asked. 'I don't know,' said Vali. 'Obviously he's got permission to see you, though. He's an old man with a white beard and there are some large dogs with him. He has snow on his clothes.' I appeared as mystified as the others and went off with Vali. A few minutes later a bearded old man came bounding into the cell with a sack over his shoulder speaking a language that could have been Lapp or Icelandic, calling out Jon and Helmut's names in a guttural accent and handing them gift parcels. 'Where's Cooper then?' he asked my astonished cell-mates. 'Give him these and tell him I can't wait, my reindeer are champing at the bit,' he said, and off he went. I returned to the cell a few minutes later with bits of cotton wool still sticking to my face. The presents were not up to much, a scarf for Jon and a pullover for Helmut, items I had received myself after Paul's visit, some fruit and other odds and ends, but it was wonderful to see Jon and Helmut laughing at last and saying, kindly, they had been quite taken in.

My daughter's visit coincided with the second anniversary of the Emam's *fatwa* against Salman Rushdie, a good excuse for the extremists to stage a demonstration outside the British embassy, from where she set off to visit me, calling for my execution. There were pictures of this event in the local papers and I was glad to see that there were more gawking onlookers and policemen guarding the embassy gateway than actual demonstrators, although these were headed by several prominent parliamentarians.

Gisu took all this in her stride, but she was soon visibly upset by the hostile tactics of Governor Pishva, who was even more unpleasant to her than at her earlier visit. He made it clear from the start that the visit would not last one minute more than half an hour, yet whatever subject we tried to discuss he objected. She brought a number of gifts from the FRCS and other well-wishers, but I was not allowed to take anything back to my cell. They would be sent to me later, he said, but not one ever reached me.

After twenty minutes of this farce I had had enough. I suddenly stopped trying to communicate with my daughter – although we had agreed to talk Persian so as to avoid wasting time with an interpreter – and asked to be taken back to my cell. Gisu immediately realized that this was the only way of dealing with such a person, and any disappointment she may have felt was cancelled out by knowing that this was the right decision. Thus ended the last of the eight family meetings I had during my detention in Iran. The total time involved was not more than four or five hours at the most, much of it wasted on procedural disputes and translation. They were always closely monitored and tape-recorded, and there was never the slightest warmth or humanitarian spirit on the part of the officials, except Mohammad, and that probably got him into trouble. On expenses alone these visits cost some £40 a minute, according to my calculations, and they were only agreed to for propaganda purposes. Iranian prisoners in Evin in my category were entitled to two family visits a month, and prisoners in Britain's medieval dungeons are allowed four visits a month, not necessarily from family. If Governor Pishva ever finds himself behind bars again, which given the unpredictability of Middle East politics is a distinct possibility, he will have plenty of time to ask himself whether he was acting in an Islamic or humane fashion.

By February 1991 the case of Mehrdad Kowkabi had become the leading local news story. We had read about a number of Iranian students in Britain being arrested on vague grounds of threatening national security, but most of these were simply expelled. Kowkabi, however, had been in Brixton prison since December 1989, on charges of conspiracy in the planting of incendiary devices in bookshops selling *The Satanic Verses*. The Tehran newspapers made a considerable fuss over the fact that his pre-trial detention lasted over a year, without of course mentioning that mine had been almost three years, with a further year before I heard the verdict. It was said that his fingerprints had been found on one such device that had failed to detonate. I knew that in English law conspiracy to commit a crime was often a more serious offence than the crime itself, so I could not help hoping, assuming the charges were well-founded, that he would get a hefty sentence, five years or so; if so, a second opportunity would present itself for some sort of deal resulting in his release and mine. The Iranian papers, both hardline and pragmatic, were openly linking my case with his and the guards were saying that I would 'definitely' be freed soon in exchange for this heroic Islamic combatant. I could not help asking them what would happen to a British subject in Iran if he were caught bombing a bookshop, or encouraging others to do so, for selling anti-British books. They saw no paradox in saying that such a person would be executed. That, after all, was the just deserts of a terrorist. What about Kowkabi, then? If he did what he is accused of, isn't he a terrorist? Not at all, came the answer, he did it for the defence of Islam.

Kowkabi's trial was adjourned several times, but finally took place at the Old Bailey in March 1991. He had called for some witnesses, other Iranian students expelled earlier from Britain and now back in Iran. David Reddaway, whom I saw about that time, told me how he had arranged visas and a promise of safe conduct for these witnesses, but they changed their travel plans at the last minute and arrived unexpectedly. Despite their having valid visas, the immigration authorities at Heathrow apparently subjected them to intense questioning and asked them about the evidence they intended to give at Kowkabi's trial, clearly a most improper thing to do. Whether they really became worried at this, or just thought it a good excuse, is not clear, but after being given permission to enter Britain they all got back on the plane and returned to Tehran. When Kowkabi's counsel told the court what had happened the judge stopped the trial and Kowkabi was expelled from Britain by the next Iran Air flight, returning to the kind of reception accorded to Fuladi, although surprisingly he did not make so much mileage out of the medieval dungeon called Brixton.

I was devastated by the news. It seemed to me iniquitous that just because his witnesses in effect refused to give evidence an accused terrorist should be freed, and I found it ironic that I, who had not been allowed to call witnesses or be legally represented at either of my trials, should still be rotting in gaol after more than five years. I wholeheartedly agree with the presumption of innocence, but cannot help feeling that the judge leaned too far in Kowkabi's favour. If the police really did have his fingerprints on a bomb, that should be sufficient evidence to secure a conviction on the terrorist charge, I thought, even if the conspiracy charge was not proved. It also seemed to me that this verdict set a potentially dangerous precedent, for what could now prevent any person accused of a crime claiming to have a witness in Iran or some other country who is afraid to come to England? Presumably he would secure an acquittal on this ground alone. And in any case, why could not the evidence of Kowkabi's witnesses have been given in the form of written depositions, as certainly happens sometimes in civil cases? Admittedly, they could not then have been cross-examined, but the court would at least have heard their evidence and been able to decide, on the assumption that it was true, whether it was sufficient for a 'not guilty' verdict to be brought in. I felt deep bitterness that once again a golden opportunity to secure my freedom had been missed.

Jon suggested that it might all be a charade and that secretly the two countries had agreed to a swop, but I simply could not believe that. To me British justice was still the best in the world — even though I had by now learned of the gross miscarriages of justice in the case of the Guildford Four and others — and it was unthinkable that an English judge would allow himself to be used as part of some behind-the-scenes deal. The only hope left was that the Iranians might be grateful that Kowkabi had not been tried, since it might well have emerged at the trial that he had been supported by some branch of the regime. This gratitude might then be expressed in a similar gesture benefiting me, but it seemed more likely that because of domestic propaganda pressures it would be difficult for the so-called moderates to release me voluntarily. A trade might have given President Rafsanjani enough to appease the hardliners, but it was increasingly clear that Ayatollah Yazdi's pious hopes that the Supreme Leader might pardon me had fallen on deaf ears.

As if to support this pessimism things had started to go from bad to worse in Block 325, especially for me, from the beginning of 1991. Jon had got permission to go to the lavatory outside the three permitted times a day because the pills he finally managed to get for his heart trouble had a diuretic effect. As a rule the guards allowed Helmut and me to go at the same time if we wanted, but this 'concession' was stopped. I succeeded in getting to the clinic because of blotches on my hands and feet (which I jokingly diagnosed as stigmata, although the doctor thought they were due to prison conditions), and while there I asked for permission to be allowed to go to the lavatory whenever necessary, like Jon. I said that the doctor who had seen me about the hiatus hernia in 1989 had told me to take plenty of fluids and it was not fair to expect me to urinate at only three set times a day, especially in view of my age. The doctor agreed immediately and told Vali, who had brought me, to tell Qasem. He probably did, but the next time I wanted to accompany Jon to the lavatory I was again refused. When Vali next came on duty he brazenly denied having heard the doctor say anything about this, and Qasem added that if it was not in writing it was not valid. I demanded to go back to the clinic and obtain written authority, but this was also refused, and for the rest of my stay none of us were allowed to go to the clinic.

This action really made me angry, so next time I was refused I simply lowered my pyjama trousers and began peeing into a plastic bucket in front of the guard, a shocking breach of decorum in Islamic society. As I expected, this led to a huge row, but I stood firm, refused to apologize, said it was against Islamic tradition and human dignity to deny a person the right to urinate or to drink when he needed to. I demanded to see the governor, who would never support such inhumane behaviour on the part of the guards – guessing, of course, that he had ordered it. Qasem backed down and from then on I had no further trouble on this score.

This was not the end of the matter, however. At my next meeting with David Reddaway the governor made an official complaint against my bad behaviour, and David actually advised me to be more co-operative. I told him the whole story without embarrassment, and said I would do it again if necessary. The bad behaviour was on their part not mine. I denied I was by nature unco-operative or badly behaved and said that if they treated us properly we would all be model prisoners.

I further blotted my copy-book at that meeting by producing

300

from an envelope three tiny pieces of meat, which together would not even have heaped a tablespoon, and saying that this was the only animal protein the three of us had received in the past week, apart from one egg each. Even the pitiful ration of feta cheese had been replaced by carrot jam. I said I knew many Iranians were suffering from food shortages, but they could at least buy fish, yoghurt, lentils, beans and green vegetables, which we never saw. I did this because at a previous meeting when I complained about the food Governor Pishva had called me a liar, saying that he personally supervised the prisoners' diet and that we were given one kilogram of meat each a month, or some such amount. When faced with the evidence he again called me a liar, but his words lacked conviction.

The governor's next move against us was to order the confiscation of all our glass objects. In solitary it is understandable that prisoners who might commit suicide or attack a guard should be denied access to potentially dangerous materials such as glass, but it had always been permitted in communal cells, and a note from Ibrahim confirmed that none of the other cells in our block were being subjected to this rule, as the guards had claimed. Needless to say, we were not supplied with any alternative containers for our food supplies, although we did manage to hide a few key glass items, such as the thermometer and magnifying glass (used to light cigarettes when matches were scarce), and the search was carried out by a reasonably friendly guard clearly embarrassed by the order.

By now I had perhaps 200 books, neatly arranged by subject, on the long shelf on one side of the cell. They were not harming anyone, and they improved the look of the cell if the rumoured Red Cross visit ever took place (Anthony Powell's *Books Do Furnish a Room* was appropriately one of them). I could not at first believe it when the order came that all but half a dozen of my books were to be confiscated: I immediately wrote a letter of complaint to the governor saying this ran counter to the ancient cultural traditions of Iran and Islam, only to be told he had personally ordered it. Two guards took away my library, pulling the books down carelessly and throwing them on to blankets and humping them off. We discovered where they were when a friendly guard

301

let me change one a week or so later. They had been put in a small room where the guards watched television, all carefully shelved by size and colour. We guessed that the real purpose of the confiscation, apart from getting at me, was that if the Red Cross did come it could be claimed that the foreign prisoners had their own library, and in due course this in fact happened.

Kowkabi's release was followed by an editorial in the pro-Rafsanjani *Tehran Times* that gave guarded praise for 'Britain's handling of the case'. Dr Larijani, the former deputy foreign minister whose downfall I had predicted two years earlier, hinted in his column in the relatively moderate *Ettela'at* newspaper that 'this sensible decision might be taken into consideration in dealing with the case of Roger Cooper', though he took care to add the politically correct term 'the notorious British spy'.

Dr Javad Larijani was an interesting person. As one of the few senior officials with extensive knowledge of the West – his doctorate in mathematics and logic was earned at the University of California – his expertise was obviously important to the regime, despite the serious faux pas he had made in differentiating between the Emam and the government. A solution had been found, with the Foreign Minister, Dr Velayati, accepting his resignation and then appointing him as his special adviser. Simultaneously he started a political newspaper column, using it at first to prove his revolutionary credentials with comments that could have come from a hardline politician, then gradually altering course until he once again reflected the moderates' position, with a thin veneer of radical rhetoric. This is entirely in line with medieval Persian politics: I can see parallels with court manuals of the twelfth century that Machiavelli would have approved of.

It seemed to me that the moderates might be testing the waters for my possible release, and this gave me fresh heart. The more sophisticated of the guards smiled and nodded, saying, 'You'll be going home soon, Cooper.' But the hardliners soon retaliated with newspaper editorials urging the authorities not to free the British spy and, as seen from inside Evin, they appeared to have the upper hand. Once again, the moderates seemed powerless to carry out their good intentions.

It sounds like hindsight, but neither Jon nor I were at all surprised at the outcome of the blitzkrieg launched by the West against Iraq on 15 January 1991, although we had expected Saddam Hussein to back off at the last minute once it was clear his bluff had been called. Quite a lot of my secret correspondence with Ibrahim was on this subject. All the Iraqis in his cell except one actually believed that Saddam would give the West a bloody nose, and for all their hatred of Saddam most Iranians also hoped for this. When the inevitable happened our credibility as military experts soared, and Ibrahim's cell-mates wanted to know what would happen next. This was much more difficult to predict. I personally hoped that General Schwarzkopf would carry on to Baghdad, which would not have presented any serious military problems. 'Stormin' Norman', incidentally, had spent some time in Iran as a young man, both when his father, a retired police officer, had been an adviser to the Iranian gendarmerie, and later when he himself had served on the US Military Mission to Iran. Sadly, however, President Bush reined him in on the grounds that the UN resolution only authorized force for purposes of evicting the Iraqis from Kuwait, not for invading Iraq itself.

My view is that President Bush ordered the ceasefire on the basis of faulty advice. There is a common fallacy that if a powerful dictator is assassinated or overthrown a 'power vacuum' will result, something that in the real world almost never happens, at least not for long. Either another dictator fills it, as the Emam quickly did in the case of the Shah, or else civil war breaks out. I believe that George Bush was advised that if Saddam were toppled there would be a dangerous vacuum in Iraq, which the Shi'ites would soon exploit to form a Tehran–Baghdad axis that might destabilize the whole Persian Gulf region. Far better, the argument seems to have run, to leave a chastened Saddam in power. Nothing of the sort would in fact have occurred. The Kurds, moderate Sunnis and the downtrodden Shi'ites would instead have formed a coalition. This might not have worked particularly smoothly, or lasted for long; but whatever happened there was almost no chance of the Shi'ites, always far from the levers of power in Iraq, coming to dominate the whole country. And in the unlikely event of this happening they would in any case never have formed a stable alliance with the Iranians, since they are in effect a separate sect, with their own leaders and hierarchy.

This became clear to me soon after the Revolution when I visited Najaf, one of the major shrine-cities of Iraq where the Emam had been exiled from 1965 to 1978. I wanted to visit the house he had lived in and talk to people who had known him there, expecting it to have become a shrine of sorts. The people of Najaf, I discovered, had scant affection for him. When at last I found the house the new tenant was far from friendly and no one I spoke to had a good word to say for him. There was perhaps an element of fear, because already relations between the two countries were deteriorating, and it might not have been politic to sing the Emam's praises, but that was only part of the trouble. I am convinced that if a Shi'ite government had succeeded Saddam Hussein it would soon have become as Iranophobe as its predecessors, just as Syria and Iraq, although both are Ba'athist regimes and adherents of pan-Arab socialism, have always been at daggers drawn.

Tehran, 1 April 1991

EARLY ON EASTER Monday I was musing on such matters and not feeling particularly optimistic about my own case. It also happened to be the first of April, and I was wondering what pranks I could play on Jon and Helmut, and even whether April foolery existed in their cultures. Ramadan had begun a few days before, which meant that no tea would be brought round, and I was just thinking of getting out the immersion heater for a brew-up when I was told to get dressed for a visit. This was most surprising as 1 April is Islamic Republic Day, a major holiday, and no one ever had meetings, visits or interrogations on holidays. It even occurred to me that Jon and Helmut might be getting their revenge over the Santa Claus jape, and that the summons might turn out to be an April Fool staged with the help of a guard.

I was taken to a part of the prison I had never been to before and told to wait in a small office, where I was soon joined by a man who told me to remove my blindfold. Although he was dressed in ordinary clothes (mufti seems an inappropriate word) I gradually realized that he must be a mullah. I could not understand the purpose of the interview, which went on all morning and ranged over many ethical, philosophic and religious topics, but I began to think he was simply getting to know me, perhaps to make a report. I gathered he had once had something to do with Evin, either as an inmate before the Revolution, or perhaps through some administrative or spiritual connection afterwards. He said he had not been there for several years, 'to his regret'. He was patently an intelligent and humane person, and by shifting the discussion from theoretical to practical morality I was able to tell him of the injustices I had suffered, most of which were quite contrary to the provisions of the Constitution. This seemed to interest him, but noon was approaching and he wanted to perform his prayers, so he asked me to write a summary of what I had told him and give it to him by 3 PM. In answer to his question I told him that I had kept the Ramadan fast for several years in solitary and found the experience rewarding, but being in a communal cell with two non-fasters, for whom I cooked, it was not really feasible this year. He said he quite understood.

Since it was a holiday it took me some time to get back to my cell, where I found the others had already eaten. Although I was hungry I decided to finish my report before eating, and I was still scribbling away at two o'clock when a guard came to collect me. I objected, saying my meeting was at three not two, and I had not eaten yet. 'So what?' he replied. 'I haven't eaten since last night either.'

Off I went, this time to the usual interrogation centre, where I sat for an hour finishing off my report and wishing I had at least brought an apple or a piece of bread, which I could have eaten surreptitiously, although eating in public, even by a non-faster, is forbidden and in any case bad manners. I was also getting rather thirsty, but expected to be taken back to the cell as soon as the mullah had collected my report. Suddenly someone came into the interrogation room where I was sitting. Instinctively I pulled my blindfold down – it might have been Hosein and I still feared his ballpoint – but a voice told me to remove it and answer some questions. Before me stood a youngish man with a pleasant, care-worn face. He was wearing a shabby suit of cheap electric-blue material, and his shoes had seen better days. Although I had never seen his face or heard his voice, I instinctively felt comfortable with him. My first guess was that he was a graduate student or intelligence officer who had come to seek my opinion on some political subjects. He spent a few minutes making polite enquiries about my health and prison conditions generally, which I took to be a preamble to such questions as 'Do you think the West will blockade Iran?' or 'How long do you think Allied forces will remain in the Gulf?' For him to visit me on a public holiday might even mean that some crisis had occurred which I was unaware of.

Suddenly he asked a totally unexpected question that made my heart leap: 'What would you do if you were released?' At midday

306

Jon had taken my morning meeting as a sign that something was happening about my case, but I was sure that the best I could expect was to be allowed a further appeal or a judicial review of my case. I replied cautiously, saying that I would return to Dubai, where I had lived and worked before my arrest, and after a few days of recuperation would probably fly to London to see my family and friends, have a medical check-up, and so on.

'Is your question purely hypothetical?' I asked him, 'or is there a chance I really might be released?'

'I would say that there is a very good chance, but it is far from certain and much depends on you. There are powerful people in the next room who are totally opposed to your release and I can only persuade them with your full assistance.'

'May I ask who you are?' I said.

'I won't give you my name, but I can say I am an unofficial member of the President's staff.' This was heavenly music to my ears and I assured him of my full support.

He left the room for a while, saying that they were reading and discussing my report. When he came back he said I had made an excellent case, but some of the people had disagreed with it. I pictured Governor Pishva, that arch-liar, sitting there and denouncing me. 'We'll leave that side of things for the moment, because another serious obstacle has occurred. They say you have been conducting an illegal correspondence of an espionage nature with other prisoners, and I have been given photocopies of your letters. This is said to be an extremely serious offence that carries a correspondingly high penalty and they want to put you and your correspondent on trial. What do you say?'

For a moment my heart seemed to stop and a tingling chill came over me. So they had discovered my exchange of letters with Ibrahim, and this was going to blight my chances of freedom. How unfair fate has been to me, I thought. At every stage when prospects for my release looked promising, some totally unforeseen disaster struck. There had been the Chaplin affair, Nicolas Nicola, Salman Rushdie's book, the Iran Air plane, the Gulf War. This time, for once, I had no one to blame but myself. It suddenly seemed madness to have tried to communicate with Ibrahim, when *antennas* abounded, even in the foreigners' block. John Bowden was right not to have got involved. I also remembered the insults Ibrahim heaped in his letters on Governor Pishva, who was now about to get his revenge. Here I had been more cautious than Ibrahim, never committing to writing what I thought about the governor, as it served no purpose and was dangerous. The only good news was that my new friend had only two or three letters in his hand and a quick glance showed they were all recent.

In self-defence I told him that there was nothing inherently illegal in our correspondence. We were friends and had been for months in the same cell, and there was absolutely no reason for us now to be separated. I admitted to the breach of regulations, but the correspondence was in itself harmless. Why could not Ibrahim and I meet in the yard and talk? There was no connection between our cases, and in any case we had both been tried and convicted. Iranians in that category were able to associate with whomever they pleased. Why were foreigners discriminated against? Since Ibrahim was in a much more vulnerable position than I was, I stressed that the idea of corresponding had come from me.

He seemed to like this spirited defence and went off to the other room to put my case. After a long delay he returned with a prepared confession for me to sign, assuring me that this would satisfy them. I smelled a rat, but after a few moments of reflection I realized I had little to lose. The letters themselves, in my own handwriting, would be sufficient evidence to convict me, whether I confessed or not. I did not like the wording, however, which included such phrases as, 'I, Roger Cooper, the British spy' and 'secret exchange of letters of an intelligence nature', which I reworded or crossed out. I also had to insert the date when the correspondence started. I had always destroyed Ibrahim's letters after reading them, tearing them into tiny pieces, soaking them overnight in water and then putting them in small batches down the WCs – my first effort had clogged the pipes and a plumber had to be called in, although luckily the true cause never came to light – but I could not know what Ibrahim would say. In the end I wrote that I could not remember the exact date, but it was less than a month ago and we had only exchanged a few letters. There was some trouble over this, but eventually my watered-down confession was accepted.

Slowly the afternoon dragged on. Progress was apparently being made, but it was a hard slog. The hardliners were sure I would start a virulent anti-Iran campaign if I were freed, much as Fuladi had done against Britain. I was tired and thirsty, but even when the dusk cannon marking the end of the fast was heard on the radio there was nothing to eat or drink, and still the strange trial continued. Eventually, after I had outlined in considerable detail what I would do if released, I was taken back to my cell, without knowing the outcome of the day's events. I had promised to be as 'positive' as possible in public about my time in captivity and in return had been given to understand that Jon Pattis's case would be favourably reviewed. I told the President's man that Jon would have served five years by 15 June. His health was poor and I did not think he would survive if he had to serve his full ten-year term. Releasing him after five years would be a humane action. This idea was well received. 'There will undoubtedly be difficulties for us if you are released and we would need time before doing anything about Pattis, especially as he's an American and a spy,' said the man in the blue suit. In the meantime it was essential for Jon to see a heart specialist, I went on. It would do Iran great damage if he were to die in Evin. This was agreed to.

Finally, I asked for efforts to be made to release the hostages in Lebanon, not just the British four, but all of them. I would in return campaign for the release of the 200-odd Shi'ite hostages in Israeli captivity, making the point that they should not be considered ordinary prisoners, having been taken across a frontier in violation of international law and on the whole never brought to trial. This was particularly true of the cleric Sheikh Obeid, who had been seized by Israeli commandos, abducted by helicopter and still not put on trial, although described as a terrorist leader.

My new acquaintance finished by saying, 'There are very few people in the West who know Iran as well as you do. We count on you to put this knowledge to good use.' I was deeply touched by the compliment and said I would never forget it. We shook hands and said goodbye, but he was unable to give me a categorical assurance about my own release, or indeed about the prospects for any other hostages or prisoners. He simply said he had done his best and it was no longer up to him.

I did not get back to the cell block until after 10 PM and immediately sensed that the attempt to release me had failed. As I entered the corridor I was told to place my hands on the wall and not look round. I was not allowed to enter my former cell and there were long delays while decisions were obviously being made about where I should be put. Finally I was taken to another cell further down the corridor, where to my surprise I found all my books, papers and other possessions piled up. Perhaps I was going to be freed after all? By now I was extremely tired, too tired to be hungry but desperately thirsty. I asked the guard if I could have some tea and any supper that was available. He seemed surprised that I had not been given *eftar*, the ritual fast-breaking meal at dusk, but said he would see what he could do. He came back with two cold potato croquettes, but said there would be no tea till *sahari*, the pre-fast meal served at about 2 AM. He got me a glass of water instead, which I gulped down quickly.

When I asked him what was going to happen to me he was at first evasive. They had heard I was going to be freed, but this had fallen through. Now I was going to be transferred to solitary as a punishment for having written secretly to 'Blackie', as they usually called Ibrahim. I would probably be moved later that night. I pleaded to be left where I was until morning, saying I was too tired to move my things. It would take me over an hour to pack everything up and at least as long to get everything into my new solitary cell. But he said the orders were that I should be moved quite soon. He went out, leaving me lying on the floor and browsing among my books. At least they appeared to be all there.

Before long I could hear the rattle of the old trolley and I was told to start loading up my things. It took me three trips to get everything to the front door of the building and despite the cool night air I was sweating from the effort. Several guards were standing about watching me, but none offered to help. On the last trip I asked if I could say a quick farewell to Jon and Helmut and tell them where I was going, but this was refused.

After a while the prison minibus appeared and I began loading my things in, no easy task as I had hardly any containers. Suddenly a Mercedes Benz 450 saloon drew up and an important-looking mullah got out. It took me a few minutes to recognize him as the man who had interviewed me that morning. I could not think what he was doing here. To my surprise he offered to drive me to the Sanatorium, but said sharply, 'Why aren't you wearing proper clothes?' I told him that I was much more comfortable in my pyjamas and I still had a long job ahead of me unpacking everything when I got to the Sanatorium. 'Put on your proper clothes anyway,' he said. 'You are going to have another meeting.' 'At this time of night and on a holiday?' I asked, but he insisted, in far less friendly tones than he had used that morning. So, watched by the guards and the drivers, I unpacked my suit and shirt, took off my pyjamas, and changed. He then told me to get into the back of his car and to my surprise got in on the driver's side himself, while his driver, who presumably doubled as a bodyguard, sat in the passenger seat, half-turned around and watching me warily.

At the first junction he turned right. I said, 'The Sanatorium's to the left, up the hill.' He did not reply, so I assumed we were going to yet another meeting. 'You can take your blindfold off,' he said as we drove fast down the hill, now speaking in the friendlier tones of the morning. For the first time, at least legally, I could see the buildings and gardens of Evin lit by street-lamps and spotlights. We drove right past the interrogation centre, on down towards the main gate. What on earth was going on? As we approached, a guard came out and peered into the car. The mullah rolled down his window and looked at him silently. The guard immediately opened the gate without apparently having seen me through the smoked glass windows. We drove towards the highway and I asked where we were going. 'Yes,' replied the mullah. I thought for a bit and said, 'Are you taking me to the British embassy?' 'Yes,' he said. By now we were barrelling down the highway at 120 kph. 'In that case, you should have turned left,' I said. 'The embassy is closed now and David Reddaway is staying in the summer residence in Golhaq.' 'Yes,' he said. 'Are you taking me to a hotel,' I asked, 'or to the Foreign Ministry? Where is this meeting going to be?' 'Yes,' he said. I was baffled. Things seemed to be going well but where were we going? I looked behind, but there was no sign of the minibus. It had probably never left Evin.

Without warning he turned into a slip road and I knew what was

311

happening. 'You're taking me to the airport.' 'Yeees,' he said with a laugh and I knew that this time he meant it. 'Hang on a moment, sir,' I said, 'I don't want to leave Iran yet. I have things to do in Tehran, bills to settle, and I want to see my daughter's family and visit my former father-in-law's grave. Can't I stay on for two or three days?' 'No,' he said, 'you are flying to London this evening, with Lufthansa, I think.' 'That's not right,' I said. 'I live in Dubai, my home is there, I work for a company there. I don't want to go to London. Please let me speak to David Reddaway and try to get this changed.' 'You will be seeing him in a few minutes,' he said and that was the end of the conversation until we reached the airport.

When we arrived the mullah faded away without giving me a chance to thank him for his efforts; whoever he was, I knew he had been largely instrumental in my release. I was taken over by a young man who had the air of an intelligence officer. I said I was thirsty and we went to the cafeteria for an orange juice. I sat looking in a daze at the two beautiful women at the next table who were obviously about to fly off to foreign parts. Their *hijab* was just about acceptable, but strands of auburn and blond hair peeped out. Subtle use of make-up and colour schemes gave them considerable sex appeal, at least to me. We checked flights to Dubai: nothing until Wednesday, so with luck this would give me at least one day in Tehran. A phone call was made and we drove a short distance to the old VIP lounge, where I had once doorstepped visiting dignitaries as a journalist. I was told to go in by myself. There was no sign of David, but I received a friendly welcome from two senior Foreign Ministry officials. An imposing butler, who must have had the job since before the Revolution, approached us with a silver tray, on which stood three beautiful glass *estekans* of hot tea. Addressing me first, he said, 'Would you like some tea, sir?', making a slight bow as if I were a departing ambassador. I thanked him in Persian instinctively, but he continued to show off his English, so I quickly switched, making small talk about the excellence of Iranian tea. It was certainly streets ahead of the Evin brew. He hovered Jeeves-like in the background, ready to replenish my tiny *estekan* the moment it was empty. I gradually rehydrated.

David came in, beaming at me with obvious joy. We chatted briefly, but in a quick aside he said, 'We'll keep the serious talking

312

till we're on the plane.' I did not want to prick his balloon, but I protested politely. 'David,' I said, 'I'm in no shape to arrive in London straight from gaol. Let me go to Dubai for a few days. Surely that's my right.' 'Shut up and get on the plane,' he said with a laugh. 'I'm coming with you.'

There were still a few things to do. Contrary to my expectations the minibus had arrived and David went off to check in my baggage. He was annoyed to find I had been wandering about in the terminal: 'Someone might have recognized you,' he said. I gathered that my departure was supposed to be strictly secret in case the hardliners tried to prevent it. The tickets had been booked in the name of Mr and Mrs Reddaway, and David had himself issued me with an emergency passport, a single sheet of paper without a photograph. Where one should have been he had written 'Not available'.

Things were happening so fast that my head was spinning. It was obviously real, but just did not seem so. Lufthansa flight 601 for Frankfurt was called and still we did not move. While David was away I joined a group of half a dozen Foreign Ministry officials. We spoke in Persian, but I had to remember to speak English whenever the butler appeared with more tea. The surroundings were sumptuous, obviously unchanged since the overthrow of the Shah, who always liked to impress foreign guests, and I felt perfectly at home discussing politics with these suave diplomats. Apart from the tea and their lack of ties it might have been an embassy cocktail party of the kind I often used to go to in the old days. No one seemed to regard me as the 'notorious British spy', or if they did they were too polite to show it.

David returned saying my things were safely on board. Lufthansa had apparently provided sacks and bags to put my loose possessions in, without batting an eyelid at Mrs Reddaway's unusual luggage. We bade farewell to the officials and I thanked them for their efforts. I almost shook hands with the butler too, but decided he would have been shocked at this breach of etiquette. He opened the doors for us, bowed, and right in front was the Lufthansa airbus. We went up the ramp and into the First Class compartment. The doors slammed, the engines roared and we taxied towards the runway.

EPILOGUE

I T   M U S T   H A V E been well after two when David suggested we
should try to get some sleep, and he soon dropped off. I calculated
that by now we must be safely out of Iran, but felt happier when
I saw day breaking over the foothills of the Caucasus in eastern
Turkey. Exhausted as I was, sleep was out of the question as we
chased a cold dawn across the Balkans and the Alps to Frankfurt.

The London flight was packed with commuting businessmen,
none too happy when a BBC television crew came forward from
Club Class to interview me as I tucked into a substantial German
breakfast of beefsteak and omelette. A pop star across the aisle
looked cross when he realized they were not interested in him.
Knowing how tight the BBC always are on expenses, I assumed
the TV people were there by coincidence; only when I learned
that they had taken the flight simply to get the first interview
with me did it dawn on me that my release must be a big news
story. The interviewer told me that there would be a press conference at Heathrow, so I spent the last quarter of an hour trying
to prepare myself.

Gisu and Paul met me at the plane and we were taken to a
VIP lounge for a family reunion. Much of what followed in the
next few days is a blur, but my half-brother George's report to
the FRCS recorded the highlights:

> Roger's appearance was shocking. He looked thin, pale, stooped
> and tired. Close up, his face had a paper-like quality, without
> expression, but his voice was strong, full of vigour and pleasure.
> He telephoned his father, posed with a glass of champagne, but

had a sip of tea. The Foreign Office told him of the enormous interest from the media and he chose to hold a press conference there and then. The room was so full that the family couldn't get in, and the noise of cameras, questions and laughter drowned out most of Roger's answers for us. From the news bulletins later it was clear his performance had been a great success. His most quoted remarks were 'sheer bloody-mindedness' (in reply to how he had survived) and 'Anyone who has been to an English public school and served in the ranks of the British army is perfectly at home in a Third World prison'.

The latter remark, although it had more than a grain of truth, was not as spontaneous as it appeared, having been thought up on the plane as we came in to land.

What I said at that first press conference and in subsequent interviews was aimed at making things easier for President Rafsanjani when my release became known, as I had promised in Evin the day before, knowing that this would help him over the release of Jon Pattis, Ibrahim, John Bowden, Captain Rosales, and the hostages in Lebanon. So I did my best to parry questions that might have highlighted the serious breaches of the Iranian Constitution, the Vienna and Geneva Conventions, and human rights in general, that had occurred, and stressed instead the positive side of my experience.

The very first question I was asked, even before I got to the press conference was, 'Were you a spy, Mr Cooper?' I replied, 'Have you stopped beating your wife?' I soon realized that the question was in many people's minds, although most were too polite to pose it as bluntly as that *Daily Mirror* reporter. There really is no useful reply; whatever the truth in any given case, a denial is inevitable. Later I developed a more sophisticated response, analysing in detail the four possible answers (yes/no, true/false) and suggesting questioners should make up their own minds on the available evidence. If some journalists and even a certain Cabinet minister chose to imply that I had been working for MI6, there was nothing I could do about it except wonder what their motives or sources of information were.

One positive thing I said was: 'The Iran that released me was not the Iran that arrested me.' By this I meant that under President Rafsanjani the country was adopting more moderate policies, a trend we in the West should encourage. I also forecast that the hostages, at least the British hostages, would be released within the next two or three months, provided the trend towards better relations between Britain and Iran was not sabotaged, and with slight delays this is what did happen. It was clear to me that the President and his supporters wanted to see an end to hostage-taking, and my release was very much a test case. True, Brian Keenan had been released the previous year, but that was largely because he was seen to be Irish rather than British: the Irish government had been sympathetic to Iranian overtures during its EC Presidency, and Iranians consider the Irish, like themselves, victims of British imperialism.

From Heathrow I was taken to Paul and Lili's house in Wimbledon. Here I learned of their son Simon's brave offer in 1989 to take my place in Evin so that I could attend my mother's funeral. It had not been accepted, nor was I told of it at the time. On we went to the family compound at Wardington in Oxfordshire, where my father, now nearly 85, was waiting to greet me, surrounded by large numbers of photographers and reporters looking for an emotional reunion – rather a lot to expect from my very British father. His first remark, after years of telling me I was overweight, was that I should now put on a few pounds. As some left others arrived and the photo-calls went on for several hours. George, who had by now become in effect my manager, or minder, was constantly fielding requests for interviews. David Reddaway had told me on the flight home that George had been instrumental in persuading the Iranian government of the need to release me if they wanted to improve their relations with Britain and the West generally. Unlike Paul, who somehow managed to upset the Iranians, George (who had worked in Tehran in the late 1960s and spoke Persian) got on well with them. Now he was managing the family's core business, a nursing home specializing in the care of patients with Alzheimer's disease.

The drive at Wardington House was choked with outside broadcast units from the BBC's *Newsnight*, ITV's *News at Ten* and ABC's *Good Morning America*. Around midnight my 42-hour day ended, but at five next morning *TVam* and *Breakfast News* arrived for more live interviews, made with only 60 seconds between them. Then came the photographers wanting shots of my first English breakfast. Although I had already had my Weetabix and toast, I obliged with more toast and a mug of tea incribed 'Home Sweet Home'. There were requests for sentimental shots with Father on a steep bank of daffodils, until he rebelled, and more breakfast shots for late-comers – George reckons I had five breakfasts that day.

So it went for several days. The *Good Morning America* broadcast triggered off interest from the North American media, including CBS, CNN and CBC Radio, the last-named wanting interviews in both French and English, and I was also in demand from Australia. Bush House then got into their stride and there were interviews for the World Service in English and Persian.

Having been a freelance writer most of my adult life I found it difficult to refuse requests for articles and soon bit off more than I could comfortably chew. Somehow I managed to write four full-length articles in those first few days, all from completely different angles. I did a political analysis for the *Daily Telegraph*, a piece on cooking in gaol for the *Sunday Express*, another on the hazards of working as a journalist in the Middle East for the *Mail on Sunday*, and a description of my early days in solitary for *The Spectator*. I knew my pen would never be in such demand again and was determined to take advantage of it. By the tenth day requests for interviews had almost stopped, which perhaps explains the phrase 'a nine days' wonder'.

Friends and family alike assumed I had made, or was making, a trouble-free re-entry into the orbit of normal life. I soon had premonitions that there might be difficulties, but I pushed these aside, while agreeing with my daughter that a medical check-up would be a good idea. I emerged with a relatively clean bill of health; no one suggested I might need any psychiatric help. Once I was out of the limelight, however, and gradually getting used to freedom, I began to notice some unusual behaviour patterns. I could perform my 'core' activities – writing, being interviewed on radio and television, giving impromptu speeches and talks – but I had difficulty with peripheral tasks such as household jobs and

317

driving. I have always enjoyed cooking and during my last year in gaol had become efficient, given the extremely basic facilities. Now I had difficulty in boiling an egg. This did not matter at first, as my stepmother Anne, although only slightly younger than my father, was turning out wonderful meals. But as I spread my wings and started venturing up to London and fending for myself, problems arose.

First there was the question of transport. Not having been on public roads for so long I was terrified of the traffic and decided not to take up driving again. I would go by train from Banbury to London and use buses and taxis when I got there. Sadly, I found rail travel inconvenient and stressful. The trains were almost always late and it could take three hours door-to-door to travel the 70 miles from my flat in Kensington to Wardington, besides involving one of the family to shuttle me to and from Banbury station. The open-plan carriages were noisy and dirty, with a constant stream of young passengers passing up and down, rarely shutting the doors and putting their feet on the seats when they sat down, a breach of regulations to which the railway staff turned a blind eye.

I had told George that I could not face driving, but one morning he simply threw me some car keys and said there was no one else available to drive one of my nephews into town. This shock treatment worked. Gradually my confidence increased and I soon ventured out on the motorway, but for at least a year I was exhausted after even an hour's motoring: in the old days I thought nothing of driving all day or all night in the far more daunting conditions of the Middle East. I was not just apprehensive of other vehicles, but of something worse. I would be driving along, and suddenly have a feeling that I was about to crash into the car in front, or into the barrier. These panic attacks only lasted a few seconds, but they were frightening. Doubtless the other drivers would have been equally frightened if they had known, although I doubt if I ever lost control of the car even momentarily.

I have never liked loud or unnecessary noise, but now it became intolerable. I could not enjoy going to a pub or drinks party, and two or three conversations going on at the same time, say at a dinner-table, got me quite confused. I began to sleep badly, often going to bed late and waking up early, something I had done deliberately in gaol, whereas now I felt tired even after a proper sleep. Another worrying symptom was the effect on my memory, which had always been good. Whereas I could still recall events from the distant past, especially my time in gaol, I would often forget remarks made to me or by me moments earlier. I had difficulty remembering whether an event had happened yesterday, last week or a month ago, and whether I had heard about something in conversation, by telephone or from reading about it. I found myself telling people things they had recently told me and making other embarrassing blunders.

A Friends of Roger Cooper Society party was held in a large room above a south London pub. Apparently I made a speech, but the whole evening remains a blur in my mind, and when I meet friends I have to ask if they were there, to my embarrassment if they were and theirs if they were not. My concentration became abysmal, my decisiveness non-existent. These memory lapses could prove expensive. Three times I started to run a wash basin and was distracted by a telephone call, flooding my own flat or other people's. As I got slowly back into cooking, saucepans or frying pans burned regularly and pressure-cooker safety-valves peppered the ceiling.

In gaol my dreams had almost always been positive and amusing, now they turned morbid and sinister. Sometimes I was back in prison, but usually these nightmares were fraught with other forms of angst, and the wonderful seafood platters that I dreamt of in Evin now became bowls of putrefying food. I would wake up in a cold sweat unable to go back to sleep. Even when I was awake memories of my captivity intruded into my thoughts, often tinged with unreasonable guilt that I was not doing enough for Jon, Helmut, Ibrahim and Captain Rosales. Even in a curtained bedroom I slept with my airline eyeshade on as a kind of security blanket just as I had worn my blindfold in gaol to keep out the non-stop lights of my cell.

George must have got some idea of what was going on and mentioned it to his wife Rene, who had recently resumed her medical career now their four children were at or about to go to boarding school. She showed me an article on Post Traumatic Stress Disorder by Dr Stuart Turner of the Middlesex Hospital and through Gisu I arranged to see him. Dr Turner is a busy consultant who does not see private patients and the earliest appointment I could get was for mid-October. Unfortunately I could not accept that date as it clashed with a talk I was to give at an international conference for military psychiatrists organized by the Royal Army Medical College. I had met Brigadier Peter Abraham, the British Army's top psychiatrist, on a television chat show of all places, and he had invited me to the conference as a kind of live exhibit. So, ironically, instead of receiving the treatment I belatedly realized was necessary I found myself addressing a packed hall of experts on symptoms associated with PTSD. Luckily Dr Turner was able to see me not long afterwards.

This was my first ever visit to a psychiatrist and I must confess I looked forward to it with a mixture of excitement and apprehension. Given my ability to read fortunes from Turkish coffee-cups, what might I not see in Rorschach ink-blots? With Americans I would henceforth be able to say 'according to my analyst', even though one would have to keep quiet about it in British circles. Suppose I fell asleep on his sofa? Should I have been recording my dreams? None of these expectations proved right. Dr Turner's consulting room looked like, in fact was, an office. There were no tests or questionnaires, no sofa. He was not interested in my dreams. But I was able to talk freely about the bad aspects of my captivity and the problems I was having in readjusting. He confirmed that what I was suffering from was quite typical of PTSD and that I was making good progress, although further ups-and-downs could be expected.

While John McCarthy, the Beirut hostage, was on his way back to Britain on 8 August, the *Evening Standard* contacted me to ask what sort of debriefing and counselling he would receive, assuming that I had undergone this sort of processing. I had to say that I had no idea, not having been debriefed or counselled myself. The reporter tried to confirm this with the Foreign Office, and quoted a spokeswoman as saying that 'He had a full debriefing at our embassy and also at the Foreign Office. He had a thorough medical check-up in Tehran prior to departure. Any medical tests he had in the UK were a matter for him.' Staggered as I was by this assertion, I refrained from reminding them that I had been taken from Evin straight to the airport and had not had a medical check-up for six years. Nor did I mention that at my only meeting at the Foreign Office, on 4 April, Douglas Hogg, the junior minister with responsibility for Middle East affairs, having arrived late, brushed aside my views on Iranian politics and the hostage crisis, preferring to favour me with his own extremely hawkish opinions. Gisu wrote to the *Evening Standard*, contradicting the Foreign Office statement, and months later I received a half-hearted apology for what was described as a 'cock-up'.

I have sometimes wondered why I was not offered the immediate psychological care given to the Beirut hostages on their release, at the special centre set up at RAF Lyneham in Wiltshire. Perhaps the facilities were not ready at the time of my release, or they may have been overstretched by the large numbers of personnel suffering from PTSD as a result of the Gulf War. Maybe it was thought that the Iranians would say, if I had been openly whisked away to a military base, 'That proves Cooper was a spy.' (On the other hand, in their convoluted way, they probably said, 'The British Government totally ignored Cooper when we released him. That proves he was a spy.') Then there was the fact that technically I was a convicted prisoner, not a hostage. It may have been argued that to offer me counselling could set a precedent for other British citizens returning from prisons abroad. Knowing the prospective problems I pressed various officials to give some counselling to Ian Richter, like me technically a convict, when he was belatedly released from captivity in Baghdad. He was not invited to RAF Lyneham, but did receive some counselling at the less conspicuous RAF Ely.

I am convinced that hundreds, perhaps thousands, of cases of PTSD go undiagnosed every year. One does not have to have been in combat, gaol or a towering inferno to suffer from this disease: a bitter divorce, a bereavement or even witnessing an accident can trigger it off. It is all the more insidious because of the delayed reactions: the key element in its rather cumbersome title is the word 'Post'. It does not strike until the traumatic event is over and nature has lowered her guard. Although, as I discovered at the conference of military psychiatrists, effective counselling treatment is now available, the NHS simply does not have the necessary resources and most doctors are still unaware of the prevalence of PTSD.

Almost as soon as I was released people began asking me what I was going to do next. In a way, I answered the question by immediately getting back into my long-term occupation, that of freelance journalist and broadcaster. The editors I wrote for immediately after my return seemed pleased with what they got and several of them wanted more in the months to come, and there were others besides. I love working on radio and there was still some demand for interviews not only on my personal experience in Iran but on more general topics too. I even did a radio phone-in. I am less attracted to television and have often been disappointed by the people who work for it and the way it deals with events, but I did agree to do one interesting BBC project. It was called *Talking to Myself* and involved being interviewer and interviewee at the same time. I wrote the script myself and it was filmed only six weeks after my release, which perhaps gave it greater spontaneity. I never understood the electronic wizardry that stitched the two sets of images into a single-frame.

Of course, I was still nominally an employee of McDermott, but shortly after my release I was made redundant with a month's sick leave. It was explained that structural changes in the company's Middle East operations, the Gulf War and the world recession, leading to sharply lowered demand for oil, had caused my job to disappear. Even though I was in no fit state to return to work at once, I was depressed by the news. I had no desire to become a professional former hostage and I would have liked to have continued to work in the offshore oil industry, which I had found fascinating. A few more years in the Persian Gulf would also have given me a financial cushion against an uncertain future. In my 57th year I stood little chance of finding a similar job.

The obvious thing was to return to journalism, and I was therefore delighted when Trevor Grove, the editor of the *Sunday Telegraph*, commissioned four weekly columns about how I found Britain after my long absence. I chose the pen-name Rip Van Winkle, intending it to be a serious if satirical view of changes in British life and society. In fact I was pressed to make it more humorous than I had intended, although I did stir up some controversy with my opinions on education, word usage and drinking habits. To my surprise, and I suspect the editor's too, the readers seemed to take to this somewhat crusty and opinionated character, and the four columns stretched to six, eight, twelve until I had completed well over a score.

I also travelled to the north-eastern Spanish region of Galicia to meet Captain Rosales' family and try to help them unblock the impasse over his continuing imprisonment. The invitation came from the dedicated mayor of the small town of Noia, Dr Pastor Alonso Paz, a friend of the Rosales family, who was waging a war against the local drug *capos*. I was able to come back with an exciting exclusive on this shocking traffic, which stretches its tentacles all over Europe, and it was good for my morale to be doing some real reporting after a gap of ten years, especially on something risky yet totally unconnected with the Middle East.

Several months after my release David Rabhan came to England to look at Belgian Blue cattle at the Royal Show. We spent a pleasant couple of days catching up on each other's news, our often stormy relationship in Evin forgotten.

By mid-summer 1991 I had heard that the powers that be in Tehran were fairly satisfied with what I had said and written about the regime and that other releases would soon follow. John McCarthy's was the first of these, and the most important in view of the message he brought from his kidnappers for the UN Secretary-General. Although the message was in itself an unimportant piece of propaganda it provided a vital gambit for the UN to become directly involved in ending the hostage crisis. Its significance was therefore so great that in my opinion John's advisers should have persuaded him to carry straight on to New York to deliver it, by Concorde if the RAF felt they could not take him there. This would have avoided the bizarre sight of Secretary-General Perez de Cuellar going, mountain-like, all the way to an RAF airbase to collect his letter. It would also have spared us the sight of Mr Hogg basking in the limelight of Lyneham and apparently taking credit for John's release, when his colonialist posture can only have delayed the hostage process. A month later Jon Pattis was freed from Evin, still suffering from what was later diagnosed as congestive heart failure, and soon after so was Captain Rosales, admittedly after the Spanish government had made an unexpectedly generous aid concession. In November, Terry Waite and Tom Sutherland were freed in Beirut, and early in December the last and oldest of the British hostages, Jackie Mann, was also released. Finally, John Bowden was home for Christmas.

While still in Evin I had learnt first-hand of the work of Prisoners Abroad, the only registered charity devoted to helping British prisoners in foreign gaols, both while they are incarcerated and after their release. Among the first books I received were two from Prisoners Abroad, and they later sent me a subscription to the *Economist*, which began to reach me, about one issue in three, during 1990 and was also much enjoyed by Jon and David. I had received a fee from *The Spectator* for publishing my open letter to the Parliamentary Mission and asked for it to be paid towards life membership of Prisoners Abroad, a status that gave me much superstitious comfort. When I discovered, after my release, how much the organization did on very little I determined to help them as a fund raiser, promoting their work whenever appropriate. I was asked to give a charity lecture in Bristol about Iran and Islam, the choice of charity being left to me; but when I suggested Prisoners Abroad there was some foot-shuffling and it was suggested a medical or children's charity would raise far more. I chose the Alzheimer's Disease Society and the lecture made over £5000 for a cause dear to my family, but I felt something of a traitor to the 2000 British prisoners languishing in foreign gaols.

At a Foyle's Literary Lunch I was more successful when my impromptu appeal brought a generous offer of assistance from, among others, Taki, the millionaire-socialite-journalist. I also spoke for Prisoners Abroad at a fringe meeting at the Labour Party Conference in Brighton, along with Daphne Parrish, who had spent six unpleasant months in a Baghdad gaol in the wake of the Bazoft affair, although that only raised £57. Many people take the view that most such prisoners are drug smugglers getting what they deserve, completely missing the point that a lot of them have been denied a fair trial and are living in appalling conditions. British consuls are often dedicated and sympathetic to citizens detained in their jurisdiction, but there is an urgent need to supplement these efforts and to provide basic necessities to those detained.

In the early days of my imprisonment I fondly imagined that Her Majesty's Government would mount a *démarche diplomatique* on my behalf. Even before the Iranian Revolution there were signs that the European Community had begun to co-ordinate diplomatic activity. Once a week the EEC ambassadors in Tehran used to meet, usually at the British embassy under the chairmanship of Sir Anthony Parsons, to exchange information about what was happening in Iran and what the Community's response should be. I felt sure that the British chargé d'affaires would persuade his colleagues that my long detention without trial was intolerable to the Community as a whole. The senior diplomat, I naïvely thought, would soon be donning his cocked and plumed hat, girding on his blunt diplomatic sword and officially informing the Foreign Minister of Strasbourg's (or was it Brussels'?) displeasure. That would be sufficient to set the telephones jangling between the offices of the President, the Prime Minister and other organs of state, the outcome being my prompt release, with excuses or apologies.

Alas, there is little solidarity yet among the EC members, and nothing of the sort happened. In the real world each country has to fight single-handedly for the protection of its own nationals, more's the pity, since there is no doubt in my mind that in such cases a common front would really work. If an Italian, say, is wrongfully imprisoned or unfairly tried in country X, not only will the European Community collectively do nothing to help him, but even Rome is likely to sweep the matter under the carpet because of the importance of trade links with X. A breach of relations, or even the threat of a breach, could lose Italy a vital contract, harming exports and job prospects at home, and this could have serious repercussions on the government's electoral prospects. That is why, whenever someone abroad suffers an abuse of human or constitutional rights, the advice given to his or her family from their own foreign ministry tends to be 'Keep a low profile', 'Give quiet diplomacy time to work', 'Don't rock the boat', and similar palliatives, which all too often send the wrong signals to the offending country. After my release I met or spoke to the families of several other prisoners questionably held in the

Middle East and always advised them to press their government to take a harder line, if possible a collective one.

By this I certainly do not mean a return to gunboat diplomacy, although in truly recalcitrant cases, such as that of Saddam Hussein, that is sometimes the only way. But it is intolerable that an individual's rights can be savagely abused while his own government does nothing about it, or at least nothing effective. In an ideal world there might be some department of the United Nations to investigate cases where foreign prisoners' rights have been abused, but such a body would need sanctions to uphold its findings if moral suasion failed. I do not want to single out Iran for condemnation in this respect, since there are many other countries where such abuses are allowed to happen, and where sovereignty is hypocritically invoked to counter any protest or attempt at investigation. In this connection I was amused to receive a letter from my father while I was in Evin that contained the sentence: 'In your grandfather's day' (he was a naval officer killed in the earlier Falklands campaign before the First World War) 'the Royal Navy would simply have sent a warship to the Persian Gulf and you would have been instantly released.'

One person I was particularly looking forward to meeting was John Lyttle, the man Archbishop Runcie appointed in 1987 as his secretary for public affairs to put order into the situation left by Terry Waite when he was abducted. Sadly, his heart condition deteriorated about the time of my release and by the end of April he was dead. Despite my long meeting with him in Evin I did not know the full extent of his activities until I read the obituaries and spoke to some of his friends at the memorial service, but I came to realize then that he was the man most responsible for the upturn in Irano-British relations in 1988. If *The Satanic Verses* had not appeared I could have thanked him for winning my freedom two years earlier, and I shall always admire him as a great humanitarian, the only British politician or diplomat, and he was both, ever to be praised by officials of the Islamic Republic of Iran.

Even short-term celebrities like myself have an enjoyable time in the fast lane, with charity and show-biz lunches and prize-givings, rubbing shoulders with the great, the good, and the merely famous. As well as all this, and the radio and TV interviews, to the astonishment of my friends I was also selected as one of the fifteen best-dressed men of the year in an *Esquire* fashion supplement, because they had heard of my habit of wearing my pinstripe suit, bow-tie and silk waistcoat when I was summoned to the prison governor's office. At the photo session, however, my own wardrobe was rejected, and instead I donned £1000-worth of high-fashion clothes that were far too small for me, robbers having made off with most of the collection the night before. The photographer cleverly angled his pictures to hide this fact.

But being in the limelight is not all fun and games. One tiresome by-product caused me weeks of anxiety. An Iranian woman in her mid-twenties decided that she was my real daughter exchanged in error for Gisu at birth. She telephoned constantly and came to Wardington to see me, when Rene made an immediate diagnosis of schizophrenia. Discovering I was in London she got my address and began ringing the doorbell at all hours of the day and night, upsetting the neighbours as well. When I went out she would follow me on to the tube and it was difficult to shake her off, even for a 'notorious British spy'. Eventually I had to call the police and through them I discovered that she had indeed received treatment as a schizophrenic. She reluctantly agreed to return as a voluntary patient, but continued to pursue me, and the hospital seemed indifferent about the effect of all this on me. I put up with the harassment for as long as possible, but when I discovered she had told some of the tabloids that she was my secret daughter and/or lover I applied to the courts for an injunction to prevent her from contacting me in any way. I was grateful to the judge for hearing the case *ex parte* and in such a way that the press did not get wind of it.

All these activities were perhaps helping me to readjust to the real world, but time was slipping by. The Beirut hostages were now free, but as far as I knew, Helmut and Ibrahim were still in Evin. Galindo Pohl, the Special Representative of the UN Commission on Human Rights, was in Geneva in December so I went over to meet him there and told him everything I knew about Evin Prison that might help him when he made his third visit, and asked him to do what he could for my friends. While in

Geneva I also had a long meeting with the International Committee of the Red Cross, who were hoping to send a mission to Iran shortly. Sadly, the conditions imposed by Iran for the visit were unacceptable to the ICRC, so the much-awaited Red Cross involvement in Iran was put off yet again. A few months later Ibrahim was released, although it was almost as difficult trying to get him home to Ghana from Ethiopia, to where he was deported penniless as being the nearest Black African country.

I had done everything I could for the time being for hostages and prisoners in the Middle East, so now it was time to start on this book. I knew I could not write it in England and found a quiet location in France, a vast thatched manor house on the edge of a forest in Normandy. In December, however, my father had a stroke in the aftermath of what should have been a minor operation, and I decided to spend more time with him. There was also understandable pressure for me to spend Christmas with the family for the first time in nine years, so I did not settle down in France until late January 1992.

My first attempt at writing about myself proved more difficult than I imagined, just as my friends had warned. The symptoms of PTSD came back to haunt me from time to time and I suffered the customary spells of writer's block, but my physical strength quickly returned, sawing and splitting logs in the cold to keep the huge fires ablaze in my borrowed refuge, and walking for hours, sometimes riding, in the Forêt de Brotonne. Evin had taught me the joys of solitude, but occasional visitors kept me from being too much of a recluse. The house has the largest kitchen I have ever cooked in, complete with a wood-burning stove and a proper larder, and it was soon filled with cast-iron pots and other utensils and gadgets which, like many male amateur cooks, I adore. A village woman came in to polish the tiled floors and clean the windows and teach me how to make apple tarts and rabbit stews in the Norman manner. When spring came I rediscovered the joys of gardening: my lettuces, strawberries and basil did well, but I did not get a single edible tomato or aubergine, thanks to mildew. My cooking gradually improved until now I am ready to accept the day in his kitchens offered to me by the Swiss chef Anton Mosimann after he read my article on gaolhouse cooking. Norman meals rely heavily on butter and cream, and wine is still reasonably priced in France, so by November I was clearly overweight, almost 20 kilos more than when I was released, but as the book neared completion a fat-free diet had begun to work. A slimmer, fitter Roger Cooper is ready for whatever the future brings.

As the natural euphoria that comes with freedom wore off, to be replaced by frequent bouts of depression, indecision and inactivity, I began to feel bitter towards the people in Tehran who had trampled on my rights and used me as a scapegoat to vent their anglophobia and dislike of the West in general. Their attitude was nicely encapsulated in an editorial that appeared in a Tehran newspaper in March 1991 when I was still in gaol. It said, 'The Muslim Iranian nation condemns Roger Cooper as a Briton in the first place and a spy in the second place,' echoing Hosein's comment early in my interrogation about the British in general and journalists in particular: 'You are all spies.' (This national paranoia, by the way, is not confined to Iran.) But as I slowly returned to normal my genuine love for Iran grew stronger and stronger. If you love a country, or a person, you have to take the rough with the smooth, and I found myself hoping that one day, before it was too late, I would be able to go back there.

If I draw up a balance sheet there is much on the credit side to offset the 'waste' of almost six of what should have been among the best years of my life. Among the benefits are that I am now a (slightly) more tolerant and patient person, who knows himself better and regards death with less apprehension. My formal religious faith grew little, if at all, but paradoxically I have become a more spiritual person. I am more self-confident, having replaced an insecure heartiness with a better understanding of other people of all kinds. I certainly appreciate my freedom and look on it as a kind of gift or borrowed time, and I love the good things of life as never before. But I have also learned what deprivation means, and if required I know I can be content sleeping on a stone floor and living on bread and water. I think I am less materialistic than I was and now regard the acquisition of wealth not as an end in itself, but to a great extent as a means of helping others and doing useful things. I have relearned the pleasures of reading and studying, and above all that our most precious resource comes from within. Milton's lines that inspired me so much in Evin will continue to be my guide now I am free:

> The mind is its own place, and in itself
> Can make a heav'n of hell, a hell of heav'n.